Solomonder's Iron

By James Anderson

Dedicated to Ann, Kate, Ned
and Molly (daughter of Sean)

Solomonder's Iron

ISBN-10: 0648113418

ISBN-13: 978-0-6481134-1-6

Chapter One

The road hummed under the tyres of his ancient station wagon as Tobias Stanley Buchanan drove into his New District, far from the turmoil of Sydney. A dutiful servant of the Raj off to the far frontier, he mused, while Fred Astaire sang from the sole remaining car speaker of picking up, dusting off and starting all over again. The dawn flooded across as Toby put other words together:

Driving through the barcode
Of the shadows on the road,
The early morning sunlight through the trees,
Warms the weary traveller
And shows him on his way,
Something something something something…

…breeze? please…? sneeze?? Fair enough, but the barcode was doing his poor jagged head in. The dappled romantic light was scouring his eyes out and his headache had not improved.

'Sunglasses...' muttered Toby, rummaging through the glove box, ignoring a low growl.

'You bloody bastard cat!' he bellowed, his arm slashed by the thoroughly pissed off Sean. Being flung into the car and driven far away from his window cushion, grazing bowl and cat door was not what the 14-pound Siamese cross wanted. Very cross. Toby inspected the ripped sleeve of yet another shirt while Sean curled back down on the passenger seat, purring. Probably remembering the Goulburn Service Station where he had taken a much-needed pee, beaten up the servo tomcat and faced down a local Alsatian before sauntering back into the Toyota.

Toby began to take notice of the steep hills, scattered farms and faded weatherboard houses among the tree ferns. The Barangan Valley was too rough for an AGCORP takeover and too far from the city to become hobby farmlets. He morosely imagined a main town staggering down a fifty-year decline and the prospect of turning up at Barangan High School, Barangan St., Barangan on Monday was starting to appear a not-such-a-good-plan-as-it-seemed. District School Counsellor (Toby avoided the new title of School Psychologist) to the rural poor. Back to basics. Slow talking beefy children, anxious teachers counting transfer points and bugger all else, he thought gloomily. And yet - Toby force-framed some positives... quiet life, clean air, an affordable house, on to the future, can't go back, committed.

Or probably should be, he thought...sectioned and committed. He drove on.

———~~———

Twelve year old Solomonder Henderson of Tilda watched the overloaded station wagon drive past and noted type/direction/mass/velocity/energy/and... Not that he consciously thought about these things... he just knew them. And more. He could have spoken of the molecular structure and interrelation of the composite alloy of the smallest part; but nobody outside talked to Solly much. He returned to the maze of accumulated electronic parts, wires and oddments on the bench and became lost again...

Julie ignored the screaming racket of her father's angle grinder. She watched her little brother with amusement, and just a bit of concern. She was used to Solly being lost in space, spending hours in odd little games with bits and pieces of their Dad's ginormous collection of spares but this was ridiculous. He had spent the entire Christmas school holidays in the workshop of the Top Ace Electronic, Appliance and Automotive Repair Centre (no job too small or difficult), and for what? Her Dad Steve and his grease-stained library had taught her how most things worked, but majorly weird this new thing was. Definitely O.T.T. And now he was giving her his 'put it together' sign while he bobbed with impatience. She sighed.

Over the years she had been Solly's maker, fixer, and self appointed bodyguard, and had never ceased to be amazed at his way of doing things. She knew he could read (though the teachers didn't believe it), and did it in ten second pages, starting anywhere but the beginning. At least he didn't start at the bottom and read up any more. In Kinder he had driven Miss Lorimer into a first time admission that "this student has not achieved any Key Learning Areas or even basic pre-reading skills."

WE know though, she thought. Two years ago on a frenzied weekend Solly had skimmed every one of Steve's text books, magazines, manuals, stock order books and identification charts, then rifled through all his cabinets, drawers, tins, shelves and cases. No small feat as their Dad Steve was a compulsive hoarder, a Top Tip Scourer and veteran Container Constructor; the Top Ace EAARC was the repository of every piece of technical information, dismantled device or gadget thrown out by the good citizens of the Barangan Valley for decades. The family were bemused by Solly's seemingly pointless activity, then forgot about it until a week later when Steve was tantruming loudly about not having a bloody 35 ohm field dependent transistor for Mrs. Harris's Sony CD and Solly went to the fourth cabinet second drawer seventh box and gave it to him. Gobsmacked. Solly never missed a beat after that. 'My integrated retrieval system' Steve called him.

Jules sighed again and dug out her tools. With gestures she asked 'so solder these here, here and this bit here? OK, lets stickit, bro!' She always loved and melted at the slow wide smile that crept across Solly's face when she built his dreams. And to think some girls at school call me a mega bitch…tsk tsk.

―⁓―

Toby slowed a little for the 50 sign and smiled at the graffiti modified community-unifying signboard. 'BARANGAN - A TurDY TOWN' lay spread out below him in its early Saturday morning haze of mist and wood smoke. He pulled over and his cat sat up to look out the window.

'Well there it is Sean, our new home nestled in the mountains... large bank buildings (doubtless closed), six hotels,

5

now down to two still alive... Deranged Derek's Bargain Bazaar, the Combined Unemployment and Social Services Office (thriving), Barangan Nemesis High School... and unless I'm mistaken, there's our delicious continental breakfast!' Toby exclaimed, pointing to a ramshackle fibro palace proclaiming itself proudly as Addison's Fuel Tyres Batteries Burgers O'Nite Cabins. He whistled the first few bars of 'Deliverance.'

A tad delirious from lack of sleep, Toby was probably at his careless and pompous worst. The entrance was grand enough for his liking; a successful fling of his coat onto the rack and with Sean playing the Lion King.

'Full cream double shot Latte, Pan au Chocolat and a bowl of tepid milk for my feline friend, if you please... or whatever else passes for breakfast!' The waitress looked up coolly over her paper to take in the scruffy, slightly swaying figure, then walked out through the kitchen plastic strip doorway.

A little later, a low, appreciative growl pulled Toby from his slumped doze.

The sound of 'A Man and a Woman' drifted from the servo speakers as he lifted his head to stare in wonderment at the apparition in front of him. Black high heels, silk stockings, a white pinafore apron and a mobcap perched above amused green eyes. She bobbed in a curtsey.

'Pardonez moi monsieur, mais le chef est tres inconsolable. Le pan au chocolat est finit, 'ow ev air, la cafe latte et croissant est tres bien zis matin.'

She whisked a red and white checked cloth from the inlaid cedar tray. Rich fragrances of arabica, warm full cream milk, strawberry jam, and fresh patisserie wafted to his nose.

Sean smiled, Toby gaped.

'Mon Dieu?' she suggested helpfully. 'Merci buckups?' A flower patterned bowl floated to the floor, milk globbled. 'Bon petit dejeuner Monsieur Le Chat... et Monsieur Postérieur Astucieux.' She turned and sauntered away.

Sometime later, after profuse apologies, introductions, fulsome praise and a little humble pie with the first croissant, Toby and Shirley were doing an empty cafe breakfast.

'Not much call for this type of tucker here Toby' said Shirley, 'It's more your burger and chips, or steak and chips for the big night out.' Toby helped himself to another pear tartlet while Sean rubbed against Shirl's leg, a friend for life.

'Pete at the Sunrise Bakery is a reffo from Paddington and knocks them out for the cognoscenti.'

'Reffo?' asked Toby.

'City refugee... are you a reffo Toby?'

'Ah yes... a refugee from the war and strife of a troubled world...' with a spot of the pompous returning, 'although I hasten to add I travel no more, I am in Barangan for the duration. Which I may even come to like, with the help of Pete's Perfect Pastry.'

Under Shirley's gentle interrogation, the sad tale unravelled of Toby's ten years before the Departmental mast, the hazy memory of a pre-Christmas party where his hand was discovered accidentally not his fault really inside the lambs wool jumper of the Regional Director's wife and his January divorce, arranged by his partner's barrister boyfriend.

'A person with some mileage up,' observed Shirley. She also heard of his somewhat uninformed yearning for an idyllic new life in the country, coinciding with the Director's directive that a tree change was the only alternative to a non-career and the unsolicited 'offer' of Barangan High and its Primary feeder schools.

'I found Pike's Crossing and Shelvey on the map, but where's Tilda Primary?'

'Well,' said Shirley, 'Tilda is where I live and if you came here from Canumbie on the back road, you passed it 30 kays out. It's as sweet a little Banjo Paterson spot as you could want, Toby, unless our resident wannabe capitalist gets his hooks into it. Barangan's Only Real Estate Agent, and as flash as a rat with a gold tooth.' She poured another coffee.

'Speaking of real estate, Mr. Toby... and Sean, where are you going to live?'

Later that night, Toby sat on the vinyl covered steel chair and rested his elbows on pure Laminex, feeling dejected. Addison's O'Nite Cabin # 3 was everything Shirley promised, right down to the red flock wallpaper. The bed was soft however, and they weren't too fussed about Sean as a co-resident. Toby reach down to pick up his cat for comfort... forgetting Sean was a cat who chose when it was lap time. He was lucky to get away with a growl and firm bite. Sean would curl up purring on the bed for company when the night grew colder.

———

The school corridor echoed to the familiar grating sounds of adolescence in full flood. Barangan High School had the same vaguely directed chaos as his previous city schools, albeit at a slower pace. Toby did his Carpet-Gum Index, averaging 2.5 blackened blobs per square metre... usually around 13 in Sydney. A very low Swear Index at 2 per 100 steps, and even that in sotto voce. No O.T.T hair, gruesome T-shirts or grunge caps. Toby pressed past the school bags and curious eyes. He tended to avoid the brick tunnels of education during period changes, but was late for his first meeting with the Principal.

Mrs. E. Mackenzie, School Administration Manager.

stated the very permanent plaque on the counter. Toby enquired, was told: 'You are to wait in The Lobby. Mr. McDermott will see you after his phone calls. He is Not To Be Disturbed.' A distinct pursing of lips for emphasis. Toby moved to 'The Lobby', a small room aside the office, dominated by the door to the McDermott throne room. He caught the eye of a lanky, disheveled boy and slid into his interested-but-respectful Counsellor mode.

'Good morning.'

'Morning.'

'You waiting for the Principal?'

'Yair...'

'I'm Toby Buchanan, the new school counsellor.'

'Oh yair.... Right... No worries.'

'That's good to hear then.'

'Waddaya mean?'

'The no worries bit.'

'Yair... no worries... oh right... school counsellor. What happened to the last counsellor?'

' Don't know, I just got here,' said Toby.

'Went mad so they shot her, me Mum says.' He paused. 'She was joking, Sir.'

'Toby.'

'Sir Toby?'

There was a brief break while the participants reviewed their positions and options.

'I'm Brad Denzil. I'm having a post-suspension meeting. We'll be having a meeting after the meeting. Up in your room. The other counsellor used to make a cuppa.' Toby was startled. Students Never introduced themselves.

'Howcome the meeting?'

'Because Counsellor Referral is always in The Agreement, just after To maintain a clean appearance, To show proper respect to school staff, and To arrive punctually in classes.'

'Riiight...'

'Then you get to write the Counsellor Report which says in the bit called Discussion and Recommendations that; This student although persistently becoming involved in behavior contrary to the school rules shows considerable aptitude in most academic areas, and is prepared to improve his behavior.'

He paused then added, 'And should return to complete his school career.' Brad smiled. Toby smiled. This remarkably eloquent student had obviously been down the path before and knew the way.

'Sounds very reasonable.'

The imposing door swung open, and a sharp-faced man in suit and tie emerged.

'Denzil, you will remain silent in the lobby. Your mother was supposed to be here with you at 9:15. It's 9:20. Is she coming?' demanded The Principal Barry McDermott, petulantly.

'I came early to say she would be a bit late, sir.'

'Well sit silently. Stop wriggling. Pick your bag up.'

The Principal swiveled to Toby. 'Come in mr. buchanan.'

Toby noticed the expensive coffee pod machine, silver tray, china teapot, cups and saucers and matching cake plates in a glass cabinet. An entertainer of those above. Gold coloured tie with small black motifs. Amazingly well shaved and clipped. Toby's Upward Mobility Index (UMI) gave high ratings to all of these...

The Principal looked suspiciously at Tobias Buchanan. His network had passed down a highly salacious version of what had happened in Sydney, but he couldn't see it. Buchanan was a bit weedy and definitely worse for wear.

'We won't be having any difficulties... will we. Another point. We expect male staff to wear a tie and be addressed as Mister or Sir at Barangan.' The Principal's eyes were narrowed and Toby got himself ready for a joust.

'Actually... Mr. McDermott... I like to establish an easygoing rapport with students, which requires less formality. It has the Psychological Purpose of enhancing communication, generating mutual trust and facilitating positive outcomes... it is very helpful.'

'Hmm. Hrrummphh… Found your office? It has all the mandatory equipment. You also have a $115 annual counsellor requisition allowance, from My Global Budget.' Toby sensed a whiff of smoke from past battles. The Principal pushed forward a neat stack of documents. 'Here is the Departmental Code of Conduct (meaningful glare), the School Discipline and Welfare policies, copy of Staff Timetable, Staff Dress Code and Staff Carpark Restrictions. Any STD calls go through Mrs. Mackenzie. Leave applications, funding applications, stationery and photocopying requests all go through Mrs. Mackenzie.' Toby suspected that nothing went through the retentive Mrs. Mackenzie with much ease. McDermott straightened his golden tie.

'You will stay here for Bradley Denzil's post suspension meeting. He's a smart aleck, getting up to no good and backchatting staff ever since year 7. I can tell you, if he were older, this would be our last little chat with Mr. Denzil. And his mother can be bloody difficult.' He pressed a button. ' Send them in please, Mrs. Mackenzie.'

Brad and mother walked in; the penny dropped for Toby with a distinct clink.

'Hello Mrs. Denzil, I'm Toby Buchanan, the School Counsellor,' he said, standing.

'Well... good morning to you as well,' said Shirley.

The meeting proceeded on tracks already predicted by Brad, concluding with conduct cards, written apology, final warning and referral for counselling. Toby and Shirley thanked each other formally in the lobby and Brad led Toby off to his room for counselling, the corridor almost deserted as Toby followed at an adolescent face-saving distance. Brad, on the other hand, didn't seem to be fussed about the association, even stopping to introduce Toby to a pair of furtive boys sliding past.

'Me mates, the Dodgey Brothers,' he said. 'Probably buggering off from Technics. Mr. Malcolm is about 90 and doesn't notice much,' he explained with a theatrical wink. 'Keep up Sir Toby, I'd hate for you to get lost on day one.' Barangan High would be so hard to get lost in. Two levels, two sets of stairs, a canteen and a hall.

They rounded a corner and into a not unusual high school tableau. A beefy boy with his back to them was pressing a terrified youngster up against the wall. Expletives and threats were being delivered in low tones. Brad looked at Toby, rolled his eyes, shook his head slightly and then advanced on the pair.

'Put him down Jonesey, there's a teacher...' he whispered conspiratorially.

'You think I give a shit you little queer?' muttered Jonesey, turning to look at Toby. Solidly built, indeed like a brick shithouse, and with the calculating look of a smart, in your face young thug. John Paul Jones' arm casually dropped to brush some imaginary dust off the small, trembling child.

'Good morning Sir... just giving this kid a hand. He's a new year 7 and I think he's lost,' he said with a synthetic smile. 'Are you a new teacher, Sir? What do you teach Sir?'

Toby went on the offensive. 'Aren't you supposed to be in class?'

'I had permission to go to the library... sir.' The tableau expanded. A muscular, red-faced teacher with school sweatshirt, shorts, long socks and trainers came up to the group.

'Any problems here John?' Toby noted this was addressed to Jonesey, not himself.

'No Sir, I'm just talking to the new teacher. On my way back to class Sir.'

Jonesey smirked at Toby, and then sauntered off. Sir grunted approvingly then turned to Toby, looking him up and down with the hostility due to a person out of uniform. Toby suppressed his aversion to PE teachers (he was never good at sports) and smiled back.

'Bruce Pearson, PDHPE. And you are...?'

'Toby Buchanan, the new District School Counsellor.'

The look of distaste lingered after the brief blokey handshake.

'Yeah. Well these two will probably be yours. Bradley Denzil Year 9 and Henderson, the new fruit loop Year 7 who wouldn't answer his name in my roll class this morning. Speaking of Hendersons, here's its sister. You're welcome to the lot, mate.' With a final glower at Brad, Bruce Pearson stalked off. Julie Henderson arrived from the far end of the corridor, summed up Toby with a glance then ignored him.

'What's happened to Solly?'

'Jonesey being a prick...but Sir Toby here stopped him,' added Bradley, diplomatically. 'Mr. Buchanan, this is my mate Julie and her little brother Solly.' Julie looked less dismissively at Toby.

'Thanks, Sir. I'll take Solly back to Miss Scott so she can sort out his classes.'

She took Solly's hand and marched off. Toby received a brief, disconcertingly direct stare from him as they turned the corner.

—/νν—

Toby opened up his modestly sized but comfortable new office. The posters of soft-headed puppies with saccharin aphorisms had to go, the bark painting could stay.

'Not bad, considering,' he said, 'Better than the average broom cupboard.'

Brad was already filling the kettle from a small sink and had the mugs, tea bags and sugar jar out. Toby emptied his bag out on the desk, and tried to look marginally in charge. On impulse he stepped into 1930's movie-mode...

'I say. One sugar thenks Denzil.' Brad looked up momentarily.

'Roight you are then, Zurr.' No hesitation. 'If'n you loike oi can go down to village shop for zum milk... and mayhaps zum teacake or biscuit zurr?'

Amazing, thought Toby. Just like his mother; must be a theatrical family.

'Umm, this village shop...?'

'The school canteen Mr. B. All I need is a note. Mrs. Evans will set you up with a tab, pay at the end of the month. Very accommodating. Wide range of produce.'

Tea and something large with pink icing later, Mr. B and Denzil had resolved counselling requirements satisfactorily. Brad would refrain from making inappropriate/sarcastic comments in class, would sort out his uncompleted assessment task in Geography and attempt to turn up on time on most days. Toby suggested that at this stage of his educational career, Brad probably needed to sink into the background a little. Brad agreed, then gave Toby a guided tour of his office, stationery cupboard, filing system and how to call up students. He opened the Counsellor computer to Records of Student Contact, then to his own file. Passwords would obviously need to change.

Recess arrived, Brad left, and after the traffic cleared, Toby went exploring. He was seeking the bold Ms. Scott, the Support Teacher for Learning who apparently had the temerity to address staff meetings and defend students. He eventually found her in the grandly named Educational Resource Independent Centre, the ERIC, which resembled an ancient computer shop set amidst the Daintree rainforest. He pushed through the fronds.

'Dr. Scott, I presume...' Maria Scott looked up from her cluttered desk and gave a broad smile.

'And you would be Toby Buchanan, District School Counsellor, lately fled from Sydney due to mildly shocking circumstances and servant to a formidable cat.' Toby shook his head in wonder. Small country towns.

'Shirley Denzil is my friend and staunch supporter in the fight against the dark forces of uniformity.' Toby was staring at the dark, animated face opposite.

'You seem strangely familiar, Ms. Scott, have we met before? A conference perhaps?' Maria groaned dramatically.

'I came back to teaching six years ago, Mr. Buchanan, to remove myself from a difficult situation, much like yourself. Does 'Update Host Resigns' ring any bells? Barangan didn't receive ABC TV in those days so I could slide in here unnoticed. I need not say more.'

Toby recalled fiery exchanges after a much needed airing of Corruption in Exclusive Places. Key players quietly submerged and the messenger became a casualty. As a determined city escapee (Definitely not a 'refugee', Toby), Maria had been making the best she could under the McDermott/Mackenzie Junta. Over coffee he heard of reading schemes cobbled together from the ether, discarded computers restored, older students press-ganged as tutors, materials extorted from local businesses and small but significant moneys extracted painfully from Regional District Coffers. He was given a run down on notable staff and students, Maria's own cat, life in Barangan and the Sunrise Bakery sourdough. Toby relaxed in the glow of civilized conversation, chatting about the Sydney Festival, plays, movies. He even slid into his ancient but favourite alien acronym joke: What is E.T. short for? It's because of his little legs.

He described his corridor contretemps with Jonesey, and Maria went to serious mode.

'I wondered what happened. Julie bought her brother back here in a very frozen state before recess, most peculiar. I kept them both here, Julie to cool down and Solly to warm back to life. For brother and sister they are very complementary. Jules talked to Solomonder, did a run around on the computers and took him off to period three.'

'Solomonder?'

15

'Yes, Solomon-der. They get some great names in Tilda.'

'Sort of a very wise lizardy thing?'

'Whatever. Young Solly is away from the safety of Primary School and doesn't like it much. Don't know much about him; dear Miss Lorimer of Tilda Public says in his record card, "Delightful boy, may have language problems, is very good at mathematics, loves the computer. Small friendship group"... which seems to consist of the Denzil boys, although even there I'm not sure he gets on too well' she added. 'Another thing - there doesn't appear to have been any useful testing. Maybe you can find out what the story is when you're out wandering the countryside like a proper School Counsellor?'

—⁓—

Much happened over the following few days. He discovered that Barangan High led the Regional Rugby Competition, due to the Coaching of Brucie Pearson and Captaincy of Jonesey. Depressing, but it explained Jonesey's untouchable status. Toby had also been forced to visit Jonesey Senior, Barangan's Best (Barangan's Only) Real Estate Agent and Mayor, after deciding to move out of town. His Addison O'Nite cabin was getting a little crowded with Sean as his station wagon emptied.

'You want to live out in the bush? What for?' snorted Glen Jones. 'I've got a vacancy at the Glen for you, prime spot, even got a dishwasher. Special teacher's deal... what with me President of the P&C and young John Paul doing so well...' Jonesey Senior tapped the side of his nose and winked. Toby didn't fancy life with the unmarried teachers of the 'Glen's View Park' brickblock of flats. It was next to the Barangan Arms, where the majority drank, a lot, most afternoons. He resisted other offers until Jonesey leant forward and said, 'Ya know... I might be able to help you anyway. I picked up a nice brick house out at Tilda last year, could give you an open ended lease at 180 a week... no, make it 150... since you're a teacher. Mate. Have a look if you like...'

Toby took the keys and directions politely.

A day later and Toby was on his grand tour to outlying Primary Schools. The peregrination had taken him to the outskirts of Tilda, and opening the padlocked gate, he drove in to view Jonesey Senior's rural acquisition.

Oh God, thought Toby, to end one's days here in unsplendid isolation... a prospect too horrible to contemplate. The featureless red brick house, garage and Hills Hoist could have been lifted from a suburban desert and glued into the middle of the flat, bare paddock. Toby steeled himself to walk through the kitchen and lounge room, looked in the bedroom but had to flee outside, shaking. A pervasive, awful melancholy chilled him utterly, despite the sunshine. Two despondent cows watched him leave from across the field.

Low in spirits, he arrived at Tilda Public school as its fourteen students of various sizes decamped on foot, by bicycle or parented 4WD. Large, grey haired, fifty something and radiating Jolly, Miss Florence Lorimer organized and bustled the parents and children away.

'Don't forget to bring the tadpoles in Jimny, if you find some. Proper shoes, Farraweigh. Tiddle's birthday cake was lovely Mrs. Fenton.' Toby's mood of despair shrank before the relentless barrage of trivial good cheer, and gave up completely in the face of a nice mug of tea and a cosy chat. From Miss Lorimer's description, the Tilda 14 seemed an uncomplicated lot; 'Apart from Giorgio, but he's gone to High School and was doing much better since the tablets... and his Dad was much the same, always in trouble. I think it's just the nature of that family.' Children and their full social histories, some back two generations, were laid bare. Toby got to an appropriate slot to drop Solomonder into the flow.

'Aah... poor pet, didn't seem to be able to read no matter how much phonics we put to him, even so he just loved books. It's the pictures I suppose. When I say he couldn't read, he sometimes did written answers on the comprehension sheets but never read out loud. He didn't sit the basic skills Tests in grade 3 and 5; he was away on both those days. Anyway, he could get help because of his sister and the Denzil boys.' Toby could picture this quiet one-teacher school, where the older students helped the younger students with the very serviceable, well polished, and well used exercise sheets. Well oiled clockwork, definitely analogue rather than digital.

Miss Lorimer had been drifting. She pulled herself up.

'Now where were we. Oh Yes, Solly. So you see I wasn't toooo worried because he was good on the find a word sheets. Very quick, even though he was left-handed... sometimes… He was very good with the computer too, flipping around that internet thingy.

'What about mixing with other kids? Any problems?' asked Toby.

'Well, right at the start he tried to play with the other Kindies in the sand pit building things, but he sort of drifted off after a problem with Giorgio. Anyway, the other children didn't pay much attention to Solly, because of the talking thing...' She began drifting again.

'Talking thing?' asked Toby, rebooting gently.

'He didn't. I've had some shy children here in my time, but Solly, I don't think he spoke to me once in the seven years.' Toby was dumbfounded.

'He hadn't spoken at school for seven years? But didn't anything happen? Like some assessments? Like Speech Pathology, Paediatricians? Anything?'

'The school nurse had a look at him and his hearing and vision seemed to be all right, and Miss Wilson had a look at him, that's the other school counsellor who left and got married last year. She did some tests on him somewhere...' Miss Lorimer began to rummage, fishing and ferreting while reminiscing. 'Anyway she said that he was a bit low in ability and that we should just let him do what he could... but he never really talked, just so shy. His sister Julie used to understand what he needed so she did most of his special help... under supervision I hasten to add.' Miss Lorimer paused to think, requiring a finger in the air and pursed lips. 'Ah... yes...of course they would be with the rest of Miss Wilson's stuff, she had her own little cabinet, but I'm not sure where the key would be.' Toby smiled conspiratorially while pulling out his School Counsellor Secret Universal Cabinet Key.

The Wilson Files were neat and petite, apart from the substantial and unfortunate Giorgio Savellis, who appeared to have contracted the widest variety of behavioural and learning syndromes. He unearthed the Solomonder a.k.a. Solly Henderson folder and spent the two minutes needed to read it. Amazing. Cryptic sentences in the Wilson hand outlining ongoing language problems, incomplete assessments due to "work refusal", difficulties in parent cooperation for further referrals, and a final comment from 12 months earlier -

**V. quick but erratic computer use, can navigate internet but seems random choices. Still no language used @ school. Home???

Toby was tempted to add "can't sing, can't act, can dance a little"

It was getting close to 4:30, with Florence Lorimer putting the final touches to her school satchel and searching out her car keys.

'I'll be back in a fortnight and we can chat about anything I can do,' announced Toby.

'I'll take these files to the High School, although if Giorgio's goes over two kilograms, he will have to be deleted...' The joke slid past, unnoticed. 'Thank you very much for a delightful afternoon... this is a lovely set up you have here... most interesting and helpful,' added Toby with transparent charm. Miss Lorimer was transparently charmed and glowed a little. 'Could you give me an idea where the Henderson's place is, Miss Lorimer? I might drop around there to say hello to Solly's parents.'

'Of course, dear. You'll probably find Stephen in unless he's out delivering or picking up things. Where they live is the Top Ace workshop, in their house at the back.'

—*w*—

Toby eased the Camry off the road, around a rusted tangle of fencing wire and parked at the front of the Top Ace etc etc workshop. The large building appeared shut, but the continuous screech of tortured metal announced Mr. Henderson's presence inside. Seriously grinding. Mentally crossing fingers against imagined junkyard dogs (Oh Sean, where are you when I need you?), he worked his way around the side, threading through piles of rusted pipes, motors and whitegoods carcasses. Sidling around the corner, Toby peered into the dark recess. Showers of sparks illuminated the back of a huge cylinder in full opera style. All a bit too Götterdämmerung. Close by, he recognised the backs of Solly and Julie, intent on what appeared to be a large cube of loosely assembled electricky things. Julie was busy with a smoking soldering iron, clippers and wire. He watched fascinated by the speed at which she worked, seemingly under Solly's direction. He would select parts from a large wire basket, indicate locations and what was to be done by a series of complex gestures, with return finger moves from Julie. Was this Auslan? Toby knew a little of the non-verbal language from working in Support Units, but couldn't recognise any of the signs being used. Whatever it was, it worked well, with the precise clipping, stripping and soldering fair cantering along. Both were oblivious to the racket from the grinder. Toby moved closer and saw that the cube was held together by bolted steel brackets and resembled a deranged meccano installation, festooned with multi coloured wires which draped or darted off to the inside. Edging sideways to get a better view, he nudged a drum and …Crash! Julie spun around with the soldering iron out while Solly did a startled rabbit bolt. Toby put his hands out, mouthed 'sorry' and hastily assumed the innocent idiot pose of the lost traveller. Julie glared, but put the soldering iron down and gestured to go back around the side of the shed.

'Sorry about that' said Toby; ' I was out this way to see Miss Lorimer, so I thought I would drop in to meet your Mum and Dad.'

'Oh?' Suspicious.

'Umm... that looked interesting... what are you and Solly working on...?' Ingratiating.

Silence. Toby felt distinctly uncomfortable. 'Is it a Science project? Something for Art? An electronics thing?'

'Art project.' Obviously not to be discussed. 'I'll go and get Dad. He might be too busy. You stay here,' said Julie. And don't move, thought Toby. Julie disappeared around the corner and moments later the racket ceased. Premonitions of a bulky, belligerent sort of person who would own the possible ferocious Junkyard Dog were making Toby a little nervous until a small, grubby man with goggles and earmuffs came out of the gloom and grinned.

'G'day there. I was scouring a steel tank with the angle grinder and didn't hearya knock. Steve Henderson. Youse must be the counsellor Jules talked about.' A handshake like a lump of granite.

'Toby Buchanan... I was out seeing Miss Lorimer at the Primary and just thought...'

Five minutes later, Toby found himself on a cane lounge, under a pergola laden with Wisteria, clutching a stubby and supplied with chips. Steve had introduced his wife Liz, then declared he'd chucked it in for the day. He raised his bottle.

'Cheers, Tobes. So what's happening in the big school nowadays? Jules and Sol going OK? How's Sol settling into Year 7? What's the weather like in Barangan?'

Toby chatted trivialities then carefully catwalked into the tricky bits.

' Well… with Solly… early days yet… it's quite a transition to High School, probably just a bit of shyness but I'm wondering if I could help with a possible referral to…' He was pulled up by the Steve beer bottle coming down Firmly on the table.

'I'm not sure where you're off to Toby, but are you saying the Sol has some problem? Now I could get a bit frosty at that, but you're lucky. The word from Shirl is that you're OK, which carries a bittta weight. Are you on about him not talking too much in class? The beer bottle and eyebrows were raised. Liz Henderson's head inclined. Toby tried to process the short cut. Somehow he wasn't surprised that the Sphere of Shirley Denzil spread through Tilda and decided that if Shirley told Steve that Toby was OK, then ipso facto Steve was OK by association. Even if a bit blunt.

'Miss Lorimer was a bit vague, but seems to say that Solly never really spoke and he certainly doesn't talk at the High School. Miss Scott the support teacher and I have been wondering... how his language was... if he ever had a speech assessment... and umm, does he have any problems like that at home?' he finished lamely.

'Is there anyone worth talking to at that High School?' mused Steve. 'He's just fine at home. Take my word for it.' He upended his beer.

'Well, sometimes it's also not a bad idea if there seems to be a... difficulty in relating to other people that a good Paediatrician can help. There's this thing called... umm... Autism...' Toby stopped as he noticed knuckle whitening, muscle bunching and eye narrowing. Liz Henderson intervened quietly.

'Mr. Buchanan, our son would not be anywhere on the Autism spectrum, including Asperger's Syndrome or indeed any Pervasive Developmental Disorder, specified or not otherwise specified.' The quiet authority of the voice brooked no argument. Steve Henderson relaxed and smiled. The moment passed.

'Yer see Tobymate, not autisticky at all. He's healthy as a mallee bull.'

Toby nodded and waited a minute before lurching onto another, less dangerous tack.

'Do Julie and Solly use some other kind of... communication?'

'Sorry?'

Toby spoke of the flickering fingers directing the art project in the shed while Steve drew some hieroglyphs in the condensation on his bottle. He turned and called.

'Hey Jules, c'mere.' Julie appeared. 'Toby here reckons you and Sol were communicating a bit, like without talking, in the shed just now. Howcome?' Julie considered for a moment.

'Too noisy to talk' she said tersely.

'There ya go Tobes, that's y'r explanation,' said Steve.

The rest of the afternoon was just as fruitless regarding any exploration of "difficulties". Over the second beer, Toby heard of the horrors of boiler descaling and washing machine rebuilds. Over the third beer he popped his last question.

'Umm... would it be all right if I did some assessment with Solly in the next week or two? Just to check out how his reading, writing and 'rithmatic are going. And maybe do a... general ability test? It takes an hour and a bit, and there's a whole bunch of different things to do in it so he won't get bored.' It was the blandest description he could make of an IQ assessment. Steve looked levelly across the table for a little longer than comfortable. He's bloody laughing at me thought Toby, noting the smallest of amused crinkles.

'Well...mate, like I said, Shirl reckons you're passable, so I'll leave it up to Solly. If you reckon he'll get some amusement out of some basic skills and a psychometric workup I'll be interested in seeing how you go.' Toby had a definite whiff of the mickey being taken. 'He gets interested in all sorts of things so he might go for it. However, Toby, he's a stubborn little coot and if he decides to pull the plug half way... don't push it.'

'We will look forward to the very limited publication of your report,' added Liz. 'Circulation to us, Maria Scott and Solly. You never know, he might want it bound for his memoirs someday.' Everyone smiled.

'Nother beer?' asked Steve.

—◦◦◦—

Toby pondered as he drove... sensibly and slowly... back to Barangan. "Well that went well" didn't quite apply, at least in a conventional sense. His list of Shirl-links had increased, and presumably included Maria. Where did that particular circle come from? He had permission to see Solomonder, but not in writing, and with interesting strictures. Solly himself had not appeared again and Toby suspected there was going to be many more elusive episodes to come. And what was in Steve's remark during Beer IV?

'The answer, Tobes, to a full life, is in the Dramatic Element.'

—◦◦◦—

Chapter Two

The Henderson offspring were hard at work in the back of the shed. Julie lugged the two car batteries across from the charger and connected them together as directed. More days of work had produced a dense, cubic metre of linked components channelled into four thick wires. She was confident that it was going to do something, but just what, she wasn't sure.

It was two years earlier that Solly had gathered bits and pieces and pestered her to start soldering. This first effort had been a mystery too, until Solly hooked it up to the satellite dish and it picked up two hundred and forty-seven global television channels, all the radio frequencies, and mobile phone transmissions. Of course, operating the old sound studio eighty-six knob control board took a while and operation was always a bit inscrutable... but it worked. Steve called it 'The Combination Stirfry Dekko Omnitron', and it kept him amused for weeks while he compiled an exercise book full of all the police, truckies and town notables mobile phone settings, along with what he claimed were ASIO, FBI, CIA and probably KGB secret channels. Julie introduced Solly to the Internet at school just after that, with the Dekko quickly being modified to explore this new world at home. He had gone off practical projects in favour of www.surfing, apart from directing the wiring of their combined satellite dish / municipal band size pergola.

—⁓—

'All right, so what's next?' asked Julie. Sol was vibrating with excitement, pointing to the green and red leads from junction one and to the double battery. 'Moment of truth,' thought Julie, motioning Solly to back off some. Shielding her eyes and ready to run, she hooked the alligator clips on... Nothing happened. When Julie moved closer, she couldn't detect any smoke or sparks. She nodded approval then looked on for half an hour as he darted around the cube, prodding with his multimeter, checking, and occasionally asking for a solder spot. Finally, he stood back and quietly slipped his hand into Julie's. Didn't happen often, must be a thank you she thought. Or anxiety.

'It's all very well sitting there, but what does it do Sol?' Julie watched as he reached in and flicked the off/on switch on the side of an included forty-year-old transistor radio. Searching through a rusted pile, Solly then selected a small, solidly rusted venerable water pump and carefully attached the blue and black leads at opposite ends. He crossed Julie's fingers for her, crossed his own and flicked the switch... A soft, deep hum. As Julie watched, fingers still crossed, a very faint blue glow crept over the pump, and as it did, Solly's face cracked into a grin of relief. After five minutes he flicked the switch, the hum and glow died.

'Oh yeah... so it hums and glows?' asked Julie. Solly shook his head, raced to the workbench and returned with a hand brush. Eyes sparkling and with an elaborate, vaudeville magician movement, he swept the brush across the pump. Julie gasped as a small black cloud drifted off, revealing a shining, fresh minted steel surface.

'Bloody Hell! How did it do that? Bloody hell!' Julie walked around the pump, flicking off what looked like black soot. A beautifully glowing, albeit deeply corroded 1920's Henry Berry water pump emerged. Realisation dawned. 'Will it do bigger things?' Vigorous nod. 'Awesome! You did it for Steve didn't you. What a beast! He's gunna be mega pleased!'

—⌇⌇—

And so he was. Julie and Solly fully charged the batteries and extended the leads to either side of the tank Steve had been working on. He watched, nonplussed (Steve did nonplussed very well) as the blue glow crept quickly over the steel, patiently waited the five minutes and then jaw-dropped when they did the magic bit with two brooms. Steve walked around the tank, shaking his head in disbelief and running his fingers over the shining surface. He climbed inside, emerging soot smudged and still shaking his head. He looked at Solly, picked him up, held him at arms length then hugged him, laughing.

'Jeez Sol, how in the hell did you work this one out?' He gestured outside to the other four tanks waiting patiently for his grinder. 'If it does them I can take a holiday! What a bobby dazzler y'are… Holy Moley! Thanks!' He gave the squirming Solly another bear hug, then Jules as well. He walked admiringly around the cube while Julie tried to explain how it had grown from an ex-washing machine circuit board buried in the middle, into the monster it now was. How only some of the components of each board were used, how it didn't make sense trying to trace the circuits in a linear fashion because they constantly looped across or backtracked. Much more amazed head shaking.

'Never thought inside squares, our Sol,' said Steve. 'D'ya reckon you could shrink it down a bit? After I've done the other tanks of course!' Steve patted the cube respectfully.

'We better keep this little beauty under our belt, though. Sure as shootin those bastards out there'd rip it off...' he said, indicating the world at large.

———

A new week at school crunched into first gear as Toby unpacked his Parker Scales of Intelligence Secondary School (4th Edition, Revised). Affectionately known by its acronym, "Psissiver", it sat up on its own chair, spilling out manuals and anonymous grey containers. Makes me look like a travelling salesman in a cheap motel, Toby thought.

There was a tap on the door; it was the Office Runner with Solomonder trailing behind. Maria assured him that he would have 'a lovely time working with Mr. Buchanan,' and left.

'Come in young Sol and take a pew' said equally jolly Toby. 'This is the box of tricks, Solomonder, guaranteed not to contain anything likely to jump out at you or explode...' Solly glanced across, then back, waiting. Hmmm... Toby chatted breezily through his digital stopwatch routine, a sure fire winner with gadget kids. Nope. He pulled out his ancient, ticking analogue stopwatch; 'See, it doesn't need batteries and you wind it up and..... if I can get this open... There, you can see the little wheels and springs.... Have a listen to it.' Slightly longer glance.... but wouldn't pick it up.

'Well Solly, you may have heard of Bribery and Corruption.' He whisked out a packet of mints from its stash in the suitcase lid. 'This... is a bribe. Or a positive, tangible reinforcement to secure your goodwill and co-operation.' Solly politely reached out, took the proffered mint and dropped it into his shirt pocket. And waited. 'Now the first bit of work we can get into is a bit of a quiz. We start off pretty easy... I'm going to ask some questions and I want you to tell me the answer... like... What goes along a road?... Hmmm? Would you like me to repeat the question...well... Tell me something that goes along a road?' Solly sat patiently, arms folded. Toby waited the mandatory ten seconds, maintaining a hopeful expectancy. Nothing. He scribbled dnr. Did not respond. 'Oookay... well what about this one Sol. Why do animals and plants need water...?' dnr.

And so it went, with Toby scoring did not respond/zeros for the eight questions to reach the required failure ceiling. Nil on Vocabulary. 'Well that didn't go swimmingly well...' said Toby, 'but...let's try this little beauty.' The test board for Picture-Letter-Number Matching was laid out with a flourish.

'Now... you will have two minutes to do this' he said, sliding the box of small tiles toward Solly, half expecting to see them disappear into the shirt pocket with the mint. 'See the numbers one to twelve, and each one matches a letter or a picture.' He looked Solly straight in the eye and said, sotto voce, 'Think of it as a challenge, battling against time to finish.' Toby began with the directions. 'Now, in these squares you put the...' but had to grab for the stopwatch as Solly, after the briefest stare at Toby's face, upended the box and began swiftly placing tiles. So swiftly in fact that eighteen seconds later Toby clicked off, looking at the neat, complete and correct array.

'Awesome, Solly, awesome! Fastest I've ever seen in fact...' Toby shook his head, cleared away. 'While we're cooking with gas here, see if you can tell me what these words mean...'

—⁓—

Toby was doing recess with Maria.

'Every language item was a zero, but when the subtests didn't need language... omigod Maria, every single one the maximum score... Never seen anything like it. So what have we got here?'

Maria grunted non-committedly into her coffee. 'His receptive language understanding must be OK,' she opined, 'like he knew what to do with the directions, didn't he. I'm sure there is a good language base in there somewhere and he must be doing some reading just to navigate around the Internet the way he does.' Toby was not so sure, pointing out the bizarre nature of the sites Solly chose and the brief time he spent on each. What would a twelve year old get from advanced quantum physics, super conductivity, radioactive transmutation or quarks? What is a quark anyway? The noise a duark makes? He held forth on possibilities such as the boy being quite developmentally delayed but with some compensatory spikes of skill, such as in maths. All the indicators were that he was severely behind in expressive language, with a strong possibility of high functioning autism...nil language, obsessive nature, restricted scope of interests, poor social skills etcetera, etcetera.

'I feel that this will be a difficult and intricate case, Watson, and not elementary at all. We shall communicate further.'

The follow-up phone call to Solly's dad Steve suggesting Speech Pathology proved as fruitless as before; a bit like keeping a frog race on track.

'Yair well, we might look into that a bit later. Bit quick in a few areas is he? No surprises there. How did you get along with him then? Didn't muck up?'

Friendly enough talk, but nothing that contained a glimmer of illumination.

Two days later in the BHS corridor, Toby got more answers than he bargained for. He was walking the corridor, considering the possibility of recruiting Shirley Denzil for help when he ran into a repeat Jonesey intimidation-with-immediate-physical-threat. As the rubber soled Toby neared, he distinctly heard 'the geek that can't speak' and a suggestion of anatomical damage.

'We have to stop meeting like this, Jones. Particularly when it looks like targeted verbal harassment of a younger student, punishable no doubt by the gallows. Or something else inconvenient.'

Jones turned, mouth open to say something, reconsidered and glazed.

'Well I'm not quite sure what you're talking about Sir, Sallymandy (slight snigger) and I were just having a joke. Isn't that right Sally? Tell Mr. Buchanan then. Oh but of course... is it true that that this... kid can't speak at all? It would be OK to call him dumb then...?'

'Sol-o-mon-der is quite capable of writing an incident report, as am I, Jones.'

'I'm sure it wouldn't need to come to that Sir, but if you need to, speak to my year advisor. That's Mr. Pearson the Head Teacher for Discipline and Head Teacher of PE Sir. I'm sure he would vouch for my character, Sir.'

'Do you think Mr. Pearson would condone bullying?'

'I don't think he would see it that way, Sir.' Again, a stand off.

'You should get along to your class.'

'Yes Sir. And of course I will take care not to be Seen to be bullying younger students in future' said Jones with a winning smile and agreeable nod.

The little shit does sincere as well, thought Toby as he turned to Solly.

'Are you all right Sol, he didn't hit you did he? I can help you write an incident report if you want...' No response, but didn't appear too fussed. 'Well listen Solly, if you want to, come up to Miss Scott's ERIC at lunchtime. I'll be there from the start and we can work something out. Are you OK to go to class now? Just make sure that if you see Jones or his mates, you stay out of sight or move off in a determined and assertive manner. I'll speak to Mr. Pearson although that oily, Teflon tongued larrikin Jones probably will probably escape the long arm of the law...' Toby turned to go.

'Oleaginous.'

The voice appeared to come from nowhere. Toby turned to see who had been listening in. No one had come around the corner. He looked down to Solly.

'Oleaginous... having properties of oil. Greasy. Larrikin... a street rowdy... what about hooligan? A holleaginous hooligan?' Solly smiled sweetly at Toby. 'Dad said I should talk to you. He reckons you're too persistent, like. I will come up to Miss Scott's at lunchtime. May I use the computer?'

Toby could only nod. Solly smiled and nodded back, turned and left.

―⁓―

Five minutes to lunch time as Toby sat impatiently with Maria.

'Tell me again what he said,' she asked. Toby told her.

'And with Oleaginous, he was spot on. Nice word.'

'Bloody hell Toby, I'm impressed. You seem to be the first person to get a word out of him, and you come away with sentences like that. Sinks a few theories that you floated?'

Toby grunted his agreement. 'Yes… bit of an anticlimax really. We still need to work out what's happening. Like whom he talks to and why doesn't he talk to anyone else? Is he a selective mute with an anxiety condition? Can he only talk to some people with sign language...?'

'That would be silly because Julie and I only finger talk when it's too noisy,' said Solly. 'Like Jules said before' he added, reprovingly. Again, that startling and unfamiliar voice, this time coming from the door.

'Come in Solly, nice to see you ... and hear you' said Maria, ' I guess you feel it's all right to talk to me too.'

'Yes, Mum and Dad like you too and Mrs. Denzil says you are great.'

Toby sat back to digest this. The Shirley Effect.

'But what's the problem, isn't it silly not to talk to most people anyway? Do you have to get permission to talk to people? Why wouldn't you talk to me when we did the testing?' asked Toby.

'You weren't asking proper questions. They were silly, like asking people what colour the sky is? I was waiting for you to finish. You always stopped after four or six questions. I liked the other bits though. My dad Steve said to tell you it's all a bit complicated, but they would talk to you both if you can came out to lunch on Saturday at 12. And not to mention this to anyone else, please.' He looked at Toby and Maria. They looked at each other. Toby shrugged, Maria nodded.

'Oh good, that's all sorted then. May I use the computers now?' asked Solly.

—◊—

Late afternoon Friday, Toby opened the Lime Green door of O'Nite cabin # 3 and groaned loudly. The Soft Orange curtains at the window were in ragged strips, but not only that, the bottom half of his best school shirt appeared to have gone into a shredder, jammed and reversed out. The Ingcat had been left in again.

'You bastard Sean...' said Toby, but without any real conviction. Sean got up from the bed, did a slow and perfect stretch and made his leisurely way out the door. Toby was staring morosely into his beer when Shirley Denzil dropped in and saw the shirt.

'Afternoon Buchanan... Should I get you some moth balls?'

'You sure old Addison would notice if I put a cat door in? But I suppose it would destroy the architectural balance. We need a new home.' He opened Shirley a beer while she carefully rinsed a glass.

'You never know your luck in the big country, Tobe. And yours might be about to change'

'Why, what do you know...?'

'I also know you and Maria will lunch well tomorrow' she said, with a grin.

'Is there anything happening in The Barangan Shire that you don't know?'

'Not much...' They both took a long draught.

'Shirley, what's the story with Solly Henderson?' She gave him a slow, measured stare.

'First off Toby, I know Stephen and Elizabeth Henderson as close friends, they are very straight down the line and anything they tell you Saturday will be true. Not that Steve can't bullshit with the best if he's up against someone who's nasty or bureaucratic, but he doesn't see you as either. As yet. Second thing Toby, Solly's so-called problems are no big deal. He talks to us too. Listen to the Hendersons, see what you can do to help.'

'Fair enough,' said Toby, lifting his bottle. 'Glad to be enmeshed in the Shirley Denzil web. Cheers, Mate' There was a brief interlude while they listened to a dog yelping down the road. Sean getting his exercise.

'So what does Steve Henderson mean by 'The Dramatic Element' then?' asked Toby.

———

'Ah well, there's a thing... I daresay Liz, Maria and myself will recruit you in. There's a role for everyone in The Tilda Amateur Dramatic And Float Inspirational Committee, even if we haven't decided this year's theme yet. One always comes along.' Toby was mystified, but Shirley would not elaborate.

'Trust me. TADAFIC and you will be a good fit...'

Maria insisted on doing the driving to Tilda on Saturday morning. After helloes from the high speed blur of Liz in the kitchen, they were ushered into the Wisteria Rotunda and seated by the refreshingly animated Solomonder. 'The full Indian Feast mate, said Steve, relieving Toby of his Mudgee Red. 'We'll have a bit of a realpolitik yarn after Solly's dessert, as fine a bit of Ras Gulla as you would get this side of Bengal.'

'Cream Balls in syrup' said Maria to Toby.

'Everybody is impressed with Solly's Cream Balls' said Jules, with a smirk. Toby and Maria were amused to see a blush and a kick from Solly. Nice to be normal.

Two hours later they were replete, wined and dined, anecdoted, charmed and also mightily impressed with the Henderson cuisine. Relaxing around the cleared table, Toby reflected that these people could sell him anything after a meal like that. As if on cue, Liz began. 'Toby and Maria, we've some serious explaining to do about how normal our kids are. Well, relatively anyway... It's not very complicated and it's very much about choice. As you have noticed, Solly is quite an exceptional boy; he takes in all of the information around him, weighs it, solves it and sticks to it. Stubborn little coot, as Steve says. All this kerfuffle is about a decision he made way back on day one in Kindergarten...'

———

Solomonder Henderson and Giorgio Savellis had been mismatched as partners from the start. They wandered randomly around the large playground, Giorgio clutching his outsized dump truck; his eyes lighting up as he saw the sandpit.

'We play here' he growled at three smaller boys, who prudently retreated. 'You play with me' ordered Giorgio, pointing to an abandoned plastic car. Solly nudged it with his foot, uninspired. A dusty cloud enveloped both boys as Giorgio filled his truck.

'This stuff is shit' Giorgio pronounced. He had mountains of washed brickies sand at home.

'It's a bit fine,' agreed Solly. 'On the Krumbein phi scale... it's too little' he added helpfully. Giorgio growled. He didn't like words. 'Sand is amazing stuff though,' went on Solly, oblivious. There was a deeper growl. 'Like the quicksand you see in the movies. It's actually salty water and sand in a colloid hydrogel that's like a liquid except you don't sink in it, you just get stuck in it and die of thirst in the desert because...' The large metal truck slammed into his side, knocking him flat. It hurt, heaps. Giorgio stood over him, the dumpster raised up over his head.

'You shut up you smartie. You don't say nothing or I bury you and make you dead.' The vigilant Miss Lorimer bellowed from thirty metres, sending both naughty boys to the silver seats. Which is where Solomonder decided that social discussion at school didn't hold a lot of interest.

He would take Giorgio's advice.

Liz had finished her vignette and Steve concluded it.

'After that, the only kids he was interested in talking to were Jules and the Denzils. Dear Miss Lorimer didn't really stretch his mind much, so he just got into the habit of staying schtum.'

Toby played with his glass of red trying not to look perplexed. Even though he was.

'So that was all it was? Just Solly deciding he wouldn't talk?'

'Pretty much...'

'Pretty much? Like pretty much he hasn't made friends with any kids his peer group, won't play games or socialize apart from with a few selected adults and family?' A shade of annoyance was creeping into Toby's voice; he was moving into lecture mode. Maria's fingers brushed his arm. Liz was getting a bit moist around the eyes.

'Yes… we know. We tried lots of things, like Jules invited friends and their little brothers around, and Shirley always bought Bobby with her, but they seemed to fall out. No fights, mind you. It just never quite worked. Solly always chose to move off… Not ideal…'

'Not ideal…' muttered Steve, staring down at the table.

'We don't know' said Liz, 'what to do. Solly just says that kids ignore him, and they don't listen even if he does try. He chose not to try anymore.'

'And judging on what's happened at the High School so far, maybe it's best he doesn't attract any attention to himself,' added Steve.

'Yes,' said Liz. 'Let's keep things as they are, in the meanwhile. It's easier and it's what Solly wants. Are you two all right with that? Talk about it, have some lemon poppy seed cake while we take a walk.' Steve filled his glass and followed Liz out.

Toby and Maria looked at each other. 'Well...'

'Well indeed. We can't just leave, of course' said Maria, reaching for the cake.

'I suppose not' said Toby, with a distinct feeling that his simple life had just slid out of the station and left him on the platform. 'How's the cake?'

They conferenced. They were uncomfortable about the social isolation of Solly not talking to staff and students until they remembered the social development of most Barangan staff and students. The ethics and possible consequences of practising a deception were dismissed, as all that was expected was direct reports on Solly's work and behaviour as presented at school.

'And let people draw their own conclusions,' said Toby. It was hard enough to change some staff beliefs and expectations as it was. 'And there's the wishes of the client and all that. Confidentiality thingies too. Not that much of a moral dilemma.'

'Basically,' said Maria, 'it comes down to that great adage, when in doubt, do nowt.'

They were both uneasy, but if Solly's self-imposed withdrawal from speaking publicly wasn't causing him any great harm, they would go along with it. Something would need to be worked out eventually, though.

'Sometimes it's the grown ups that have to make the choices…' said Toby.

—⁓—

Toby, Maria, Liz and Steve smiled at each other, meeting suitably resolved.

'Drinks all round, do you reckon?' asked Steve, disappearing inside.

Some chat later, Steve raised house hunting. 'You were visiting the Jervis place last week?'

'Yes. It was a little … depressing,' Toby added. 'Whose place did you say it was?'

'Francis Jervis and depressing would be right. Poor bloody Francis went broke last year, his wife and kid left for Sydney and unfortunately, like most farmers, he owned a gun.' There was a thoughtful silence for the rural death toll. 'I thought Jonesey might have bought the place. Trust that vulture! He owns the place on the other side of Jervis's too. We're expecting a big fight if he tries to do something gross with them. Anyway... a mate of ours, Ned, might be interested in letting you stay at his place. He's got another place he's staying at, up in the bush and when I suggested you might be OK as a caretaker he agreed to a meet. Its not as posh as this,' he looked around proudly then grinned, 'but there's enough room to swing a cat.' Toby blushed a little. Sean's reputation had also spread.

'Sounds very... interesting. When should I meet this Ned?' Steve looked at his watch.

'In about half an hour. I'll drive you over. You can have afternoon tea with him.'

Steve's ute was fifteen minutes up a small valley when they bumped over a rise and he first saw "McZedcroft". He had no option but to fall immediately in love. Slab hut, wide verandahs, peppercorn trees, a tiny orchard, a creek running through rocks to the side and the head of the valley forming a magnificent backdrop of sandstone cliffs and forest.

'Good God Allmighty Steve… This is just…amazing!'

'Yair, you couldn't get much more than that onto a Christmas card,' agreed Steve. 'Now a couple of things. I've put in a good word, but Ned makes up his own mind about people. Go with the flow, and remember he's as sharp as a tack. And it might not be a good idea to say you are a psychologist. Good luck.' An imposing, grey bearded man in rough clothes watched Toby as he approached the verandah with Steve. Book in lap. Rocking chair.

'Ned McZed, this is Toby Buchanan.'

'Aye. Come on up, I've been expecting you.' Ned waved to an ancient sofa. 'Will you be staying for a bit of afternoon tea then Steve?'

'Bit of a rush order on at home I'm afraid. I'll need to be off' said Steve, sidling away. Toby, feeling distinctly abandoned, looked questioningly to his driver.

'It's OK, Ned will drop you back. Enjoy yourself! See ya Ned.'

'Aye, that's fine Steve. Say hello to the kiddies for me.' Ned lit his pipe as the dust of the ute faded on the horizon. Toby sat on the edge of the sofa, uncomfortable, but not for long.

'I'll just go and put the kettle on then. You go for a walk and have a look around the house. Take your time, I'll give you a call when we're ready.'

Ned added a smile that told of sympathy for people at sea and disappeared inside.

Strolling around, Toby slowly came to comprehend The Gem of McZedcroft. Strange devices and tableaux festooned the shelves, the bookcases were brimming with interest, the beds were all comfortable, there appeared to be a full set of necessities like fridges, TV, sound system, bathroom and stove. Working off something or other? Toby had earlier noted that the power lines seemed to stop ten kilometres away. Walking out the back door was a revelation; a massive bank of solar panels stood near the orchard and a variety of antennas sprouted from the back roof. Ned nodded to him from the kitchen in passing.

'Steve and I put the electrics in. I'll show you the Bible of Operations later.'

Afternoon tea was served. Ned had a penchant for trying out interesting foodstuffs in novel combinations. The scones were quite pleasant, albeit an unusual shade of blue, the steamed calamari and cabbage quiche didn't make it to the table, but the kangaroo and ginger wholemeal vol-au-vents proved to be surprisingly good. After some discussion, Ned and Toby decided the brightly coloured local fungi salsa might require some further research. They finished with a remarkably smooth coffee, Ned's own deep dark red liqueur (Toby didn't ask about ingredients), and a large plate of noteworthy green flecked Nori-Anzac biscuits. Ned described them as his Kakoda Reconciliation Bikkies. Conversation ranged around life, politics, films, music. Ned asked how Toby earned his crust. Toby avoided the P word.

'And what does being a school counsellor require Toby? The essential ingredient?'

'The ability to step back and remain a little detached... and you've got to keep a sense of humour. Only way to hang onto the shreds of sanity. Might I sample another smidgeon of that deep crimson, Ned?'

A half an hour of exchange of experiences, interests and attitudes later and Toby hadn't learnt much about Ned, certainly not as much as Ned had learnt about him. Then again, it was Ned's house that was at stake, so fair enough. And Toby fervently wanted to live in this house. Never had he picked up such a warm, peaceable, feeling from a place. Ned puffed on his pipe. Magpies chortled.

'You know Ned, I've never had such a warm, peaceable feeling from a place before'. After a reflective silence, Ned replied.

'Well, if that's so, you and McZedcroft should get along well together. Young Steve has given me the nod on your behalf.'

'And of course Shirley Denzil says I'm a bit worthwhile too?' hazarded Toby. One of Ned's eyebrows lifted.

'Aye, you're starting to get the picture then.' He paused, then with a mock reproving frown over the glasses said, 'You'll not be bringing sheep or other livestock into the bedrooms. Or play Doof music on the stereo. Apart from that, treat the place as your home. Steve will take the rent and sort out ... arrangements. You can expect me to retain the use of the small back room for rare occasional nights in transit. I shall phone ahead. Does that appear satisfactory?'

'Oh most exceedingly Ned. And you are sure regarding little Sean...?'

'Try and encourage him to keep the wildlife toll down.'

There was a contented sigh from Toby. Ned poured another liqueur and they toasted the arrangement. A comfortable silence.

'Since you'll be living here, I best show you some country on the way back. I keep my rock hopper in the shed out back..., which is part of the deal by the way. There's other sheds you may use for your own vehicle. We'll close shop and be off then' said Ned crisply.

———

Outside the large, closed garage, Toby took a stab in the dark.

'Would that be a vintage Land Rover four wheel drive in there then, suitably battered and in a nice shade of green?'

'Only three wheels, and black and in good order as well.' The large timber door swung up and in.

'Bloody Hell Ned!' croaked Toby. Ned walked up to the nose of the wickedly skulking black Airborne ultralight and gave it an affectionate pat. He turned and gave Toby an amused smile. Toby's face had blanched.

'Although exceeding the bounds of a chap's privacy, Shirley told me you have an extensive Biggles collection. You can take the final leg home, Ginger. Be resolute.'

Toby's mind said 'This is not a good idea. It's little. You may die. Squish.'

Toby's logic replied 'If I don't fly I walk ... and maybe lose the house.'

But Toby's inner child was saying 'Bomb doors open, banking left onto target roger wilco!'

'Well Ned, in for a penny, in for a pound.' Toby, despite his tucked away obsession with Aeroplanes and The History/Romance of Flight, had only taken two trips, both in the contained comfort of passenger jets...

In the borrowed freezerwear coveralls, ('Almost a Sidcot suit' said Ned), proper sheepskin gauntlets and intercommed helmet, Toby worked at his co-pilot role as Ned ran through the preflight checks. The triangular wing shaded them and the

———

motor purred quietly behind his back. 'I've doubled the muffling, no point in annoying the locals,' said Ned. No point attracting attention either, thought Toby. Does this person have a licence? However, the calm confidence and determined demeanour quashed all doubts. 'Would you be fine back there then, Toby?' asked Ned genially over the intercom.

Toby proffered an upraised thumb. 'Yes... affirmative...um... Roger?'

'Would that be Tally Ho then?' chuckled the large, leather clad figure in front, cranking back the throttle. Toby heard the deepened roar, felt himself hurtling out into the paddock then leaping upwards as Ned pushed the bar forward. The trees fell quickly below as they climbed, banked in a wide circle around McZedcroft and steered northwest across the lowering sun.

'Who could ask for anything more...' suggested Ned.

Barangan and Tilda lay at the edge of the Central Warrigal Range, as Ned explained, and they would do a run through the middle and out at Steve's. It sounded simple. He dropped the motor back to cruising speed and explained weight-shift steering, the throttle and the instrument panel as he ran up a small valley.

'What's the screen there?' asked Toby.

'Well... there's a thing. It's a rather nice little leftover ground hugging radar from a previous life' said Ned, switching it on. Toby listened and watched avidly, but becoming conscious that the valley walls were quickly becoming steeper and ... closer.

'Umm ... Ned, do we need a bit more height?'

'No laddie... it's fine. I know the way quite well, thank you.'

Toby's fingers gripped ever tighter on his seat as they powered on toward the cliff at the end of the valley. At the very last moment Ned banked steeply left into a secondary gully, over a rise and out into another, thickly forested wild valley. Omigod.

'Bit tricky that last bit if you miss the turn,' said Ned.

Apart from it getting a little close to the wingtips at times, the beauty of the deep Warrigals was not lost on Toby. Ned cruised up rivers, past cliffs and waterfalls, lightly playing the weight shift bar and running a quiet commentary; Toby was lost in a richly tapestried flight dream that left his Planet Cruise Sim ™ for dead.

'That's where I'm living at the moment' said Ned, pointing over to a small natural clearing.

'Harder to find than a wild Wollemi Pine' he added. Toby stared as Ned circled.

'But I can't see anything there at all!' exclaimed Toby.

'Aye' said Ned proudly.

A slow zigzag through some more valleys, five minutes flying over a jumble of ravines and they crested the escarpment on the far side of Tilda. They climbed to 6000 feet in a wide upward spiral as the setting sun dabbed its last rouge on the western clouds.

'A couple of nice things about these jiggers. Firstly, they fly just as well without a motor' he said, cutting the ignition. The whistling of wind through rigging replaced the motor's muted roar. 'And they don't need people as well!' said Ned, nonchalantly clasping his hands behind his helmet. The microlight continued its gentle descent unperturbed.

'Now take hold of those side handles young Toby, and let's be at it.'

Tentatively at first, then with greater confidence as his first manoeuvres did not result in a fatal plummet, Toby learnt to bank, dive and climb. He loved it. The craft responded beautifully to his handling. Under Ned's direction they drifted across the farmlands to Tilda, lining up on the Top Ace Repair Centre. Ned switched the motor back on to an idle.

'Gives us a few more options as we come in' he explained.

The microlight floated down to landing along the dirt road fronting Steve's workshop. Ned helped Toby unbuckle and climb out of the overalls.

'As my tenant, there's a good chance this flying business may happen again. If you were interested, that is' he said. Toby took in Ned McZed's amused smile, and striving desperately for cool, said 'Anytime at all Ned. Absolutely. Indeed. Yes thank you. Yes.'

'Need to catch the last of the light then. Talk to young Steve. Goodnight to you for now' said Ned as he… swung back into the saddle.

A bellow from the motor as the black ultralight sped down the road and lifted into the twilight. And disappeared. Like a bat, thought Toby. Did Ned do a lot of night flying?

A full audience was waiting on the verandah and cheered as Toby came into sight. He mounted the step grinning ear to ear and asking…'Who was that masked man?'

Later, over a coffee for the road, Toby learned more of the McZed aerial exploits. Moonlit glides over the Barangan Valley with Steve, his flights to Tasmania, to the Daintree, Arnhem Land, Indonesia and beyond. From the limited history they could glean, Ned had been all sorts of pilot in the past, military, crop dusting, experimental testing, freelance cargo to the inaccessible, and held a full licence with multiple endorsements. He was also an engineer, marine biologist and lecturer in aviation law.

'Very private bloke though, keeps to himself, so never push the questions. If he was born a century earlier, he would have been a solitary explorer,' added Steve. 'Told me once that things run across his path and he can do nothing but follow them into the forest.'

Arrangements for Toby to move into McZedcroft the next weekend were made. Leases, bonds and references were not needed. Even the rent was 'Whatever you reckon is a fair thing,' which left him in a quandary until he suggested the same as he paid for the O'Nite Cabin in town. A nice surprise was the satellite phone and Internet computer which Ned had failed to mention, being busy at the time explaining more important things like the solar toilet and veggie garden.

'I think it may be time to be off, Toby Buchanan, you've had a big day. As a newly aviating renter of country properties, you can shout me some tea. At The Rissole?' Maria named Barangan's premiere eating-house.

As they left, they could see Jules and Solly scurrying around the lit up workshop.

'Working on their art project like little beavers,' said Toby to Maria. 'Very commendable zeal for homework,' he called out genially to the pair. Five kilometres closer to Barangan, in the middle of Toby's enthusiastic description of Croft McZed, Maria wondered briefly to herself, did Jules or Solly actually have art as a subject this semester…?

—*∿∿*—

Chapter Three

Toby and Maria checked each other's reports for any signs of meaningful information and decided they were both the epitome of bland pessimism.

' "Has achieved very little curriculum related work and progress reports from all subjects indicate ability in lowest 5%." was nicely put,' said Toby.

' "IQ assessment not valid due to limited participation and very abnormal scatter" was fair enough too,' agreed Maria. 'Nothing is ordinary with Solly.'

'So our recommendation will be that "Solly can be maintained quietly and discreetly on a modified language program and with Support Teacher aided integration into selected classes,"' summed up Toby.

'Gives him more time for the quantum mechanics, differential integration and dysfracted multilineal astro navigation?' asked Maria.

'And should keep him out of harms way,' agreed Toby. 'Meanwhile, I might do a bit of work with him and then Bobby Denzil.' The reports went in without a ripple.

'Yes!' screamed Solly, 'I DO want to have some friends!' Tears of frustration and rage were streaming down his face. He was not taking Toby's technique of gentle challenge too well. 'They just don't want to be friends. And they can't keep up with me when I try and tell them stuff. They're stupid! All they go on about is birthday parties and TV shows and...'

The floodgates opened and Solly's frustration with the children of Tilda came tumbling out.

'It's ok Solly, it's ok. I know it's hard and you're not happy with it. There are just a few tricks to it, things you can learn that will help. It's a skill, you know, like reading; you have to start at the beginning and it takes time.' Solly was puzzled, he knew how to read after his Mum read a few stories to him. Toby jumped analogies to swimming and basketball, then just settled on "things that work" This would take time and practice.

—◦◦◦—

Bobby Denzil glanced around the empty ERIC then looked suspiciously at Toby. 'My Mum's always on at me to make friends with Solly but you can't! It's like talking to Wikipedia and he just goes on and on and he never listens to you. We sort of get on ok but jeez!' Bobby shook his head. Talk and play with Solly for a half hour until recess?

'Just give it a go, and you're missing out on Maths anyway...' pleaded Toby. He moved Bobby over to the carpet square at the back of the palm forest and drew a chalk circle.

'You can keep some of the marbles' he said, tipping his collection out. 'But not those ones...' he added hastily, retrieving three childhood treasures.

'Marbles are so primary school' muttered Bobby, but noting the green clearie and two connie agates still there.

Solly arrived and smiled (appropriately) at Bobby.

'Hi Bobby, thanks for coming.' Now how did the first bit go?

'You've got a lot of great marbles!' Solly worked hard. Bobby was happy to explain the rules of "Little Ring and Big Ring" when asked. Solly listened attentively, making comments from what Bobby said. They started the game and Solly bit his lip to prevent comments regarding the initial translational velocities and Newton's second law... concentrating instead on related questions, listening and compliments. To his surprise, Bobby was smiling and laughing. With him! And Bobby was better at marbles than him and Solly didn't care... So this was how it worked. Across the other side of the ERIC Toby listened to the laughter and winked to Maria.

Giorgio Savellis sat quietly in the sun, well away from the noisy groups of fighting, competing students. He didn't like High School. He looked up as Solly squatted nearby.

'Hi Giorgio. Would ya like to play Little Ring? I've got some marbles...'

Giorgio smiled shyly...

———

A week later, Jules and Solly were putting the final touches to the Tank Stripper Mark II, which had already been named affectionately 'Little Egypt' by Steve. Jules had duplicated the functional components of the Stripper Mark I, and assembled them... under direction, of course. This made it a lot smaller, not needing the extraneous bits like pumps, cassette decks, toaster elements and the like. The size of a small suitcase, Little Egypt was a marvel. Jules patted it.

'Dad will be glad not to lug the old Mark One around the yard, he reckons it must weigh close to ninety kilos.' Solly looked at Julie puzzled. He had not considered this before. Too heavy. Mass. He folded his arms and sat down, staring at the large conglomerate cube they had built in his frenzy of creation two weeks ago. What if... and if... His lips moved soundlessly, his fingers traced lines, his eyes darted. Jules recognised one of Solly's Archimedes' bathtub light bulb moments and didn't interrupt, stood aside and waited. Got up and found her tools. And sat down and waited for quite a long time.

Solly turned and smiled.

'I think we can change all that...'

Jules sighed and picked up her soldering iron.

———

Three hours later Jules put the iron down and stepped back. Solly was nodding and bouncing, carefully holding two leads which protruded from the side of the even larger, even more convoluted original prototype.

'Sol, what with the extra batteries, transformers and circuit boards, our magic monster must top a hundred and twenty kilos... easy!'

'Could you stand over there and watch please Julie Louise' said Solly.

Jules felt a wave of apprehension. Solly rarely called her by both names.

'Solly, perhaps we should put it off for a bit... get Dad in?'

'No.' Very final. Jules moved. Solly, as gently as he could, touched the leads briefly together. The small spark showed the leads were live, there was a faint creak from the cube's bowels, but nothing else.

'So what was that about?'

'Just wait.'

Solly touched the wires for a fraction longer. Jules thought she saw a glimmer of the familiar blue glow flicker over the cube's surface.

'So it cleans itself? Bit like a cat?'

'Wait'

Solly joined the wires for a good two seconds. This time, the blue spread over every exposed metal section. And ... to Julie's amazement, the cube groaned... and hopped! It was so unexpected she started back and knocked a welding stand flying.

'BloodyhellSollyyouscaredtheshitoutofme!'

Solly gave a long, contented sigh.

'I wasn't really sure what it would do actually... it's a sort of direction thing really, the iron that gets turned into... energy, only goes one way when you ...web it into the spiral. I just had it... push downwards.' He beamed. 'It works, doesn't it!' Solly flicked the toggle switch to the batteries, then wrapped insulating tape around the leads for good measure. They trudged back to the house to join Mum and Dad for tea.

Sunday morning found the family in the workshop, working industriously on the cube. After a demonstration hop, the flabbergasted Steve ('I'm just... flabbergasted Solly') also got to thinking and suggested fitting a swing arm rheostat he salvaged from a lighting set.

'If it had just a trickle of juice through it, it mightn't jump as quick. I don't fancy that lump landing on me.'

'And maybe a bit of a shield on top in case it bumps something' said Jules, gesturing to the jungle of metal dangling from the rafters and the particularly fragile agglomeration of transistors, resistors, capacitors and unrecognisablors on top of the cube.

'And wooden handles' said Solly. They all agreed. None of them were overly keen on actually touching the blue glow but it didn't seem to travel through wood.

'And, you boys be careful. Very careful' added Liz.

They gathered around after Jules hooked up the rheostat, a venerable brass model, and Steve had put the final screws of the shield support into the frame. The cube now resembled a cross between a chip heater and a post-modern palanquin. The family looked at Solly. Very stylishly he swivelled down, flicked the power switch on.

'Nothing happened. Which is to be expected. Which is good.'

Very gingerly he slid the rheostat to its first notch. Faintest glimmer of a glow. Steve touched, then took hold of the wooden handles and lifted.

'Bloody amazing. I do believe it's a bit lighter Sol'

'Notch two coming up ladies and gentleman, and forty-eight to go!' exclaimed Solly. Second, and then third and fourth resulted in a very apparent lightening, and a more definite blue blush.

'Crackerjack. Be about sixty kilos now I reckon,' said Steve, excitedly. 'Grab the other handle to steady it Jules, and just take it up slow, Solomonder my dear.'

'Steady as it goes, father.' replied Solly.

The cube lightened, the glow deepened until, as Solly said later, that thaumaturgic moment on notch sixteen when the cube rose ever so lightly, ever so gracefully, off the concrete. To be held in place by the smallest, downward pressure. Steve, Jules and Solly were all beaming at each other.

'Drop her back eight notches, my beaming boy.'

'As you wish, oh glowing elder' replied Solly.

The cube settled to the floor with a slight groaning of joints. Steve, ever sentimental, was in for a grand family hug and burled around, gathering Solly in his arms and making for Jules. Who croaked 'Watch out for the rr...' just as Steve's gaping overalls caught on the brass rheostat knob.

Ziiiiiiiiiiiiiiiiiiiiiiiiiiiiiiiiiiiit !!!

Steve and Liz hauled the kids back as they all watched in horror.

The soft blue glow glinted, flared and blazed. The cube lifted itself, hurling up to the roof, paused momentarily with a crunch, then burst through as several of the galvanised iron sheets joined its blue charged irresistible urge to be up, up and away! The stunned Henderson family watched the blue dot quickly shrink and disappear.

'Bit like the dot on old black and white t.v. when you switch it off,' Steve later observed.

At 100,000 feet the cube cracked Mach five, and at 200,000, just as it reached escape velocity, a lead bounced past the apparently protective blue glow and flared. The glow ceased, to

---

be quickly replaced by the red...orange...yellow...white one that Shuttle passengers once, briefly, saw.

Like a reverse meteorite, what was left of the cube popped into a permanent orbit.

And the last, recorded fifteen seconds of this remarkable flight were noted with great interest by several sophisticated, snoopy, and for some, sinister agencies.

Wheels were put in motion.

Life at Barangan High ground on through the mid week. Education proceeded with some gains and some losses. Mostly effective teaching with positive outcomes, but in some cases... well, it only takes a blowtorch to make crackling out of a silk purse. Wednesday, known amongst education employees as 'hump day', came around. A short day. Sports afternoon.

Solly loathed and detested sports afternoon. Despite interventions on his behalf by Maria, it could not be avoided. Sport for boys was limited to football or football, because it was in the pre-early stage of the season and it was the Passion of Brucie. Barangan HS boasted four teams of varying ages and ability who played each other on a weekly rota, mainly to allow Mr. Pearson's selected 'A' team the opportunity for supervised thuggery. Team D was this week's sacrifice.

Acutely embarrassed in oversized shorts that highlighted his skinny white legs, Solly waited anxiously on the sidelines. As second reserve...last resort, he was next to go on. Jonesey, Captain and Tyrant of the Alpha Team smirked at him in passing and ran a finger across his throat. The inevitable happened as Jonesey's lumpy fullback Robbo creamed a player.

'Get out there Henderson and don't be a woos' yelled Mr. Pearson.

Solly trudged onto the field of slaughter and tried to make himself as inconspicuous as possible. He figured that if he moved slowly enough, the dreaded football might never come his way, and it worked well enough up to half time. Sitting apart and sipping his bottle of water, Solly looked up when Bruce loomed.

'Listen you gutless little runt, ya here to play football. Keep up or you'll be doing detention for a week.' Bruce left. Solly then watched as Jonesey spoke to his hapless D teammates. He appeared satisfied, leered at him and moved off. Not good. Bruce blew on his whistle and the game resumed. In a transparent effort to follow directions, Solly's team tried very hard to pass the ball to him, while Solly tried equally hard to lose it. Finally, while the game moved at a snail's pace, one spotty and terrified boy ran up to Solly and pushed the football into his arms. Solly dropped the ball and turned to run, just as Jonesey's solid, 65 kilo body crashed into him like a bull bar into a jumping rabbit.

Solly lay huddled and shaking on the ground while Jonesey swaggered back to his mates.

A hundred metres away, a horrified Brad Denzil looked up and ran to help.

'Get up you snivelling little feral' Umpire Pearson bellowed as he reached down, grabbed and hauled Solly to his feet. Brad winced as he heard Solly's wail, then saw him crumple back down, fainting from the pain of a dislocated shoulder.

———

A white faced Julie heard the story from Brad as she waited with Solly for the ambulance. Later, she sat with her mother and father while the Principal read out the incident reports from the very caring but won't take any nonsense Mr. Pearson and the exceptional student John Paul Jones. Even if the truth were known, Julie knew the Principal would never take action against the star teacher or the golden son of the town's mayor.

'Pusillanimous' she muttered, using one of Solly's favourite words, and adding 'Prick…'

There was a suitable resolution the following day after a terse parental note regarding sport, placement in the Resource

Centre for sports afternoons, the mention of duty of care and a distinct whiff of future litigation and/or formal complaint to the School Education Director.

'Useless for Rugby anyway' said Bruce Pearson.

'Keeps him out of sight' said Barry McDermott.

'About bloody time' said Maria Scott and Toby.

———

'Jules, you can't do that. It's not what… girls do' said Brad doubtfully. 'Anyway,' he said with some embarrassment, 'I'm not much good at that sort of thing, to do it properly, anyway.'

'I'll just have to do what I can then' said Julia with finality.

Brad brightened. 'Check out with Bobby though. He actually did some for a while at the gym and got pretty good at it. He reckoned.'

Bobby was very helpful, with the enthusiasm of expertise before elders.

'No, not like that, put your foot forward, yeah, bit more, swing and lean into it, right, then you can go back, or follow through…'

Jules called a halt after ten minutes. It didn't seem that complicated.

———

John Paul Jones and his mate Robbo were alone, well out of bounds and having a smoke at the back of the Science block. Jonesey turned to see what Robbo was looking at and came face to face with Julia Henderson.

'Yeah, whatever. I'm fucking busy Henderson.'

'You don't ever, ever, go near my brother again.'

'Waddya mean? Yeah? So what would you do then? You Hendersons'r'all weir…Oooff.'

Jonesey's breath whooshed out and his stomach exploded in pain. He was realising how much it hurt when a right cross, delivered without much precision but with a lot of commitment, laid him on his back on the grass. Blinking through tears, he saw the red face of Jules looming above.

'That's what. Sorry about that, but that's what.'

The following morning Jules sought out Jonesey and apologised. He stood back warily and shuffled his feet a bit, said that was ok, he wouldn't go near Solomonder and also he didn't want any stories going around about being decked. By a girl, Robbo had added and smirked, but only briefly. Jonesy looked past Jules and mumbled that he might catch up sometime. Jules muttered whatever (in your dreams).

Suitably armisticed, they drifted apart.

—⁓—

Wednesday again. Short hump day. An unseasonal day, with rain since the weekend and a thick, overcast Barangan misty sleet. It was recess, with students told 'stay out of the rain.' Staff were not quite prepared to go to "wet weather indoors" with additional supervision…

Under the arch, a shadowy figure with turned up collar, checking left and right. Around the corner, the staff car park is shrouded in fog. Another mysterious and seemingly hunchbacked wraith eddies through the miasma. It sinks at the back of a car blob. Brad, playing P.I. Marlow in this morning's production, peers anxiously into the murk, and thinks he sees a faint, blue glow…

—⁓—

Home time in the Tilda bus line, Jules, Solly Brad and Bobby leaned with nonchalance on the chain link fence. Solly found nonchalance difficult with the sling, so he sat on the concrete. Quick off the mark, teachers were loading into cars. Bruce Pearson gazed lovingly at his just run in, six point zero litre V8 Commodore SSV six speed blah blah and sighed. With the metallic Prestige option in Sizzle Red, and in the late afternoon sun, it glowed. Radiantly. The distinctive and satisfyingly loud Brrilleeep-eep of remote unlocking attracted the attention of bus-line apprentice petrol heads. Two more blips on the remote and the boot sprang open for his Adidas Bag and towel. A different blip and the boot pulled itself shut. Small cheers. Nice timing thought Brucie as the new languages teacher with the big tits, Sharmayne, walked toward the gate.

'Hey Shazza! Would yer like a lift downta the Narms?'

'Well, I dunno Brucie. Are you gunna do the right thing and buy the drinks this time?'

The gum-chewer girl bus-liners became interested and exchanged looks. Bruce put on some charm, leaned back on the car and parried 'Well I reckon I'll get the first round in Shazza. And I reckon that…' Bruce got no further as the uneasy feeling he was moving sideways was followed by a long, ragged tearing ripsound, not unlike that of broadsheet newsprint being shredded for a chookhouse… Loud cheering from the entire bus line as Bruce landed on his arse.

'Bloody Hell! Shit!' said Bruce Pearson, looking up at the side of his car. He scrambled to his feet and gingerly prodded the flaps of paint surrounding the shiny, bare metal rear panel. His lower lip trembling, he picked up a beautiful sizzle red with grey undercoat sheet of paint and appealed to the staff crowding round 'What's happened to my fucking car?'

Sharmayne gently rubbed the drivers door. The paint wobbled.

'Wiee-erd Brucie. It's not stuck on very well…'

'Yair Bruce, look at this!' said Johnno Baxter from Maths, stripping the chrome off the racing mirror in one lump. Various staff members and a few students prodded, picked and peeled. Some offered observations, suggestions and even sympathy.

'STOP IT' screamed Brucie. His car now resembled a badly unravelled Chenille bedspread. Devastation! He moved around his HSV, back to everyone, breaking off the sticky-out bits. Staff sidled off to their cars, mumbling.

'Shouldn'ta gotta bloody Holden' said the Ford owners.

'Lightning strike? Didn't hear any thunder' said Garry from Geography.

'Poor undercoat preparation' said old Mr. Malcolms from Technics.

The Barangan North and Tilda bus line lost interest as the familiar whine of the Addison's Bus Line wreck became audible. There were four who kept glancing down onto the scene however, semi straight-faced, with the occasional snort and shoulder twitch. Later in the bus, they had the joy of being overtaken by a gleaming, high powered, bare metal two door sports sedan, complete with the entire section of roof paint flapping like mother's bed sheets in the wind.

'Julia Henderson tells me that we don't have to worry about Solly being bullied anymore,' announced Maria, 'because she had discussed this with Jonesey and he agreed to back off.'

'Maybe that explains Jonesey's black eye' said Toby, smiling. 'Must have used the "Kick-ass method of shared concern" then.'

'Oh dear. Quite a strong girl, our Jules…'

Chapter 4

Saturday afternoon and Toby relaxed on the couch with coffee and surveyed the vast vistas that radiated out from his new front verandah. Sean, unusually friendly, unusually purring, sat on his lap and unusually, had his claws in and paws crossed. He impetuously indulged in a scratch behind Sean's ragged ear. The purring stopped, as did Toby, obediently. Purring resumed.

'Ahh.... Bliss, Sean. And do not bite please' he added, but Sean was not interested, too fascinated by the interesting bird life and dark spaces under bushes.

The move from the ridiculous O'Nite Cabin #3 to the sublime McZedcroft had been relatively painless and there was so much room to spread the pile from his station wagon... He had hit the supermarket before leaving Barangan so food was abundant. The sound system had been worked out and Stepan Grapelli competed softly with the magpies. Even a promise of future excitement: a note from Ned, saying he would drop past Sunday to run him through some takeoffs and circuits and a flight out past Shelvey.

Toby concluded that although he had never been on such a merry-go-ride of strange situations before, everything seemed to be progressing in a strangely logical way. 'It's A Relentless Pursuit of Connectedness,' he mused, remembering a Regional conference, 'and I'm not quite used to it.'

Toby decided he was now totally enmeshed with an entire small community, and surprisingly, not unwillingly! But what on earth was happening here? A conspiracy to maintain a student's fictional disability until he was mended? Learning to fly in a scrap of a plane? Living in Paradise? Well... it'll keep me off the streets, he thought.

Sean, watching his new territory from knee-vantage, was particularly entranced by a group of three large black and white birds. Different to the high speed flying things of the city; here were flyers who preferred walking! Standing out like Collingwood players on a Sunday afternoon, perambulating as his hunting brain plotted creep lines, leap-twist-snatch-killerbite moves.

Jumping down, he locked on to the smallest, the one that advertised with a constant feed-me bleat, and slid silently off the far side of the boards. Padded (soundlessly) behind the first shed, slid (furtively) between the boxes, and crawled (invisibly) through the tall, savannah grasses towards his prey. Ears flat, eyes slitted, tail trailing. Sean loved David Attenborough shows about his relatives.

Magpie Four whistled softly in incredulous amusement to Magpie Five and the three walkers. Was this large, clumsy, ragged cat for real? The walkers lifted their heads to watch the classic, synchronised double powerswoop flanking attack. Quick jabs, en passant.

Sean felt the stabbing pain from his rump as the beak clacked shut and tore out a lump of skin and fur. He spun around in time to see a magpie flap leisurely up into the gum tree, only to be hit a second time and lose a small triangular lump of ear. The walkers lifted off, joined in a perched circle and leered down at him. Blood dripping, Sean began a new experience…ornithological anxiety. He stood cautiously, and with stiff dignity walked back toward the house. Whistle-whoosh-clack-pain; the walk turned to a mad dash up steps and under the couch.

The magpies stayed around for a while, hoping for more fun, chortling and inspecting the cowering cat from the verandah railings. Eventually bored, they took off in file for the dam and a drink. Sean slunk inside. Birdlife at McZedcroft was safe.

―⁓―

'This is a goddamn major concern!' stated Under-Secretary Senator Kelvin Dobrovich, glaring at the collected executive. 'We get a radar contact at orbital velocity over Australia of all places but no tracking to say how it got there! Is our best little ally putting up private satellites and not telling us? And after a huge payout to rent a Russian shuttle, all it picks up is this lump!' He threw the downloaded photos of an amorphous blob onto the table and lifted out a transverse section. 'And what the hell is this? The only bit in the middle that they can identify turns out to be part of a 1973 Kelvinator compressor! Someone has built one helluva big rocket to put a vintage fridge in space?'

'Very curious about the fridge part,' said Homer Spiggott, Chief of Overseas Security, 'and Australian Security doesn't appear to know how this object got up there either. To smuggle in, assemble and secretly launch a rocket the size needed would take a very well organised and funded group, which is a great concern. Why the rocket could not be tracked earlier also means there's a big gap in our surveillance.'

There was a concerned muttering around the table.

'So what are we doing about it Homer?' asked the Under Secretary.

'We'll certainly need an undercover investigation Sir.'

'Quite right. And information like that needs to be… carefully managed. I wonder when their elections are coming up? But, whatever it is, we need to be on top of it.'

'Sir, as we speak we have two special agents flying to Sydney Australia to give their security a very limited briefing, then heading south to the area of concern.'

'That would be South New South Wales then' said Kelvin.

'Yes sir. Very good sir.'

—◠◡◠—

High above the Pacific, Agent Jason Graupner had complained profanely to Agent Graeme Horowitz yet again.

'I know Jase, the agency should have some sort of priority on flights,' said Graeme tiredly, 'but we don't. We're stuck in economy. Every time. And yes the food is crap.' He paused and groped for something placatory. He seemed to spend a lot of time placating his co-agent. 'But what the hell, we're on overseas expenses and you haven't seen Australia yet. Nice place. We liked it anyway.'

'So you took the little wife and little Horowitzers down under for a happy family holiday did you?' said Agent Graupner, voice dripping. Graeme sighed, pulled out his headphones and returned to the movie. Jason was one of the nastiest workers he had known in his twenty-five years with the Agency and was also seriously warped when it came to family values, children and community spirit. Probably wouldn't eat apple pie, on principle. Not that Jason would hold to any principles.

Totally unjust, to be partnered with such an arsehole.

———〰———

Ned parked his flat bed Bedford truck outside the Top Ace workshop and untwisted the ignition wires to stop the motor. It died with the usual snuffles and a worrying new long rattle. Pulling out his biro, he wrote 'ignit swit & tune' on the back of his hand, then a reminder on the other hand. Coming around the back, he faced four massive tanks glistening with newness, neatly balanced on wood blocks. Steve emerged from the first, put down the spray gun and peeled off his respirator.

'Omigod, you must have been going some! And how did you get them up on the blocks?' asked Ned admiringly.

'All this is down to my amazing offspring!' Steve switched off the compressor. 'Time for morning tea?' Empty mugs and crumbed plates later, Ned shook his head.

'So have I got this right, Solly's machine generates some kind of current that detaches the rust off steel?'

'Not quite' said Steve with a smile, 'We reckon it actually converts the top few iron molecules into some sort of pure energy, cos all it leaves is a bit of carbon behind. Puts up a real nice blue glow while it works too. Sort of somewhere between an Ultramarine and a Cobalt...'

'Turns iron into energy? Come on! That's impossible except at some incredible temperature. I mean any physics I know says so...'

'Solly is into some physics that goes a bit past that' said Steve with a degree of smugness. 'Come with me Mr. McZed Sir, and I'll show you something else.'

In the workshop Ned looked with wonder up at the hole in the roof.

'Lucky the whole roof didn't go, but we reckon it happened so quickly it just ripped out the three sheets. Hasn't rained yet, but I better fix it soon.' Ned sat down on a portable generator and tried to digest the wild story he had been told. Somehow this improbable energy had been changed into a directional force, hurling a hundred kilo, machine designed by a twelve year old child through a steel roof and up out of sight. Madness. Or was it a joke? Definitely not on.

'Watch and be amazed, Ned!' said Steve, snapping an aluminium suitcase open with a flourish.

Ned peered in at a jumble of electronic components, wires, dials and knobs. Two protruding wires were clipped to the sides of a massive V8 engine, and resting the case on his knees, Steve flicked a switch to produce a soft hum. 'Yer ready?' he asked, raised eyebrows. Ned nodded uneasily. 'Got to be careful, don't want to lose me motor...'

As Ned watched, a blue glow crept across the motor. Definitely cerulean, he thought. Lumps of grease-encrusted dirt slid off the sides but not a lot else seemed to happen. Steve walked to the motor with a hand broom. 'Voila!' he said, lightly brushing. The sweep revealed a gleaming metal surface. No rust. 'Impressed? I certainly was the first time. Now, demo two...' Steve sat back down, picked up the case and confided to Ned 'I'm getting pretty good with this now...'

Again, that strange blue glow, and then... with a smooth slow movement, the whole motor slowly lifted a metre off the concrete and... hovered. Mid air. Only the two wires to the case connecting it to… anything. Ned rubbed his eyes. The engine was still there, impossibly floating. He got up and walked the full circle around it. He picked up the broom and waved it uncertainly over the top and under. Gave it a tentative prod, to see it move slightly to the side.

'Well bugger me…'

———~~~———

Three hours later Ned was deep in earnest conversation with Solly and Jules. So deep indeed that he felt he was drowning, but he pressed on. Lunch had floated past unnoticed, as did Steve reading the back of Ned's hand and sorting the ignition switch for the Bedford. It had taken a long time to get a grip on what he had heard and seen, but once he climbed over the unbelievable, a starburst of possibilities had fired his thinking. Lots of questions.

'So what would happen if you could tilt this… field thing? Or like if the field generates a force upwards, could it also push sideways or down? In any direction?' Ned asked Solly, feeling a little like a mendicant traveller at the feet of a diminutive Guru. 'Would that work oh great and amazing Solly?' Solly paused to think. Seeing Ned's eagerly attentive face he rolled, then crossed his eyes for effect. He already knew this one.

'Oh Ned, the path to enlightenment on this matter is one of simplicity. One of the attributes of the force is its rotationally spherical nature and the strategic placement of another five loci of final phase subset… umm… aggregations would cause the effect ye seek.' Solly's eyes uncrossed and he giggled. Actually it was… different to that, but he couldn't explain how. He consulted with his sister for some time as to the practical aspects.

'Take that as a yes, Ned. You'd need six feed wires with slave units and some form of switching device. Easy Peasey' said Jules. Ned's sigh of relief was most gratifying.

'Thank you Solomonder and Julie. And now, a humble request. Weight is not an issue? Say two to three tonnes?'

———

63

'No, but power input and consumption goes up a bit. Why?' asked Solly.

'I think I know what Mr. McZed wants' said Julie. 'It was the way his face lit up when we said Stripper was out of sight in seconds. He wants his own rocket ship.'

Solly considered. 'Oh' he said. 'Wow.'

—⁂—

Ned had been on a shopping spree at the Top Ace and the Bedford was loaded past groan point. A chubby, ancient but essentially sound, riveted iron boiler had been de-rusted and levitated onto the tray by Steve. Several sheets of steel plate, weld rods, four heavy duty glass observation panes from a furnace, parts off a variety of Top Ace junked cars and numerous bits and bobs were roped on. The McZed wallet rained cash, while his cards sponsored a grand order emailed off by Jules and Solly to their favourite electronics distributor. Better get a dozen of everything he had suggested.

'I shall be refreshingly and totally engaged for some time, but we will stay in touch. Doubtless I have forgotten many items. And I urge this entire assembled Henderson family to very seriously consider what you have done. Absolutely wonderful and thank you, but omigod the implications... Farewell for now!' The Bedford sprang to life (thumbs up for the new switch) and moved off, cautiously.

The family of four looked at each other. Jules and Liz both sighed at the same time.

'He's right you know' said Liz. 'Very much. Implications.'

—⁂—

Graupner and Horowitz sat in front of the ASIO Senior Executive Officer while he politely explained the restrictions applying to the firearms that they insisted they needed. Graeme sold their cover story of tracking down a missing low level US security risk suspect and settled for a pair of reasonable handguns while Graupner could only grunt and seethe. Jason was a little better in negotiating their massive SUV hire car by being downright unfriendly. Still, twenty percent off, and Graeme approved of a bargain.

Four hours later and they were on the road south, Graupner driving as usual while Graeme navigated and worried. He was remembering a particularly nasty incident in Spain two years back where Graupner had used a similar vehicle to mash their target against a wall… He buried himself in the roadmap, finally choosing Canumbie for the initial base. Quiet intro to the local police to check any groups of new people moving in, some story telling with real estate agents about isolated rural lettings, a night or two at some bars… or was it 'pubs'? Always a good place for information. Give that two weeks, then Barangan seemed to be the next large town in the interest area. That sorted, he put in his earplugs and cranked up Handel on his i pod in an attempt to drown out Jason's grunge from the car's CD.

———

To Toby's great relief (hard week at mill) it was Friday afternoon and he was pulling into the home paddock of McZedcroft. The sounds of grinding and clanging alternated from the larger Bedford shed, as it had the past four days. On Monday he had found Ned setting up an ancient steel boiler on blocks and sorting his welding gear.

'Patching … and a few modifications' was all he had gotten for his questions.

Toby dumped his ancient, wounded-in-action school case on the verandah and walked over to see how Ned's rural labours were progressing. Pushing in the back door he was faced by a strangely angular vision of … the Lochabie 747 nose section? With little stubby wings and steel skids underneath? Four angled windows glowed briefly with light from the welder inside. Toby walked to the back of the tank to find Ned at work on a massive, hinged steel door.

'Ned mate, what on earth or wherever else have you got here? It's a bit like a 1960's Venusian Landing Shuttle … or is it a flight simulator thingy?' Ned pushed the helmet up and looked seriously at Toby.

'This is the Ladybird, about to come into the world like a freshly hatched new species of eagle chick and destined to have an enormous impact.' Toby looked inside to find a timber paneled cabin, two early model bucket seats with full harness facing a dashboard and the windows. On close inspection the thick glass panels were bedded in silicon, set in welded steel framing.

'Certainly... sturdy enough, and a whole set of flying instruments as well. Is it for training purposes...? Or for an entertainment thing? A children's playground feature?'

'Well there, I suppose it could be a training device,' agreed Ned, 'but you are also right the second time, it will be most entertaining if it does what I think. We shall see.'

Toby knew it would be pointless to ask further. Besides, afternoon tea and the prospect of another forty-five minute microlight flight lay ahead. He had negotiated flying lessons formally with McZed by phone and was delighted to find himself in the air every afternoon since. Ned had said that aeronautical enthusiasm was to be encouraged, and it was always handy to have another pilot on hand. Toby diligently studied Ned's battered textbooks, could answer most questions put to him, and was inordinately proud of his recycled exercise book / pilot's log.

—–ᴧᴧ—–

Ned put the log down and looked at Toby over his mug of tea. He judged his student to be of a good reasonable average, not necessarily gifted, but quick and suitably motivated.

'This afternoon, I was only a passenger. Of no help at all. We survived, so tomorrow you will do your first solo circuit' he announced. Toby quailed a little but strove to maintain the expected coolth. He nodded. Ned's technique of teaching was a bit WW1 Lafayette Escadrille squadron, or even early Battle of Britain, so he had no option. You couldn't get off an express train… or was that the back of a tiger? 'And while I remember, I've ordered some charged sealed unit batteries from Addison. Could you collect them Monday week on your way home from school? Then again, maybe bring half on the Tuesday. Six each trip should be enough.' Toby groaned inwardly.

—◦◦◦—

Chapter Five

Toby ran through his pre flight checks for the seventh time. Did a visual check on the transparent fuel tank under the idling motor. Nervously scanned the sky for planes. Checked and pulled on the straps on his harness.

'Toby, you'll do yourself a permanent injury if these are any tighter' said Ned soothingly, loosening off. 'You will be fine, or I wouldn't trust you with the machine. You won't crash... or if you do, try and avoid the house. I'll be in radio contact at all times. Push for up, pull for down. Break a leg. Now bugger off!' he exclaimed, pointing to the distant horizon. Toby breathed in deeply, counted to three and breathed out saying 'relaaax' to himself, just the way he advised students to do before exams. Didn't really seem to work for him. He looked at Ned, who shouted 'Chocks away! Tally Ho! GO!!' No escape there.

Toby pulled the throttle back and felt the familiar surge of power and juddering ride across the grass. Wing level. Glance check speed. Look up. Bloodyhell! One of the rams too close running wrong way   stupid sheep   bouncing rump of ram rapidly looming   jink left   bloody ram jinks left   no choice push forward   stagger into the air   just cleared the horns close to stall pull back not too much   brushed the ground   but speed picking up and climbing 20, 30, 40 feet ... and away!!

Toby stopped holding his breath and swore. The headphones crackled to life with Ned's terse voice; 'You'd be better off on the motorbike if you intend chasing the sheep. Now set a course for Mount Thompson, cut round the back and steer up the creek line to Pikes Crossing then back to here. Stay at about 1200. Check back to me at the turns or if anything... interesting happens.'

'Roger, Group Leader. Setting course Mt. Thompson' Toby acknowledged briskly.

It was a beautiful day for flying, still, cool and clear. Toby flew on, constantly scanning for other aircraft and possible landing sites. The motor purred quietly behind his head. He snapped the occasional photo with his camera, called base at Mt. Thompson, a lazy circle around at Pikes Crossing school with six shots (for the kids) and the last slow descent back to Tilda. Toby circled the home paddock, located the ram peacefully grazing well away from the strip, did another circuit and lined up. Aware he would be watched, he concentrated on a perfect landing and was pleased with the result. He trundled back to the shed, climbed out of the microlight and walked up to Ned.

'Yes … fair enough Toby. Should have told you about the little dip where old George likes to camp sometimes, but you managed to avoid him. Landing was fine.' He fished in his pocket and handed Toby a small woven badge.

'Better sew this onto your jacket,' he said solemnly. Toby looked at the blue and silver wings.

If Ned said so, that was good enough. He was a Pilot!

—‌ᴧᴧ‌—

Agents Horowitz and Graupner had argued all the way out of Canargen. Jason Graupner had stuffed up big time again and Graeme was sick of it. It was bad enough that Graupner's method of gathering intelligence consisted of herding a group of the town's low life together, getting shitfaced drunk with them and announcing they were looking for any suspicious looking foreigners like Arabs or Dagos. Why did he then have to pull out his automatic and batter two of them unconscious over a joke from the Italian guy that the only foreigner in town was a fucked up American? Expecting police trouble, Graeme had dragged his drunken colleague back to the hotel, packed, paid and got out of town as quickly as possible. Half an hour of side roads and Jason had finally shut up; snoring, with a dribble of saliva running from his open mouth. Graeme discreetly cruised into Barangan and settled on the quietest, seediest and most isolated accommodation he could find.

Shirley helped the quietly spoken American drag his insensible companion into O'Nite Cabin #2 and then went back to the Café to make up some coffee. Very curious pair, she thought. Obviously had money, judging by the clothes, luggage and big 4WD, so why stay at Addison's? And did she glimpse something like a shoulder holster as the drunken one sagged on the bed? The other one had quickly stepped in front. She bought the coffee back to the room and accepted the generous tip from the polite one, quipping that tipping was unusual at Addison's but since they were American...? He didn't engage, thanked her again and closed the door. Cops? Salesmen? Evangelists? Shirley decided they would need watching carefully.

Next morning Graeme introduced himself properly to Shirley over breakfast in the Café. Said they were on holidays, apologized for the state of his absent friend and that he was interested in photography and collecting old and odd bric-a-brac from junk shops. Which was why they had the big SUV. A smooth talker thought Shirley as she played the chatty waitress. He was particularly interested in, please don't laugh, old whitegoods and electrical items from the sixties and the seventies. Some people would pay a lot for them in the States, he said. Like old Kelvinators for example. Shirley, nonplussed, suggested the St. Vincent's store in town as a place to start, and recommended the Mt. Thompson Lookout for photos. She admired his large mobile phone on the table; unlike any she had ever seen. He explained that it was a satellite phone, he could phone home from anywhere in the world. How interesting said Shirley, wide eyed. Were there any other little towns up in the hills he asked, 'for the photography.' She talked about Pike's Crossing and it's old general store. Graeme thanked, paid, tipped and left. Shirley simpered suitably.

Later, she caught a glimpse of the other registered guest, Mr. J. Graupner, as he sullenly drove the pair out for their day's 'sightseeing.' Curiouser and curiouser. Nor was she satisfied when she cleaned their room. Everything was neatly tidied away, the jacket pockets were empty and the solid aluminium suitcases were very securely locked.

—⁓—

Toby's old Camry groaned and he muttered sympathetic encouragement to get it up the final hill. His school test equipment was piled around him on the seats; the last six of Ned's heavy, fully charged batteries filled the back of his wagon. Addison hadn't loaded the batteries - crook back mate - and Toby would try the excuse at the other end of the trip. Ned wanted them at the Top Ace for some reason, and lots of strong backs there. Threading through the car bodies and wreckage of the yard, Toby was surprised to see Ned's Bedford with his strange project loaded on the back. Perhaps it was ready to do…whatever it does, he thought. Obviously an electrical thing, judging by the batteries. He parked and strolled to the house.

'Good man,' said Ned. 'Just what we are waiting for. We should get them loaded in no time.' He organized the work party, brushed aside the 'crook back' and had Toby staggering under the weight of the first battery in short order. As Ned fitted it into a boxed casing behind the seats, Toby looked around in admiration. The interior was now beautifully panelled with lacquered veneer and gleaming brass work. Instruments and controls, including a Nintendo joystick and the radar screen from Ned's microlight were mounted on elegant walnut.

'Wow! Dashboard's genuine leather eh Ned? Wonderful carpentry… and a full racing harness on the seats.' Ned grunted and sent him back down; Steve was waiting with the next battery. A Flight Sim with real style mused Toby, heading back to the Camry. Now was it about dramatic entertainment, or did it have a serious training function to it?

—⁓—

Afternoon tea was laid out as Ned completed the connections and stowing.

—

'Well,' said Toby as mugs were lifted, 'here's to your first trial run Ned. You'd be using back projection on the windows I suppose?' he added knowledgeably. 'Would it be better off the truck and on the ground... if it throws itself around a bit?'

Ned and the Hendersons exchanged glances and laughs. What was he missing?

'Anyway, as the Conveyor of Batteries, I think I could claim the spare seat? So you could show me... the show?' Ned peered over at Toby and considered.

'I don't think I could argue with that, young Toby. Besides, you do have your wings.'

There was a small round of applause from those gathered and Toby blushed.

————

The old bucket seats were very comfortable, and to Toby's amusement, Ned insisted they were both fully strapped in.

'Do we have sound effects too, Ned?'

'Of course' he replied, scrolling the i-pod to the Barber of Seville.

'I'll expect a close shave later' commented Toby, predictably.

Pre-flight checks seemed to involve putting the power switch down and checking the dials. The radar screen was switched on, to show the jumble of metal surrounding them.

'12 volts, 480 amp hours. Good. Solly thinks that should be good for a few days so we have plenty of leeway' said Ned. 'Now Toby, prepare yourself for some serious entertainment and don't get alarmed. I know this works.' Toby grinned and settled back.

A low hum began to start up from a previously unnoticed small cabinet tucked away in front of their feet. A faint blue crackle of light appeared around the rim of the plate windows. Nice. Back projection? The hum increased and there was a little wobble. Leg hydraulics thought Toby, gripping the side arm. Then the show commenced. After a very convincing lurch the nose dipped down realistically to show the Hendersons (waving), the Top Ace workshop, the house and surrounding paddocks, all rapidly receding. The nose lifted with a lovely floaty sensation to show the vast vista of the Warrigal Ranges out on the horizon. Beautiful graphics. Even the smoke plume from some burning off, just as he had seen on the drive out, but… Just… Too Real.

'Ned,' said Toby's small voice, 'How the fuck are you doing this? I know we're not, but are we actually… flying...?' Ned beamed beatifically.

'Yes. Absolutely flying. Works a treat doesn't it. We're at about 800 feet. Only problem is, the radar seems to have gone on the blink. Might get you to keep a visual check to port in case we have any traffic…'

'Traffic…' repeated Toby. 'Ned, please tell me that we're not 800 feet up in the sky inside a nicely decorated ex steam boiler. With little wings stuck on the sides. Please.' Ned looked sympathetically at Toby.

'Sorry Toby, we couldn't resist winding you up a little, you do astonished so well.' Thank God, thought Toby, it's a joke. It's not real. 'Young Solly came up with an amazing device which converts electricity into a field that excites and decays the top molecular layer of solid iron. He's further developed it to make the field directional. It's quite powerful. Simple, when you think about it. Although I'm buggered if I can work out how it does it. I just applied the principle with this little jigger.' Oh God no, he's serious, thought Toby.

'At the moment its directed downwards to support the 2.6 tonnes of the vehicle hovering, and when we also direct it backwards by moving the control here, we move forwards… good acceleration eh?' Pressed back in his seat, the countryside began to reel past faster and faster, the Warrigals becoming larger.

'SHIT NED JUST STOP FOR A MINUTE HERE!!!' Toby screamed. Ned obligingly pulled back on the control and slowed back to a hover.

'Toby,' said Ned in a reassuring, conversational tone, 'I've done quite a bit of testing with the device. Ladybird is purpose built to be a radically new and safe aircraft.'

There was a long pause as Toby struggled with reality.

'No. It's science fiction. Antimatter proton hyperdrive thingies. 1967. Doesn't work. All those interminable articles in the back of Analog. Not possible.'

'Hmmm' said Ned. He gestured to the window, nudged Ladybird to rotate slowly in a full circle, and then tapped the altimeter for emphasis.

'Well Toby me boy, if you're right, we're in deep trouble.'

Toby shuddered, sighed, slowly adjusting himself to the improbable. In a crisis, resign. Or perhaps he was still in bed about to wake up? He could do no more but wait… Ned smiled and nodded.

'Would you like me to set you back down at the Top Ace? Or if it's all right, we should get on with the test flight.'

Although he knew the sensible answer, Toby said 'Why not…?'

—⁓—

Ten minutes of flying and Ned had decided that the northern end of the Warrigals would be best due to being well away from people and flight paths.

'Not that we'd be easy to see anyway, the drive field comes up in a nice sky blue.'

'Does it come in other colours? Lime Green? Tangerine?' asked Toby, somewhat recovered. Ned declared he had flown most types of aircraft in his long career, but never one like this. After twenty minutes of gut wrenching g-force manoeuvres he declared Ladybird to be fully aerobatic. Toby had learnt how to do a barrel roll, and his favourite Biggles trick, the Immelmann turn. After Ned demonstrated flying backwards, inverted (an absolute first!), he complimented Toby on his strong stomach. Toby said he would rather not discuss that at the moment. In a three minute run down the entire length of the Warrigal Chain, they calculated having reached Mach 4... at least. The very old ex-RAAF air speed indicator only went up to Mach 2.5, but a good guess. Ned explained his belief that the field also acted as an impervious shield against the wind, so he had extended a ceramic tube into the slipstream past 'the edge of blue' to activate the altimeter and air speed anemometer. As an afterthought, he had also hooked it up to an air pump so they could breathe...

'One last thing I would like to try for is some real altitude' Ned said seriously, 'We have to seal the hull off completely to maintain pressure, but that's easy enough.' He switched off the air pump and closed a large brass tap. 'Are you all right with that?' he asked Toby. Toby took a deep breath and nodded. Ned slowed to a hover, and then directed power downwards.

'Not unlike a very, very fast elevator on the side of a very, very high building' said Toby, trying to sound detached as the Ladybird accelerated drastically, vertically.

'Keep an eye on the air pressure' said Ned, tapping a small dial. Toby did so, in between glancing out the window. 'Fifteen thousand feet and rising' said Ned cheerfully, and a few minutes later, 'forty-five thousand.' There was only the soft hum of the 'motor', along with the occasional creak as the hull adjusted to the pressure difference. The acceleration was constant.

'Losing pressure very slowly Ned, no problems though...I think.'

'Sixty thousand.'

'Umm... Ned, passenger jets only go up to thirty thousand...'

'Yes, don't they. Seventy thousand.'

'And we seem to be climbing ever faster.' Toby stretched forward, using his feet to lever himself. 'I can see a bit of a curve on the horizon...'

Slight changes occurred that took a moment to register. The soft hum stopped. The blue glow died. The steady upward thrust diminished. Toby looked at Ned. He was furiously tapping dials, flicking switches. He was looking distinctly worried...

'Power's gone ... circuit break somewhere...' he muttered. The momentum faded and a moment when things stood still. A very distinct down sensation took over. The nose slowly fell away below the horizon as the little stubby wings started to bite on the air...down to vertical and falling towards the ridiculously tiny little mountains so far below...

'Toby watch the power dial and the slightest flicker yell' said Ned, planting his feet on the console and unclipping his harness. He contorted himself down and around to reach behind the instruments and began to desperately feel, tug, twist. Toby, hanging face down, stared at the dials and tried to ignore the soft sound of wind going past growing to a whistle.

'Nothingnopoweryet.'

'Buggeration. I can't find anything loose here,' said Ned, 'have to check the batteries. Don't panic, we still have a couple of minutes.' There was an edge of anxiety in his voice that didn't help Toby at all. Ned hauled himself up using the back of his seat and attacked the battery cover. Wing nuts and washers rained past Toby's head, then the cover itself tumbled down clipping his ear as it went. He extended his foot to kick it off the instrument panel and to the side.

'Still nothing happening Ned.'

'Yes. Nothing loose here. Shit.'

Toby could hear loud mutterings from behind, just audible above the dull roar of the wind. It was starting to get quite warm in the cabin. The mountains were not so tiny anymore.

Ladybird was beginning to vibrate. Toby was realizing he was going to die.

'What was happening just before the power cut off?' shouted Ned in his ear.

'Oh Christ... um … I just said I could see the curve on the horizon' said Toby through chattering teeth.

'Yes but what were you DOING??' roared Ned.

Toby thought desperately. He hadn't touched anything. It's not my fault was no help.

'I pushed myself up a bit to get a better look' he cried. Ned looked down past Toby's dangling legs. Think!

'Bloody junction box. I should have known it!' He scrambled and fell past Toby, ripped at the carpeted floor and yelled 'Screwdriver in the glove box!'

'Where?'

'Next to you!' Toby found it, ripped it open and a torrent of tools, tissues and travel sweets crashed down onto the instrument panel. 'Thanks' muttered Ned, scrabbling through the broken glass and rubble. Toby watched as the impossibly twisted Ned ripped a plastic cover, pulled out his penlight torch and feverishly probed with the screwdriver.

'Ned, it's getting bloody hot and I think there's something burning in the bow.'

'I know, I'm down here. Friction. Remember Challenger Three? No, don't even think about it. Ah… maybe this one!' He shouted in triumph as a sheet of sparks arced.

'Power's on' croaked Toby.

'I'll have to hold the lead on. Pull back on the control a bit and get the nose up horizontal then hit the down power.'

Toby eased the stick back gently. Nothing happened.

'Nothing's happened!'

'Damn. Wait a minute… There!' More sparks. Blue Rim on the windows. Nose lifting.

'Full power now and hang on' Toby shouted. Ned jammed his foot onto the seat and grabbed a bracket as the g-force rapidly built up.

'Not so much or you'll black out …' said Ned straining to breathe.

'Not enough and we're mince' gasped Toby.

'It's getting extremely hot too, the field is not letting the heat out…air pump's not working… we're still going down too fast to cut the field. Up to you, Toby…'

Toby's last thoughts on the matter were unbidden and regarding mince in an oven and a recipe for spiced meatloaf.

―∿∿―

Ethan Blunt, unusually drunk in Canumbie that night, told the story to anyone who would listen how the blue glowing flying saucer came barrelling down from the sky to briefly hover and land with a thud in front of his tractor. The blue glow faded and two doors swung open. How two black, smoking, vaguely human looking figures leaped out. How they would have abducted him had he not fled from the scene, and how they were gone when he came back with the shotgun but there was still a big mark in the paddock… Most folk bought him another drink. Eventually Mrs. Blunt got to hear about Ethan from another member of her church group and fetched him home.

―∿∿―

From far above, in a different space entirely, the geostationary SAGINT automatic detection systems called down urgently to technicians at Pine Gap, who in turn conferred and expedited imperative signals up the line. In the space of twenty minutes the comprehensive report was on the desk of Homer Spiggott.

'So this time it appeared at eighty-two thousand feet. What the hell are these things? How can they get so high but avoid detection? Was our equipment working?' demanded Homer.

'Perfectly Sir,' said the aide deferentially. 'It was going up vertically at around Mach 6 and then seemed to go into free fall before disappearing again at around 4000 feet.'

'Has to be a damn rocket. No aircraft can do that. Although if this information gets out of Pine Gap, the loony tunes will be saying it's another damn flying saucer' said Homer.

'We got a fix from two of our satellites so if it crashed, it should have hit around here' the aide said. He placed a map in front of Mr. Spiggott Sir.

'About 40 miles south-west of this town… Can-arr-gan? Same district as the last sighting.'

'Right' said the Chief of Overseas Security, 'We've got agents Graupner and Horowitz out there somewhere, brief them to get onto it and report back.' He scowled at the aide. 'I suppose I'll have to brief that cowboy klutz Dobrovich' he said gloomily. He sighed, pulled his polite professional face down and reached for the phone.

—*vv*—

Ladybird, with back doors propped ajar and smouldering a little, dropped down gently in front of Ned's Bedford. The blue glow flickered and died, the intrepid aviators emerged, blackened, bedraggled and coughing. The Hendersons gathered, concerned, enquiring.

'Bit of an incident. Need a drink, please. Beer.' said Toby. Liz and Solly shepherded them off to the Wisteria Rotunda, while Steve and Jules looked in wonder at the charred shambles inside the craft.

Ned poured a large glass, handed it to Toby and solemnly regarded him for a few moments.

'Toby, I am ashamed. In my haste to get into the air, I broke every basic precept of test flying. What is worse, I endangered your life needlessly, probably because I wanted to show off. That thing I took you up in had no back up systems, no safety reserve whatsoever. We didn't even have an escape option. I apologise, profoundly.' Ned sat uncomfortably, looking away and not touching his beer in penance. Toby lifted his and slowly drank, looking all the time at Ned's face.

'Too bloody right, mate. I have never been so terrified in my life. Culpa maxima, big-time.' Toby finished his beer slowly, savouring Ned's very atypical embarrassment, then grinned and passed his glass over. 'However, I accept your apology. We made it back… and I presume you may drop your fee for the last training flight?' Ned filled the glass and passed it back.

'Thank you' he said gravely. 'Yes, we did get through, despite the odds. Cheers.'

The companionable silence was shattered by a loud expletive as Liz slammed the drinks tray on the table and rounded on Ned. 'That's all very well but you can cut this returned air heroes crap you seem to be both basking in. Do you mean to say, Ned McZed, that you took that pile of recycled junk and nearly killed the pair of you?' Before he could answer, she turned to Toby. 'And, Mr. Buchanan Sir, I'll warrant that you were quite happy to stay up there as well. You are a pair of irresponsible, stupid, juvenile fools! I've a good mind to tell Steve to get his torch out and slice the bloody thing into… breadboards!' She stormed off to the kitchen.

'She is absolutely right you know' said Ned after a while.

'I'm afraid so,' said Toby, 'the swash has quite rubbed off our buckles…'

Ned chuckled. 'For a while, at least.'

'Breadboards are wood usually,' said Solly. 'And what you need is at least two motors for a start, double wiring and maybe a big parachute thing as well. It wouldn't fly very well if you had a component failure,' he added, helpfully.

'Amen to that' said Toby. He closed his eyes and tried to take in all that had happened. He hadn't woken up in bed, what happened was real! He had actually been in a small aircraft thing, plummeting earthward and desperately repaired at the last moment. These things just don't happen to Tobias Stanley Buchanan! If he had any sense, he would carefully get up, walk to his boring, safe motorcar and get the hell out of here. But then... a fierce, wild thrill he had never known before was coursing through him. This was essential stuff!

And the other thing, for the first time in his life, he was an important part of a small, vibrant group of close friends doing amazing things! He was a Tildan!

He could see what it all meant and he had to go along with these mad, lovely people.

One thing though, safety would have to be paramount before he would ever go up in Ladybird again. He would demand an O.H.&S. conference. No more foolishness.

Chapter 6

Agent Jason Graupner had a fabulous, fully secure satellite cell phone. The built in decoding computer enabled the agency to speak to him anywhere on the planet despite the most sophisticated intercepting surveillance. Unfortunately for the thick and loud Jason, thin O'Nite walls and an unsophisticated middy glass were sufficient for Shirley Denzil. While cleaning the adjoining cabin, of course.

'Goddamn it, speak up, the reception with this thing is goddamn lousy! Now is what you're saying we have to get the hell up country somewhere near Canumbie. Gimme the references... Right... another mid range missile... right... code red-2? There's nothing worth code red-2 in this country buddy... Yeah right... probably crashed... full team if we need it... OK... I'll go collect Horowitz... we'll call back in 24.' Shirley heard the screen door slam and the 4WD roar out the entrance. So what on earth was that all about, missiles crashing at Canumbie indeed. Shirley was sure she would have heard of any such nonsense. 'Code red-2' and 'team' sounded definitely beyond suss as well. Shirley could feel a full-blown mystery investigation coming on.

—⁓—

The Top Ace Electronic, Appliance and Automotive Repair Centre was in full production, a hive of industry, humming with activity. Toby and Ned had returned from McZedcroft at first light to strip and rebuild Ladybird in one of the side sheds. Steve, Jules and Solly were hard at work assembling a back-up engine. Liz, a little mollified by Ned's earnest entreaty that his chief concern and focus now was Safety First, was busy on the Net researching power and politics. Morning tea was a scattered affair, bread, jam and tea on the run in three locations. Toby broached a worry while he and Ned munched.

'Ned, you know this blue field thing and how it generates energy by breaking down iron... Well do you think it might be dangerous? Nuclear radiation or something? You know, like the early X rays where they thought it was harmless but…'

'Yes, of course, and what happened to Marie and Pierre Curie,' said Ned sombrely. 'Trust you to ask embarrassing essential questions.' Both chewed glumly on their jam sandwiches.

'I suppose…I have an acquaintance that works at the CSIRO station at Cambrawarra, so I might borrow some equipment and do some testing. We best tell Steve and the kids not to run any of the engines until I do. I suppose we've all had some exposure…Do you think that we might try a small experiment however? Very carefully, of course. I've been trying to work out as to why the radar on Ladybird didn't work.' He indicated one of Steve's tanks, which was sitting well away from the others. 'I want to hook the engine onto that tank, we can activate it at a distance of course, and then run the radar across it…' The radar unit had been removed and was sitting up on a workbench. Toby nodded absently, still somewhere in Fukishima. They finished morning tea and set up the equipment. The tank blue-glowed faintly on a low setting as Ned swivelled the antennae across it, onto an old tractor and back to the tank.

'Aha! As if it did not even exist!' exclaimed Ned. The screen was totally blank. He disconnected, and as the blue haze faded, the radar image sprang to life. Like a child with a new toy, he switched it off and on with gleeful comments of 'Wonderful! Well look at that then! Now you see it now you don't! Oh my!' Turning to Toby he proclaimed 'It eats radar! The radio pulse must be absorbed into the field so you don't get any reflected signal. What the Air Force would give for this!' Ned paused and reflected. 'I must admit that in my rash enthusiasm to get airborne, we might have got some unwanted attention from Regional Civil Aviation radar, but it seems that the field would have screened us from that,' he said, smiling in satisfaction.

'Apart from when the field was not on…' reminded Toby gently.

'Oh dear yes' said Ned, blanching at the memory of the death dive, 'We were up at around eighty, ninety thousand when that happened too... probably picked up by all the military stations as well. Bugger... at least we were out the other side of Canumbie I suppose. We best tread very carefully in future, Toby. And I think we'll move this beastie back to my Warrigal hideaway as soon as the main repairs are done. Now, young Solly in his wisdom was suggesting a parachute and I believe I can lay my hands on a large cargo chute in good condition. We need some solid hooks about here, here and here and a casing welded ...'

—*∿∿*—

'Ya there Liz?' came from the back door.

'In here Shirl.'

'Would you believe that there's espionage happenings back at the O'Nite Cabins?' Shirley was haemorrhaging with news as much as Liz was desperate to unburden. They had known each other when the Top Ace was just a run-down hayshed in a paddock, and shared everything. Trust based on years of successfully maintained confidences. Closed shop. Two glasses of red appeared; this was beyond tea.

'So what's this about spies in town?' asked Liz.

'Well ... there's two Americans who turned up on Wednesday, and...' Shirley gave chapter and verse on appearance, character, activities, and finished with Jason Graupner's loud, not so secret conversation that morning. Verbatim. Liz sat for some time thinking. He was talking about something flying then maybe crashing over towards Canumbie. It had to be Ned and Toby. She nodded. They were going to need Shirley, arch-conspirator and seeker of all truths...

'Shirl, you know how Solly and Jules built that wonderful radio? Well... he's come up with another little device... This time, it was Shirley's turn to listen. She was incredulous at first, especially after Liz walked her out into the workshop yard and pointed out Ladybird. Sounds of industry were coming from inside, the lads at work.

'You've got to be joking! That…lump was what the Americans were talking about? You're saying Ned and Toby actually flew in that thing?'

'Yes.' Liz was adamant. 'And it almost killed them too, stupid boys.' Shirley had no choice but to believe. It was Liz talking. She shook her head and marvelled.

'Well! I'll be damned! I would have loved to have seen that.' The idea of a huge, flying, Made in Tilda steam boiler appealed to Shirley. Liz and Shirley retreated back to the lounge. They had a large, complicated jigsaw to sort.

———

Arabella Swift, dedicated Junior Journalist, had her first fully sensational story in the Cambrawarra Pastoral Times. Much to her chagrin, the elderly editor had cut it down to 200 words, put it on page 12 and had told her to 'make it more humorous.' Fuming, she had complied, modifying Ethan Blunt's statement to give it a hillbilly flavour; deleting two other reported sightings (from pub contacts) and re-titling it 'Beam Me Up!'

Arabella had a quill in more than one inkwell however; the original (incisive and challenging) 'First Contact? Rural UFO Scare' had been sent off freelance to all the nationals in Sydney. Arabella had ambitions well beyond Cambrawarra and District…

———

At Canumbie Police Station, Graeme Horowitz waited while the desk sergeant confirmed their story and looked for someone to talk to them. Graeme squirmed, remembered Jason's blood stained debacle at the hotel and expected serious questions/negotiation. Jason practiced his excuses and built up some bluster.

———

Detective Sergeant Paul Hammond jiggled his foot impatiently while Graeme quietly explained their connections, presented their documents and outlined the help they might require. He glanced over the documents, but the desk sergeant had already confirmed the pair were kosher. He looked at Jason.

'So you would have been the bastard who put Angelo Costardis and Bazza Johnston in hospital the other week then. Been looking for you. Motel said the two of you cleared out just after the fight.'

'Don't know anything about a fight buddy' said Jason petulantly, folding his arms. Graeme sighed and prepared to step in. Paul Hammond smirked at the American discomfort, then held out his hand to Jason.

'No fucking worries mate, both a waste of space. Since you blokes are on our side, I'm sure we can keep it quiet, know what I mean. Better not go back to the pub though. You can stay at my place...'

Graeme stared out the window resignedly as the parallel personalities of Jase and Paully bonded in mateship. Their like minds shared the same intense interests in fine beers, violent forms of football and uncomplicated sex. Sure enough, before ten minutes were up, they both had their handguns out for comparison and discussion.

Unfortunately, D.S. Hammond couldn't identify any suspicious groups of middle-eastern appearance in the area, but agreed that if they could find any, he would be happy to hammer them in the interests of homeland security. Calling the meeting to order, Graeme pulled out the map references of the 'area of interest' and solicited more information. With the help of the desk sergeant, they located the site in the centre of lot 537/a, Kingston Road, property of Mr. & Mrs. E &V Blunt.

'That'd be Ethan Blunt' said the grey haired, well-informed desk sergeant, 'and funnily enough there was something about him in the Cambra this week mate.' The desk sergeant had a lot of time for the newspaper. He lifted it from under the counter and smoothed out Arabella's snippet. Graeme and Jason read the account with interest, but made no comment.

'Probably pissed, or into the wacky baccy…' opined the sergeant, 'I can't see why old Ethan would bring you fellers out here though?'

'Security stuff, just leave it George' said DS Hammond portentously.

With copious directions to the Blunt farm, as well as to the Hammond residence for after (The Missus won't mind), Jason and Graeme took to the back roads.

—∾∾—

Valerie Blunt was very reluctant to allow Ethan a second interview and only gave way after Graeme showed his impressive Bureau badge and swore solemnly on his mother's grave that they were not from the press. The genuine badge made up for his Mom being happily alive in an expensive Miami retirement village.

'That woman made a complete fool of my Ethan,' complained Valerie bitterly as she led them out toward the machinery shed. 'EEEETHANN!' bellowed Mrs. Blunt with the practice of thirty-five years of self imposed empowerment. Graeme winced at the level of governance. 'Whatever you're doing, stop it and get out here now Ethan. There's two American policemen come out to see you.' She turned and left for the house.

Ethan shuffled sheepishly into the sunlight and squinted at the agents. He took them back into the recesses of the machinery shed to a cleared area, which complete with a fridge, enough broken down chairs and a square of once-was carpet. Graeme was comforted by the universal male need for a private space and passed a compliment. Ethan looked around his workshop and seemed a little puzzled at this suburban viewpoint.

'So you reckon a bloke's gotta have a shed do you, Mr…?'

'Horowitz, Graeme Horowitz, and this is Jason Graupner, and we're very interested in what you might have seen… from a research point of view of course.'

Under tutelage from Valerie, Ethan's story had become considerably truncated. Yes, he had seen something that could have been a rocket of some sort. Yes, it did seem to come down on his property but then took off again and disappeared. No, the newspaper story about him seeing two aliens was not true and as everyone knew there was no such thing as aliens and a bloke would have to be an idiot to say something like that. No, he didn't think the thing was damaged when it landed. There wasn't anything much else he could add and he was sorry that they had come all this way out for nothing. Graeme was nodding and formulating his next questions about size, shape and appearance of the UFO when Jason Graupner jumped in with both boots.

'You fucking dumb hick! You think we buy this crock of shit?' He stepped toward the alarmed Ethan, hauling out his handgun.

'Look, I told you all I know.'

'Stand fucking still' snarled Jason. 'I know you scavenging backwoods bastards. I bet you've pulled it to bits and stashed it away. You are going to tell me where it fucking is right now.'

'I told you it didn't crash, it flew off…' quavered Ethan. He looked to Graeme despairingly. Graeme shrugged his shoulders sadly and looked away, he knew what was likely to happen next. Jason advanced menacingly… 'OK OK OK so it crashed. Look, I'm sorry. You don't need to do anything' Ethan wailed. Something ever so slightly wrong in the voice bought Graeme's head back around.

'So where the fuck is it?' said Jason The Dominant Male Aggressor.

'Well I did get some… technical bits off it and put them in the trunk back there…' said Ethan the submissive. Jason sent a told you so smirk to Graeme and strutted after Ethan. Graeme listened and watched fascinated. Although Ethan was speaking subservient very well, the accent was… studied. Although he was walking backwards and hunched, there was a hint of feline spring. Graeme opened his jacket a little for quicker access and settled back down onto his chair.

'The stuff's in there, I'll get it out for you.'

'No way, stand back where I can see you and keep your hands up.' Jason was not about to have Blunt pull some weapon out of the trunk. Ethan lifted his hands and moved back obediently while Jason carefully lifted the lid and peered in.

Graeme reflected later that the positioning and timing was perfect. A heavy metal bar mounted on a swivel was given a generous push; Jason caught the movement in the corner of his eye and brought his head up. There was a dull thud as the two objects neatly intersected and Agent Graupner crumpled to the floor. Graeme rose smoothly and pulled his jacket fully back to reveal the butt of his gun. Ethan appeared relaxed.

'Sorry to clobber your mate, he just wouldn't take no for an answer.'

'He is a bit pushy. He does have a remarkably thick skull so I think he'll survive' said Graeme indifferently. 'Did you learn that on a farm?'

'Ran a pub for fifteen years' explained Ethan.

'Do you mind if I pick up his gun and look after it?' asked Graeme politely. 'I suppose I better check if he's breathing too.'

'You don't think much of him, do you' said Ethan, standing aside.

'Not a lot' agreed Graeme, picking up Jason's gun and casually dropping it into his coat pocket. Jason's pulse and breathing were regular and Graeme decided he would recover, with a hell of a headache, in a half hour or so. He looked at Ethan speculatively. 'Whatever it was didn't crash here, did it,' he said. 'If it did, there would have been a fair hole and wreckage that a satellite scan would have picked up.'

'Suppose so' said Ethan.

'What did it look like? How big?' asked Graeme.

'About the size of a small truck. Cylinder thing.' Graeme shook his head in wonder. He was getting some dialogue but it could hardly be called credible. He was about to ask his next question when he became aware of a slight lessening of light from the shed entrance behind him. Ethan was looking over his shoulder and smiling. He slowly moved his hands well away from his coat. 'Valerie would have been outside listening to this galah' said Ethan, pointing to the recumbent Graupner, 'and she likes to look after me.'

'I think it's time you took your foolish friend and went away, Mr. Horowitz' came the steely voice from behind.

'Probably the best thing mate,' agreed Ethan, 'nothing else I can tell you anyway. I'll give you a hand with muggins here.'

They dragged Jason to the 4WD and hoisted him across the back seat. Valerie cradled the vintage double-barrelled shotgun comfortably, clearly a country-schooled shootist. At least it was no longer pointed at his abdomen.

'I don't suppose if I left my mobile number and you remember something more...' said Graeme hopefully.

'No... I don't reckon so mate' said Ethan.

'Definitely no point' added Valerie.

—⁓—

Graeme drove carefully down the back road to Barangan, trying not to avoid the larger potholes and enjoying the resulting groans from the back seat. The choice between staying at the DS Hammond residence or Addison's O'Nite Cabins had been easy, and the drive gave him time to think. Ethan appeared to be straight regarding something landing in front of him. About the size of a small truck? Landed and took off again? What the hell had Ethan Blunt seen then? Some sort of a VTOL rocket plane maybe? Such a thing may be possible... Graeme was originally an engineering student before he fell into the Agency, and loved unusual machinery. He remembered the beautiful simplicity of the Messerschmitt Me163 Komet, a tiny rocket-powered single seater which looked too ridiculously Buck Rogers to fly until he saw some WWII German film footage of it taking off and blasting straight up to 39 thousand feet in three minutes. Everyone investigating this thing seemed obsessed with the idea of missiles but why not a manned aircraft that could lift to the stratosphere and then slam into any chosen target? He liked the idea... He was mulling it over as he drove through Tilda, smiled and waved to the kids leaving the Public School and noting with amusement a large, run down shed and junkyard grandly named 'Top Ace Electronic, Appliance and Automotive Repair Centre...'

Shirley watched as Graeme struggled out of the lofty 4WD with the groaning Jason and smiled as the whingeing one was let fall. She offered to help lift Graupner to the room. 'Need some Panadol?' she asked, surveying the large bruise and lump. 'Don't suppose he might have concussion?' she added hopefully.

'Nothing to concuss,' muttered Graeme. 'Thanks for the offer, but I've got something stronger here... at least I might get some peace for the night.'

Graeme looked and sounded very pissed off, so Shirley slid into the flow.

'Café's empty, come on over when your offsider is unconscious and I'll make you some tea, or do you say dinner? Food. Don't argue.' She turned and left.

Graeme walked in gratefully an hour later to meet a gloriously comforting pan-fried high carb 'n cholesterol meal, the kind his health conscious wife had banished long ago. Shirley had an extra plate on the table and two bottles of 'a nice sort of red' airing.

'You haven't got a family to go home to?' asked Graeme.

'Yes, two great kids, Brad and Bobby, doing a sleepover with friends tonight.'

Fast phone calls had sent Brad and Bobby off on their bikes to Liz and Steve.

She was attentive, wide-eyed, respectful, and with a line of chat as smooth as the cab sav in the oversized glasses. The meal began very well and in the rosy glow Graeme felt his cares slipping out the door with the closed sign on it.

'You have kids at home Graeme?' asked Shirley.

'Two girls, Rosa and Juliana, both at High School. Gave them a call earlier, and Jenny, my wife.' He gazed wistfully at his glass.

'Long way from home...' added Shirley softly, while pouring. Graeme found himself telling Shirley at length of his family history, the home, the dog, his hobbies, and the amount of time he had to spend away on account of The Damn Company. She was such a good listener. He liked Shirley. He didn't have to drive anywhere. They started on the second bottle of red. Superb dessert was complemented with a potent liqueur muscat pudding wine. Shirley's natural talent as an interrogator lay in her assiduous guidance of conversations and her genuine, absolute interest in what other humans thought, did and felt. It was irresistible.

'Your grumpy Mr. Graupner seems to be somewhat accident prone...'

'He's stuffed up every job I've ever been on with him. And yet the... company... still keeps him on! How he got the latest smack to the head is a prime example.' Graeme paused and helped himself to another small glass of muscat.

'How was that then?' tinkled Shirley, eyebrows arched. A muffled alarm bell rang faintly in the back of Graeme's mind. He knew what it was. The same reason that agents never got to reminisce or write their memoirs. He had so many entertaining stories his friends would never hear around the fireside, and that was... sad. He sipped, and then pursed his lips. Frankly

Scarlet, I don't give a damn he thought as he reached in and switched the bell off.

'Well…of course this is all very hush hush' he said. Shirley murmured about her undying discretion. 'The company I work for got to find out about some mysterious high altitude flying objects…' Graeme launched into the whole tale of radar sightings, space shuttles, Ethan doing Jason over and his own theories, encouraged by Shirley's rapt attention. He had a lovely time, told some other tales of exotic foreign parts he had in storage, had thirds on dessert, an Irish Coffee and more muscat. Developing quite a taste for the good old muscat in fact, he decided.

In the morning Graeme vaguely remembered standing up and falling over around one a.m., then being helped back toward his room. He didn't really want to think about the night before, what he said, how he got to bed… and he certainly didn't fancy breakfast.

———◠◠◠———

Jules and Solly stood back, satisfied. Resurrected, a nice coat of red paint, the Dad-built plywood MG pedal car of their childhoods sat proudly on the concrete.

'I reckon you can still fit in Jules. Dad made it pretty big and the pedals are gone.'

Jules grunted as she squeezed herself in. With her knees up, she could still fit one hand on the steering wheel. Tentatively she eased the joystick controller forward.

'Whoaaa!!!' The car shot forward but she managed to brake with some reverse thrust.

'We need to cut the voltage down a bit before we try the next bit.' said Solly.

Liz sang softly as she bent, lifted and pegged. It was a good drying day and the first load was almost ready to take down.

'Hey Mum.' She turned around to smile at Solly, but where was he?

'Up here Mum.' Liz looked up, gasped and fell back into the laundry basket. Above the Hills Hoist, Solly was laughing at her from his pedal car! A metal plate bolted to the underside opalesced with a familiar soft blue light…

'Get down here straight away you little brat!' she roared. A giggling Jules rushed forward and helped her to her feet while Solly landed the MG and clambered out.

'Sorry Mum. Solly and I just thought we'd put a motor in our old car. It's great!'

'Really good,' added Sol. 'We went down the back paddock and I took it up. I could even see the McPherson place and Mr. McPherson on his tractor!'

'Well! I hope Mr. McP didn't see you! And the first thing you can do is take the up-down controls off that sports car. Right now. I'm not having another near flying disaster!' Liz harrumphed as she lifted the last of the sheets. After a while she added 'but you can leave the other bits on… I think I've got a bit of an idea for tomorrow.'

In Barangan Police Station, Sergeant Ken Baker ran his hand softly over his favourite handgun, the fabulous Colt Magnum. He sighed, put it away in the bottom drawer and pulled out his third favourite, the Smith and Wesson 38. Which although superseded, was at least police issue. It reminded him of Rubber Bullets, his favourite 10cc song. He tunelessly mumbled it, giving the bit about Sergeant Baker being cool and clear and always in command big licks. Ken's brain didn't really run to irony.

'Harris, get in here!' The much-oppressed Constable Ernie Harris appeared. 'We've got another one of those loopy farmers putting in a flying saucer report out the back of Tilda. Total horseshit and a waste of time so it's yours. Piss off!' He crunched the report into a ball and threw it at Ernie.

Ernie drove out of Barangan thinking dire thoughts about "Dirty Ken," as called by most Barangans. Not due to the movie, as the sergeant believed, but more down to his mouth and personal habits… Just concentrate on your exams for next week, Ernie reminded himself.

———

Ned and Toby were finishing up their afternoon tea in the Henderson garden.

'Ned,' began Liz carefully, 'back before you built Ladybird you said we should all consider the implications of what we had done. What exactly did you mean by that? Hmmm?'

'Well now,' said Ned tugging at his moustache, 'I suppose I was talking about the device being applied to flying… but what with my Ladybird project, that's about as far as I got.'

'And other implications? Anyone?'

'As soon as you come up with a good gadget, someone always tries to rip you off,' announced Steve. 'They steal it… they put a tax on it … they make it illegal … that sort of thing… you have to be careful anyway' he added defensively.

'How much did the device cost to build then?' asked Liz.

'The big one, Stripper 1 was $134 because we made it from second hand spares,' said Solly. 'Little Egypt was $427.37. Ned's ones and the next four will be $349.67 each. We got a discount on the big order.'

'Much charge in the batteries when you got back after the crash?'

Toby and Ned conferred. 'Sixty-eight percent. Pretty economical I'd say' said Steve.

'Yes indeed. We have something we would like to show you,' said Liz, gesturing.

The very small MG glided silently around the corner of the house, driven by a beaming Solly. He neatly reverse parked in next to the wall and climbed out.

———

'Pretty cool, hey? Jules and me reckon with the one motorbike battery we've got in it, we could get from here to Barangan and back, at least.'

'And a full size car could do it too, with not much more…' added Liz, smiling. It would only take a minute to sink in. Jules grinned and drew a dollar sign in the air.

Two hours later, Solly had just announced that the world used about 30 billion barrels of oil a year and at, say, $100 each, that would be $3 trillion in the short scale and Ned was explaining the linkages between the three bits of The Iron Triangle when there was a quiet rapping on the back door. Suddenly, the real world was intruding, and it came in the form of Constable Ernest Harris. All discussion stopped as Ernie came in and gravely acknowledged everyone. He had known the Hendersons since childhood, was on nodding terms with Ned and Toby. Ernie's embarrassment radiated in waves from his open face.

'I'm here on account of a report received yesterday afternoon from a Mr. McPherson. Lives near here. Said there was a… um…car flying up in the air near here, yesterday afternoon. Like those flying saucer reports but it was a car.'

'Oh,' said Ned. 'Amazing. Gosh.'

'Well thanks for that news Ernie' said Liz.

'He thought it was a fair way off, but it looked like a red sports car… A bit bizarre, eh? Don't suppose any of you folk saw anything?' enquired the Constable, hopefully.

'Flying, like up in the air?' asked Toby. 'Bit like in Harry Potter?'

'Yes,' said Ernie. 'Oh thanks, very nice,' he said, accepting a mug of tea from Julie.

'Maybe it was one of the kids in their pedal car,' said Steve, pointing at the innocent red MG by the wall. 'You been flying around the McPhersons, Solly?'

'Not apart from yesterday, Dad…'

Ernie snorted into his tea. The Hendersons were renowned for their jokes.

Later, they all saw him off, wishing him luck on his search.

'Thanks for the cup of tea. I'll let you know what happens.'

'Totally unbelievable,' said Toby to Ned later. 'As the man said, bizarre!'

—*∧∧*—

A Top Ace Sunday Lunch had been declared with the usual suspects summoned, including Maria and the Denzil boys. Maria had accepted the whole story with remarkable aplomb.

'Fantastic,' she said to Toby. 'Literally.' Jules and Solly said that as best friends of course Brad and Bobby were already fully informed and were waiting for an invitation to see things and do stuff. Toby nodded to Brad and was introduced to the bro.

Shirley took the floor over entrée and gave an account of The Inveiglement of The American Agent by The Tilda Mata Hari and what he said before unconsciousness. She added the tucking in of the comatose Graeme - a nice family man - and the cursory check that Graupner breathed. Shirley cared for most of her customers. The main meal arrived.

Steve decided they must have found whatever was left of Stripper 1 and hoped there wasn't much. Ned thought that as there was a radar sighting, the field must have failed at that point and hitting even a thin atmosphere at a huge speed … Toby grimaced as he remembered their recent warm trip. Liz expressed concern that if the spy agencies were talking terrorism, the recent anti-terrorism legislation could be a threat to everyone. Ned said he knew a good barrister in Sydney. Shirley suggested that 'this thingy' should be patented, Steve said they would still rip it off, Ned said the oil companies would want it all buried deeper than the electric car. Toby suspected the patenting process itself might not offer protection, but more likely would call attention to the device and provide a tool to control it. Shirley and Ned briefly touched on the fact that the field would be worth gazillions. Ideas and counter ideas continued to circulate regarding dangers, usefulness and potentials until dessert was served. Toby tapped his spoon on his glass for quiet.

'The big question,' he said with gravitas, 'Is how do you get an idea of this size and importance actually out into the world? Put it on 'The New Inventors'? Trot up to the Patents Office with a full set of plans and hope for a copyright? I don't think so! Because there would be so many powerful groups of people determined to tie up and exploit the device or stop it entirely as soon as it emerges. There would be so much at stake that anyone who got in the way would not stand up for long.' There was a long wet blanket hiatus.

'That's my family you're talking about Toby, and I realise how easy it is to have inconvenient people put aside' said Liz, angrily, 'You're not just talking about little holidays away either, are you.'

'No I'm afraid I wasn't,' said Toby glumly. Dessert proceeded without the customary joy.

Ned quietly opened the forum again.

'Solly and Jules are the only ones here who really know how the devices are made and operated, and must be protected at all costs until they have powerful and principled allies who can be trusted. Tilda is too isolated as a safe base, and when news of Solly and Jules' little project gets out, I think they will have to leave.'

'How that news is broken will determine if it is squashed or not' said Maria. 'The story will need to be sudden, dramatic, and spread world-wide so fast that the powers that be can't pull the plug on it. So appealing to people that the media will find it irresistible, despite pressure. A media blitzkrieg! Along with the Internet.'

'Dramatic... sudden... appealing and irresistible...' said Shirley. 'Certainly sounds like a job forrrrrr.... TADAFIC!!!' There was a general round of applause.

Toby looked around puzzled until Maria whispered a reminder.

'Tilda Amateur Dramatic and Float Inspirational Committee.'

Suitably inspired, the assemblage fell to planning.

With the lunch cleared and coffee served, Ned sprang the surprise he had been nursing impatiently for a week. He placed a large cardboard tube on the table and pulled the stopper off with a hollow, mysterious plonk. The chat stopped.

'In a fit of madness I did some bidding at the decommissioned Mullawang power station auction a fortnight ago. Picked up a bargain or two. I've been at the drafting board since then.' He carefully pulled out two large, translucent sheets and spread them out, borrowing cups to hold down the corners.

'I'd just like to put this up as a possibility. Along with some of your communication schemes and a couple of japes I have in mind, it may help answer some of the questions raised this afternoon' he said modestly, moving back. The Hendersons, Denzils, Toby and Maria crowded around. Bobby Denzil broke the stunned silence with a comment that later earned him a clip over the ear from his Mum.

'Holy Shit Mr. McZed!'

—◦◦◦—

Chapter Seven

Stan Addison looked at Toby with disbelief.

'How many more bloody batteries did you say he wanted? McZed took twelve just the other week mate! What the hell's he doing with them?' McZed was always a great customer for batteries, but this was getting ridiculous. Toby muttered that there were plans afoot to make the Top Ace solar and laid out $2500 in cash on the counter. The cash settled the Addison curiosity and he quickly scribbled a receipt from his special book. Must check out this solar malarkey though, thought Stan. Might be a bob in it…

—⁓—

'What do you think about this material for some curtains for the side windows then, Ned?' asked Liz, holding up some heavy wool fabric in a nice shade of plain. Ned curbed his first response, thought, and said they would go very well with the carpet. He added curtain brackets to the ever-growing list, underneath 'remove stove/fridge/air-con/toilet from caravan and fit.'

Toby looked with pride at the classic curves he had chalked, cut and smoothed from the large steel plate over the past three hours.

'Nice one Tobes,' said Steve, 'now you can get started on that one for the other side, then we better get onto the fin…'

Toby stretched and looked again at the thirty feet of ex-power station coal fired high-pressure steam boiler, which had arrived at the Top Ace a week ago. De-scaling had been easy, thanks to the field, but the amount of cutting, grinding and welding to do was horrendous! The blisters started to hurt again.

Maria and Shirley, exhausted from the laughter, had finished the final speech of the fifth annual TADAFIC presentation for the Barangan Festival.

'Exit stage left' said Maria with finality.

'Not falling off back of truck' added Shirley.

'I think they might be talking about this one for a good few years, Shirley.'

'Reckon. Cracker of a finish, eh?' said Shirl.

—*∿*—

It had been a slow news day in Sydney and Melbourne. Not a single politician had committed an obscene or even mildly indiscreet error. There were no multiple fatalities on land, sea or in the air. No damning reports had been released. Editors faced with very thin papers sighed, scrolled further and further down, reluctantly took uncomfortable decisions… and so it was that the complete Arabella Swift masterwork 'First Contact? Rural UFO Scare' had made it to page one or two. Padded with some archive photos. Sharing the page with the unfortunate Balmain Vespa riding commuter who was taken out by a matched pair of fashion statement Irish Wolfhounds. An elated Arabella hit the road scouring for a follow up, notebook in hand. Graeme and Grumpy received a directive to check out the 'other reported sightings…' and set off in pursuit of Arabella…

—*∿*—

Ned McZed, aka Edward McCannigle, had been sent at age 15 and with numerous scholarships to the University of Edinburgh to study Pure Physics. Three fretful years and a degree or two later, he had traded the ivory towers for an engineering post in the New Guinea Highlands… but that was another story. Albeit, his love of science and argument earned him a guest spot with the Cambrawarra CSIRO Five at their Friday Afternoon Drinks. They had been moved to the back room ('We can't hear the races because of those geeky bastards'), where much dark ale and house red fuelled their expoundings.

Ned carefully plied Dr. Gavin Melvin, Head Scientist of Electro-Magnetic Research with drinks and compliments, gradually cutting him out of the flock. During a meal at the Blue Lotus Chinese (Gavin liked exotic), Ned (humbly) put forward his problem. He had developed what he believed may be a useful food irradiation device but alas, did not have the expertise or equipment to do an evaluation. Gavin blinked owlishly and Ned hoped he hadn't overdone the impulse disinhibitor.

'You see Gav, I wouldn't know where to start… I suppose I could go to the Sydney Uni laboratory…' Gavin had graduated from Melbourne University.

'Buncha wankers. Wouldn' know a quark from a lepton. Even wi the equiment I got, I c'd do a better job. No worr's. Jus gotta run id thrr… through th'… Twenny mints.'

'Really?' said Ned with child-like hopefulness and awe. 'Gosh.'

'Yeah. Jus bringit in. Anytime.' Ned lifted his backpack up onto the table with a thump.

'Twenty minutes you reckon?' he said, firmly.

A slightly sobered, very sceptical Gavin looked through the thick glass at the anonymous wooden box with its steel plate screwed to the side. It had been placed inside his very expensive dosimetric instrument and Ned had run a rheostat switch to the outside. The plate was glowing ever so slightly.

' 's not gunna blow up or burn is it?'

'Never has so far, Gav' said Ned reassuringly. Little Egypt was tucked into the case and limited to produce a non-directional field, so Ned was reasonably confident it wouldn't take off either.

'Wind it up a bit, very very slow then' said Gavin…

Half an hour later and Gavin was pleased to announce that the McZed project had been a complete failure. The curious blue glow appeared to be entirely ineffective as a steriliser. Not lethal at all, Gavin repeated with relish as he passed a bundle of printouts over. Ned scanned them quickly and nodded absently to the Head Scientist.

'S'why are ya grinning then?' asked Gavin with querulously, 'I thought you'd be pissed off that y'r bug killer is… buggered.'

'Just my way of hiding my deep despair at failure, Gav' said Ned hurriedly. 'Back to the Drawing Board then. All those sleepless nights and two years just wasted' he added sadly. 'I suppose you've cleared all the data out regarding this trial? It wouldn't do to have a record for a CSIRO auditor to find' said Ned solicitously. Gavin duly deleted.

'Only thing I can't figger out' said Gavin as Ned drove back to town 'is that weird sort of oscillation at the third level.'

'Don't you worry about that Gavmate' said Ned, jollymode, 'probably just the machine playing up. Now, take a look in that glove box there and you'll find as nice a bottle of single malt whisky as you'll find this side of Speyside…' Ned grimaced as he watched the cork casually dropped on the floor and the bottle upended. Such a Sacrilege, but the sacrifice would guarantee that the night would only be a painful blur.

In the small hours of the morning, after retrieving and corking the remaining half bottle of Abelour, he left the snoring Doctor to the tender mercies of Mrs. Melvin.

'Must have been something he ate at the restaurant,' he confided to the grim faced wife before he drove off. Gavin would not have much time, capacity or headspace for physics when he woke up.

—⁓—

Mid morning saw Ned back at the Top Ace, running through his midnight CSIRO excursion. Nothing remotely toxic appeared in the printouts, apart from one curious anomaly. Gavin had gone for a pee giving Ned a chance to play, and when the test apparatus was stretched to its limit, it did detect a hint of an unknown waveform.

'Yes,' said Solly, 'that's just the field. It's like a harmonic, but a bit different, like the top layer's randomised chaos, but the ones under that have a different structure. Won't hurt anyone though.' Ned added some more reassurance: when he had put plywood in front of the detector, the waveform had disappeared. Wood shielding worked! Steve and Toby smiled and nodded enthusiastically, problem solved. All they needed now was a bit more research to back it up.

'So where and when might that be done?' asked Maria. 'It seems to me that all you have is a half finished script here. We'll have some great attention grabbers with the TADAFIC play, the Internet and papers but then what? Sure, the publicity might make things safer, but it's never stopped "the powers that be" before. Publicity is media, and media is controlled. As I know, to my cost.'

'Yes!' agreed Liz vehemently, 'it's a world that turns on money and like Toby said before, there's a lot of interest groups would move very quickly to either stop or control Solly's invention. Political, military, police, the justice system… they can all be manipulated "in the national interest" and then nothing said due to "security concerns." I know how incredibly important this work is, but I don't want my family sacrificed for it! So what are we going to do about it?'

Liz and Maria, having thrown the gauntlet, waited. The men were nodding, but not smiling.

'Well,' said Shirley, filling the gap. 'Damn right. Either you bury the whole thing, and knowing you lot that's not bloody likely, you might need to get out of town in a hurry when the balloon goes up.'

'Yes indeed,' agreed Ned. 'In a crisis, decamp. Done it before, many a time. Like I said when I first proposed the big Ladybird, it's what we can use to take the Henderson family safely away. Nothing will catch the Ladybirds,' he added proudly.

'And where will you take them to? Where will you get this "bit more research" and powerful people of principle who can protect you while it happens?' asked Maria.

'Yes… well, there's a thing. No one's quite worked that one out yet…'

Toby rose and did his glass tapping for quiet. An hour of arguments had piled the table with

ill formed arguments, good but wispy ideas and random gems. He had made notes.

'Seems we're agreed on a few things, correct me if I'm wrong of course, but mainly…

Both Ladybirds need to be finished and made as safe as possible. Hear hear! We can't really explore getting help until that's done and we're ready to leave. After that, Shirley and Maria are prepared to keep the information going out and to recruit support and allies. Some possibilities are the Scottish Universities (thanks Ned), maybe some of the more independent U.S. state universities, or as Solly suggested, Scandinavia. Japan? Western Europe? The climate here doesn't seem quite right,' he added sadly, 'and anywhere else is definitely out. And the TADAFIC play will need a bit of re-writing.'

He sat down amidst general agreement.

'No worries,' announced Steve, 'something always turns up…'

Afternoon tea was rustled up. Liz asked pointedly about improvements to "that damn flying Ladybird breezeblock," returned from the Warrigals. Ned took them out and carefully explained his new safety features; the doubled circuitry and twin motors, thicker wood panelling, additional battery monitoring and twin steering/power controls. Jules and the lads had been very busy over the past week! All of these features were to be fitted to the larger craft, of course. For want of a better name, the committee had called it 'Ladybird 2'

'My final contribution to peace of mind' he said, climbing up and patting three securely welded steel boxes on the roof, 'are these spring loaded Havelock MarkVII cargo parachutes I picked up from disposals. Mechanical operation, guaranteed to open in emergencies, capacity four tons. We'll put six on the big'n as well.' The new instruments and sumptuous panelling were admired. Ned had also added a small fridge, carpeting, storage lockers, a wall clock and some framed prints.

'I expect there'll be a chaise longue and a small piano in the corner soon' said Liz.

'Piano...? No, but a small pull out bed might be the go maybe...' said Ned, unconcerned.

Around lunchtime the Sydney Morning Herald arrived with Shirley and offspring.

"First Contact? Rural UFO Scare' (page 2) with picture supplement (page 7) and additional interviews" created much laughter, however, the reminder from Shirley of spies in town and what was at stake bought everyone back to a siege mind frame. Ladybird 1 would be taken to the back shed at McZedcroft. The three completed motors and Little Egypt would be hidden amongst the workshop junk. The spare 'Aerial' radio set, a mini version of the Dekko Omnitron, could easily pass as part of Solly's mail order Junior Electronics Project Kit. As indeed it was, added Jules.

The afternoon wound down with Ned shyly showing the assemblage his genuine Air Force high g flying suit picked up for next to nothing in 1989, followed by a hilarious reading of the modified TADAFIC Play; The Whizzer of Oz.

—◯◯◯—

School Holidays bought Acting Senior Constable Ernie Harris to drop in on the Hendersons. He was quite pleased really, the exams had gone well and even more surprising, Baker was off his back. A multitude of local complaints over years, carefully redirected by him, had seen the Sergeant ordered to attend a very expensive "Redirection" therapy course in Sydney. At last!

Ernie walked to the rear of the workshop and noted with interest that Steve, Ned McZed and the new School Counsellor Toby Buchanan were all hard at work on a massive steam boiler up on chocks. Grinding, cutting and welding with great enthusiasm.

'Ello Ello Ello, What's all this then?' he asked, sauntering over.

Steve looked up startled, but recovered quickly. Bit edgy.

'G'day Ernie… Ahhh…Yes mate. This is the new float. The Committee are going with a bit of a space theme this year… the flying saucers up at Barangan and all that…'

'Apart from that one that looked like a sports car,' said Ernie with a snort, 'aren't flying saucers supposed to be round?'

'Ummm, yair, usually, but not necessarily mate. They're whatever shape you happen to have lying around at the time. The beauty of this one is that after the parade we could set it up in the park for kids, with a few ladders. And it's a hundred percent vandal proof too!' Steve exclaimed as he banged the quarter inch steel plate side proudly.

Ernie nodded approvingly. A succession of Swedish pirate ships in Barangan Memorial Park had been reduced to smoking puddles of plastic or little busted bits over the years.

'You'll round off the rough bits and get it through council then?'

'It'll be all space ship-shape' called down Toby, pausing from cutting a large porthole.

Ernie strolled back to his car, musing on last year's TADIFIC production, the giant watermelon which opened up to become the stage for a highly libellous play around a 'fictitious' development scheme. Ernie noted that despite his fury, Barangan's Best Real Estate agent, Mayor Glen Jones did not press charges and instead rearranged certain of his affairs hastily. Ernie approved of self-regulating communities.

He continued on with his rural neighbourhood rounds.

—〜〜—

Chapter 8

Ned sat in Ladybird 1 at McZedcroft and switched on the mini Dekko Omnitron.

'Mr. Watson, come here, I want you' he called.

'My God, it talks!' came back, clear as a bell, from Toby in Ladybird 2 at the Top Ace. Ned smiled. Totally unbreakable, Solly had encoded the VVEHF (modified) voice signals, using Winnie the Pooh as the encryption base. Ned agreed with Solly and Jules that it was not high on Security Agency reading lists...

He looked proudly around the rebuilt cabin and sighed contentedly. Extra batteries, radar with an extendable dish, external ceramic aerial for the Omnitron and a very nice piece of figured walnut veneer for the new instrument panel complemented the new radio.

'Ah well,' he said aloud, 'As Duke said to Sam, Let battle commence...' Jules and Solly laughed and left. Flicking the switches to power up the drive, Ned eased Ladybird off the floor and gently out of the back shed, rotated 360 to check for aerial traffic, blasted up to a thousand feet and set course for the hills.

———

Steve glanced at his watch, grunted thanks as Chazza gave him a fresh tinnie then joined in boisterously with the third obscene verse of 'The Footie Lament'. The annual Pre-Season Afternoon Barbeque and Piss-Up of the Barangan Tigers was in full swing and he didn't want the troops to miss out on their big surprise. Again he stared north, just to the left of Spenser's Knob and frowned in concentration... yes, there it was, a distinct blue dot.

'Watcha looking at Hendo?' asked Nick Bronson, one of the more alert club members.

'Funny lookin blue thing flyin around out near Spensers, mate' said Steve, pointing.

Nick peered.

'Yairrr… Coming this way too… Hey youse blokes, what do youse reckon that is then?' he obligingly bellowed. The club turned as a team and saw the dot grow to a sizeable blob, then streak at an incredible speed over their heads and off to the north-east, leaving a deep rumbling sonic boom in its wake. They stood awed, mouths open, cans unmoving. Well done Ned and very impressive, thought Hendo. Conversations in Barangan and District were well primed for the next two weeks.

Arabella Swift had her next national feature, complete with colour shots of the Tigers.

Maria Scott got in touch with her old mates at the ABC about a very entertaining rural drama production at the upcoming Wool 'n Hops Festival. Would segue well with the Current UFO Scare. Quirky, evocative and above all, cheap. She'd do all the legwork, free. Some email chat to other selected friends ensured leakage to the commercials.

Liz and the Denzil boys fed the net. Stuffed it full.

Accommodation in Barangan for the weekend 22-23 became expensive and scarce; Canumbie and Cambrawarra became choked with the overflow. Enterprising locals offered B&B, Glen Jones filled all his 'cottages'. The Council doubled the portable dunnies… just about everyone was happy.

———

Under-Secretary Kelvin Dobrovich was not happy, and told Homer Spiggott, Chief of Overseas Security just so.

'What the damn hell are your agents doing out there? How can a drunken football team see this damn flying saucer thing and our multi-billion Security Surveillance Stations can't? Is this a secret Australian government project? I want answers, Homer!!!'

'I'm sorry Sir,' sighed Homer with delegated unhappiness, 'we still don't seem to get any radar info on whatever it was and they can't work out why Sir. One of our office staff did manage to find a visual track of sorts though.' He handed across two very pixelated landscape photos with a faint streak encircled.

'Where are these from?' asked the Under-Secretary suspiciously.

'Well... um... Google Earth actually...' said Homer, with deep embarrassment, 'we don't have any visual surveillance in that area yet...bit of a gap...' The Dobrovich explosion elicited a sincere promise that a 10,000 square mile fixed spy sat visual coverage was being organised as they spoke, hopefully for next week Sir. Signals to the agents concerned had been sent, and they were working around the clock. Sir.

———

Agent Horowitz had been working around the clock, Agent Graupner was chronologically impaired. Graeme had rented a small family sedan to scour the district. Jason had taken the SUV to go drinking and plotting with his good buddies over in Canumbie, and to maintain surveillance on the Blunt farm. That fucking hick was hiding something for sure. Graeme was on the road, following up a 3 a.m. night-light bulb moment. The words Kelvinator compressor, workshop and appliance had jigsawed and he was retracing his steps to the Top Ace Electronic, Appliance and Automotive Repair Centre. Vintage jazz on the CD player, maps and snacks on the nicely empty passenger seat. God, it was easier without Graupner. Graeme vowed again to stay solo in future. Way to travel, Yessir.

Agent Horowitz had picked his ploy and done his research. He parked politely and knocked on the front door of the Top Ace until Steve appeared around the side.

'Hi there, name's Graeme Jenkovich and I'm a freelance journalist from Utah, that's in the States, friend, and I'm doing a journal piece on your 'outback' garages for the American Garage Association Journal. I was sure hoping I could do an interview with you folk. You've got a real nice looking operation here.' Graeme smiled and stuck his hand out.

Steve wiped his hands with a blackened rag and regarded him with interest. Definitely the Horowitz of Shirley's description. He grabbed Graeme's hand with enthusiasm and shook it.

'Steve Henderson mate. Yair sure, why not, eh? So what sort of stuff you American blokes interested in then?'

'Well there,' said Graeme, keeping his hand away from his clothes, 'I guess the kind of machinery you use, marketing, kind of repairs you do, that sort of thing. One of the things I've found so far has been the way you fellers can improvise some pretty fancy things out of nothing, mighty impressed with that...'

'Yair... Guess we're well known for that sort of thing mate. Could make anything in a place like this.' Steve launched into one of his favourite conversations, how Australian blokes had invented most things in the world, from combine harvesters to Furpheys to the aeroplane, well the box kite anyway, as well as... Graeme listened patiently, took notes with interest, but was still stuck outside the front.

'Well that's great... so what work are you involved in currently?' he asked more directly.

There was a long pause, then a Henderson wink.

'Dunno if your Utah readers'd believe this, Mr. Jenkywitch... but we're building a genuine, proper Startrek, lightspeed Spaceship!' Steve grinned at the confusion.

'Yer better come and have a dekko at it then mate.' He led Graeme down the side.

Graeme gasped, hand automatically reaching into jacket/crouch for cover/check sides back/escape routes. Steve watched with obvious amusement. Towering above them, with multi facetted nose stretched back smoothly to stubby delta wings and tailplane, was a massive, iridescent blue...rocket spacecraft. From his childhood. Almost a space shuttle. Graeme straightened slowly, took his hand out from his jacket. The only other person in the vicinity was the grinning mechanic.

'Sorry about that mate, should have warned you. She's a bloody ripper don'tcha reckon?'

Horowitz walked slowly around the craft. Thick grilled windows were fitted into the nose and sides. Where in hell were the rocket exhausts? Was it sitting on skids? He looked closer at the hull and tentatively patted it; riveted steel plate! He shook his head at his own stupidity... flying? Sucked in! Two large steel doors were open at the rear.

'So they can lock it up at night and the vandals won't get in' explained Steve. 'We can bolt it down so they couldn't push it over too, not that they could cos it weighs close on eight tons, but those little bloody demons'll try anything won't they? Ya know, if they put as much energy into getting a job...' Light dawned from the PTA section of Graeme's domestic brain. Play equipment! He nodded and agreed wholeheartedly, they had the same problems in his hometown. Invited inside, he marvelled at the wood panelling, the seating with harnesses, elaborate instruments, screens and lighting.

'We'll probably run it off solar panels and batteries... or something... should be great fun when it all lights up eh? You can just see the kids in here, off on adventures, arguing over who's Captain, manning the ray guns... eh?' Graeme could. His own kids would love it. Terrific. He wanted to strap in, himself!

'What goes here then?' he asked, patting the casing on the drives. Steve told his first lie.

'Big water cooler mate. Don't want the little tykes dehydrating do we.'

Graeme learned that the 'Ladybird' would start its life as a float in the Barangan Wool 'n Hops Festival parade in a week's time and promised to be there. He jotted down details as he chatted and strolled around the workshop, exchanging on families, hobbies, amusing anecdotes. Henderson didn't fit any known terrorist profile, but Agent Horowitz also scanned for signs of light alloy workings, high tech equipment, propellant tanks… This however was very much the run down and ancient machinery of a backwoods establishment. He duly photographed Ladybird, the workshop and Steve Henderson, probed a little regarding other 'garages' in the area and then set out to check the suggested Barangan Aerodrome workshop. Might be a possible…

—⁓—

Arabella Swift had been well pleased with the response from her Second Saucer article and when people in the office were not looking would often do the double fisted 'YES!' thing. She was not really surprised when the two American Journalists from a Big Syndicate asked for an interview, with a promised byline and maybe stringer connections. She happily re-ran the unexpurgated Ethan Blunt interview, the pub reports and an embroidered version of the Tigers' Barbeque Revelationary Fly Past. The nice one, Graeme, asked for precise details of what the players had seen; Arabella explained the blurred nature of football barbeques, the consensus that the object glowed blue, was the size of a small plane and very, very fast. She couldn't add much more and the other not very nice one had sworn a bit and they had left. Arabella realised later that they hadn't even asked for her mobile number or left theirs. Bloody journalists!

Bought back to more mundane matters by the Editor, Arabella Swift (Entertainment, the Arts, Obituaries and Dining) was dispatched to interview a Mrs. Shirley Denzil, out at Tilda for God's sake, about the local dramatic society's next play. I am a slave to my craft, grumbled Arabella, but brightened up on the road as she recalled the watermelon saga of the previous year. That had been interesting and had a whiff of potential investigative journalism in it but no one had been that interested in her questions once the play was over. Even so, the play had been very funny and Arabella felt that her review (fabulous, incisive,) had been really excellent.

Shirley welcomed Arabella with open arms and some Proper Journalist coffee, then chatted at length about the TADAFIC new play, The Whizzer of Oz. Arabella was again well pleased; the play seemed based on her Flying Saucer stories from what she could see glancing through the script. A topical, light-hearted skip through alien space ships in small country towns suggested Shirley, noted by Arabella. Speaking of which, would she like to see some of the stage props? Just a kilometre up the road.

Forewarned, Steve and Liz pampered The Press, gave the guided tour and provided quotable quotes. Arabella took photos of the very impressive 'space ship', promised support for the proposed Council Playground application and was able to make some very helpful suggestions about adding rubber bits on the edges of the hard bits. Liz took a photo with her in the pilot's seat. Captain Swift at the controls! Had a nice ring as a byline? Arabella felt she had all the makings of more great special correspondent articles to send to the nationals before and after the festival…

—⁓—

Friday saw Maria transported back to the frenetic, chaotic world of a film crew on location and loving every minute. Two weeks of hard work had paid off; the ABC Rural Events crew (bushfires, floods, dog shows and fetes worse than death) arrived in convoy. Headed by Roger The Director, who had been washed up, dried out and recycled several times. He was quick to take her proposal for a vintage newsreel format, was mildly interested at "some possible controversy" though a tad sceptical. Happy to play along. Might be a laugh.

The cameraman and sound technician, proper drinking mates, took her more seriously.

'Make sure you keep up with the cues and directions that Shirley in the Oracle of Delphi costume gives to the audience. Particularly when she goes Wagnerian… never mind, you'll see what I mean. I'll put the remote mikes up for you on the stage and I've got the High School rugby team keeping you a clear space for shooting.' She got more drinks from Dylan, then came back collegially earnest. 'Listen. Make sure you download what you shoot and forward it to a few people. Can't say much at the moment, but I would hate for someone to shelve this for being too … rude.' Much nose tapping and no worries mate.

Maria also did the rounds with the two commercials to make sure they knew where to be. She was very pleased that one crew were shooting live to their kids show Hi Ho Rupert…Thoroughly satisfied that everything was tucked in, Maria headed out to the Top Ace.

—◦◦◦—

It was foggy there in Tilda and the word had gone around
That the Ladybird would spread its wings tonight
The core of great TADAFIC had come out to the ground
To witness it rise up and then alight…
And as poetry it's shite, thought Toby. The meeting to finalise plans had been run around a slap up feast and followed by a full rehearsal of The Whizzer. By 1.00 a.m., Ned judged the countryside would be quiet enough for a trial of the 'big yin'.

Toby looked across at Ned illuminated by the myriad instruments and grinned, thumb up. The pre-check and circuit testing had all gone as planned, the field was slowly being powered up and the ground crew waited outside the open workshop doors.

'Have to respray' said Toby, as a large sheet of detached blue paint sashayed to the ground. Ned grunted, concentrating on the slow lift and watching Steve through the side window, a little annoyed at his impression of pensioner parking signals. At last, Ladybird 2 lifted gently off the blocks, smoothly, and without a creak or groan.

'Altitude seven and a half centimetres,' said Toby 'break out the champagne!'

'Just keep an eye out on your side and we'll get out of here' said Ned.

Ladybird slowly crept forward to the applause of the Hendersons, Denzils and Maria. They formed two columns of torches, picking their way through the fog, a silent procession flanking a ghostly, luminescent elephant.

'We should be middle of the paddock by now' called Steve in through the open back doors.

'Thanks,' replied Ned, 'clear a circle and we'll go up a two hundred feet or so and I'll check the altimeter, sat nav, radar, battery charger and landing lights...'

Where does he get all this stuff from, Toby wondered, Council throw-outs at Bankstown Airport? They floated up, mist swirling past the blue glow.

'I must confess that this has broken the bank, but what a privilege, eh? The first of a new advanced species of aircraft. It's like flying at Kitty Hawk in 1903 in a prototype Lancaster!' Ned waxed aeronautically lyrical as they rose. With sensors fed to the edge of the field in ceramic tubes, all the instruments worked well. Fog swirled in the back doors as they switched on the landing lights and descended. The ground crew of seven peered up into the mist a little nervously; the prospect of being squashed did not appeal. The faint glow of lights from above grew into an opalescent ball; Ladybird sank in front of them.

'E T go home...' croaked Steve pointing. Inevitable.

They crowded around the back doors as Toby proudly fed his DIY collapsible wooden stairs out. All his own work and well done, even if a bit shuggledy. Liz, Steve, Shirley, Maria and the kids boarded.

'So where are we off to then, Mr. Ned?' asked Liz.

'Since the OH&S appears acceptable' added Maria. Ned peered back serious.

'We have to be very careful of security just now' he said, then smiled, 'but a little cruise in the fog would be in order!' Steering from one familiar landmark to the next, Ladybird drifted like a galleon through back paddocks and bush reserves, brushing over trees, following up creeks and witnessed only by the foxes, owls and cats. With lights off they crept close to the Farnham's posh plate glass lounge window.

'So that's what they watch at 2.00 a.m.' tutted Liz.

'And her, the President of the Church Guild…' said Shirley. Brad and Bobby, Jules and Solly crowded forward wide eyed; Ned reversed discreetly back into the mist. Ladybird crept back to the Top Ace, following the fence lines. Ned scrambled down the stairway and guided Toby to settle gently, gently, onto the back of the borrowed hay wagon.

'Time to shut up shop and get some sleep,' said Steve, 'and I'll need to be up at sparrow fart and re-spay this jigger as soon as the mist burns off.' He waved and disappeared inside. The rest dispersed - Maria was staying at Shirley's, Toby and Ned were back to the cold comfort of McZedcroft. Alas no power, as the house battery bank had become part of Ladybird 2.

―*∿*―

Eight a.m. glorious weather and the cars pulled back into the back yard at the Top Ace. Steve was gazing at his artwork; a blue metalflake Ladybird, now complete with tasteful vermilion flames, lightning bolts and a rainbow shooting star.

Two hours later and Ned was waving the small motorcade off to town. The Bedford would be growling with the overloaded trailer, but Ned was confident it would labour heroically and make it to the parade. Time now for his own preparations.

The High School oval had become a sea of decorated trucks, floats and bikes. This year's theme SAUCERTOWN! had turned the 37th Annual Barangan Wool 'n Hops Festival into The Biggest and Best Ever. Excited infants in fairy wings had sprouted antennae and traded wands for ray guns. The crowd of onlookers was liberally sprinkled with Spocks, Wookies and Aliens… Deranged Derek's Bargain Bazaar had made a killing by a shrewd, extra-terrestrial plastic stock-up. The Narms and The George had opened early with specials on Saturn Slabs,

Martian Mixers, Robot Rum; local farmers and townies were well fuelled and enthusiastic.

'Shall we do a stroll around the perimeter Sergeant?' asked Senior Constable recently promoted Earnest Harris. Sergeant Baker agreed with an amiable nod. His medication, along with the surprisingly illuminating Cognitive Restructuring Life Therapy sessions, gave him a new space cadet outlook, well suited to the day. Sergeant Baker was out and felt at one with the world. Now, how did it go in the group session... brief eye contact, acknowledging nod and smile, appropriate sociable comment, listen carefully for reply....

Ernie watched in amazement as his former sergeant walked up to Mrs. Swanston and her three small aliens and engage with Kiddies going well at school? Janeen muttered her yes thanks and we're leaving this afternoon for a holiday down the coast and hurried off. The twin girls both stuck their tongues out and the new Sergeant Baker smiled. Remarkable! Was Dirty Ken becoming respectable, responsible and reasonable? The "Redirection Clinic Inc." deserved congratulations and those drugs must be really something!

Ethan Blunt was transfixed as the TADAFIC Ladybird arrived.

'Jesus Valerie, that's it! Just bigger! The bloody space ship! Look!'

'Stop being stupid Ethan. There's a dozen space ships here and the chance of any of them landing in front of your tractor is nil. You know what I think about that nonsense.'

'I know what I know...' muttered Ethan.

Steve Henderson eased the Bedford into position behind the Shelvey Public School's float, a delightful floral conversion of Bert Jordan's drilling rig into a Saturn rocket on the launch pad. The Pike's Crossing Public Giant Venusian Sheep backed up to make room.

'Really, with a space helmet on, it's just last year's float re-jigged' said Shirley tartly.

The previously absent TADAFIC extras gathered up on the Bedford tray, breaking out the thermos flasks and passing compliments on the 'Fabulous Ladybird' prop. They had small-but-important roles and nervously fingered their scripts. Shirl, resplendent in her Delphic Oracle costume, quickly chalked positions on the Bedford tray.

'This isn't dangerous is it?' asked Miss Lorimer, holding the polystyrene shotgun at arms length.

'I thoroughly dislike guns.'

'It's made of polystyrene Miss Lorimer.'

'D'ya reckon me farmer's costume's OK?' asked Nick Bronson, TADAFIC's favourite butcher. 'Do I get to say anything?' he asked hopefully.

With reassurances all round, Shirl, Maria and Liz powered the team through the script twice more before the Grand Marshal's Acme Thunderer got the show on the road. 1:45pm and the whole shooting match was heading for the Showground.

Arabella Swift scribbled observations as she strode purposefully up, down and through the procession * down Station / up Main *est. crowd over 10,000 cheered wholeheartedly record 37 floats *wonderful children's costumes a delight *everyone happy….

'Press! Clear away there! 'Scuse me sir, madam! Press!' Small children were sent flying and drinkers shoved aside as she forced her way through the crowd. Jim Dobson, the Cambrawarra Times work placement photographer, struggled to keep up with Arabella's rapid-fire directions.

As the parade passed, the crowd joined in behind, surging up Main Street like an ever expanding clot pulsing up a vein. The High School Drumming Group and the Barangan Municipal Band had finally got into synch with Colonel Bogie. Squadrons of alien children capered and screamed, gaggles of chattering parents unconsciously marched in step, hangloose ganggroups of disaffected hoody teenagers straggled, smoked, spat and swore at the tail.

The Bedford fell silent after a long, grateful rattle. The wooden steps were quickly extended to form a bridge from Ladybird to the truck tray, the cast assembled in a silent tableaux and TADAFIC was ready to rock'n roll. There was a loud crackle from the official podium.

'G'day everybody, I'm Glen Jones the Mayor and it's lovely to see such a fine turnout for the 37th Annual Barangan Wool'n Hops Festival. I'd just like to thank...' Jonesey Senior droned for ten minutes about all the Main Street stalls, the RFS sausage sizzle, lost and found children, the Real Estate Notice Board and the Country Music Tent Show starting in half an hour. When reminded by the Grand Marshall, he grudgingly mumbled that a local group had a bit of a play on in a couple of minutes... if they wanted to stay. He scowled at the loud cheering this caused and carried his grudge off left. Maria whispered softly: the ABC cameras turned to the TADAFIC Bedford.

Shirley, head bowed, flowing Delphic Oracle robes and best golden summer sandals, glided stately forward while Karl Orff's "Oh Fortuna" theme built and faded. Wonderful silence, audience heads turned, chatter stilled. Attention was focused.

'Mummy look, Mummy look! It'th Printheth Leiaya!' The pristine pre-school voice carried clearly to the audience and there was muttered agreement, Oh yes, just like her, you remember her, in the first episode when she talked to the little robot...

'Good layer then?' called a drunken poultry farmer from Shelvey. Oh bugger, thought Shirley, try and bring in some classical culture to Barangan... still, whatever works... In her maximum projection Delphic Oracle/ Galactic Princess voice she began.

'Long ago in a far off galaxy... on a planet called Earth... technology had become locked into a form controlled by a rich and powerful group of Dark Lords...'

Toby moved back into Ladybird and started his final checks while "The Whizzer of Oz" got underway. Carefully, humorously crafted, it outlined the story of the Stripper's space flight, the building of Ladybird, the near fatal crash and the spies visit to Ethan's farm. He stopped to watch Miss Lorimer send them packing with swats from her shotgun, to loud cheers from the Country Women's Association and dutiful clapping by husbands.

At the back of the crowd, Graeme Horowitz blushed as the story fell in place; Shirley had obviously adapted his drunken dinner disclosures. He glanced uncomfortably at the television crews then relaxed and started to chuckle. The pure absurdity of his professional life as a pantomime appealed to Graeme as much as the breach of security troubled Agent Horowitz.

Agent Graupner had finally figured out the scene and was hopping mad. Even more so when he saw agent Horowitz, cheering and clapping along with the crowd.

Shirley waited while the crowd settled, taking the moment to toss Graeme a wink. She willed seriousness out into the audience, stilling the shuffling and chat.

'The family and their friends realized that this wonderful invention would be of great benefit to the world but that the Dark Lords would do anything to keep control...'

Most of the crowd settled back. After four years of TADAFIC plays they knew this was the talking bit. Not sure what was happening, but it would wind up soon, with lots more laughs.

*startling allegory of the modern world??, scribbled the scribing Arabella, *delivered with panache, or was that popcorn... *good vs. evil *rural battlers etc., etc.

'But isn't it like a bit weird?' said Sharmayne to Bruce.

Shirley finished, Steve told of the building of Ladybird 2, then it was Toby's big moment. Strapping on his vintage leather flying helmet, he declaimed:

'Was the world ready for such a thing? Some would hunger for the power over others it would give… but we can't let villains stop positive progress, can we!' He spotted an uncomfortable Barry McDermott in the audience and called 'Ah, Principal, I'm away to seek powerful allies in far off lands and have left a 475 leave form in your pigeonhole. If you could sort that I would be much obliged.' He exited into Ladybird, smiling.

'This device must now be fully checked for its environmental and human health safety. Initial tests had good results but more advanced trials would be sought,' announced Jules. Solly stepped forward, unscheduled, determined. He gestured toward Ladybird.

'It will cause Gargantuan Changes. Enormous. Mega! Uber Massive!!'

He grinned at the effect his words had on the students in the audience. The geek speaks!

'Sorry, should've spoken to you all earlier about this stuff. The thing is, we're off to prove that it's all working OK. See you later' he finished simply. Solly and Jules waved, walked up the ramp and the rear doors swung closed with heavy-duty thunks.

Graeme clapped and cheered but in a distracted manner: his mind was racing. How did they get every aspect covered? Why did it sound…correct? Shirley glided onto the stage.

'Ladies and gentlemen... It's Showtime! The family and their pilot prepare Ladybird 2 for its flight. The message is sent out that all is ready.'

The ABC cameraman glanced around as Maria clapped him on the shoulder.

'Follow directions.' He nodded. Always a few surprises with Ms. Scott.

—w—

Ned adjusted his flying suit and wriggled uncomfortably. It wasn't that he had put on much weight, it had just … moved around a bit over the years. Toby's decoded voice hissed in his headphones; 'Ready when you are, Group Leader.'

'Affirmative, LB Two.'

'Folks, you're about to get a real treat! If you look carefully just to the right of the War Memorial and up a bit, you can see a small blue dot… Yes! Let me tell you now, that blue dot the famous Captain McZed and the Escort craft! All part of the show and nothing to get worried about…' She cued in "The Peasants Revolt" from the William Tell Overture and strode forth and back across the stage.

'Yes madam, you can see it moving on the skyline there; it's the real McCoy. The genuine Barangan Flying Saucer! Get that phone camera running… what a great picture this would be for your sister or brother. George! Time to use the last six shots you have left in that disposable! Ms. Arabella and others of the press… En Garde!'

The audience was one part oblivious to what was happening, two parts getting rapidly anxious, but the other seven parts were happily doing what they were told. It was in the show so it must be all right. A thousand recording devices were being readied with varying degrees of competence. Infants were being shoulder mounted. Blokes were mounting eskies. Adolescents were ascending onto roofs or into trees.

'It's the same bloody thing what was at the Barbie!' shouted the Tigers, mostly.

'It's moving, look, there it is, look straight down the street near that mountain' explained family members of the visually challenged.

'Don't let the twins go and where's Justin?' said Mrs. Swanston.

'Sir, we have a situation here at Barangan Code red repeat code red…' said Agent Horowitz urgently into his satellite cell phone.

Ned pushed Ladybird 1 up Main Street at a shade over 100 knots, pulled up into a vertical climb, ending with a barrel roll and wide, slow spiral back down. The mass of people rotated with him, transfixed. He slid to a halt, hovering above the spire of the war memorial, surrounded by the silent, stunned mullet crowd. For effect, he dipped the nose and slowly spun a full turn, inspecting and waving to the upturned faces. There were a few nervous giggles and squeals.

'A big hand for Captain McZed! A warm Barangan welcome for the Intrepid Aviator!' boomed out Shirley's voice. The claps, whistles and shouts started from Ethan Blunt then did the whole chain reaction, hall full of mousetraps Grand Final Winning Goal thing. Ladybird 1 floated serenely in the deafening, primordial roar, lit by the sparkle of camera flashes.

'Told you it was real, didn't I!' shouted Ethan exultantly to Valerie. He turned and extended his finger at Agent Graupner: 'Told you it flew off too but you wouldn't believe it! Loser!'

Graupner looked at Ethan, Ladybird hovering and that woman from the motel who seemed to be running the whole show. Had to be terrorists and somehow that fucking thing was the missile! He snarled and pulling his gun out, started pushing his way forward.

Sergeant Baker stared up at the floating, glittering blue cylinder. 'Real, isn't it Ernie?'

'It bloody well shouldn't be, but it is!' agreed Ernie, fervently. Ken Baker shook his head in the wonder of it all, thought it through and began to chuckle. All these people could see it too. Look at them, looking at it... Apart from that one though! Ken focused and morphed himself back into a policeman. Bloody Hell! Guns were bad, especially the small ones.

'Harris, there's a nutter with a handgun pushing through there!' Barangan's finest sprang into action and bulldozed through the skygazing citizens. Ernie's full body tackle bought the perpetrator down and Ken's large police boot squashed hand and gun. The screaming profanities of thwarted Graupner rage were stopped short by a sharp rap over the head from Ernie's large police truncheon. Not an excessive rap, mind you.

'Well done Senior Constable, can't have him spoiling the fun now, can we!'

'Yes indeed Sergeant' replied Ernie. What a good and positive thing it is to be a keeper of the peace, he thought. There was the hubbub of a thousand excited theories and predictions. Shirley came forward, hand over one earphone and a listening expression on her face. The crowd hushed.

'Yes… right Toby, ready here too…' she muttered into the throat mike.

'Ladies and Gentlemen, girls and boys, if you would step back from the stage a little… Now it's time to wish our brave local adventurers a fond farewell. I'm afraid none of us can tell you where they are off to… we simply don't know… but join me in a round of applause for their amazing achievement!'

The space around Ladybird 2 was rapidly cleared by back stepping clappers. As well as 'The Ride of The Valkyries' now pumping out of the stage speakers, something strange appeared to be happening to the TADAFIC Spaceship. There was a blue, sparkly haze forming around it and its paintwork was getting… well… rubbery. Before their eyes the entire blue/lightning bolt side gently peeled away and flopped over the side of the trailer. The clapping stopped.

'Three guesses what happened to your car Brucie' whispered Sharmayne to her open mouthed boyfriend. The blue shimmer intensified and Ladybird 2 silently lifted a hundred feet. Its smaller companion lifted with it and together they turned to face down Main Street. Barangan and District waited expectantly. Only three of the quicker local petrol heads knew what was happening… both sets of Barangan's traffic lights were on red.

They chanted the mantra:

'Yo Bro! Time to Go!' as lights dropped to amber... Green.

Ned and Toby pushed the power on, LB1 and 2 rocketed the length of Main then climbed into the sky, blue dots disappearing out over the Warrigals. The crowd roared, applauded, whistled and screamed, and the show was over.

'Cowboys!' said Shirl to Brad and Bobby, all three beaming. She turned to the audience.

'Bon Voyage indeed! Off down the path into the bright future! TADAFIC hopes you loved our little show and we know you will enjoy the rest of the festival. See you again next year!'

There was a scattered round of applause. Everyone seemed to be busy with mobiles.

Graeme had been busy too. His digital video clip with detailed voice over had flashed back to The Agency and battling with souvenir hunters he had snatched a strip of the blue paint for analysis. Passing the two policemen he confided that he knew the inert Graupner as a fellow American and suspected he had serious mental health issues.

'Told me he was a Secret Service Agent. I believe he might be delusional... I think you guys call it mad as a cut snake.'

'Know just the place for him then, mate...' said Ken jovially.

Graeme moved off to take an urgent call from Chief of Overseas Security Spiggott.

'What in God's name were those things, Horowitz? Was that for real? Do you have casualties? Can you secure that area?' came barking.

'Negative, There's only two of us... one of us here. What you saw is what happened here, Sir. No tricks. They both flew and I have no idea how. I saw the big one close up, it was made of quarter inch steel plate and would have weighed four... five tons. No noise, no jet or rocket exhausts, just a blue glow. I'm buggered if I know' he added, repeating the predominant local opinion. There was a long silence.

'We've had visual satellite surveillance in that quadrant for twelve hours now. If they're airborne we'll see them. Australian Air Force can put something up. We'll shoot those bastards down. Was there armaments mounted on them?' Homer Spiggott demanded.

'Sir, my assessment is that they are unarmed. Unless someone else was hiding, it was a local family of four and a schoolteacher that went in the big one. Suicide bombers don't usually make their missions family outings Sir. Also, they were part of a… drama production before they left… talked about developing a new technology… saving the environment, that sort of thing.' Graeme tried to explain.

'What the hell are you talking about Horowitz! We've got no idea who they really are and what they'll do. We ask questions afterwards! Find out what you can.' The link cut abruptly. Graeme frowned, shook his head and then went looking for Shirley Denzil.

—◦∿∿◦—

Chapter Nine

As Jules and Solly had crossed the threshold into LB2, Steve and Toby hauled in the steps, swung the heavy rear doors closed and dogged them shut. Everyone strapped into position: Toby and Jules (Trainee Pilot) were up front checking flight readiness, Liz was at the transplanted big Dekko Omnitron, chatting to Ned and listening to selected channels. Steve checked the drives, Solly sat behind his Flight Engineer panel sampling the travel sweets. All reported everything as AOK.

'Ready when you are, Group Leader' said Toby and got his reply. Liz rolled her eyes. Moments later, as Jules announced she had spotted Ned, Liz declared that the new Dekko unscrambler had 'cracked the spies secret security phone'.

'Reckons its Code Red out there.' Everyone ooohed, sarky.

The roar of the crowd filtered through the vents and they could see Ned above the War Memorial. Toby spoke softly to Shirley, got her reply and turned to the crew.

'Time to Rock and Roll, folks! Close the vents. Power on Jules.' A gentle hum from the three motors, the paint slid off and Toby lifted away, chatting to Ned while he lined up with Barangan's main drag. The pressing surge of power caught the Hendersons by surprise, Barangan flicked past and the earth dropped away far too quickly. They sat in silence as they hurtled over the Warrigals. At last the acceleration eased.

'Problem LB2?' hissed Ned's voice through the speaker.

'Power seems to have plateaued when we hit Mach point 9, Ned' said Toby. He looked around to Solly inquiringly.

'Don't know' said Solly shrugging, 'but it might be a component in one of the extra feed thingies. Even so, the other motors should make up for it. We'd have to set down so I could disconnect and test it proper. I could only have a bit of a look now. Sorry.'

'Can't set down, we have to get out of here fast LB2.' Ned had been listening in.

'Yes indeed Ned,' said Liz, trying to keep her voice calm, 'that secret agent Horowitz has just had a message from his base saying they now had a satellite that could see us and suggesting we should be shot down by the Air Force. Would they do that?'

Ned digested that. His reply was not reassuring.

'They might try. We didn't think it was possible before; these ships should easily get away from any current aircraft. We have to head for the coast and hope we can get out from under the satellite. It's a bit of a mess I'm afraid…'

—ᴧᴧ—

Shirley had parked her car at the showground, planning to get away with the kids straight after the show. They were creeping through the crowds when Graeme slipped unannounced into the back seat next to Bobby. She swore.

'Lock the doors and keep on driving Mrs. Denzil.' He looked and sounded grim.

'Should I brain him Mum?' Brad had lifted the steering lock off the floor.

Shirley told him to put it down. Although it was Graeme, she knew he carried a gun and was not quite sure what would happen. She drove as directed, pulling up outside the deserted Addison's O'Nite. Graeme politely, firmly invited them into his cabin.

The three Denzils sat.

'Mrs. Denzil, Shirley, I don't know what happened today but I suspect that you folk could be in a whole heap of trouble. I know you aren't terrorists but there are some people out there who could be thinking that way. They don't fool around.'

'People out there… over there? Are these the people you work for, Mr. Horowitz?'

'Yes.' said Graeme.

'And?' asked Shirley.

'If the play is true, that those children invented an entirely new way to fly and the family has just taken off in a supersonic ex-boiler...' he shook his head, 'then I hope they know what they are doing. After nine eleven, there's open season on anything flying without a clearance and... I've been told as much about your friends and their gadgets' he admitted.

'Everything in the play is true. Solly and Jules invented a brand new, alternative power that's cheap, doesn't pollute and doesn't use oil or coal. Thing is, what would your Iron Triangle of Corporate Industry, the White House and the Penthouse do if they got it?' Graeme looked puzzled.

'That's the Pentagon Mum' said Brad, while Graeme ran the information through his head.

'I see what you mean Shirley...'

—⁓—

'Alpha Zebra six five operational training to base, have both bandits in visual contact below at height 9000, course south-east, speed 600 knots. Can't get a fix on them, radar scanning contact nil repeat nil, but have detected radar coming from bandits. Holding at 12000. Twenty minutes fuel for shadowing. Request instructions.'

'Base to Alpha Zebra six five, maintain but do not close. ETA by Alpha Tango 7 and Alpha Whisky 3 Squadrons 18 minutes. Repeat arm status.'

'Nil, repeat Nil arm status.'

'Just sit there then Jacko.'

'Izzat you Kev? What are these guys? Look like wheelie bins with fins. Are Whisky and Tango gunna whack them?'

'Dunno.'

The decoded Air Force exchange crackled out of the Dekko. Ned tutted.

'Dreadful RT procedure Toby,' he said, 'but good news is they don't know we can listen in; they're unarmed and can only stay twenty minutes. Not so I fear the two fighter squadrons, probably FA18 Hornets out of Williamtown. Can you put on any more speed?'

'Solly is working on it but it's not looking good. Bloody hell, Ned. All these lethal Alpha males chasing us… so what do we do?'

'Hmmmm. Uh huhh. Mmmmm. Yeeaaarrrse. MmmHmmm… Ah-Hah!'

The crew of Ladybird 2 listened anxiously to the cogitations-at-work.

'What does the last Ah-Hah mean Mr. McZed?' asked Liz, eventually.

'Sorry my dear. We have to go to plan B. Tell Solly to leave the motors and strap himself back in. Good thing I checked the B.O.M. You're following me Toby, we're dropping to 500 feet and changing course. Switch off your radar, they can pick it up. Now… what I propose is that…'

—⁓—

Maria had pocketed her thumb drives and DVDs and was chortling with the mates over a rewind of the spectacle when Roger The Director arrived. Had been stuck the other side of the crowd. Over at the Tigers' Drinks Stall & Bar, actually.

'You could have fucking well told me, Scott,' he complained, 'I would have bought a whole production team down here!'

'Stop whining, if I had told you everything, you wouldn't have come. You wouldn't have believed me. This could be your finest hour Roger! Go with it!'

'But I don't have a presenter or writer or anything. What can I do?'

Maria sighed then smiled. 'Roger dear, you're looking at your presenter. I do have a little experience you know. Get on your phone and set up a news flash… tell them to look at what Channel 7 is doing if they won't move on it!' She indicated across to the furious activity of the commercial crew. 'The lads and I will do the rest. I might even have a bit of a script here…' she said, rummaging in her bag, 'and tell them we can do a two minute cut in, 4 minute main news and … twenty minute follow up report. Now do hurry up, call Sydney.' She turned on her heel to the mates, who were already hooking up the computer for play/incident cuts, a presenter mike and the direct feed link for the main station. Professionals. While they worked, Maria sketched in the first Intro and consulted about which shots fitted.

'Ten minutes tops!' she shouted to the red-faced, frantic, mobile-talking Roger.

—◠◠◠—

'Alpha Zebra six five to base, targets still maintaining new course, now at height 500. Light cloud build up so closing to 1000 to maintain visual. Request time to Alpha Tango Alpha Whisky rendezvous.'

'Estimated three minutes Alpha Zebra.'

Toby blanched as he sighted the range of steep hills and ravines dead ahead.

'Ned, we're going hell of a fast and low for that lot, can we slow down a bit?'

'No. Not much worse than the Warrigals this lot Toby, coastal range, know it well. Just tuck in tight, I'll put my lights on to help. You know what to do.'

'Yes,' said Toby glumly, 'that's the problem.'

Ned banked hard to port, Toby swung in behind and they rocketed up the narrow misty valley. The fighter above followed suit, radioing directions. The Ladybirds banked starboard, over a ridge and into another series of valleys.

'That's more like it' said Ned, ' those hills at two o'clock. Fog looks thicker there. I'm slowing to 90, don't run up my bum but stay close…'

Toby went a whiter shade of pale and concentrated. Another tricky bit. The blue field on Ladybird 1 ahead flickered briefly and it dropped, back on and rose, flickered again, all the time nearing the mist shrouded granite crags.

'Alpha Zebra six five to base, I'm getting an intermittent targeting signal from these guys, whatever was blocking it must be breaking down. Where's the cavalry?'

'Alpha Whisky to Alpha Bravo we can see you now and picking up target signal. Break off, return to base.'

'Roger Alpha Whisky. Good hunting.'

'Up this one Toby, my radar shows it to be pretty clear ahead, get ready…'

The mist closed around and with visibility ahead two hundred metres, Toby could just pick up the bobbing ex-Bedford orange taillight. Through the Dekko speakers they could hear the excited messages from the rapidly closing Alpha Whisky fighter wing.

'Got a suitable gully on the left Toby lad. You're 150 above the valley floor. See you all later at the first halt. If not, good luck my dears. Ready… Now, Toby.'

'Roger. Go well, Ned…' Toby spun Ladybird 180° and reverse accelerated; as ground speed quickly dropped to zero he banked right. Dropping to a hundred feet, Ladybird 2 crept forward.

'Leader One to flight, target has lifted speed to 750, weaving a lot, getting a ground hug radar signal too. No visual but still getting targeting signal. Two and three go port four and five starboard. Looks like they're headed for the coast. Good. Alpha Tango is closing.'

The clear, in charge voice of Alpha Tango Leader came through Ned's Dekko.

'Unidentified aircraft this is the Royal Australian Air Force. You are in contravention of air security. You are directed to immediately increase altitude to 4000 feet, slow to 300 knots and follow directions.'

'Unidentified aircraft to RAAF,' said Ned firmly, 'we are unarmed civilians on a set test flight and are unable to comply with your request. We are not approaching any built up areas or population centres, are unarmed and are no threat.'

'Repeat, you are in contravention of air security. If you do not climb into plain view immediately you will be shot down.'

'Sorry about that lads, for the time being we have to maintain this course and height. I suggest respectfully that you bugger off.'

There was a long pause while the squadron leader considered Ned's reply.

'Look mate, I don't know who you guys are or, but we've got our orders. I'll give you half a minute to comply, but after that we've got no choice.'

'Tally ho chaps...' muttered Ned to himself, focused on the glowing screen in front of him. Banking right and praying the mist lasted, he headed south down the range. With a bit of luck he would be out from under the fixed spy satellite by the time the cloud cover broke.

—◦◦◦—

With the Dekko on receive only and the radar off, Ladybird 2 crept up the misty ravine. Toby and Jules peered ahead, stopping to lift carefully up a massive cliff face and sliding back down into the next valley. Liz and Steve fiddled with the Dekko, still picking up the Air Force RT chatter. Staying at tree top level, Toby and Jules pushed along as fast as they dared into the increasingly rugged wilderness area, searching. Cresting a rise, they caught another segment of Ned's drama…

—✷✷✷—

'Buggeration,' said McZed loudly. He had been just at the point of angling up and applying full power: he would come blasting out of the fog at Mach 2 plus, through the jackal pack like a whippet and away. Unfortunately, in the flicker of an eye the valley sides had dropped, the mist disappeared; he had crossed an estuary and was out over the empty sea. Moreover, he was totally surrounded by two squadrons of fully armed FA18 Hornet fighters, stacked in more layers than lasagne.

'Alpha Whisky to Alpha Tango, we've lost the big one, maintain boundary. Target going due east, increasing speed, has crossed coast. Targeting signal gone again. Whisky 1, 2 and 3 engage, repeat engage.'

'Clear shot… shit, how did he do that?'

'Still in view Whisky 1, Whoaa, almost got him, he's going straight up, yours Whisky 3.'

'Breaking left. Bloody hell; see that, he's flying backwards now. Where'd he go?'

'Whisky leader, open season but watch for our guys…'

Ned was pushed to the limit, had come close to blacking out twice and was desperately looking for clear air. The glowing streams of cannon shells were too close and he knew that the steel plate of Ladybird 1 offered as much protection as blancmange. A quick rotate and he could see he was boxed in. Two more were closing in, others circling above and radar dots were ranged over every escape route…

'Tango 6 engaging… Yes! Think I clipped him, diving, have a smoke trail…'

'Tango leader, follow him down Tango 6, cease fire unless he recovers…'

'Target spiralling, lots of smoke, seems to be slowing, think he's going in for a crash landing… target down… come on man, get out of that thing… bloody hell… Tango 6 to Tango leader, target sank immediately. No sign of crew.'

'Roger Tango 6. Tango 1 and 2 stick around ten minutes, put markers down and get coordinates for the debrief. The rest of us, home.'

Chapter Ten

Somehow through the fog and tears Toby had found a long, narrow ravine to creep into. A ledge under one of its overhanging cliff faces; just enough room to hide.

The rain dripped gently from the dark trees and blew a little into the open back doors of Ladybird 2. Jules and Solly sat wrapped in the arms of Liz, heads buried. Toby and Steve sat morosely, looking into the darkness.

'Another fine mess, Stanley. Silly bastard had to play the hero didn't he. Deliberately blipping the field so they could get a fix on him and lead them off. All a game' said Toby angrily. Steve put his arm around Toby's shoulder and gave him a consoling hug.

'Listen mate, Ned knew what he was doing, known him a long time and he never took a risk unless it was a calculated one. Probably figured he could outrun those buggers and would have… but it went wrong.'

He passed another bottle of Coopers. Toby unscrewed and raised it to the forest.

'Here's to Ned McZed, Engineer and aviator extraordinaire. Astounding Cook. Good mate.'

'Yairs… generous old sod as well.'   They upended their bottles.

'Bureau of Meteorology' said Solly.

'Pardon?' said everyone.

'B.O.M. It's where Mr. McZed got his clouds from.'

'Oh…'

The crew of Ladybird 2 had pulled down the canvas screen, set the beds up and had a quiet dinner. The purr of the battery charger competed with a waterfall and the nightlife somewhere. An additional crunching, thumping sound was coming from something large.

'Sounds like a wombat' said Steve

'Sounds like cardboard' said Jules.

' Sounds like it's coming from your locker Toby' said Liz.

'Ummm, yes probably, sorry, meant to tell you…' said Toby, gently opening the locker door. A shredded cardboard box and jumper fell out, followed by a fuming Sean. Toby was not quick enough and got the full set of claws and teeth in his calf. He hobbled away as Sean first inspected the new home then set to work washing his paws and face.

'Well I couldn't leave him with anyone and he… travels well… usually.'

'Dettol and bandaids in the first aid kit, Toby' said Liz. 'I trust you've got kitty litter and cat food, or is he just going to eat someone else's leg?' she inquired.

'All his supplies are there' mumbled Toby 'and none of mine. He only ever bites me, no one else. He's a nice cat, really.' As if to prove the point, Sean ambled over to the apprehensive Solly and with a graceful, claws-in leap arrived onto his lap. Solly tentatively patted his head and was won over immediately by an impressive, deep rumbling purrrrrrrrrrrrrr.

The crew bedded down for the night.

———

Across the other side of the planet, Under Secretary Senator Kelvin Dobrovich had been picked up, bought to the secure unit and briefed. He had been expecting another long distance, vague u.f.o. sighting and was staggered by what was laid before him.

'Now this is one helluva interesting event here Homer,' announced the senator, 'and you just run that film footage from Australia again.'

Homer Spiggott, Chief of Overseas Security and Kelvin's main man, nodded to the aide. Graeme Horowitz's stills of LB2 at Tilda, the ABC film of the play and of the two Ladybirds cavorting over Barangan, followed by the RAAF combat shots of LB1 ran on the screen.

A highlighted map of New South Wales and Victoria replaced them.

'Current situation hasn't changed from the briefing document Sir. The smaller one is accounted for; a search is still underway for the other. They both went into the mountains here, the small one came out alone here and was shot down here. Satellite tracked them visually from Barangan and they didn't seem to be heading on a direct course for any major cities or bases when the RAAF picked them up. A report from Agent Horowitz suggests the group flying these things were unarmed but even so the possible threat to the safety of military bases or population centres is paramount...'

'Yeah sure... paramount... sure...' Kelvin said absently. His mind was elsewhere. Kelvin was a keen pilot, had his own Very Light Jet, an early test prototype at a very good price from the company that manufactured them. He had a lot of friends in the industry. Goddamn! Those things could rotate 180° while still going forward! And although this pair was pretty slow, the earlier satellite reports had one going at over Mach 3.7! The report confirmed that radar was totally unable to pick them up: they were not just stealth capable, they were damn invisible. They would outfly anything on the planet and if the right people had hold of them...

'Homer, the way I figure it, threat ain't what we concentrate on. The little one's shot down and if there's a bomb on board the big one, I'm sure the Australians can handle it. What we've got to get all paramount about is how the hell we get hold of one of these things and pull it to pieces! Get an American salvage ship there, or if the Australians have got to it first, stall bringing it up, tell em it's likely to blow up or something. Need us to defuse it.' Senator Dobrovich sucked on his coffee. 'If that damn crazy story this bunch are putting up is legit, then these things were built at...'

'Little town called Barangan Sir.'

'Right. Says here some sort of workshop? Have the rest of the group connected to these people been rounded up? I want everyplace connected to these people sealed up tighter than a penguin's ass. Get that subcontracted George Morton's crew onto it pronto. They still operate out there don't they? And get more information from those two lazy bums the agency has had there for weeks. Get onto it Homer!'

'Yes sir…'

—ᴧ₥—

Ten p.m. in the back lounge of the Royal George and Roger The Director staggered back with a sloppy tray of drinks.

'Znot my fault. They put th'noozbreak on an w'sayin it was triffic. Then th'main news at seven and nothin' happens. Nothin' on th' eight o'clock report either. My bes' work too' he said plaintively. Roger looked over his glasses at Maria. 'That Sir Peter Whasisname was on the phone to me in the dunny y'know. He was asking lossa questions about you. Kep on talking to someone else too. Said he shoulda been tole bout it fore they put th' noozbreak on. Reckon he pulled the rest of it. Gu'less bastard.' Roger returned to his drink. Maria quietly talked to The Mates.

'Thought that might happen. Hope you don't get into too much trouble.'

'No worries' said the cameraman, 'We're workers in short supply mate. Shitproof.'

'Yeah, no worries' added the sound technician, but not as confidently. He indicated his laptop. 'This is big time stuff. It's been pulled from all the ABCTV websites and there's nothing on the commercials, or radio. The guy from Channel 7 said their filming ran live on Hi Ho Rupert but got canned from then on. There was heaps on the net though, little clips and still shots, but I can't show you because ten minutes ago all the landlines, mobiles and satellite to here went down. The whole dam lot!'

'Bloody radio doesn't work either' added Dylan from the bar. Maria pulled her chair closer and dropped the decibels to proper conspiratorial. The three versions of the news had been emailed to her overseas contacts within an hour of the event. Shirl had the DVDs and stick downloads and The Mates were confident they could push quite a few copies when they got back to Sydney. Hunky Dorey. Maria stood up to get the next round.

'Ah, just who we were looking for!' came the genial voice of Sergeant Baker. 'Finish your drinks if you please, then we'll give you a lift along to the station.'

'I'm afraid there's a warrant came through from Sydney,' apologized Ernie. Protesting to no avail, the Rural News Team and their new presenter were off for a ride in the Barangan Paddy Wagon.

―〰―

Graeme, after two stops for directions, had found the Denzils at home.

'Sorry about dropping in like this, but thought you better know what's happening.'

Brad and Bobby complained their computer was down and Graeme nodded. 'If you suddenly seem to get through, don't send anything you wouldn't want the umm... dark lords becoming aware of. Same with your phone line and mobiles. Sorry.'

'Thanks,' said Shirley, 'so what else is going on then?' Graeme shuffled his feet. Selling out The Agency didn't sit easily.

'Your local police have already collected the rest of TADAFIC, the ABC news crew and your friend Maria Scott. Federal Police, ASIO and umm... staff from other agencies should arrive in Barangan quite soon and I imagine all of them will want to meet you and your sons... personally. Interesting to see who gets their act together first, actually. It mightn't be a good idea to be here when they arrive, Shirley.' Shirley looked at Graeme, realizing what he might be sacrificing to warn them.

'Thanks... mate. We never saw you here tonight.' Graeme pressed a mobile phone into Shirley's hand.

'Use this prepaid to reach me if you need help but only use text. ECHELON, their scanning thing, does voice recognition too. And dump any other mobiles you've got. They'll be looking for your car too.' Graeme sighed and looked plaintive.

'Yes?' asked Shirley after some more shuffling.

'There's something else. I'm afraid there's been a report that the smaller... um... Ladybird may have been shot down by air force jets, just off the coast. I don't know any more. The big Ladybird got away. I'm very sorry.' Shirley, Bobby and Brad looked aghast.

'Ned...' muttered Shirley.

'I'm sorry' repeated Graeme, reaching out to pat Denzil backs. After an awkward pause, he moved to the door. 'I've got to get back to Barangan, so... good luck. Sorry. I'll let you know if I hear anything else... anything at all.' Brad and Bobby shook hands with Graeme, solemnly, Shirley gave him a hug and he left.

'Swap the battery into the ute Brad, it's still registered to your uncle... or it used to be, anyway. Bobby, come and help pack, and dig out the old Lands Department maps.'

The Denzils were getting out of town.

———

Three massive, black SUVs full of dark suits and one police uniform arrived outside the police station just after midnight. Graeme quickly picked out the suit-in-charge, George, 'Head of Morton Security,' to explain the whereabouts of Jason Graupner.

'Had a breakdown you figure? Police hauled him off to some clinic? Well, goddam it Horowitz, we better just leave the

142

useless prick there then. We'll grill these fanatics straight off; someone's gotta know what their target is! We've got half the Aussie Air Force looking for their buddies, shot one down but can't find the other.' Graeme patiently tried to outline the TADAFIC group and its aims, but George was not comprehending. Two wagons were dispatched to Tilda, while an 'interview' room was set up at the station.

'And tell those local cops to butt out!' yelled the suit-in-charge to his subordinates.

George folded his hands over his enormous gut and glared at Maria Scott. The other prisoners obviously knew nothing but this one had arrived at the showgrounds with that damn flying tin can, was organizing the TV crew; she was a player!

'Full name and date of birth ' he barked loudly.

Maria was not fussed, she was used to dealing with rude adolescents.

'Maria Shelley Scott, 22nd December 1982. Might I ask to whom I am speaking?'

'We'll be asking the questions here' snarled George.

'Ah, ' said Maria, 'reminds me of Toby's dreadful knock knock Gestapo joke.'

'What? Listen lady, you're in real trouble here so cut the crap. I could turn into being your worst nightmare!' Maria looked at him coolly. 'Well, Mr. Nightmare, just settle down there. Might I suggest that anger and clogged arteries are not a great combination? I intend to be fully cooperative, so how can I assist you?' George fumed. At this point in many countries, he could have called on the specialists in pain and fear to get even. He looked at the impassive two local cops hovering outside the cell door. Later maybe.

'You can "assist" me by telling me where your friends were going, what their purpose was and what in god's name those machines were.' Maria launched into a detailed description of the Ladybirds, their crews, their goal of further assessment of the technology that she was not privy to, their destination and that Toby had put in for three weeks leave. No forwarding address. She described the nature of the ship's cat Sean and her evening low cruise through the mists of Tilda, her only flight and very comfortable too. She had helped collect and pay for the grocery supplies on board, still had the supermarket receipt, and was getting onto a description of the fittings and furnishings when George demanded her to stop. He was totally unused to suspects monopolizing the conversation and providing too much information. Interrogations generally involved tricky questions and painfully slow extraction. Compliant to the smaller rules of law he grumped off outside for a cigarette.

'So what happens now?' Maria asked the remaining Federal Policeperson. He took his hat off and rubbed the back of his head reflectively. The nice cop, thought Maria.

'Well, Miss… mind if I call you Maria? Not that I like to see it being used, but you've been arrested under the new Australian Anti-Terrorism Laws of 2014, which means that you can be held for 14 days without charge or evidence with no outside contact. For starters, since you bought and supplied groceries for these people, it brings you under Division 103, that's the 'Reckless Funding' clause… could be up for 'Urging Disaffection' as well. I'm afraid the maximum for those is life imprisonment. Category 5 in a high-risk prison like, the orange suits and leg irons. At the very least you could end up under a control order for 12 months, no reviews, lots of restrictions.' The Fedcop sat back and sucked his teeth, studying Liz with sympathy. 'Maybe it would help if you tell us more about these machines, where the plans might be kept, prototypes, that sort of thing?'

'Like I said, Solly and Jules built them, entirely without plans, and as far as I know they left nothing behind. No doubt you have a few people looking around who'll tell you as much.' Liz looked at the Fedcop. Did she detect an American accent? She sniffed, to see if he would offer a tissue from the box next to him. He did. Definitely American.

'Anyway, doesn't all this anti-terrorism stuff depend on it being... terrorism? Once the fuss is over, I guess I might be up for "friend of people who fly experimental aircraft without permission" although we could argue that they're not really aircraft, are they. Could be charged with "providing entertainment beyond that advertised"? Also, isn't it supposed to be ASIO who do the investigations and where are they then? And who's the fat American?'

'Lets just say it's a joint enquiry and ASIO will get here eventually. Meantime, as my colleague said, Ve shall ask zer qvestions...'

Outside the Barangan Police station, a growling, growing crowd was gathering.

———

Dawn found Solly, Jules and Steve stripping back and testing the motors, Liz monitoring the airwaves and Toby tying foliage over the top of Ladybird 2. Just as he was finishing, a helicopter chattered up the ravine, flying low. He cowered behind Ladybird expecting the worst, but the cliff overhang and his hasty camouflage appeared to work; it flew on.

Liz reported the depressing news that a salvage ship was dispatched to the crash site.

Solly and Jules muttered and soldered on while Steve morosely supplied them with bits.

Sean found a sunny rock and posed, absorbing heat, while Toby made a working morning tea. He sat in the sun with Sean for a while but lacked the cat's capacity for idle repose.

'Just going for a bit of an explore around, Steve' he called into the back.

'Yair OK, Tobes. Pick up some milk and papers mate.'

Sean came along as Toby followed the stream and scrambled further up the ravine. Designed for slinking through forests and in his prime, Sean found the going easy. Toby wasn't and didn't, but persisted. After twenty minutes and a scraped shin, he was rewarded to find sweet little pool and a warm rock to take a breather on. He shared a sandwich with Sean, the ham for Sean, the bread for Toby, and contemplated the Sylvan Glen. What rhymes with Idyllic? Sean contemplated lizards awhile, got bored and set off up a small path he discovered among the ferns. Must be an animal track down to the waterhole, mused Toby, setting off to follow. With the distinct track to follow he made better time, but even so, could not keep up with his cat. A faint scent had rung bells for Sean and propelled him off at a fast lope.

The hunter had detected Prey!

—ᴡᴠ—

The Swanstons enjoyed their adventures. Mr. and Mrs. S, the Grade 2 twin girls known affectionately as 'Shock and Awe' and Grade Three son just Justin all craved the same small pleasures. Pack the hamper, find the camera, fold up the rubberized blanket, fill the Thermos and hit the road for a picnic. All had their roles. John would unload the car, check the tyres for slow leaks from rural punctures and set up the folding chairs. Jeanette would set up the blanket, food and plates; unscrew the soft drink and wine, down her first glass. The twins would go roaming to find something to destroy or torment. Justin would trail behind them, sulking, and later he would wet himself because he wouldn't pee outside.

'Come and get your picnic children, before the ants do' called Janeen, as usual. Usually the children came quickly, as their overweight father was well ahead of the ants. This time they didn't and Janeen frowned. 'Darlings, where are you?' she called, louder.

'Mummy there's something furry moving in a bush and if it's a little soft baby animal we found it first so it's ours' said one of the twins petulantly.

'But I'm rescuing it so it's mine' said Justin defiantly. The parents got up, John armed with a drumstick, Janeen with a fresh red.

'Mummy, Justin's got a stick!' said one twin, 'and boys aren't allowed to play with sticks.'

'Mrs. Cavalli at Wombat's Patch said so!' the other added. Justin had indeed found a very long stick and was trying to push the bush sideways. The twins, failing in their censure motion, attached themselves to the stick to add their weight.

'Stop it, it's mine' wailed Justin. They all stopped, gaping…

———

Toby had just discovered a tree with a metal nametag and was reconsidering his animal track theory when Sean returned. Tail up, he proudly carried the torn off leg of a large, ground foraging bird. What particularly interested Toby was the covering of breadcrumbs on the leg and the faint yells of outrage from up ahead. He shook his finger at the feeding Lion of Tilda.

'Never been good around picnics, eh Sean.' Peering through ferns, Toby saw a disconsolate family on a blanket, reassembling their Jumbo-Pack Tennessee-Fried.

'Did you see the size of that fucking thing!'

'Don't swear in front of the children, John.'

'Mummy it had stripes and Big Teeth.'

'Don't be stupid Justin,' chimed a chorus, 'it had spots, like a leopard.'

'What sort of a place allows animals like that to run around attacking people…'

'As big as an Alsatian…'

Toby withdrew, feeling he was seeing the birth of another rural myth.

———

'So it's about a kilometre up the gully there, Toby? Toilet block, barbeques, car park, that sort of thing?' asked Steve later.

'Like I said, and a big sign saying Angel Falls Lookout Picnic Area.' Liz looked at Sean, still gnawing on the splintered thighbone.

'Don't suppose those people will go exploring today.'

'Found it!' said Jules, pointing to a spot on the map, 'at least we know where we are now.'

'And I think I've solved the problem here, too!' said Solly, holding out a blackened resistor. 'We better up the power rating and change it in the other motors. Can you get me a...'

He was interrupted by a musical ring tone from the Dekko Omnitron.

'It's never done that before' said Steve, 'what is it?'

'Teddy Bears Picnic' said Solly.

'It's the SMS we fitted last week,' said Jules, 'but...' The crew gathered in front of the screen. Words began to appear slowly.

if you hear reports of my death

they have been definitely overstated.

Collective gasps, expletives and exclamations.

all's well, will explain later

take care, may still be in satellite range, do not reply

see you at rendezvous one...   came slowly to the screen. Then, gloriously...

Fond Regards,

McZed.

―⁓―

Ned watched the FA18 bear down from ten o'clock high and was grateful they were taking turns to have a go at him. One he could dodge. He straightened and slowed so the pilot could take his time lining up, watched for the gun flashes and lurched hard left. As the glowing string of cannon shells whisked past, Ned rolled and dived, hitting the button for the flame and smoke flare mounted under a grill. Really, he thought, what would burn on a steel plate boiler? But this was the expected end in the movies, and these guys would have watched so many movies. A few out-of-control swerves, quick check of the vents, flatten and slow... totally stuffed if this doesn't work... definitely absolutely last resort! Ned was thrown forward violently in his harness as a massive sheet of spray obliterated the windows. It cleared in streaks of bubbles and was replaced by the cold green of the underwater world. Going down like a stone. Moment of truth thought Ned, applying a little power. Miraculously, Ladybird stopped sinking and began to glide forward. Halleybloodylulia. He looked with new appreciation at the rich blue glow on the window grill, a little darker perhaps? Foolish to think it wouldn't work underwater …

Taking Ladybird down to a hundred feet or so, he set course for the east at what he considered, judging from the occasional shoal of fish he passed, a very fast bicycle rate. He settled back and calculated that an hour and a half, maybe more, should get him well away from the 'crash' site. No doubt the navy would want to get in on the act, very keen to lift his shattered remains from the abyss… Ned shuddered at what might have been. The boiler appeared well suited as a submarine and provided the seals held, the only problem was air. What happened on Apollo 13? Not so much the oxygen gave out, but more that the carbon dioxide could build to toxic levels. Ned the meticulous had researched this of course. A plastic jerry can of water, mix in some Portland cement but not too much, add the airbed pump with tubing, simple really. Ned selected an expensive long panatella and lit up, then plugged the pump into the lighter socket, sending a thick cloud of fragrant smoke past the happily bubbling filter. Bit of an extra challenge for it thought Captain Nemo, settling back.

Two hours of steady cruising and an estimated 30 kilometres later, the diminishing light from above showed dusk had arrived. The atmosphere in Ladybird was decidedly stuffy; time to go up, work out where he was and open the vents for a bit. Ned slowed to a stop and swung Ladybird toward the west; maybe he could spot the coast. Slowly he began the ascent toward the dim pink glow. A very faint thrumming, regular, steady, came to his ears and he uneasily scanned the instruments. The motors seemed to be performing well, so what was that pulse of sound? Ned eased the nose gently through the surface into a magnificent sunset... and in its centre an immense, orange and black steel cliff bearing rapidly down on him!

The sharp bit of forty thousand tons of Swedish cargo ship.

Off the south coast of New South Wales, Sven Heyerdahl, Captain of the M.V. Tempo and a devotee of the World Wide Web was settling in for an evening's hunt when the polite knock on his cabin door interrupted.

'I'm sorry Sir, Arne was about to run his evening Yoga class on the aft deck but they can't because there is something in the way.'

'What does he mean, something in the way? There is nothing to be stored there until Melbourne.'

'I think you best come and look Sir. It is very strange.'

Sven stared in disbelief at the finned steel tank. It was the same unmistakable object he had watched on the net that afternoon, impossibly flying above a small town on the mainland. He had spent over an hour site jumping to find more images, caught a whole segment of a strange play, saw the arrival of one of these machines and the departure of both. Walking around the back he banged on the double doors. The more cautious crewmembers backed off a few steps.

'Aye, just a minute there, I'll be right with you' came a muffled voice. Some clicks and scrapes and the doors swung open. A tall, lanky individual clambered down and offered a hand to the Captain. 'Ned McZed reporting on board Sir. I hope you don't mind me dropping in unexpected like this, but I had a bit of an emergency.' Sven looked at Ned, at Ladybird and grunted. He shook the offered hand warmly.

'I see. Captain Sven Heyerdahl, MV Tempo. Was this machine flying inland this afternoon? I have seen this. Is it also why the navy and air force have excluded shipping from the coastal waters just west of here?'

'Yes, probably…' said Ned warily.

'Good. You are very lucky. We have had unwanted military visitors on this shipping line before. You are welcome here Sir.' Turning to the gaping crew, he ordered a tarpaulin pulled over Ladybird and secured.

'Have you eaten dinner? We had veal this evening and I'm sure our fat cook has saved some. Please, come and tell me your story! I have some good whisky too.' Feeling distinctly that he had landed on his feet, yet again, Ned closed the doors on Ladybird and followed Captain Sven below.

Ned found a keen listener as he explained the history of the device, the development of the Ladybirds and the decision to introduce them to the world in the most public way possible.

'Yes, I see that, so that they don't hurry this boy's invention away and keep it for themselves! I see that. This will be most difficult however.' He filled the two glasses and laughed as Ned described the Barangan Showgrounds spectacle, the fox and hounds chase with the air force, his dramatic crash, the underwater escape and almost being rammed by the Tempo. 'We would have opened up your little tin can for you no problem!' Sven said jovially. Ned agreed, with less Jove. The old sailor became serious. 'So my friend, how can we help you? This is a great work you are doing. We can put your little tank away and take you to Sweden, but this will take a few weeks.'

'Thank you Sven, I appreciate that, but I need to meet up with my friends' said Ned. 'You are sailing south-east and well out to sea, so your kind lift will take me well away from this area. After I charge up my batteries and contact the others I will need to leave, tomorrow.'

'Well… if that is how it must be. Just you remember there is a floating refuge for you and your friends somewhere on this planet anytime. We got lots of room and these boys of mine, they keep their mouths shut too. You send me email, I send you my position.' Sven glanced at the half bottle of whisky. 'We finish this tonight then' he said, laughing aloud, 'and since you got two seats in your tin can you will take me for a quick ride before you go! I never fly in a boiler before! I give you a good big Swedish battery too, you can never have too much power…'

'This is a bugger of a track, young Bradley' said Shirley, swerving to avoid a stump.

'I know Mum,' said Brad, waving the map, 'but we reckon that about ten more kilometres or so should get us to the Jerangamere back road, and if we go through here, to here, it brings us out to the coast road!' Shirley groaned. It was going to be a long night.

Dawn found the Denzils bleary eyed in the first open roadhouse on the first bit of serious bitumen. Over breakfast (not up to her Addison's Fuel Tyres etc. standard), Shirley discussed strategy.

'We need to start the publicity campaign in Sydney quickly because our mates in LB2 are getting a very hard time! Can't go to your auntie's place because they can track back to her, and the friends I had way back in Sydney won't want to know. We might have to go with the only remaining option.' The boys frowned, then twigged.

'You can't mean Dad! You said we'd never go back there after last time!'

'I know, I should have done more planning, I know already. Although he's a total dipstick he's all we've got and if he's not in prison, he might have some useful acquaintances. Also, he's changed his name and address so many times that he'll be impossible to trace.'

'So how are we going to find him then?'

'Ah yes. That means we have to pay a visit to your dear old white headed Granny.'

Both boys groaned. Dad was bad enough, but Grandma Bess was the absolute pits.

—⁓—

Bess Dyce flung the door open and squealed at the sight of her grandchildren, totally ignoring Shirley. Pressed to the Grannybossom, Brad and Bobby struggled to breathe. Bess relented then glanced at their mother.

'Shirlgirl, you seem to be a bit famous lately. Saw you on Hi Ho Rupert.' Bess's TV habits and tastes hadn't changed then. 'Get yourselves inside then before the neighbours see you. We got a lot of catching up to do and those boys look as if you've been starving them.'

'They need a bed if that's OK, been up all night' said Shirl.

'Shirley Denzil, you know that can't be good for them,' began Bess angrily. Start of round one thought Shirl, but no. 'But you're right, bed first' said Bess, pointing to Bobby asleep standing. She moved across to him and tugged off his backpack, grunting in surprise at its weight. 'God, what's in this? The crown jewels?'

'It's his crystal set, never leaves it' said Shirley.

'CB radio actually, and I'll take it' said Brad, with equal haste. Bess shrugged.

'Whatever. Double bed in there young Bradley, take the zombie and climb in. Take off your shoes though.' Brad led Bobby off.

Over a coffee and compulsory cake, Bess announced to Shirley that she had a new hobby and proudly waved to the large computer in the corner of the lounge room.

'My young Bradley got it for me at a nice price.' She grinned, expecting a comeback from Shirley about her ex husband's business dealings. None came, so Bess continued. 'I did a lot of searches on the net after I spotted you on TV and it seems that everyone in that hick town of yours has posted photos or film shots of your flying saucers. Lots of bits of you, in your fancy dress and carrying on. How mad was all that stuff? I downloaded most of it.'

'I'm very impressed Bess.'

'Funny thing, all of it seems to have disappeared off the net since then. What actually happened? It all looked very exciting. What were those flying things? Like helicopters?'

Shirley explained as well as she could, including the secret agent and why they had to stay out of sight for a while. Bess Dyce was well acquainted with law difficulties and was quite pleased to welcome Shirley into the criminal world. Shirley said whatever and thanks and apart from staying out of prison they had to try and get the story out to the public.

'Actually, my Bradley might be a help there, he's come up in the world a bit and runs a few scams on the www dot, got into white collar crime from home as you can make more money with less work.' Shirley couldn't imagine how Flash Brad senior could do less work.

'Trick is not to have the punters get back to you after they've paid up, and since you lot don't even want money out of them it shouldn't be too hard.'

'The only thing is Bess, can I trust Bradley not to stuff up?'

'This involves his kids, so I shall be taking a personal interest, dear.' Shirley wasn't sure whether the 'personal interest' or being called 'dear' was the more disturbing. All in all however, it wasn't a bad offer. If Bess took charge, she was wickedly efficient, or efficiently wicked, and as well, they might not be sold out as the Dyces did have a thing about family... 'Shall I get onto my Bradley then dear? Good-oh.

Now, are there some things you would like him to get for you? A little shopping, maybe…?'

Later that afternoon, Shirley tucked the boys in and cranked up Bobby's "crystal set", the Denzil Dekko. Nothing in from Maria or the Hendersons, but she sent off a quick report.

———

'Yair, is that the country freight section there? Oh, good one mate. It's Bryce Davenport here, production manager with Alphabet Films and we're doing a special shoot tonight just outside of Jerrunadie. Period piece, 1800s, can't have the noise of a diesel electric in there so could you give us a bit of info about…' Toby juggled the phone, map, notepad and pencil stub while he wheedled more information from the bored Regional State Rail clerk. Piece of luck the phone still worked too! A last glance around the deserted Angel Falls Car Park and he set off through the fading light back to Ladybird 2.

'No word from Maria, but Shirley and the kids have made it to Sydney and will start broadcasting tomorrow" said Liz on his return. By agreement, Shirley was "Publicity and Stirring the Possum", while Liz had taken charge of "Overseas Negotiation." Nice to be well known, but even better knowing where you were going thought Toby. He was having serious misgivings about the lack of a clear plan, the massive opposition they were facing, the near loss of Ned… lots of things actually. But, there was always the buts, of course, like But you're helping save the planet, But these people are relying on me, and but you can't just get off and walk home. Bear up!

They then got into the escape discussion. The problem was, of course, the superb, clear weather. Yesterday's fog had gone, there was a three quarter moon tonight and any optical satellite above would pick them up in moments. The crisscross of con trails, chatter of helicopters in the distance and radio babble monitored by Liz testified to an intensive search. Despite Solly and Jules' confidence that the speed problem was sorted, everyone was well aware what could happen if they were found flying slowly in open country…

A wallaby looked up startled and skittered away as a very large bush edged around the cliff corner and advanced silently down the gully. Ladybird was moving camouflaged through the moonlit forest, drifting around the massive gums like a kelp festooned whale. Toby slowed to a hover while Steve evicted Jules from the co-pilot's seat and spread a map out over the glowing instruments.

'I reckon if we follow this creek across country to the main line, it might give us some cover most of the way. No towns or roads anywhere there either,' he said hopefully, 'so turn left at the junction to go downstream.' Toby nodded and Ladybird crept forward. Steve returned to Solly at the open back door, listening for aircraft, trucks, voices, anything. An hour later they were hovering at tree top level looking at their creek, grown to a small river and snaking across rolling pasture land.

'Could've left more trees' grumbled Toby.

'Well, it's pretty patchy but if we stick in to the river bank and go slow, we shouldn't stand out much' said Steve.

'No more than your average moving clump of trees. Bit like being Birnam Wood' mumbled the pilot. He was about to elaborate when Steve grinned widely and struck a quoting pose,

'Be lion-mettled, proud; and take no care
Who chafes, who frets, or where conspirers are…'
Liz, Jules and Solly joined in with enthusiasm.
'Macbeth shall never vanquish'd be, until
Great Birnam wood to high Dunsinane hill
Shall come against him.'
'Act 4, scene 1, kid with a crown on his head' said Steve

'Who happened to be Brad Denzil when TADAFIC did Macbeth four years back. All about the local member and some wood chipping issues, bit of a complicated plot, but it worked out OK' explained Liz to Toby.

'The good guys carried the trees' stated Solly.

'And we have to be a bit more lion metallicised' added Jules, as she deftly dropped Ladybird back down to the river surface. Toby gestured downstream and reluctantly marvelled. Smartarse kid had learnt how to fly about sixteen times faster than he had.

'Better watch out for power lines draped across the river and any farmhouses up on the bank. Not that anyone'd be up at two a.m. We should be about an hour away to the main bridge' he directed. Jules nodded, slipping into videogame mode.

Forty-five minutes later Birnam Wood rounded a bend and faced the squat railway bridge.

'Nice going,' said Toby. 'We should make the 3.10 mixed freight and empties for Melbourne according to the eventually helpful Robert at the SRA. Park it over on the beach there and we'll defoliate'

Had the train driver been less interested in his paper and checking his mirrors, he may have spotted the silvery blue shape rise behind his train as he crossed Colnighte River bridge.

'That one looks the go' said Toby, indicating a low flatbed wagon. Looking down through the ground observation windows, he talked Jules through the landing. They shut down quickly and opened the back doors to check their situation. Ladybird 2 fitted neatly onto the flatbed, well parked first go, and they were rattling through the countryside at a good fifty kilometres an hour.

'Reckon we should just clear the overhead bridges with the tailfin,' said Steve clambering up. 'Those milk tanks ahead would only be a few centimetres lower.'

'Looks a bit like a milk tank I suppose ' said Toby, dubiously.

'Doesn't have to!' said Steve, 'Liz and I knocked up these when I worked out the idea about the train trip.' He held out two large cardboard signs and gaffer tape. Toby read them.

COLLINGTON'S NOVELTY RIDES 04284954844 or collinovel@hotech.net.au.

'Well, that's bound to put them off the scent, and I'm sure it explains the fins.' A tarpaulin was pulled over the nose windows and they settled in for the night.

Liz took the first watch; the others tried to get some sleep.

—⁓—

Toby awoke to Liz shaking his shoulder urgently.

'Shhh. Get up front, we may have to leave in a hurry.'

He scrambled out of his bunk. They were creeping at a snail's pace down a large country railway station platform, the fluorescent blocks of light swinging slowly across the cabin walls. Murphy's law at work, they came to a squealing halt in front of the only lit window, framing the glazed face of the only station attendant. Steve and Liz pulled back into the shadows.

Greg's wits worked pretty slowly in the early morning and took time moving from unfocussed boredom to slight frown puzzlement and final blink-squint mild interest.

'He's coming outside. Stay down' whispered Toby.

Greg sauntered over to Ladybird buttoning up his coat against the cold, walked up and down a little, tugged at the tarpaulin rope and slapped the metal side with his hand. Sounded empty. Inside, Liz slipped silently to the bunks as Jules stirred and mumbled. Toby watched the internal debate flickering across the attendant's face and groaned when a bulky Railway cordless phone was fished out of a pocket. At that point Greg didn't quite know what to do. What the fuck was this thing doing on the otherwise empty freight train? It didn't even look properly secured. He could be sure the driver wouldn't know anything about it because drivers were arseholes and the engine was a good 500 metres away down the track and it was bloody cold.   He didn't want to phone the duty supervisor in the middle of the night because he would be asleep with consequences, but this thing needed sorting.

Greg pondered, then noticed a sign taped down toward the rear of the tank. He brightened; at least it had a label! Toby watched as the lips moved and the debate continued. After a while, the peering intensified, the phone was raised and numbers were tapped laboriously.

'Liz…' hissed Toby; 'I think he's calling the phone number on the sign!'

'Oh bugger… that's the number on one of the new pre-paids.'

She scrabbled in her bag, flustered but thinking. Greg walked back to the warmth of his office as the call connected… funny echo…he shut the door. Probably no one there but he might get some answer machine details…

'Collington's Novelty Rides 24 hour answering service, this is Karen speaking, how may I help you?' said the bright young girl with the I'm wide-awake voice. Greg was taken aback, but rallied. Big company then, 24-hour service!

'Umm, it's Greg Posten the umm acting station master at Wangernal and I was wondering if you could umm tell me about one of your ride umm thingies on a train here… like.'

'Could you describe the machine in question and where this Wangernal is please Sir? We have a lot of machines to keep track of,' the cheerful professional voice enquired.

'Well, umm, we're about 120 km north of Melbourne and it's on a train heading south. It's about ten metres long, sort of a big tube thing, and its got windows down the side, doors at the back and wings on it. Little ones.'

'That would probably be one of the new Interstellar Mars Rockets, very popular, just hold the line for a moment please Sir… Yes indeed, that is a KA465 and it should be on a freight train going to Tottenham Yard for collection tomorrow. Special request from the Premier's Department… short notice… needed it for the Festival of Science… Now, were you interested in hiring a KA465 for something at Wangernal, Mr. Posten? I believe we may have one from the Gold Coast coming back soon.'

'Oh. Not really, just wondering howcome it was on the train.'

'I believe the transit and paperwork was personally organized through the Victorian State Rail Regional Director. Would you like me to contact him for you Mr. Posten?'

'Umm, crickey no, no worries. I'm sure it's OK... What's this rocket thingy do anyway?'

'I believe it goes up and down and spins around a bit Sir.'

'Oh. Umm, sorry to bother you.'

'My pleasure Sir. Thank you for your call. Have a nice day.'

Five minutes later and the train got the green light to proceed. Greg studiously ignored it, head buried in his magazine, Hot Rods 'n Chicks. Didn't know if he'd spend much to have a go on the Mars Rocket if it ever came to the Wangernal Show, sounded a bit of a fizzer. He had ducked out however, to take a picture on his mobile, show the blokes at the pub and see what they reckoned.

—◦◦◦—

An uneventful hour later and well away from under the satellites, Solly found some BOM cloud cover while Toby and Jules plotted a course for the coast. A quick vertical lift to 10,000 and they sped off into the night, very subsonic to be quiet. Air pressure seemed to be maintained, Liz monitored the Dekko, Steve did the rounds of the windows checking for aircraft while Toby and Jules wove through the cloudbanks and Solly slept on. The coast slid past as the fires of sunrise glowed ahead on the horizon. Fifty miles off the coast they changed course to southeast, with two thousand kilometres of open sea ahead. Toby quietly requested the power bought on and Ladybird surged calmly up to Mach 4, not a hiccup. Rounds of applause and cheers. Successful repairs. They wound back to Mach 2.5.

'Just cruising then, Captain' said Jules smugly.

'Yes. Life on the open road eh, young Julie' said Toby, pulling on his fake Aviator green sunglasses against the golden new morning sun. 'I'll take the helm for a while if you want to get some breakfast, we should be there in less than an hour. If Solly emerges, maybe you could check the motors over with him. Everything, touch wood, seems to be operating OK' he said, waving across the instruments.

The crackling and smell of bacon roused Solly. The motors checked out fine, the egg and bacon sandwiches even better. Sean extracted a can of fish from Toby. With the Dekko feeding out Satnav positioning and a large atlas, Steve and Liz plotted their way across the icy ocean until Jules announced she had spotted the massive granite sea stacks of North East Island. Toby slowed, banked to the right and they circled.

'Welcome to the Snares my dears' hissed the decoded voice of Ned McZed from the Dekko, 'and you're a sight for sore eyes. If you steer due south, you'll spot a small bunch of huts in a clearing just to your left of the peak…' Ned talked them down to a low hover, then with very professional gestures and many silly grins, backed Ladybird in under the trees. He was well pleased to see his friends, safe and sound. The back doors swung open, Solly and Jules rushed out with hugs then stood back embarrassed, there was a big kiss from Liz and then blokey handshakes from the blokes.

'Ned McZed

Back from the dead.

More lives than a cat...!

And all of our thanks for that…' proclaimed Toby.

Ned's face glowed to the ear tips… then cooled rapidly as Sean sauntered down the steps, sat and stared insolently.

'Toby Buchanan sir, if you think that we may be in trouble for taking on the armed might of the upper echelon of world power with a device that challenges their entire economic base, it is nothing to the shite we will be in if the New Zealand Department of Conservation finds out we've introduced a cat into the Snares. This is the home of the Southern Buller's Albatross! People freeze their bums off in the roaring forties just to measure the weight of the chicks! They do not like cats!'

'Is that why the huts are here?' asked Solly, trying to change the subject on behalf of Sean. Ned snorted, glared at Toby, and then regained his composure.

'Yes. You better come in. Including you' he said tersely to the offending carnivore.

The hut was clean, functional and above all, warm with a fired up slow combustion heater. An interesting savoury smell came from one of Ned's better, publicly tested recipes and some fresh baked bread. Over an early lunch Ned explained his choice of venue, that he had worked in The Snares island group briefly in the last century as a researcher, knew it would be deserted at this time, and was the essence of remote and desolate. Just the thing for their needs before going on.

'Our problem is,' said Ned, waving a chunk of bread, 'the surveillance satellites which have optical capability. That's how they got onto us when we left Barangan. The bulk of the others use electronic, microwave, infrared or radar systems and shouldn't be a problem. Some of the GPS satellites might run to cameras and they cover most places, but hopefully, not in this neck of the woods. Even so, there's so much unknown stuff floating up there that we better keep on moving. Always a good policy when you're on the run.' The others didn't ask regarding his experience in this matter.

'There's still nothing from Liz and only that earlier message from Shirley, so we won't be moving anywhere for a while. Ned, you said you would explain how you escaped a certain and dreadful death when you caught up with us. Please explain,' asked Liz.

'Ah yes, and went on to meet new friends!' exclaimed Ned. He settled back.

'Gather around children. Well, there I was, the mist disappeared and I was alone in the sky, surrounded by enemy planes…'

Chapter Eleven

'Goddamn it Homer, tell the Department of Defence that it's all under control and we'll brief them at the right time. It's an agency matter.'

'I'm afraid Senator it's not as easy as all that,' said the Chief of Overseas Security. The DOD began monitoring the whole operation since the Barangan story broke, are linked in with the region's Air Forces and have their satellites searching. They know the potential and want those machines in their own hands... just as much as other people' he added, glancing at Dobrovich. No response apart from a scowl, so he continued. 'We pulled on a whole ball of strings to keep it quiet in Australia, but not all of the media is on board. As well, there's a load of stuff on the Internet, and some of it professionally produced. That damned silly play that they put on is a cult hit right across Europe and has crept into our own domestic channels. We're also getting new material, like interviews with the kids who are supposed to have invented these machines and discussing about how they need to be available to the whole world...' Senator Dobrovich fumed and paced. As much as he hated it, he would have to 'open a meaningful dialogue to foster a collaborative interagency approach' as Spiggott had put it. Who in the hell did he know in the Department of Defence?

'Get in touch with the CEO in Procurement, Henry Sommerton, for a conference.'

'Mightn't be a good idea, Sir, he's currently under investigation, or so I heard.'

'Damn. Well...' he ran down his mental list of unpaid debts, 'General Roberts then. As a sweetener you can give him all we know from the Barangan interrogations and how the search for the shot down one is going and line me up a meeting with the old fart.'

'So tell him nothing then' said Homer. 'The questioning went nowhere and the search found zilch. The aircraft must have fragmented or exploded underwater.'

Either that, mused Kelvin to himself, or the thing has underwater capability as well! What a machine…we must have it. I must have it! Available to the whole world be damned! We have to cut these people out of the herd and destroy their support.

'Homer, get me George Morton on line. We need to make an example of one of these terrorists and find the ones that got away. It has to be them who are putting up this new propaganda. We also have to dig that big ship out of the mountains; it obviously snuck off while the air force chased the little one. Satellite updates? That area was covered, wasn't it?'

'Yes Sir,' said Homer, directing scurrying aides, 'but you better have a look at this first Sir, we just lifted it off the net. Seems it was posted by a railway employee from well south of the mountains in question, as a joke.'

Kelvin Dobrovich looked at the photocopy and swore. Sitting on a flatbed rail truck in full view was the same mother ship they were searching for! Goddamn!

———

The wholesale detention of TADAFIC was having its impact in Barangan and district. First hit were the folk who had developed addictions to the fine pastry and exquisite sourdough breads of the Sunrise Bakery. It was shut. After they heard the story from Pete's wife and complained bitterly, they drifted as a group toward the Police station.

'My husband Glen the Mayor will be hearing about this!' exclaimed Lady Mayoress Mrs. Jones, 'and he better do something quickly!'

'Yes, and we will be getting onto the District Superintendent of Police, who's in The Lodge with My Barry' added Mrs. Reynolds, wife of Major Retailer.

'I've got four people coming for lunch and no baguettes. Peter promised me a dozen Bichon au Citron as well' said Margaret the minister's wife, very careful with the vowels and affricate.

'Perhaps we could arrange a meeting' said wonderful-organiser Susan Armitage, scenting a committee.

On the way the group of seven was joined by the much rowdier Barangan Tigers Football Club and lady associates. They coalesced warily.

'They can't lock up our bloody Full Forward today, we've got the big game with Wimbarra!' complained Jimbo. He'd not been drinking for several days. Close Encounters will do that.

'So what's Nick supposed to have done?' growled Chazza, 'Mucking around in a bloody play! Didn't pinch anything or hurt anyone. What's the charge?'

'It's not like the play was obscene and they didn't swear or anything' said Chazza's fiancé Sharmayne, 'and Nick's supposed to be bringing the snags for the barbie too!'

'Nick Bronson does make excellent sausages,' agreed the Lady Mayoress. 'Have you tried those lovely chicken, fetta cheese and rocket ones?' The Tigers ignored this social gaffe about Nick's nouveaux sidelines and got on with how the bloody hell they were going to get their key player sprung.

'Anyone know anyone who's important?' asked Jimbo.

The outraged rural Parents and Citizens of Tilda had been phone conferencing since the milking finished at 7 am. Miss Lorimer had taught most of them and the idea of her in prison was appalling. Well used to lobbying and protest, the faxes and emails had flowed to the Director of Schools, the local member and the Minister of Education. Correspondence to all the national TV, radio networks and newspapers followed. The editor of the Cambrawarra Times and the Federal Opposition Spokesman for Agriculture, both ex Tilda Primary students, had been summoned from their beds. The entire population of

Tilda and district was now driving to a demonstration outside Barangan Police Station.

Barangan High School's Teachers Federation Representative had also been on the phone with far less success; the staff was not noted for industrial or any other action and anyway, the energetic Maria Scott had always been a bit on the outer. He was told to bugger off and you don't call people on Sunday mornings by a majority; three agreed to come to the station and protest, the rest would wait until Monday.

The ABC was also a bit of a curate's egg regarding support of its workers. The upper upper levels had been told not to go there and were comfortably compliant. Some of the middle upper levels had moral twinges regarding the ABC charter of independence, but the older generation at least of the middle middle and down to shop floor was spoiling for a fight. As was the Camera Operators and Sound Technician's Union. Two of the current affairs programs had Serious Questions to ask regarding The Legitimacy of the Current Legislation. 'Mechanism', the very popular science show, had cut straight to the heart of the matter with very pertinent points about the potential of the device to revolutionise the transport industry and cut carbon emission.

—⁄⁄⁄—

Evangeline Parsons QC was striding bluetoothed through the supermarket collecting her provisions for the week. Corporate law with politically correct pro bonos, she knew what worked in her city. Her conversations with the unseen were sharp, professional, concise and very directive. People always listened and obeyed quickly; except mother.

'Yes Mum, I know he's a silly old fart but we can't leave him in jail. Yes Mum. Yes, typical. No, as far as I know he hadn't been drinking. No, she's not his fancy tart as you put it, she's an ex ABC presenter and they were just working together. They were not doing anything wrong, Mother, and he's just got himself mixed up in something political…'

There was a long pause at the Dairy Fridge. Evangeline glared fiercely at a curious mother-with-toddlers and they scuttled away. Lite White, crumbly sharp, yoghurt full fat six-pack, olive marge; they all went hurtling into the trolley. On to the veggies. 'Mum as far as I know so far he was clueless about what was going to happen. Yes I know, as per usual. I've got three people onto it already. I have no idea what your Quilting Club will say. No Mum, of course I care. Just tell them he's taking a principled stand on our democratic rights to free speech or something... that he's becoming quite famous and you are supporting him. No, not like that...' The pre-packed salads flew through the air, none missed. The singing chicken above the meat section began its inane ditty. Bugger. 'Yes Mum I'm in the supermarket but I don't have time to... just the milk and bread then... toothpaste, apricot jam... they don't sell that here...that means I'll have to drive to... yes mother. Have to go now... yes all right...Bye.' The Parsons trolley did a swinging U turn and the fuming Evangeline headed back down the aisle. For sure, several junior members of The Firm would suffer for the rest of their abbreviated weekend.

—◦◦◦—

At the tops of a dozen glistening buildings in different cities on the planet, the immaculate, expensively dressed leading representatives of vast pyramids of power were observing information, conferencing with each other and bluetooth murmuring back to their leaders, controllers, partners or subordinates. Using ahead of state of the art fully secure technology. Not national groupings, more a gathering of agents of planetary commercial and industrial tribes. New York spoke.

'The data and its analysis is very clear on that point, the larger of the two machines must weigh over five tons, the smaller one was earlier noted as moving at over eighteen hundred miles per hour, and the only power source is a limited one from batteries. Construction of both was at a small country workshop, no special equipment.' New York paused. Even the sharpest, hardest minds on Earth, in his opinion, needed a bit

of time to get around this. Each group conferred, the occasional glance at the other members on screens.

'No evidence of hydrocarbon fuel use at all?' asked Dubai.

'Can we obtain this technology and how much do they want?' asked Munich.

'Where are they going? Do they have backing, connections?' asked the London trio.

'Can they be removed?' chorused the Shanghai committee of five.

'Why have they not been removed already?' demanded Singapore.

'All we know has been presented to you. They do appear, at first glance, to be a very small and poorly organized group without security back up. There have been no moves to establish patents or any commercial approaches. From looking at the presentation made at their departure and subsequent releases, our analysts indicate an extremely high risk of this group establishing widespread use of the technology in the immediate future.'

There was a shocked silence, followed by urgent, within group murmurings. Questions, suggestions and statements. New York called a plenary.

They knew what they were facing, and were unanimous in what they wanted; immediate capture and complete control, or total destruction.

'Thank you Ms. Montague, that was very well organized' said New York when everyone was off line. Ms. Montague nodded. She had achieved 98% coordination and 100% unanimity for this meeting and sat back, quietly satisfied.

—ᴧᴧ—

Sunday evenings in Barangan were always ghost town dead, but not tonight! The protests had continued, growing in size as locals either realized that the rights of Barangan Citizens were being compromised, that the people responsible for the best ever festival had been nicked for it, or at least that something exciting was happening down at the cop shop. Teams were shouting impromptu slogans such as 'Free the Barangan Seven!', 'Go The Tigers!' and 'Let Miss Lorimer Go!' Groups of students held up well spelt placards, including 'We Need our Support Teacher' and 'What price Demokracy?'

Arabella Swift, now loosely contracted to several national radio stations and newspapers, dashed happily about with voice recorder and notepad. Jim Dobson, the work placement photographer, had shimmied up the learning curve and was almost keeping pace. He had pushed his uncle to lend his new, expensive (look after it Jim or I'll bloody well brain you) DSLR camera. Arabella was pleased; she had intently watched Maria at work on Saturday and figured they/she might branch out into Television with some incisive interviews/humorous interludes/action shots. A good chance came with a loud delegation hammering on the front doors at 2:00 am, producing Constable Harris and Sergeant Baker, who quickly quietened the more boisterous and patiently explained that under the legislation, the 'suspects' could be detained for up to two weeks without charge. They weren't being released, according to their "visitors". Not that they had all the paperwork yet. And they couldn't do much about it but would make bloody well sure everyone was well treated. Jim filmed away; Arabella pushed to the fore and was about to start incising when the crowd noticed three black, dark windowed SUV's creeping out of the lane from the back car park. Jim, with remarkable reflexes, raced across to film them as a ragged yell went up and the crowd surged. Headlights flared, horns blared and people scattered; the vehicles accelerated away. Ernie looked at Ken and they both hurried back inside, locking the doors.

A further delegation, knocking politely after the Police Talk, gave up after 10 minutes and returned to the barbeques. Arabella went back to interviewing, the crowd went back to socializing and drinking. The Salvos set up a coffee stand and did well.

Just as dawn was breaking, two 4Wheel Drives, in a nice shade of grey beneath the mud, arrived out front and sat patiently. The suited occupants stared fixedly ahead, uncomfortably packed in behind the tinted windows. More dubious official visitors, and quickly surrounded by sleep deprived, angry Barangans and Tildans.

'Stand back there or we'll be breaking some bloody heads!' bellowed out from the Police Station. The Trunchioned Police Force of Two had again emerged and subdued the crowd by dint of their superior crankiness: people fell back when they saw the thunderclouds above Ken and Ernie. The grey 4WD's were allowed to go around the back.

Ernie and Ken had been furious for the past four hours. They had come back into the Police Station to find the entire swag of "Security Section" staff and the Federal policeman had decamped, taking one of the prisoners with them! Without a transfer authority! The American, Graeme Horowitz, was still hanging around.

'They just gathered that Miss Scott up and said they were going back to Sydney, Sergeant. The other Federal policeman went along with them and was saying it was all OK. Don't know what they're doing, not my department.' Unable to contact any regional executive staff, (not to be disturbed), unable to chase after the perpetrators (the crowd situation), they fretted and fumed.

〰〰

The newcomers had impressive papers, stated they were ASIO Officers, were here to take charge and were unaware of any other agencies being involved. Their tale of woe around problems with mis-directions and losing a vehicle in a river cut no ice. Particularly when the rumple suited Officer in Charge confided that there had been a lot of pressure on the Minister, particularly from a top Queen's Counsel named Evangeline Parsons whose dad was one of the ABC prisoners and that after a brief interrogation, sorry, interview, the film crew and TADAFIC cast were to be released without charges…

'Brief is five minutes' snarled Ernie.

'Tops' barked Ken. 'And you can get straight onto whoever is in charge and ask how the hell a foreign security mob think they can abduct an Australian citizen from an Australian Police Station!'

The assembled throng, in the throes of discussing their next move, cheered mightily when six of the Barangan Seven were shown the front door. Bit of a problem that Maria Scott had been taken away, but now no one was locked up they could all adjourn for breakfast.

Arabella Swift and Jim were reviewing their notes and images as the last of the crowd trailed away with their empty eskies. Arabella recognised the nicer one of the two American journalists coming out of the Police Station.

'Mind if I join you?' said Graeme, 'We need to talk, but not here, my car's around the corner.' Jim looked to Arabella who shrugged.

'American newspaperman I know. Big syndicate.'

'Oh' said Jim, shaking hands with Graeme. It was quite cosy in Graeme's economy two-door rental as they drove to a barren nature reserve on the outskirts of town. Jim in the back seat was instructed to keep an eye out for anyone trailing them, Graeme ran his police band scanner. The milk delivery van was the only other vehicle on the road, and the Canumbie Police Station breakfast order the only message on the airwaves.

'Quiet little place isn't it' commented Graeme, parking behind the only bush. Arabella and Jim on Assignment... sounds like the title of one of his twelve-year-old daughter's books thought Graeme. He asked for and switched off Arabella's recorder. 'Before I start,' he said gravely, 'I must have your absolute guarantee of confidentiality. You must both protect your source. I will be in very deep shit if this gets tracked back to me, it's ultimate sanction territory.' Arabella agreed immediately, the confused and anxious Jim likewise after a glaring nod. Graeme accepted the assurances, baulked a little at Jim's spat-on handshake but made the most of it by immediately insisting on shaking Arabella's hand as well.

'Joined in spit,' said the discomforted Arabella. 'So what's the big secret?'

'Well. I can't use the story because my passport and work permit depend on it. As you saw, I managed to talk my way into the police station, so I saw and heard most of what went on. I won't tell you how I did it, but it wasn't easy.'

'Tricks of the trade,' Arabella explained to Jim.

'The three black SUV's you saw leave were supposed to be full of American Embassy Security staff on official business but I'm not so sure, because their paperwork was minimal, they were over-armed and embassy staff don't snatch prisoners. You might find they work for a private intelligence agency.'

'I got some shots of their four wheel drives' said Jim helpfully.

'That's good work, you'd be a great man to have on a stake out' opined Graeme, 'and you might find Sergeant Harris was prepared to check out their number plates, Arabella, if you told him the right story.' Arabella scribbled furiously. 'These people interrogated your 'Barangan Seven' but were mostly interested in Maria Scott as she was the closest to the Hendersons, Buchanan and McZed. I believe they took Miss Scott to stop her being released and so they could… question her at length, well away from prying eyes. Have you ever heard the terms 'rendition' and 'enhanced interrogation?'

'No' said Jim, lost again.

'You mean take her illegally out of the country to somewhere she can be tortured?' asked Arabella, horrified. 'But that only happens in foreign countries!'

'Australia is a foreign country for these guys Miss. They have the resources, know where your security gaps are and can get it done while bureaucrats dither around. Getting this information must be helluva important to someone...' he mused.

'Where were they going to? Did you hear? How can we stop them?' asked Arabella.

'Poor Miss Scott must be terrified!' said Jim. It was only six months since he had been in her class. Her help in Maths and Photography had got him his HSC.

'I've got a few contacts,' said Graeme, 'so maybe I can ferret out some more information. See what you can find out from Sergeant Harris, give me your mobile number and I'll get back to you in half an hour. We may have to work very quickly...'

—◦◦◦—

Monday in Sydney was the start of a busy working week. Despite Bess Dyce's protestations that the home desktop was very secure, Shirley and the boys decided on a 'roving distribution' for their networking. Bradley Dyce, ex-partner and father, sidled in early and accepted the coolish greetings of his ex-family. Things warmed over breakfast; the Denzils conceded he was trying hard, and the charm was infectious. Brad Senior now carried a genuine leather briefcase, in keeping with his 'new lines of work', and from it produced a high power wireless modem, a laptop, a new registration sticker and set of number plates for the ute which he assured them would pass any reasonable inspection.

Back on the road and Shirley pulled into a quiet side street; her bag full of mobiles ringing.

She fished through and pulled the flashing one out.

'It's the secret agent phone Mum' said Bobby. Shirley switched it on.

'Hi there. Just to let you know a few things, and don't say anything.' The voice had an odd, muffled quality, obviously a security thingy. Didn't sound like Graeme at all. They had looked up ECHELON on Bess's Internet and knew the massive electronic monitoring system picked up voice patterns as well as key words. 'Your friends were all collected after the event, have just been released apart from the high school person. The group from Sydney left with her before the Alpha Sierra India Oscar group arrived. I'm afraid they may be planning a nasty overseas trip.' There was a pause. 'I need to know if our school friend was aware of our absent friends plans, where they were going and so on. If that's the case, can we contact them? Guess it's a matter of trust if you tell me or not. Send me a text.' The phone cut off. Shirley thought it through. If Graeme was setting them up, he was an amazingly good dissembler, but wasn't that what secret agents were? Was the earlier help just grooming? Bobby and Brad said it was up to her. She sighed and sent her SMS.

Friend and I both aware. May be possible to contact.

Glad you are on our side. Stay in touch. Love, S.

'We better start raising a bit of hell on the internet,' declared Shirley, 'then let Ladybird know Maria has been kidnapped. Get the laptop fired up boys!'

'Lots of nice utes around Mum' said Bobby, as they slowly cruised the streets of Bondi. Sparkling, fat tyred, lowered utes with longhorn cow heads on their back windows.

'Yes Bobby, but we've got the genuine mud, rust and blue smoke' said Shirley.

'Found a new one Mum, can you pull over for a couple of minutes' said Brad, pointing to a loading zone. He had tracked down yet another potential zombie; an unprotected, left on wireless linked computer. Brad and Bobby typed, conferred, chuckled as they jumped into its remote access, firing off emails with attachments and setting it up to continue doing so for the next week. The boys finished, Shirley glanced at her watch and pulled onto the road, heading for Centennial Park. The urbane prattle of Billy Styler, your favourite talk back host, oozed from the car speakers, inviting callers. Shirley handed a pre-paid to Bobby.

'Get the text up that Maria loaded and we'll send it off to Billy-the-Bigot's mobile.'

Maria had made contact with Billy a week ago and Shirley hoped fervently that his lust for an exclusive would outweigh his desire to dob them in. The mobile was linked back through one of the zombie computers, but even so, she would make the call in a CCTV free environment and keep it very short...

Turning in through the Park's ornate gateway she nodded to Brad, who fired up the pre-paid. Billy Styler's theme music abruptly faded and he launched into the agreed intro.

'Well folks, some of you may have caught the excitement which happened in the small southern town of Barangan on Saturday, either on the telly or on the www dot since then. Seems that during their annual Wool 'n Hops Festival - don't you love it - some of the locals took off and flew out in two - wait for it - flying saucers! These amazing craft seemed to...'

Shirley gave the thumbs up to Brad and Bobby who switched off the car radio, put on headphones to monitor the station and dialled Shirley through.

'Shirley Dee here.'

'Putting you straight through Shirley. Billy suggests you keep it short.' Billy's voice was patched through, Brad confirmed they were on air.

'... and yes indeed folks, we have Shirley Denzil who was the MC for that whole event, actually on line... so what really happened down there Shirley?' Shirley quickly launched warm and genuine into the message.

'Well Billy, what we have is an aussie family of battlers who developed and built a new, revolutionary motor which uses very little power and...' Shirley quickly explained the implications of the device, the risk of it being hijacked and exploited, the need to leave to get support for further testing before releasing the technology. She voiced her concern about Maria and was midway into some human interest on the Hendersons when Bobby signalled termination; they were off air. Shirley was pleased to hear Billy Styler mutter about a 'technical problem' and 'speak to you later Shirley' before they shut down. At least he wasn't trying to keep her talking. They quickly took the next exit out of the park and burrowed into the back streets.

Twenty minutes later the Denzil ute was pulled up in a deserted picnic area and Bobby was unpacking the backpack-that-never-left-his-sight. The mini Dekko Omnitron was a heavy, squat plywood box with a hinged lid and an assortment of odd dials, knobs and switches inside. Solly's hand painted pictures of Tilda scenes and a family portrait of the Hendersons on the sides made them feel wistful for missing friends, but they busied themselves hooking up the cigarette lighter power lead and mounting the large folding metal vegetable steamer/satellite dish up on the ute's roof. A trial transmission two weeks back from Barangan to Tilda had worked fine, but god knows how far away the big Dekko and LB2 were now.

'We'll try a coded SMS first' said Brad, holding up crossed finger as he folded out the battered keyboard. Fingers flashed, switches were clicked, the baby Dekko hummed.

'Told them about Maria being kidnapped, that we were fine and spreading the word in Sydney. We're getting through 'cos there's some stored messages coming back…' The Denzil heads bumped as they all tried to read the flat screen mounted in the lid. Brad pushed his Mum and brother back, read aloud. 'First one… LB2, hiding out in the mountains, think Ned might be in big trouble, will let us know.' The family looked glumly at each other. So Graeme was right. 'Second one… HOLY SHIT!' Brad yelled, 'It's from LB1! If you hear reports of my death they have been definitely overstated all's well will explain later keep up good work take care love Ned.' The Denzils all grinned hugely.

'Trust that bloody McZed' said Shirley eventually.

'Third one… we're at the Snares and Ned is here all safe and sound. Waiting to hear from you again, hope you are well…. That's it. Isn't that great. Jeez!' He tapped out an additional message of congratulations, told them how the opposition thought Ned was sunk off the coast and that they would get back later on. Added a little personal sentence to Jules.

The Denzils were right pleased as they headed for the next random suburb; the Ladybirds had got through the first stage of the big trip, and Billy Styler would have reached out to nearly a million listeners. Useful for something. Tonight they would do a bit more filming and editing, re-jig the package and tomorrow start all over again.

—⁓—

What's happening with these Australian terrorist hippie bastards? Did my boys get that organizer tucked away? Has she broken yet? Have we tracked down the one that got away to Sydney? She's been too damned busy stirring up trouble down there!' Senator Dobrovich was giving Homer the inquisition.

'Well sir, the team got Maria Scott out of Barangan without hitch but haven't left the country yet. Shouldn't be any problems, transport's arranged and they're getting clearance. Shirley Denzil's been very careful, but can't hide forever. Some problems with the newspapers and talk shows since she got some airtime, but TV is pretty well sorted. Apart from the ABC channel which is painting the Hendersons as Revolutionary Heroes who made an Amazing Aussie Scientific Breakthrough. Not a big coverage though.'

'What about my health scare?' asked Kelvin.

'Ah yes. Very good that one sir, at least to begin with. The radioactive spray on their truck went down well but it turned out that the idiots used a manufactured medical isotope that was easily identified and the story had to be pulled, along with the 'patients with radiation sickness' they had lined up. Some of the mud will stick though and after all, no one has proved these things are safe. A blue glow; its got to be dangerous hasn't it!'

Kelvin grunted. Good idea, poor implementation. Just can't get good agents nowadays, all these half-assed private contractors.

—〜〜—

Graeme, the good agent, was happy and very efficient in his work. Senior Constable Ernie Harris had been attentive and helpful; the vans were traced back to a company called Morton Security. Graeme had accessed their accounts, followed links to a charter aircraft company's logged flight plans and now knew where the SUV's were headed.

'Arabella, your Miss Scott is in big trouble and I doubt if any of your government agencies will raise a finger to help her. Listen carefully…'

Ernie stared incredulously at the journalist and her offsider.

'Being flown out overseas from Moruya airport so she can be tortured for information? Bloody hell Miss Swift, can you be sure your source has got it right? One thing's for sure, they're spot on that those clowns over there won't help. It's taken them two hours to work out that the first bunch with their so called Federal Cop were fakes!'

'We best be leaving to sort it ourselves then, Senior Constable,' said Ken Baker, unlocking the gun cabinet, 'I know now that handguns are wrong for me to be involved with, but these little fellers we confiscated last month should be OK.' With a wide grin he passed two lethal looking sawn off automatic shotguns and a box of shells to Ernie.

'Bit recidivist Sarge, but those blokes did seem to have a lot of hardware. Reckon we should take the press along too, keep it all above board. The Commodore?'

'Of course. Feel like a bit of a drive. Youse blokes can lock up when you leave!' yelled Ken to the gaggle of ASIO agents clustered around the coffee bar.

'We're pulling into the servo to fill up and since we've only got three and a bit hours to get to Moruya, it's the only toilet stop' said Ernie to Arabella and Jim.

'Yair,' said Ken from the bowser, 'and ask Bazza for a few packets of chips, drinks and some minties. Get some plastic bags too, it's a bit bouncy sometimes in the back seat.'

Ernie nodded sagely; he had ridden with Ken in Pursuit before.

Four minutes later and the SSV, blue lights flashing and siren screaming, bellowed out of town and headed for the coast.

Chapter Twelve

Sean stretched on a log, out of the wind and into the sun, watching morning tea.

'As we said before, Ned,' said Steve patiently, 'it's a hell of a long way, half way around the world. In fact, we'll probably be stretching the friendship to get LB2 there. It's just too far for LB1. We have to strip it and lift it out to sea... sorry.' The others looked on sympathetically. Solly patted Ned on the arm.

'Perhaps we could hide it in the forest and come back for it later?' suggested Liz.

'Such a shame, it was a ripper flying machine,' said Jules.

'It's OK to be upset, mate, but we can't do anything else' said Toby counsellorially.

Ned seemed quite unperturbed. 'No. That will not be necessary' he said decisively. 'All the gear and the batteries, apart from the large one from Captain Sven, gets loaded into LB2. Then, what we do is this!' With a flourish he whipped out a large, well-worked sheet of paper. Steve groaned. More mad plans.

Everything went remarkably well, considering. As the sun set, they stood back and looked at the result. Ladybird 2 was now double-decked, with LB1 securely bolted to its roof.

'Reminds me of a monster Winnebago I saw once' said Toby, 'which had a tiny 4WD attached to the back to go shopping in...' Steve shook his head.

'You know, I always wondered what you put those lugs up there for. So you reckon that with the extra field generator set up on the roof inside, the field'll extend to cover LB1 as well? Good thing we had some spares then, eh, but I suppose you had that figured too... You're a bloody wonder, Ned' said Steve.

'Yes,' agreed Toby, 'but if it doesn't work, we'll have a large blob of molten metal upstairs and those looking for us will have a big, unshielded radar blip.'

'Well, no. If there's any problem at any time we can jettison my small friend. The fasteners I used are called pyrotechnic bolts, similar to the ones that hold the space shuttle onto its rocket boosters,' explained Ned. 'I've hooked it so we'll be able to fire them from LB2 using the Dekkos.'

Toby shook his head in wonder. Where would Ned get explosive bolts and why?

'Mail order engineering works. So I could lift things, then drop them' said Ned.

Drop things? On whom?

'Photo opportunity!' yelled Jules, flourishing the Henderson camera and shepherding all to the front of the fly united Ladybirds. She set the timer and ran to join in. Flash.

'Could we test the extra motor?' asked Ned.

'Give it a burl Jules, we'll watch what happens' said Steve. Jules and Solly climbed aboard and fired up the motors; the familiar blue fuzz crept readily over both hulls. Looked good.

'We're just going down the street, Dad' Jules called out and before anyone could argue, had lifted a hundred feet and steamed off down the hill. Ned roared, Toby and Liz complained, Steve just smiled proudly. Chips off the old once around the block.

The final modifications were worked out over a tea made more interesting by the addition of Ned's supplies. Not too bad, really.

'Seems to fly just as good,' said Julie, self appointed test pilot, 'or should I say that the essential flight characteristics are unaltered due to the unique application of force across the entire surface of the craft.' She'd worked on that one.

'Solly and Julie calculate that with the extra batteries we have more than enough range, and if we cut down through Antarctica we might be able to keep out of most trouble' said Toby.

'Might be problem staying out of sight once we get closer.'

'Now however, since everything is working fine on the big yin, we won't be very catchable' opined Ned, sipping malt.

'All very well Ned, but we have to stop sometime, and judging from your reception on Saturday, they shoot first and pick up the pieces afterwards' chided Liz.

'Yair. Just remember you had a big hole through your tail fin, so the shield doesn't make us bullet-proof' added Steve, 'and it's harder to hide Ladybird too, now she's grown a bit.'

'I suppose so,' conceded Ned regretfully, 'but we do need to move on soon anyway, just in case the buggers are on to us.'

'Lets just hope that it's not a case of "little did they know" then,' said Toby hopefully. 'Our problem is, where do we go? With Maria abducted, we've got no-one negotiating for help in Europe. We're still in a bit of a limbo…'

―⁓―

Little did they know, of course, that as they spoke, the blunt, chunky finger of Senator Kelvin Dobrovich was hovering purposefully over the New Zealand Sub Antarctic Islands.

'From the satellite info and the visual sighting halfway to New Zealand, this has to be where they went, Homer. The next damn place in line would be Tierra del Fuego!'

'Well sir, I believe New Zealand is one of our allies, despite what some of its citizens may think. We could get them to locate the craft, land some troops and secure it for us very quickly. The islands are quite close to them.'

'No way!' roared the Senator. 'You think they would give up that gadget? It's landed on their sovereign territory! We'd have a hell of a time extracting it from them. Have we got any of the Pacific fleet nearby?' Chief of Overseas Security Spiggott consulted his staff.

'The aircraft carrier Oklahoma could be in strike range in ten hours sir. We can organize a reconnaissance flight from Australia in the meantime; two of our long range F15K Eagles are visiting there. New Zealand and back is just within range and they can scan the place.'

'Do it. Tell them to fly high and quiet; don't want to spook them if they're there. Oklahoma would have a marine contingent, wouldn't it? Lets hope General Roberts has enough pull with the DOD; otherwise, who do we know in the Navy and Air Force? This damn thing's getting bigger than Ben Hur! Try and keep it tight, Spiggott.' Homer Spiggott reflected privately that if it was any tighter, he wouldn't be able to walk. Too many questions were being asked and he was getting anxious. He knew where buck stopped; with the underlings.

'We would have to clear any flights or landings with New Zealand of course.'

'The islands are uninhabited aren't they? We can let them know later...maybe,' said Kelvin dismissively. Move on. 'And increase the satellite coverage for that area, five hundred miles all around.'

—⁓—

Shirley read through the long text from Graeme, whistled softly and passed it over to Brad and Bobby. They also whistled. The whistling Denzils were taking a break in one of the immaculate North Shore suburban parks, their white rental anonymous sedan parked to the side. The ute had been left in a backstreet; too conspicuous and on its last legs.

'Our espionage person did well, tracking down the kidnappers and setting the dynamic duos onto them,' Shirley commented. 'We'll get some political action in Canberra as well. I know just the radical ratbag senator to stir the possum a bit. Might feed that Evangeline Parsons too, if you can ferret her out, Brad.'

'No worries Mum, we've got a zombie across the road there. Anything else you want? Did you know we got about eight thousand hits on our last web site before they shut it out? Good stuff eh?' The Denzils were doing well; the possum was well stirred. With their skilful mix of fact, sentiment, jingoism and scientific logic, public opinion was gradually coagulating.

—⁓—

Bradley Dyce was maudlin after an extended beer and deals morning. He was not happy. The unfamiliar familial feelings spurred by seeing his kids and Shirley were fading as he realised how much money he had laid out. Now a rental car for them to run around in, and to do what? At times like this, Bradley Snr. had only one person to turn to. 'Yes Mum, I know the kids are great and it wasn't my fault we broke up. Yes Mum. Yes Mum, it's costing me a fortune…' Bradley was in full whinge and didn't need much encouragement from Bess.

'I know son, you've always done the right thing, even when she ran off to the country without a by your leave and you never got to see them for years' complained Bess, cheerfully ignoring the zero maintenance, open access availability (never taken up) and dutifully forwarded school reports (unread).

'Too right. As well as never giving the kids my name. Should have been Bradley and Bobby Dyce, not Denzil. Bloody Shirley!'

'Shirley Bloody Denzil!' agreed Bess…

Backward and forward the cranky little Dyce signals flew, to be scooped up and relayed to the Pine Gap Defence Signals Directorate. LED's flashed; it met criteria on four points in the ECHELON Dictionary and was forwarded as programmed. The message streaked across the Pacific, re-flagged, sped on up to the Office of Overseas Security, walked across to the Chief P/A and trotted into the hand of Homer Spiggott. He scanned it and the orders zipped back to the antipodes.

—⁓—

Bess opened the front door and swore silently at the sight of Mrs. Marge Brindon, the street's ancient font of all gossip. She appeared to be highly amused.

'Hello Mrs. Dyce' she cackled, mysteriously handing Bess an empty egg carton.

'What...?' began Bess, only to be interrupted.

'It's my excuse for being here. It's supposed to be me returning the four eggs I borrowed last week dear. Now don't look around because I've seen it on Crime Investigation Squad and they would have those binocular things and the camera. I don't know what you and your Bradley have been up to and I don't want to know unless you want to tell me but when I was down the corner shop for the milk and the papers Mrs. Johnston said that Mrs. Angionopolis said she saw three men with guns and cameras and those funny jackets being let in the back gate by Mrs. Fenton over the road and you can see the black van they came in still parked down the back lane.' Mrs. Brindon smiled the smile of one who had a story that would last for weeks. Bess willed herself not to even glance over Mrs. Brindon's shoulder at the Fenton upstairs net curtains. She carefully opened the egg carton a little, looked in, smiled and nodded to her.

'Thank you so much for the eggs Mrs. Brindon, and I promise I'll come by and tell you the whole story in a day or two. It's not what it seems... but we better not be chatting for too long. Once again, thank you and bye for now.' Mrs. Brindon winked, Bess shut the door carefully and ran for her mobile praying that the old woman wouldn't look at the Fenton's. Shirley and the kids were due in any moment.

As luck would have it, the Denzils were still four blocks away when Brad answered Shirley's number two mobile.

'Bloody hell! Turn left here Mum! Go go go hurry, get out of here!' Shirley didn't need telling twice. Brad quickly switched off the mobile, pulled out the battery and for good measure, threw the phone out the window. He'd watched the movies. Bobby had too, and was anxiously looking for the inevitable out the back window.

'Mum, there's a big black four wheel drive turned into the street and catching up!'

'Bugger,' swore Shirley, glancing in the mirror and looking desperately around for options. The Denzil brain lightning-noted the blocked main road up ahead, choked with traffic, only two streets left to go, garbage collection day, back lanes and wheelie bins…lots of wheelie bins… 'Hold on kids!' shouted Shirl, lurching into Little Wentworth Lane. The Black Behemoth followed, its massive chrome grill mouthing 'Gotcha!' as it accelerated for the ram. Shirley was not for ramming and being snatched however. She clipped a wheelie bin, noted with satisfaction it bounced off the back fence and leapt out; she weaved ricochet left and right, sending wheelies flying. Inside the black monster the driver laughed, he could climb mountains, what were a few bins? The few bins however quickly became a tumbling tidal wave of ten, fifteen, thirty, loaded with heavy inner city garbage, jamming up against the fences, climbing onto the bonnet. He swore, engaged 4WD and planted the foot. Wheelie bins have to be tough, the massive SUV grunted and clambered through and over them, but they were not to be crushed and cast asunder…

'Goddammit, get moving Frank' roared the Executive agent to the driver, but they weren't moving, despite the thunder of the motor. Nor could they get out, a solid block of wheelies was wedged between the doors and fences. Not until the four agents clambered out the sunroof did the whole catastrophe sink in; their shiny new vehicle was balanced up on a mangled mass of chunky green plastic, embedded in a mound of fetid rubbish and was not for going anywhere. All along Little Wentworth keys were rattling in back door padlocks; the residents were coming out to see what was happening in their back lane to their bins and they would not be happy, John…

⁓⁓⁓

Half an hour later in a deserted industrial car park, the Denzils had transferred their meagre possessions from the battered white rental back into the resurrected ute. Bobby sent an email advising the company of its location, and they all agreed Bradley Senior could sort out the paperwork later.

'Which might be a while,' as Brad explained, 'because Grandma Bess was swearing at some blokes who had just broken through the front door when I switched off the mobile.'

Mother and son would be busy.

Two suburbs worth of backstreets later and they pulled over to conference.

'I would say my dears, that we have worn out our welcome in Sydney so it's the Blue Mountains for us. I just hope that my old mates up there are still as keen to see us and stay anytime, as they said.'

'Didn't you say that was just what we write on Christmas cards because it's Christmas anyway?' asked Bobby innocently.

'Yeah, right. We'll see. Meanwhile, we need a nice loopy trip through the suburbs, away from the tollways and main roads across to Richmond. Then up Hawkesbury Road… shouldn't be any cameras,' said Shirley, adding 'provided this wreck can get up the hills.'

'It's a good ute Mum, don't knock it!'

With Brad monitoring the Dekko and Bobby plotting courses, the family headed west.

—⁓—

Jim Dobson was revelling in the situation while Arabella hunched over her third plastic bag and unravelled. She was never a good traveller but she was a determined one. Ernie Harris sat stoically, feet firmly wedged and sucking on a mintie while Sergeant Baker, hunched over the wheel, wove through the coastal traffic with a constant flow of sotto voce obscenities. Ken was getting to be a worry again; perhaps he needed a refill at the clinic.

'Did you see that bit on the freeway Arabella, we musta been doing over 200 and Jeez when we went between those two semis… I got all of that!' enthused Jim, waving the camera. Arabella grunted sourly, put her plastic bag out the window and rummaged for a notepad and recorder. At least that fucking siren was off and they had slowed a trifle (no don't think about trifle) and must be getting near the airport so they could stop. Please.

Ken took the side road to the hangers and Ernie pointed out the severely bent gate used recently to get access to the aprons. The police Commodore grumbled quietly down the side of one of the hangers.

'Is that them over there?' asked Jim. Four hangers down, the black four-wheel drives were clustered near a twin engined Piper.

'You two get in the front and keep your eyes open. If there is gunfire or other drama, drive to the terminal building and get their security guys to call the local police. Shouldn't be any problems though,' added Ernie as an afterthought. The policemen climbed out, gathered their shotguns from the boot and started walking toward the plane. Arabella and Jim got into the front as directed. As Arabella later recalled, a number of things happened quickly. Ernie and Ken had just set out when they were noticed by one of the agents. There appeared to be some shouting, the plane's engines suddenly coughed into life, five suited figures formed line abreast and started to walk toward the police. Jim swore.

'The buggers are going to get away! Jeez, they're off to torture Miss Scott! No way!'

Jim started the motor, found Drive and planted the foot. When the fishtailing stopped and he had narrowly avoided hitting the policemen, he took aim at the plane, which was beginning to move forward.

'Don't hit it Jim!' screamed Arabella envisioning an aircraft fireball disaster. Nonetheless, she managed to switch on the siren and lights.

'No worries, they're gunna have to stop though.' Jim skidded the Commodore face on to the Piper. All Arabella could see was whirling propellers, getting closer. The nose dipped, the plane stopped. She locked the doors, lifted her notepad and put her professional, albeit somewhat tight smile on. Jim pulled on the handbrake, picked up the camera. They waited to see what would happen next. A gasping George Morton was first to arrive, hammering on the windows. Jim switched off the siren, left the lighting on for effect.

'Move it boy, this plane has clearance and is leaving, now!' wheezed George.

'Could we have a statement from one of the passengers on the plane, Miss Maria Scott, regarding her removal from her home town please' asked Arabella politely, poking the microphone of her recorder out the top of the window.

'This is none of your fucking business. Maria Scott is a terrorist suspect and isn't speaking to anyone. It's illegal to stop this aircraft!' said George, face glowing cherry red. He had pulled his gun out and was emphasizing each point with it. War correspondent intrepid cameraman Jim filmed on.

'I'm afraid you will have to discuss that with our legal team sir' replied Arabella, pointing to the Barangan Police Force facing the uncomfortable line of George's employees. She zipped the window up.

—◦◦◦—

'Bit of a Mexican standoff, Sarge,' said Ernie to Ken. The small, dark suited army had pulled out an assortment of guns, cradled in readiness.

'Yair,' said Ken in a loud voice, 'but a bit unfair on them though. The blokes we took these shotguns off used them for pig shooting… reloaded the shells with ball bearings as I remember.'

'Have to shoot low' added Ernie.

'Probably take both legs right off at this range' reflected Ken cheerfully. A small crowd of interested mechanics and pilots gathered at hanger doors. George Morton came forward to remonstrate.

'Sergeant, we've got full authority to remove this suspect for further questioning. Now since you probably haven't been formally notified as yet I'm prepared to overlook this crap if you remove your car now. This plane has to get to Sydney.'

Ken looked at George with distaste.

'Bullshit, mate. At best, all you've got is a nod and a wink from some bugger in Canberra who would withdraw at the first whiff of scandal. You're not flying to Sydney; you're off to the Marshall Islands or some other overseas base. You illegally removed one of our prisoners, you're forcibly taking an Australian citizen out of the country and one of you coots impersonated a Federal Police Officer. Bring Miss Scott out here, now!' Ernie and Ken glared at George, who glared back. The private army seemed transfixed by the large bore muzzles directed at their reproductive organs, but still kept their own guns ready.

In the end, it was the charter pilot who called a halt; the engines stopped, he climbed down, threw the plane's keys to Ernie and strolled back to his mates at the hanger. George swore, his underlings put their guns away and a very bruised and dazed Maria was carefully helped out of the Piper. She was steered into the back seat of the Commodore and collapsed there.

'Well George, that's a lot better, isn't it' said Ken softly, 'and I can see you've been looking after our Miss Scott.' Ernie winced; Ken's soft voice was his usual introduction into GBH.

'Y'see George,' continued Ken, 'the way I see it is we now have a couple of options to look at. One is that I arrest you right now and take you back to Barangan, have a look at kidnapping, threatening police, assault of said illegally removed prisoner… apart from the $10,000 fine for bringing firearms into an airport. Dunno what the gate would be worth. I reckon these workers of yours are a bit over the idea of stopping us, what with the audience over there, the press, and this artillery. So what do you think there, George? Might wriggle out of it? I guess your company would still have to close up shop and your boss wouldn't be too happy about that, eh?' Ken concluded dolefully. George's face had gone from beetroot to blanched celery. Ernie relaxed; Ken must have learnt acceptable alternatives to gross violence. 'So that leaves a second alternative mate. Maybe Miss Scott travelled with you blokes to have a chat about, umm, Barangan's history and community spirit and we tagged along as an escort. You fellers were so impressed and friendly you decided to give a sizeable donation to the... kiddies fund... in cash, cos I know blokes like you would always carry a bit of a wad... in fact the press were here to record your generosity. I figure $600 would be fair enough. On the spot fine sort of thing.'

'Six hundred fucking dollars! That's extortion! You're fucking joking, you asshole!' George was getting his colour back.

'Make that nine, mate,' said Ken, changing his grip on his shotgun. 'Each. And it would be a good idea too if you and your fake federal took the little plane trip you had organised,' added Ernie, 'because Australia might be a bit difficult for you two. The rest of the blokes can bugger off to Sydney. So what's it to be then. Number one or number two?' asked Ken.

George looked down at the enormous gun barrel. Not much of a choice really.

———

Driving sedately back down the coast with their three passengers, Ernie broached his concern to Sergeant Baker. 'Ken, we can't really keep that money you know.'

Ken looked mortally offended. 'Ernie mate, you've cut me to the quick. Those days are long gone! Apart from a couple of hundred we'll post back for the gate, this bundle is the start of me next project, a bit of a fund for hard up Barangan families. School shoes cost a bloody fortune nowadays.' He handed the roll to Ernie. 'You better hold onto it in case I change me mind though,' he said with a wink.

A little later, heading up into the foothills, Arabella raised her own concerns.

'Ummm, excuse me Sergeant... but do we have to keep the real story quiet, on account of the Kiddies Fund and what you said to that George Morton? I mean, we've got so much good material here, and it's the public's right to know... sort of.' Ernie and Ken looked around at the battered face of Maria and the two young defenders of press freedom. They nodded to each other.

'I reckon in that case, you should do whatever Miss Scott wants,' said Ken.

'Get your notepad out, Arabella, and which side looks worse, young Jim?' said Maria with difficulty, on account of the split lip. 'And Sergeant, could you get us home as quickly as possible please. I have rather a lot of messages and calls to attend to.'

Arabella grimaced, reaching for the plastic bags, along with her notepad.

Ms. Montague sensed the power of history beneath her fingers as she typed the last dispatch and sent it sliding off on very secret paths to all of the branches of The Alliance. Ever since its formation deep within the great imperial trading John Company of the 17th century, The Alliance always had unsurpassed communications with the best horses, the fastest ships and no expense spared. And such a structure! Over three centuries, the development of the Courts of Directors and Proprietors and operational groups under the leadership of the Head Factors. All who would be lost, she knew, unless supported by the Council of Arrangers. Initially the cosseted living repositories of information, the Arrangers provided safety for The Alliance when written records had become dangerous. Their memory skills, organizational ability and a natural freedom from emotional and social reciprocity had propelled the Arrangers into their pivotal position. As the Principal Factor, New York, had once tried to explain to her:

'The Court of Proprietors are the owners and passengers of this great ship, The Alliance. The Court of Directors are the ships officers and the Factors are the ships masters. All are important, but you, my dear, as Principal Arranger, are the ship's navigator and helmsman. You are the one who knows where we are and where we are going.' New York had then explained what an analogy was. Ms. Montague understood her role completely and didn't like analogies.

She had gained her position as Principal Arranger when Mr. Allen retired some nineteen years earlier. Mr. Allen had spent three months inducting her into the complete history, the running and magnificent scope of the Alliance. At the end, he had formally handed her the small, highly ornate Arrangers Key and for the first time she had seen him displaying... emotion. He had quickly recovered his composure when her distaste became apparent, but it was a most uncomfortable moment!

'I apologise for my lapse, Ms. Montague, but the prospect of leaving this position, which has been my entire life, is a little difficult. I look forward to my retirement of course,' he had said, visibly brightening, 'with the opportunity to at last complete my collation of Virginian Railway Timetabling 1870 to 1898.' Mr. Allen poured tea. 'You understood that up until the Annual Alliance Meeting of 1892, Principal Arrangers were expected to kill themselves immediately upon completion of their great task. This is no longer permitted by the Court of Directors, of course.'

He appeared to be waiting. Ms. Montague understood. Although the Directors may have banned the tradition, the possibility of a retired Principal Arranger sliding into babbling dementia or somehow exposing the Alliance was too great. She sipped her tea.

'How long will it take for your timetable collating to be completed, Mr. Allen?' she had asked conversationally. Mr. Allen had almost beamed.

'Fourteen months to the day, Ms. Montague.'

She made a mental note. Later, she had made arrangements.

Ms. Montague moved into her next tasks. Her specialists had located the two machines south of New Zealand; her sleepers in the Department of Defence had fed in negative risk assessments and the Pentagon was reacting usefully. The interest shown by Overseas Security in this affair was being carefully monitored but so far they were not in any position of power. Unlike, however, the Denzil woman and her two sons; remarkably successful in gathering support for the Tilda consortium. Taking this new, uncontrolled technology into the world economy posed the greatest threat since The East India Company Act of 1773! An even worse threat, as the Company Act merely pressed The Alliance to greater secrecy and ruthless efficiency. So, to deal with the Sydney problem. She quickly reviewed records, sent off an anonymous email directive and a funding transfer...

—∿∿—

'Dammit Homer, Morton blows a simple rendition, the Denzil woman escapes again and now you tell me Horowitz may be involved in both these stuff ups!'

'It's the most likely scenario Senator, but no solid evidence of course; he's a good agent. There may be a positive aspect though...' said Homer Spiggott, soothingly. 'It is just possible he is still in touch with Shirley Denzil, who may or may not know where the devices are going to and how to communicate with the crews.'

'Lots of maybes there Homer, but if Horowitz has gone native, we can use it. I've got to fly out there so get onto the airfield and have my plane fuelled.' Homer sighed. The Senator had done a lot of hard flying over the last year in a plane, which, in Homer's opinion, had been cheap to buy for good reason. As a prototype, it had been chopped and changed, pushed to the limits, rebuilt and sold off. On its last flight a month ago, with a terrified Homer on board, both engines needed re-starting mid air. Thankfully, not at the same time. The manufacturers, made aware of the public relations disaster a dead Senator might generate, were still overhauling the very, very early model Cougar. When Homer told his boss about his return to passenger status, he sank into dark brooding thought and scribbled mutterings. Always lots of arrows and boxes on the Dobrovich desk pad. Homer waited patiently.

'Fifty thousand Australian currency, first flight you can get to Sydney, gun, secure cell phone, trackers, scanners, passports, clearances, whatever else I'll need Homer. No one else to know. I'm home sick with the plague. Get Horowitz up to Sydney and waiting, no briefing and let him sweat.

I want my jet back together and flown out to me as soon as. Three hours, Homer!'

—◦◦◦—

Solly, Jules and their Mum sat back from the Dekko screen.

'Heavens above! Well, it's the best chance, I suppose,' said Liz.

'I guess so,' said Jules,' but it means we've got to do more modifications.'

They sat for a few moments, each thinking through the plan.

'All right,' said Liz decisively, 'get the blokes to the table and we'll have a cuppa…'

Over sandwiches and tea, Toby pre-empted what he thought they were facing.

'It seems that those chasing us are able to track us as well. They'll probably pick us up again once we're airborne and I dare say have a welcoming committee there whenever we slow down. Sorry to be gloomy.' He chewed on his sandwich, reflecting that the bread was getting a bit stale, too.

'If they've tracked us here,' added Ned, 'they probably will have set up surveillance. I'd say that they could use optical satellite scanning tuned to the blue spectrum for night-time and daytime would be easy. I'm afraid my dears, that we're up against it. We may have to head back to Australia, make ourselves very public and hope for the best…'

'Indeed,' agreed Toby, 'we don't seem to have planned this very well. Stay here and freeze or go back to Australia and get shot down, blown up or whisked away.'

Ned and Toby looked morosely into their tea.

'You're right, big problem, but we're way ahead of you' announced Jules.

'Rock my soul is the only way, in the bosom of Abraham. It's a good plan,' added Solly.

'So how does the old testament fit in?' asked their father.

'So wide we can't get round it and so low we can't go under it, except underwater but it's too far' said Jules. 'However…'

'They do have a plan,' said Liz, 'but it scares the living daylights out of me…'

The blokes again looked enquiringly.

'Well… do you think that your carbon dioxide scrubber could be boosted up a bit?' asked Jules, 'and do we have much oxygen left? Will the seals handle a vacuum?'

Ned finally twigged.

'Holy Mary Mother of God!'

—⁓—

The temperature outside the hut had plummeted for those working in Ladybird.

'Next bloody model will have an on board toilet' said Steve later through chattering teeth as he came inside. The ever practical Liz announced that they had designed an en suite; she would set up five litre plastic cereal containers and a screen.

'It's great!' announced Solly to the blokes with joy, 'It's got this flip up lid… '

Steve, Toby and Ned shuffled back out to continue their work while the rest of the crew, cosy in the hut, monitored the Dekko and packed up. Sean of course, was curled in front of the stove absorbing most of its warmth.

—⁓—

Shirley shivered as the cold Katoomba wind whipped around her legs.

'They need proper Dr. Who boxes up here Mum, not these things' protested Bobby, rapping on the flimsy plastic sides of the public phone. Shirley could only agree. A thousand metres higher than Sydney, the Blue Mountains generally ran to frosty. She shushed Bobby as the connection came through.

'Hello, Senator Kelly, can you talk at the moment? Good. Yes, no names or identifiers please. You obviously got the phone and the material I sent to you then. Yes. I thought you might be interested and all the information in there is first hand... Now, about the statement to the Senate and the list of questions I included... you're happy and want to add in... well I can only agree with you there, Senator...' Shirley finished the call a few minutes later, grinning at Bobby. 'No wonder they named him Dan after Ned Kelly's brother! Said he'd have the phone on midnight to six am and is dead keen to 'get stuck into the buggers'. He wants a royal commission into Maria's abduction and a protection order for us. Reckons the 'Ladybird Jiggers' are bloody marvellous and need full government support... Now for the next call.'

Shirley's call to Evangeline Parsons QC was equally successful. Ramifications, legal loopholes and available lawful avenues flowed like a river from the Parsons' brain. Evangeline guaranteed the full weight of the Parsons Team behind the Barangan 7, Ladybird crews and themselves. Pro Bono and Toot Sweet. Evangeline's VIP list of owed favours could be called on. Anything else they needed? Cash? Place to stay in Sydney?

Shirley and offspring were well pleased as they drove down the winding, rain-forested road to the isolated farmhouse in the

Megalong Valley. They were welcomed at the door by Sue Nelson; Shirl's old mate from Sydney days, and most of her numerous children. Her scruffy partner Danny, vague and unchanged since Shirley had last seen him, left to split wood for the stove. Sue herself had evolved from the self-centred, floaty-love-power-flower child into a plumper, far wiser earth-business mother. She had summarised their history for Shirl while they finished cooking tea:

'Been up in the Megalong fourteen years and almost locals now… bloody well should be; this brood is the only reason the local school has stayed open… moved here because they did proper winters… Sydney's choking in its own wastes…done a lot of things with the farm, free range game birds, chooks and the organic Pinot Noir seems to have been the best bet so far, supply the best Blue Mountains restaurants and do an Internet niche market with the wine. Danny does some fencing and woodcutting as well. Guess most of the kids will end up back down in Sydney for work though… bit of a circle, eh?'

After an impressive dinner of organic pheasant, fresh veggies and harvest pear cake, they settled into the best pinot and chat. The impressive sandstone cliffs nearby meant no TV reception, but Sue and Danny remembered newspaper accounts of the flying saucer shenanigans. Danny dug out an unmulched back issue showing Shirley holding forth majestically to the assembled Barangans and Ladybird 2 framed in the background.

'Never picked it as being you Shirley,' said Sue incredulously, 'though I knew you lived down that way from the Christmas cards. Your friends built these things after the young ones came up with the idea? Holy moly! You reckon they're off to get it tested somewhere? Well we could certainly do with one; this place is a bugger to get out of if it snows. Can't deliver the chooks. What you reckon Danny?'

Danny had been sitting quietly, looking off into space. Shirley wasn't sure he had been keeping up with the conversation. He had been.

'You are aware of just how much a change this 'Ladybird' machine will make? We're talking major unemployment and disruption here. The oil industry just for a start, and sure, at the sucking it out of the ground end we can do without Dubai's obscene conspicuous consumption, but at the other end add up all the service stations, motor mechanics, whole car industry turned on its head, shipping, transport …Then there's all the other carbon based industries… coal miners, power stations…' Danny launched into a ten minute speculative economic discourse, which left Shirley reeling. Three parts incomprehensible but very authoritative. 'It's going to stuff up the entire trade, industrial and fiscal structure of the world!' he finished bluntly. Shirley looked at Sue and slowly blinked.

'Yeah. Danny finished a doctorate in Business Economics early nineties,' said Sue proudly, 'smart bugger. Still took a long time to get this place working economically, mind you. Too many variables, at least that's his story…'

'Well we did talk about disruption a bit,' said Shirley defensively, 'and we thought that once things settled down everyone would be a lot better off, economically and environmentally like. We figured that people at the top end would lose out most and would be pissed off on account of that and try and stop it going ahead…'

'Wouldn't be at all surprised' said Danny with a grin. 'I was wondering why energy stocks were doing a nosedive. You and your mates have certainly stirred the possum, no worries! Might be a bit rough for a while I suppose, an entire new industrial revolution arriving in the space of a few weeks… but it would certainly clean up the greenhouse. There'll be a whole lot of things needing sorting. Anyway, Cheers! Here's to living in interesting times!'

The discourses continued into the night with spirited excursions into many problem and possibility areas. Shirley hammered key points into a document on the laptop, along with a progress report, some radical suggestions and numerous felicitations/congratulations from all in the Megalong

Kelvin Dobrovich paced his second DVT circuit of the Airbus, eyes surreptitiously scanning faces out of habit. He stopped by the window at the rear of the aircraft, staring down on the moonlit clouds. Fourth row economy, third across… who the hell was it? Goddamn brain was packing it in. Concentrate! Starts with a P… Patrick… Peter… Paul… Paolo! Paolo Cappaldi! Goddamn Paolo Cappaldi, one of the most cunning and successful freelance killers to come out of Europe. A lot older of course, different hair and a beard, maybe a nose job, but definitely him. Kelvin did some half-hearted stretches on the window frame. Top echelon killer flying to Australia… expensive… and as far as he knew, there wasn't any current high cost assassination risks in the land down under. People like Capaldi didn't go on holidays either… sort of professional a major player might commission to remove annoyances. Kelvin did not believe in coincidences. He took a tired business executive stroll back to his business class seat without a sideward glance and got to work on his agency satellite phone.

Paolo Capaldi did not expect any trouble from immigration or customs; he was essentially a quiet, polite, law abiding citizen with immaculate paperwork and nothing to declare. He was patient with the delays in unloading the plane; after all, this was to be expected in anonymous economy class. He lifted his blue suitcase from the carousel and moved out to the taxi rank, unaware of the tiny scanning transmitter now embedded in its frame. Kelvin was sitting well back in the "taxi" ASIO had provided for their high profile visitor. He instructed the driver to be very, very damn careful not to lose his target.

'Great tracking bug, fresh out of our lab, but it aint no damn good until it's switched on,' he said amiably to the fiercely concentrating assigned agent. He would activate after Capaldi had a chance to check his bag over, after which the EB-J275/F would track positions, listen in on conversations, phone calls, radio, or obligingly blow itself to bits if requested.

Capaldi checked into a motel outside the CBD and Kelvin slipped into the one next door. After two hours, agent

Dobrovich switched on his whiz-bang monitor and was rewarded with a carefully worded phone call, almost certainly organizing some hardware. Nice. The backtracks would give ASIO a good lead to a high-class arms supplier... later. Agent Dobrovich (he liked the sound of that, after so many years) gave the assigned driver a job.

'OK friend, it doesn't look like Capaldi is going anywhere in a hurry, so go fetch me one of those little cars you drive in this country. Find one with air conditioning.'

'They all have air conditioning, sir,' muttered the driver, through clenched teeth, 'It's just that the department wants us to limit its use... environment and economy thing.'

'And two bottles of Jack Daniels' added Kelvin as an afterthought.

Later that night, Graeme tapped on the door using the code and was let in by Agent Senator Dobrovich. Carefully placing his handgun in the bar fridge as directed, he collected a soft drink and sat. His boss obviously had serious issues to discuss.

'Horowitz, you've got one thing between you and a quick flight back to the States and a life in prison. You don't switch sides if you work in my department.' Graeme ran arguments like lack of evidence, a good service record and natural justice briefly through his head. Then remembered whom he worked for.

'What's the one thing then, Sir?'

'Me. Along with the fact that I know you can probably put me in touch with this Shirley Denzil woman. Let me also add that I am prepared to help these folk you've hitched up with and that they are in serious danger. Everybody wins.' The senator looked at his agent shrewdly and lifted his glass of bourbon. Graeme slid into the new arrangement.

'What is the nature of this danger Sir? We are talking about a family unit here, very vulnerable and with a positive public profile. They deserve our protection.'

Kelvin gave Graeme a bourbon and a clap on the shoulder. He ran through the flight encounter, his suspicions, bugging, trailing, and arms order.

'Since then, Homer's got a definite connection between Capaldi and that badass bunch The Alpha Club. Twenty minutes back Capaldi sent a brief text, probably confirming his arrival, and Homer says it is opening up a whole new box of links for us. Interesting. Capaldi's target has to be the Denzils. Enough of a clear and present danger for you boy?'

Graeme sat and thought it through. Shirley, Brad and Bobby had no choice but to work with Dobrovich if they were up against an organisation employing someone like Capaldi. He looked at the corpulent, grey senator and wondered if his field and weapons skills were up for it. Kelvin caught the appraising glance.

'I might be a little rusty, but I'm not out to pasture yet, agent,' he said sourly. He snapped open a large suitcase and displayed a high-powered rifle, lethal machine pistols and a variety of other weaponry. Graeme whistled. 'Yeah, we've got some nice equipment on loan from the Aussies, so I don't plan on doing anything too close and intimate. We sit here until Capaldi makes his move, then follow on.' Graeme nodded, and then with a question mark shrug, asked, 'I can get in touch with Shirley Denzil, warn her to be careful…'

'No. They might have some sort of a tag on her, so we'll stay schtum until we know. Let them do the work in tracking her down.' Dobrovich downed his drink. 'That's your bed over there. You can take a walk and get us some takeout food, although god knows what sort of eateries they have out here. Leave your cell phones behind too…'

―⁓―

We can now track the location of their communicator devices Ms. Montague. They use an extreme frequency and unusual signal pattern. We are not able to break the code as yet as it changes with each signal. A number, probably a preloaded contextual base, precedes each message. Simple, but very effective,' said the technician, beginning to warm to detail, 'it means that although we can pick up semantic patterns within each particular signal text, we can't delineate enough of the...umm...' He pulled himself up as he noticed the pursed Montague lips. 'Sorry Ms., the messages have been tracked to the Sydney area and to the Snares Island group, south of New Zealand.'

'So. Monitor both communicators, miss nothing. Break their code. Keep me informed.' Ms. Montague waved the technician away and her lips unpursed into the semblance of a smile. Good. Now she that she could track her opponents she could target her actions more efficiently. Capaldi would locate the Denzils and remove them. The flying machine however would be more difficult. Ms. Montague contemplated, sharpened and chose. It was definitely the time to use her extreme option, a project she had hidden in West Africa near Matadi in The Democratic Republic of Congo. Five hours to activate?

She picked up the phone.

—⁓—

Steve switched off the oxy-acetylene torch and pushed up the welding goggles.

'Should do it Tobes, but it's the wildest exhaust system I've ever put together. The wooden bits should be OK because the generator doesn't put out much heat and the pressure bleed valves should work. The new aerial has a good seal too.'

'Just so long as the bloody thing doesn't leak with all the extras,' said Toby, 'because I'm not too sure how well Solly's Blu Tac will go in an emergency. I suppose it does constitute a plan B though....'

—⁓—

The Denzils were out next morning, climbing a small hill, which Sue assured them gave mobile reception. It was time to communicate with the friendly spook in Barangan. She settled onto a shaded rock and composed a long SMS while Brad and Bobby set up the mini Dekko. The only other inhabitants, a small mob of wallabies across a gully, lost interest and went back to grazing. Over morning tea, the family conferred.

'That Graeme Horowitz is a worry. He has to go to Sydney because his boss is coming and he might be in a bit of strife. One good thing though, he says Maria was rescued by Ernie and Ken Baker, along with that Arabella Swift and Jim Dobson. They managed to get her off a plane just before it took off. He's given her a mobile too… so many numbers…' said Shirley, busy copying the new one into her little black book. 'Crank up your baby there, Bobby, and fire all this off to our pals in Ladybird, as well as to Maria.'

'Mrs. Henderson says they are freezing in the Snares and that they are doing some more work on the Ladybird,' announced Bobby later. 'They'll probably set off again tomorrow. We sent everything to them and they all send their love. Nothing back from Miss Scott.'

'Thanks sweeties, well done.' Thoughtfully, she dipped her ginger nut. 'No worries. After that we better slip back down for lunch.'

—∿∿—

'Another two special communicator messages from the Snares Islands and one reply from Australia, in a place called the Megalong Valley, Ms. We have refined the tracking and have both locations to within a quarter mile. Still no progress on the code used I'm afraid.' The technician handed Ms. Montague a printout of the two sets of coordinates.

The Montague steel point pen swiftly scrawled onto the pad. Rip, rip.

'This to the Matadi unit and this to Capaldi.' The tech scurried off.

—∿∿—

'Get up and moving boy!' boomed Kelvin, 'Capaldi's had a call and is on the road.'

Graeme hauled himself off the bed and started packing. 'Leave that crap, just the artillery and the tracker. We'll go in that compact Ford they got me' barked the senator, pointing out the door to the Falcon. 'Homer tells me the Alphas messaged a place in West Africa, including coordinates for a research station on The Snares Islands, same place I figured the fliers would be. Question is, how can they find them when we can't? Capaldi's call had coordinates of someplace called Megalong Valley so I guess that's where your Denzil family is. Or did you already know that?' Graeme shook his head and finished loading the car. Kelvin climbed into the driver's seat and grinned at him, pointing to a large strobe unit on the dash. 'Capaldi's bound to take the back roads; we'll take the expressway and use this. Give us time to set up a little reception.' Graeme pulled out his mobile and raised his eyebrows enquiringly.

'No way,' said agent Dobrovich, 'lets give the little Aussie family a surprise...'

Just on an hour later the agent's car was nearing the Denzil hideout. Kelvin drove quietly along a dirt track, winding through a thick eucalypt forest.

'Should be about a mile further on, once we clear these trees' said Graeme, showing his boss the on-screen aerial photo, complete with its cute little glowing red car and farmhouse.

'When we get there you can...Goddamn!' swore Kelvin softly, pointing at the exposed corner of a car, a hundred metres off. 'He must have got away earlier. Took a while for the decoding. Damn.' Dobrovich was out of the car, reaching into the back seat and grabbing the suitcase. 'Drive to the farmhouse. Take it slow and ring your friend on the way so they won't freak out with the car. Tell them all to stay inside.' Graeme slid across as Kelvin jumped out and softly closed the driver's door. There was no need of further instruction. He was the tethered goat; Dobrovich the great white hunter. He keyed Shirley's number onto his phone in readiness then opened his briefcase. A quick change of dress was called for... bit like Superman, he thought.

Paolo Capaldi settled himself comfortably into his bush and slipped off the safety catch. He set the photocopy on a branch next to the high-powered hunting rifle and looked at it carefully. Tall woman, late thirties early forties, dressed in a long flowing costume standing on a makeshift stage. Rural Opera? He knew nothing of his targets, cared even less.

Clear field, 300 metres; he adjusted the telescopic sight.

'Come out little fish,' he murmured. A car emerged from the trees to his left and crept very slowly along the road toward the farmhouse. He swung the rifle onto it and studied the suited, nondescript driver. A businessman, out of place and uncomfortable in the countryside. Paolo grunted with satisfaction. He may not have to wait long for the target to appear…

Agent Horowitz fumed helplessly. Shirley's phone, of course, wouldn't answer, no damn coverage. He couldn't turn back, there was every chance Capaldi may have heard or seen the car. As much as he could do was to try and use the car as a shield and hope that Shirley or the kids didn't appear… and trust that Dobrovich was a hunter of skill. He could feel the crosshairs lined up on his head… the bullet would come from somewhere off to his right.

'Mum! There's a white car coming up to the front of the house…' said Brad urgently from the window, 'there's only one person in it… dude in a suit… it's OK though, pretty sure it's Mr. Horowitz. How'd he find us?'

'Don't know Brad. Pretty sneaky, those spy fellers' said Shirley, looking over his shoulder.

'Definitely him though. Tell Sue and Danny and I'll go find out why he's here.'

She walked toward the front door.

Graeme wheeled the Falcon in a big circle, pulling up in front of the farmhouse. Not appearing to rush but moving swiftly, he climbed out, opened the gate. His hands in front made frantic go back signs but Christ Almighty the front door was opening! The purposeful walk turned into a mad scramble up the steps... A fist smashed into Graeme's back, slamming him forward at Shirley's feet.

'Geddown' he gasped, grabbing her ankle and heaving; she pitched forward as stoneware potted ferns exploded behind her. Luckily, the Nelsons were into big pot plants and they cowered behind the largest bromeliads as more bullets whanged off the iron railings or slammed into the converted oil drums. Shirley was screaming to Brad and Bobby to stay away from the front of the house when a loud roar echoed across the front paddock... and the bullets stopped.

Kelvin dropped the Anschluss 25AZ rocket launcher, pulled his automatic out and lumbered rhino-like toward the smoking clump of bushes a hundred yards off. Hoping to God that he had got it right. Was sure he had spotted a puff of smoke and a glint of metal there. If it was the wrong bush he was easy meat, a lot bigger and slower than he used to be. Gasping, he carefully pushed a tattered branch aside to see a blood splattered shoe and ankle hanging by a strip of flesh. Other bits were scattered around a small crater.

More a case of half a dozen shopping carriers than a body bag, he observed to himself. Damn powerful thing, the new 25AZ...

Back in the house, Shirley hugged her kids. Graeme pulled off his ruined suit coat and the now somewhat shop-soiled flack vest. He gingerly felt his back and concluded he had a possible cracked rib and certainly some massive bruising. He walked over the paddock to talk to his boss.

—∿∿—

Chapter Thirteen

One a.m. saw Toby and Steve having a nightcap with Ned in front of the stove's opened firebox. The rest of the crew was sensibly asleep. Sean, with inexplicable cat logic, had leapt up on Ned's lap, was now curled and purring. Ned's initial attempt to remove him had resulted in punctured thighs, so he was forced to follow the amused advice of staying inert. At least the claws retracted. He'll get bored soon, was the tentative hypothesis.

Toby swirled his second scotch and decided.

'At the risk of sounding a bit chicken hearted, do you two think we've taken on a bit too much? That all of this is just a bit too mad? We're not exactly the stuff heroes are made of, are we. Like, apart maybe from you, Ned, none of us have done anything like this before…'

'And I'm a bit past it? Yes indeed, almost certainly, Toby.' Ned waved Toby's protests down. 'Heroes are not demigods; heroes are ordinary people who find themselves in dangerous spots and do what they have to do. Like those hotel workers at the Taj in Mumbai, staying to save their guests from terrorists. Like you, flying LB2 into hiding and saving the Hendersons!'

'Reckon,' agreed Steve. 'You did what was needed Tobes. And even though I'm shit-scared for the kids and us, this bloody field thing is so important to get up and running that we all have to stick with it. Even if it's a bit mad.'

They all sat sipping on their inner necessities.

'Meanwhile, this cat, who is not a hero, is a hell of a weight on my lap,' said Ned, 'and since I can't go to bed, he's an excuse for another drink.' He was holding out his glass when Sean's head lifted with a low growl.

'You'll not be for restricting my drinking you mangy mog,' said Ned firmly.

'Shh... I think he can hear something' said Toby, experienced cat owner.

They sat still, straining their ears. Sean leapt down, went to the door. The faintest whistle grew quietly to the softest rumble then dopplered down and away to nothingness. It bought them all to their feet.

'Twin engined fighter!' yelled Ned. 'Get into Ladybird and onto the Dekko Steve, see if he's talking. Toby, fire up the engines and get the field up. He's probably already picked us up on his ground radar. Bugger! We may have to get out of here quickly.' Steve and Toby fled out the door. Liz, Jules and Solly were wakened and hurriedly dressed while Ned bundled possessions and food into bags and boxes. The four scrambled into Ladybird, Ned slammed the doors shut.

'Field's on' called Toby from the pilot's seat.

'I think there's two of them' said Steve, 'and they picked us up right enough. They've sent a message to something called Oklahoma and want to know whether to attack. Hold on...' Steve listened intently. 'No, told to return to base in Australia... quite happy about that... Oklahoma will be in range in four hours. Don't want us scared off... That's it, they've both signed off.' Steve put the headphones down and looked around. Ned sighed and grimaced.

'We can't stay, the Oklahoma is one of their biggest aircraft carriers and I bet they're planning a surprise landing with full air cover. We need to go, as soon as possible.'

'Well we can't just leave right now anyway,' said Solly. 'Like, who's missing? Sean went for a walk when we moved into Ladybird and you might remember the first night he didn't come back till about dawn when he went out,' said Solly in explanation, 'and of course we can't go without him.'

'He's used to living with people, what would he eat?' added Jules.

'Probably everything...' muttered Ned, acknowledging they would not leave Seanless. Snared. For a cat! Also hoisted on his own wildlife conservation petard! Secretly though, he admitted to a growing affection and a grudging respect for the ruggedly independent Sean.

As it was, it was touch and go with Sean. Dawn had broken, daylight was certainly well established and according to the increasingly anxious Steve and Liz on the Dekko, a whole bunch of helicopters with fighter escort were less than a hundred kilometres off. Plaintive calls of pusspusspuss and rattling the Cat Crunchies box did nothing. Ned stormed around, demanding take-off in five minutes or they wouldn't have a chance in hell of avoiding the advancing horde.

'Do we have a microphone?' asked Toby desperately, putting the stereo speakers on the steps outside. They did, and watched bemused as he sent the amplified sound of a tin of cat food opening up into the hills. Halfway through the third tin, Sean streaked up the steps.

'You'll just have to hang onto the carpet with those claws of yours, tardy cat!' yelled Ned, slamming the doors shut and locking them. He scrambled into his seat and strapped himself in while the rest of the crew ran through a very abbreviated flight check. The field went up.

'The fighters were told to attack as soon as the field went up, must have someone up high and scanning us,' shouted Steve, 'less than two minutes off they reckon.'

'Vents all closed' called Jules.

Ned lifted smoothly and rotated, angled the nose up and fed in as much power as he thought the crew could handle. Toby and Jules, a little strained, called instruments. Somehow Ned had managed to find Dvorak's Carnival Overture on the i-pod; not quite a soothing piece, but appropriate to the occasion. At 5000 feet he rotated and they saw a multitude of dots crowding over the eastern horizon. Others had skirted around, were approaching from the west. Afterburners on, fully armed and with 20,000 feet of height advantage. Acceleration was the only way they could outrun the barrage.

'The first lot have launched missiles' shouted Liz, 'and could you drop the volume Ned!'

'Mach one point two.'

Ned veered strongly to port. Air to air missiles streaked along at Mach 3 or 4, but these would be unable to use their infrared tracking sensors. He could dodge.

'Mach one point nine, height 8000.'

'Second lot launched' yelled Steve. Ladybird corkscrewed further to port and up, traversing the field of fire rapidly. All of Sean's sixteen toe claws were anchored in the carpet. Cat Velcro. The first set of missiles flashed past on the right.

'Mach two point four, height 10,000.'

'They're firing independently now.' Getting smarter, thought Ned. Starboard and climb. A good guess pair of missiles shot past the window, much too close. Bit of left and right to throw their aim off... more height... and we should be well away from the main mob. Toby and Julie were searching for 'them upstairs.'

'About two o'clock and up a fair bit' said Jules, pointing to make sure. Toby and Ned caught the glint of six dots, well spaced out and boring down.

'Oh dear. Got a bit ahead of us unfortunately... we've got less than a minute... strap up tight' shouted Ned, levelling off and banking hard to port, 'sorry about this...'

'Sorry about wh...' began Toby, only to be slammed back in his seat as Ned bought the power up to full. Bit bloody desperate, he thought, before the world went brown, then black...

When the crew recovered consciousness, Ned apologized profusely.

'The problem we had,' he explained, 'was that their six dots were going to intersect our one dot at unmissable range unless we moved very quickly. We haven't tried full bore before, but it produced about seven g's and got us to Mach 6!' he added proudly. 'Speed freak...' muttered Toby, shaking his head to clear it.

'All right for those with g-suits on' agreed Liz.

'Oh I'm sure it wasn't too bad... its what we call in the trade a brief eyeballs-in g-loc... but it bought us up to speed in about 30 seconds...' Ned did a quick calculation and beamed.

'About 7000 kph, which is a new world speed for a manned aircraft!'

'Mach 6 at 36,000 feet is only 6356 kph' stated Solly.

'Interesting when we overtook two missiles that went past looking lost' added Ned.

'Mr. McZed,' said Liz with broken glass in her voice, 'We are not going to go through a situation like that again... ever... so stop being so bloody gung ho. Where are we?'

'Umm, about four hundred kilometres south of the Snares, cruising at 200 knots,' said Jules, 'with 60% battery left. The fuel consumption goes way up when you speed.'

'As always...' said Steve. 'We'll need to charge up again before we do any big hops'

Ladybird hovered at a thousand feet while the generator re-charged Steve triple checked all of the work done. Liz checked the Dekko.

'A message from Maria at last! Must be back from her little romp on the coast. Not good news though, she's able to send out enquiries to Europe using their Dekko, but nothing's coming back. Phone calls and Internet just drop out. Barangan must be all sealed up. Says she'll go for a drive.'

'Meanwhile, and again, where's the destination?' asked Toby. 'Going home is sounding better, from what Shirl says; she's scored a Senator, a Barrister and a Shock Jock so far. We could land in Martin Place... And a good question,' he added, 'is why the attack was so full on back at the Snares? There was no negotiation, no demands to surrender.'

'As soon as we were airborne the order went out to totally destroy the target,' said Liz quietly, '…meaning us. They know that we aren't terrorists, especially with Shirley and the kids getting the message out, so it's a quite deliberate decision. Also Toby, I think the people who are running this show have too much influence back home for us to return.'

'Scandinavia. Has to be Scandinavia' announced Solly. 'Sweden, Norway, Denmark, they've got all the good gear to check the field.'

'And the right attitude too' added Jules.

'You're just getting a bit twitchy on our travels plans mate' said Steve. 'But whatever. Which one of those countries is in the middle? We still have a very aggressive navy over the horizon so we're going. Swiftly. All agreed?' All the hands went up.

Toby gritted his teeth and nodded. No arguments there.

———∿∿∿———

Ms. Montague looked up as the underling coughed nervously. Bad news obviously.

'There's another communication device operating, from Barangan, Ms. Montague'

'And? What else?'

'We intercepted more text messages from the flying device, Ms., but the location has changed.' He handed her the data sheet.

'Was a signal sent to Matadi to abort?'

'Immediately, Ms. Montague. Luckily they still had two minutes to launch.'

Ms. Montague glowered. She held no truck with luck.

———∿∿∿———

On the wind-swept Snares, a huddled colony of five hundred Snares penguins were definitely in luck. The comfortable inner circle, with uncanny prescience and an existential urge for hypotheticals were discussing the joys being very, very cosy for even a microsecond. It was not to be. Ms. Montague's private long range tactical nuclear missile now simmered gently on 60 minute alert to go just about anywhere else on the planet.

Life can be so krill, one penguin on the outer edge (for good reason) quipped.

—⁂—

'Everybody comfortable?' called Toby from the pilot's console, 'then we shall begin.' Julie grinned and winked at him as she ran her hand over the new auxiliary control stick hastily cobbled together. Liz, Steve and Solly raised thumbs.

'Dekko's on, no radio traffic, all ready' called Liz.

'Pumps and CO_2 extractor's are cool. We're all sealed up tighter than a fish's,' said Steve.

'Sean's not happy but the cat cage seems to be holding together,' announced Solly.

'Just as well…' muttered Toby, looking at his new bandaids.

'Flight deck check affirmative roger wilco etcetera' called Ned cheerily, 'and today we have a special treat on our in house entertainment!' The haunting sitar, birdsong and water chuckle music of Sangeet floated out of the speakers.

'Ahhh…a bit quieter than our last departure,' said Toby happily. The motors were up to a satisfying, Solly monitored hum. Liz was calling out reports and locations from the Dekko; Steve tapped his gauges and made adjustments. Toby, Jules and Ned consulted on flight plans in muted mutters. Sangeet's sitar sang…

Ladybird lifted gently, high above the wild southern seas. The sun was setting, had been for the last hour, softening the scene with an overlay of pink. Liz typed quick messages to Shirley and Liz and fired them off. All the goss and more.

'We'll start our first intersection course if you could give us a hand with the calculations, Flight Engineer Solly' asked Toby politely. Solly grinned.

'Head north-northwest at about at about three thirty degrees and accelerate at around one g and it shouldn't take too long. Climb to at least three hundred thousand feet for the first intersection'

'About thirty-three degrees? Around one g? Shouldn't take too long? Solomonder seems to be getting a bit mellow...' said Ned to Toby.

'Accepting imprecision,' retorted Toby, 'lots of it about.' Ned pulled gently on the throttle and they pressed back into their assorted car seats. Steve started the generator, 'just to give it a run and keep the batteries charged up while we're still down here... and make sure it won't spifflicate us...'

It purred quietly without a whiff.

'Should be coming up from the horizon about now, out the front right drivers side window ' called Liz.

'Starboard side observation panel...' muttered Ned.

'Yairrsss...' said Jules eventually 'It's that one there, moving and very big, at ten o'clock.'

More than three hundred kilometres higher than them and traveling at twenty-seven thousand kilometres an hour, the International Space Station hurtled silently through the void. Solly looked and calculated the second leg.

'Twelve minutes fourteen seconds if we angle up at fifty two degrees, maintain one point one five g and alter course to forty seven point five' he announced to Ned, 'sort of north east and up a bit, around about, give or take...' Ladybird swivelled to the right, and the nose lifted a little. The earth dropped away and the wisps of Cirrus cloud lacing the Southern Ocean shrank away. The stars above them hardened and lost their twinkle. Jules pulled out the Henderson digital camera and snapped some shots.

Totally mad, thought Toby. The Henderson children and mother en net back on The Snares had decided that satellite observation, now it knew what it looking for, was just too hard to avoid. The first course they had set while they were climbing would give the impression they were heading for the east coast of Australia, going home. A bit of research and figuring said that at about 90 kilometres high, the visual reconnaissance satellites would lose sight of them; they were designed for looking at things closer to the surface and their cone shaped observation field was much skinnier up here, leaving lots of gaps… Pure bloody guesswork, thought Toby. The plan got even madder after that, where they would set a second secret course that would lead to them actually going into orbit. Bloody Hell! Which was why he was getting justalittlebitanxious. Be a bit like drowning, not having any air to breathe. Ned and Steve just seemed to accept the decision; Toby felt he needed a little more time for processing and reframing. Like, Air Travel Is Very Safe Nowadays. People pay a lot of money to be a space tourist. Really, it's just flying a bit higher…

The bright dot of light caught up with them, passed overhead and forged ahead. It shrank for some time, and then slowly began to grow. The crew watched fascinated as the blob began to assume a form, something like a tiny, glowing stick insect. Ned eased off on the throttle and they began to experience the first giddy pangs of weightlessness. Sean yowled, and Toby was glad they had managed to get part of a travel sickness pill down his cat's throat. Glad he had taken three himself.

'According to what I could find on the net,' said Liz, 'they won't have any visiting Soyuz shuttles at the moment. There's usually only three crew, and the real time site says one is asleep; the other two are in the lab doing experiments. Their radar won't pick us up.' She bought up a NASA image on the screen of the Dekko. 'Seems there's lots of windows, some of them pretty big like this one in the Destiny Lab, but I'm hoping they spend most of the time looking down on the earth. If we climb a lot higher and come down in behind, there's a fair chance we won't be spotted. We hope.'

'Never having snuck up on a space station before' added Steve.

'Right you are, better do a bit more climbing before we get closer,' said Ned.

'Well, let Toby and Jules do that,' said Liz, 'because you have to come over here. I need to show you where we might go. Just be careful though…' Ned unbuckled his belt and swore as his first tentative push banged his head into the roof. He clawed his way across to Liz. She had a labelled model of the ISS on screen. 'These are all the crew and experiment modules, and it looks like the only spot out of line of sight is tucked in between these radiators and the solar panels.' They looked over the model and a few more images.

'Might be a bit tight' grumbled Ned, 'but you're right. Can't afford to touch the sides, although I suppose the whole jigger is made of light alloys so the field won't creep. We'll give it a go. Only one bit of music for this of course…'

It was perfect, absolutely, thought Toby, as his fears were dissolved in the magnificence of the view. They were floating down, a kilometre off the spidery space station, with the glorious blue backdrop of the Pacific Ocean far below. Softly at first, then swelling, the strains of the Blue Danube Waltz came from the sound system…

'You bastard Ned… my favourite scene…' said Toby, tears floating off his cheeks.

Ned chuckled. 'Never thought I would get to see it myself. Bit of a high point, eh Toby!'

Jules had set her camera to video mode. Great You Tube shot! She had never seen 2001: A Space Odyssey, but Steve had told her about it. Liz, scanning for transmissions, announced that they were unobserved as they ever so gently nudged in behind the black panels of the radiators. Through the gaps they could make out windows in some of the modules, but no sign of movement.

'We better pull the curtains on this side. Bit of a chance they mightn't register a bit of extra hardware,' said Steve, gesturing at the jumble of panels and trusses around them, 'but if they spot a new face looking in at them they'll wake up, that's for sure!'

The crew settled in, adjusting to the weightless cabin. By group decision they decided Sean would stay in his strengthened cat box. An outraged ricochet projectile with claws and teeth was not needed. He had settled a little anyway, amusing himself with the last floating stuffed mousetoy. They had also lined his den with absorbent towel, hoping for the best...

'We need someone at the controls in case we start to drift,' said Ned. Toby took first shift.

'Of course, it might get very lively if they decide to do a height adjustment and go up six kilometres like they do about once a month,' said Jules, knowledgably. 'Would be slowly, though. This thing weighs about two hundred and thirty tons.'

'I'm sure they would say something about it to their base before it happened, dear,' called Liz. 'So far they're tied up with school projects, microbes and housekeeping' She had a live time show with two serious astronauts in the Columbus Laboratory, demonstrating and explaining. Solly watched amused, shaking his head.

Ned's much modified carbon dioxide extractor, now a sealed unit to deal with the zero gravity, fizzed away. After a terse comment on battery levels, Steve carefully primed and muttered over the generator. After a hiccup or two, it started and seemed to work as well as before; the balloon in the petrol tank had done the trick. He floated anxiously between the oxygen bottles, pressure gauges, valves, extractor and engines, checking and adjusting. Steve was totally focused on his machinery.

Machinery keeping them alive.

—⁓—

Back in Megalong, the Denzils, Nelsons and agent Horowitz surveyed the splintered front verandah while Senator Dobrovich patiently explained, soothed and organized. A very discreet clean up squad would be up from Sydney within three hours to collect the bits and pieces and do some tidying up. Danny, who had insisted on walking across the paddock to the site and who was now looking a bit green around the gills, nodded curtly. Sue, looking at the bullet holes and her kids, was beyond furious.

'Perhaps, considering everything, the Nelson family might like a bit of a quiet vacation?' suggested Kelvin. 'Queensland for two weeks? His company would organize transfers, flights, top accommodation and say… five thousand expenses?'

'Ten,' said Sue, 'and the front verandah had better be fucking immaculate because in two days the neighbours will be checking on the place. Which will be empty,' she added, glaring at Shirley. The Nelsons went inside to pack.

Not a lot was said over the rest of the afternoon. Brad and Bobby, holding up Graeme's bullet proof vest, made points about what if the shot was a bit higher or lower. Agent Kelvin's demolition job wasn't mentioned. The sanitation crew arrived and took direction. One was sent to Blackheath Hardware for paint, putty, some nice big new pots and best potting mix. Sue, Danny and the kids left in a small bus driven by a suit, headed for Sydney airport. Shirley had decided to leave the ute behind for them, partly from guilt, but also because it was too conspicuous and really… it was clapped out. Danny'd fix it and they could use it to deliver chooks. Or whatever. Kelvin Dobrovich continued charming, solicitous and tactful, driving them all to their new, luxury Blue Mountains Resort accommodation.

—◠◠◠—

While the Denzils were off exploring, Graeme and the Senator were taking a conference call from Homer. Kelvin Dobrovich was no slouch at scepticism; a lifetime in security and politics had honed his ratsmell and the odour of rodent was definitely abroad. He had heard the report on the Snares operation, and why the hell had they used missiles? You could salvage a shot up ship, but not one blown to smithereens! General Roberts had been evasive, said it was orders from further up, not under his control. Bullshit! Kelvin knew Roberts had run the whole show and gave the orders direct, so who the hell was he working for? Someone who obviously wanted these Ladybird gadgets vaporised.

'What's the story, Homer?'

Homer had been working hard, stretching his considerable resources to the max.

'General Roberts is definitely on a payroll, Sir, but it's impossible to track back as to whose. Interesting similarities in the money lines to the organisation you called the Alpha Club.' Kelvin remembered well. The probe into an elaborate arms shipment scam had cost him four agents, and every other trail they followed came to a halt, generally at a neat pile of bodies. Nothing since then either, although he and Homer were both aware there was a very large, very mysterious and very competent bunch of badasses still floating out there in the mist. So well connected too! He had closed down the full operation when they found definite links into the back door of Overseas Security itself, but quietly formed a very small, select team headed by Homer to continue digging. Cautiously. If the Ladybird bunch were in the sights of the Alpha Club, they were in big trouble.

'Homer, I don't want these guys and their toys disappearing. Those damn things are too important for that to happen, you understand? I'd rather see them succeed in their cockamamie scheme, whatever it is, and pick up the pieces afterward.'

Homer understood. His boss was totally obsessed by anything that flew. He would now want to become the best pal of these country radicals instead of ripping them off. Or be their best pal and rip them off later.

'Well Sir, it may be time to begin some more… positive negotiation…?'

The boys headed off to explore the pool and the games room while Graeme took Shirley to the bar for large whiskies, on the senator's tab. He had news.

'We just heard that your friends had a little run in with our navy, near New Zealand. They got away though. Your Ned McZed must be OK too, because the little Ladybird was glued onto the back of the big one! Cheers!'

Shirley worked on surprised, teary and grateful, even though the Denzils had read Liz's messages on the Dekko a half hour earlier. Talk drifted to more local events.

'So who in the hell was that guy this morning, Graeme? What was happening?'

'That guy, doubtless in hell this evening, was Paolo Capaldi. He was a particularly nasty contract killer, employed by an organisation who seem to be determined to stop the Henderson's project. As much as we know is they do business at a very high level, in great secrecy and without any scruples. They kill people. Probably because you were doing such a great job of promotion, they sent Capaldi.' Shirley thoughtfully sipped her drink, Graeme ordered two more. 'Senator Dobrovich happened to spot him on the plane coming out here and organized surveillance. There was a call to Capaldi early this morning with the exact coordinates of where you were staying. Maybe they tracked you by your mobile phone? If that's the case, might be time to dump and swap.' Shirley nodded absently.

'Yeah, call we made last night from the Megalong farm, I guess.'

Graeme looked around the room, and then dropped his voice. 'The Senator also heard that these people located your Ladybird friends near New Zealand. We're not sure how they did it.'

Oh Bugger! Problem is, thought Shirley, we only used the Dekko, and if this new bunch of bad bastards could track us by that, the Hendersons needed to know.

'Graeme,' said Shirley, 'Thank you for saving my life this morning… so thanks… Mate.'

'Just doing my job Ma'am,' drawled agent Horowitz, in a fair imitation of John Wayne.

'Yair, right. That bastard would have just sat out there until I stepped out the door, wouldn't he. Or else walked in and killed the lot of us. Remind me to thank your boss as well… after I've found out what he's actually here for. He's been very cagey.' She turned and looked directly at Graeme. Mate. He glanced over his shoulder again.

'As much as I know, the Senator came out to see if you could maybe put him in touch with the Hendersons. He told me over a bottle of Bourbon last night that their flying machine is just too important to be destroyed. Closest to emotional I've ever seen him. Homeland security and the armed forces seem to be pushed to obliterate the Ladybirds and the links lead back to a bunch he called the Alpha Club. He wants to help.' Graeme lent back in the armchair and sipped meditatively, looked sincere. 'If I'm any judge at all, Shirley, I think he's straight. He's hoping to get you on side, which is why he's being very circumspect. Meanwhile, it's been a long day and the bar's open.'

Dinner that evening was in the resort's elegant restaurant, looking out on a fading sunset over the Jamieson Valley. Bradley and Bobby were well scrubbed, suave and hungry, pointedly ignoring the children's menu and settling for the Northern Rivers Milk Fed Veal and the Grilled Swordfish. Which they added to when they discovered the exotic entrée and dessert menus. While they debated, Kelvin the Affable plied their mother with cheap talk and expensive wine.

'Cheers Kelve! Don't worry about the kids ordering too much, they're bottomless pits when it comes to a good feed. More to the point though, what's on your particular menu,

Senator, and is it palatable? As a boss-cocky spook, what devious deal will you propose? Meanwhile, you can pass that nice Mudgee red, and before I forget, thanks for putting a rocket up that bloke who was having a go at us.' Kelvin looked at her, working his way through the idioms as he poured the Shiraz.

'You're welcome Mrs. Denzil. Taking out Paolo Capaldi was a bonus for humanity and me. You can appreciate now what you and your colleagues are up against, and if I might say so, how much you need some buddies with resources for protection... Ma'am.' Shirl looked at him with some amusement.

'Yeah right. Like the sort of buddies that attacked Ned in off the South Coast, and the pals that were trying to crush me and the kids in the back streets of Sydney. Then there were those mates who did a kidnap number on Maria!'

'A rendition thingy to a secret American base to torture her horribly,' growled Brad.

'Very mega not nice at all' added Bobby.

'As far as I know, those buddies haven't changed sides yet, Senator.'

Kelvin scratched the back of his thinning head in genuine embarrassment. Difficult to explain what had happened. Goddamned Alphas screwed him and took over somewhat.

'Difficult to explain what happened there Shirley. I can only apologise for my part in the initial...hostilities. At that time I genuinely thought we were facing a terrorist group flying aircraft to an unknown target. I only had one option open to prevent a thousands dead nine eleven situation. I'm truly sorry it happened.'

'Indeed. So very polite and suitably dramatic, Kelve. Circumspectacular you might say. Then what happened?'

'By the time I had figured your friends were not a danger, this group I call the Alphas had managed to infiltrate and escalate the responses of the Navy and our Australian operatives.' Kelvin ignored his own role in initiating the unfortunate rendition. 'It's slow work, but we're sorting it out. I'm pleased we managed to stop you being killed.'

'So you're useful for something then, eh?'

Kelvin squirmed a little, sipped a little and came to the point, a little.

'Maybe a bit useful as you say, and I can vouch for my own agency and its resources. If it's at all possible, I would like to open some communication with your friends to at least keep them aware of the threats facing them. It would be a help to us all. ' Kelvin decided not to raise his last Homer communication, that the intercepted messages to the DR Congo and subsequent research suggested the Alphas may possess a long range tactical, or even strategic nuclear weapon, and be planning to use it. Too dramatic, besides, it was agency business. He was also peeved. The entrées had quietly arrived; Graeme nibbled a spring roll, smiled and gave Shirley a small encouraging nod.

'I can communicate, providing I have secure access to the Internet or mobiles,' lied Shirley easily, 'but you dropped in the words 'at least'. What's the 'at most' bit of that?'

'Well Ma'am, depends on what your friends want. Damned if I know how, when the world's scientists have missed it, but this kid Solomonder Henderson has come up with some entirely new form of energy. If it isn't lethal or a con, then there isn't a country in the world wouldn't want to get hold of it. Or a company.'

'And I wonder what they would offer?' asked Shirley sweetly.

'I understand that it wouldn't be of interest to you, however, US government… fifty, a hundred million, starters. I know some aviation companies who would be happy to match that, even if just for the flying applications. I could act as a liaison for your friends… all this conjecture just in the interest of progress, of course.'

'Placed and noted, Senator. Including your interests.'

'Yes... Well. According to what was said during the stage play at Tilda, seems your friends are flying somewhere to get more testing done to make sure this thing is safe. If you like, my government would be happy to help out with a full laboratory assessment, no charge, no obligation of course, could be at UCLA, MIT...' The Senator looked hopefully at Shirl, who pursed her lips.

'Or the Unnamed University of Langley, Virginia perhaps?'

'No, no, no of course not. Be that as it may,' he hurriedly continued, 'if they wanted to test it somewhere else independently, we would fund that too. Well, it's an offer, anyhow.' Kelvin gloomily refilled his glass. Shirley Denzil would not be an overly sympathetic advocate. 'Let them know anyway, Ma'am. We could build in some safeguards somehow if they're worried about control. Meantime, with your permission, Graeme Horowitz and I will stick around to protect you and your family. I'll pay the bills; we won't get in your way, restrict you or do any spying. I'll pass any information on regarding the Alphas to send off, and when my damn plane gets here, I'll fly you anywhere on the planet to meet your friends. Perhaps they could take me up for a flight?'

Shirley, Brad and Bobby looked at him solemnly, and then burst out laughing.

'Sounds like a goddamn fine deal there Kelve. For starters, you can both take us clothes shopping in Blackheath and Katoomba tomorrow, trail around the shops!' said Shirley.

Kelvin and Graeme groaned.

———〰———

Arabella Swift, now in much demand as special correspondent to several Important Newspapers, was conferencing with Maria Scott and Jim Dobson in the George back bar.

'The problem is,' Maria was saying, 'that nothing big and new has hit the media since the Great Departure. Your conspiracy articles were great of course, but only got a run in the smaller, leftish rags. TV seems to have the attention span of a goldfish, and although Evangeline Parsons and Senator Dan Kelly are pushing hard, change and bold initiative is not a notable feature of law and politics.'

'I know,' added Arabella peevishly, 'nothing I send to the States, Asia and most of Europe seems to get published at the moment. Like a blanket ban on anything Barangan. Is it that lot?' she asked, waving her notebook at the two obvious ASIO agents at a table by the door. Small beers, ties, earphones and a suspicious black case under a newspaper. Jim arrived back with the drinks, brimming with something significant for the agenda. He dropped his voice when Maria reminded him of the spies.

'You know that photo journal collection we knocked up, Azza? I gotta neemail back from Paris Match and they're putting all of it in next week! Jeez! Dyllo reckons it's a big frog magazine. Do you reckon the newsagent could get us a copy from Sydney?'

'That would take a month or two... I'll order it on line instead' said Arabella.

'It's wonderful news young James!' said Maria with warmth, 'and quite a feather in your cap. Paris Match is world famous, particularly for the photographs it uses.'

Jim glowed. Junior cadet scoops the pool. No, that sounded like the bloke down at the Municipal Baths. Cub Photographer scores front page? Which reminded him.

'Hey, youse blokes!'

The ASIO agents looked across startled, to be met by Uncle Frank's shuk-shuk-shuk camera in their faces. Faces that reddened as all the bar resident Barangans laughed, whistled, cheered. They packed up and shuffled out, muttering.

'Good one Jim!' acknowledged Arabella, 'Give them a stir up. Well done.'

Maria grinned at Ms. Arabella handing out compliments.

'Yes, I don't suppose undercover work works quite as well out in the country. However, we will be nice to them as they appear to be relatively harmless, almost civil servants I suppose, and their presence might discourage rougher elements…' She touched her bruised face carefully. A mobile phone burbled in Arabella's shoulder bag. She frowned, it was a different tune.

'Must be one of the phones that Mr. Horowitz gave me' she said, rummaging. 'Oh God, sorry… I was supposed to give this one to you, Maria…'

—⁓—

After a half hour of intense chatting, Shirley switched off the phone. She gave a thumbs up to Graeme, her personal minder/G-man standing at a discreet distance. Together they strolled to the cliff edge to view The Three Sisters.

'That's Maria up to date and I hope that the bogeymen weren't listening. I guess there's safety in numbers though, they can't listen to every mobile conversation and I didn't use any key words. Like you suggested, we'll set up an anonymous site on Facebook or YouTube and only use outside terminals.'

'What about contacting the Flying Tildans?' Graeme asked.

'Bit more complicated… don't suppose the kids and I could borrow the car? It would make it a lot easier.' Graeme considered. 'My boss would want me chaperoning, but you could drop me at a café I suppose,' he said dubiously, 'so long as you come back. If you don't…'

'Trust me, mate' said Shirley with a grin.

—⁓—

Timothy Branston, not to be confused with the pickles, was fucking furious. This was not unusual for the world's seventh (another irritation) richest media/transport/lots of other things magnate and happened whenever people who he didn't control wouldn't do what he wanted. The fact that he had paid $31million should also entitle him to a fair and immediate slab of the ISS communications access, so to be told he must wait two hours… The argument had ended when the large Russian engineer had grasped the floating magnate firmly and suggested that Mister Timmy might take a walk outside. The American had suited him up, reminded him about always having two lines attached and bundled him out the Quest Joint Airlock. The long-suffering ISS crews found that the reality testing of floating alone in space usually settled the tourists down…

Timothy grumbled as he clacked his lines over to the massive truss section holding the station together. This time, he decided, he would take a stroll past the JEM and the radiator, well away from the modules and those fucking technicians. As for the terrifying fucking vastness of space, it didn't impress him. Ever mindful of business however, he panned his digicam across the station, the Earth, the stars and to his face while he solemnly intoned the sententious drivel penned by his expensive copywriters. Enough already. Carefully edging around the black, ammonium filled radiator, he gazed past a large double cylinder out to the massive solar panels at the end of the truss.

'What the fuck?' swore Timothy Branston, with a classic double take as he realised the blue, glowing cylinders weren't meant to be there… were not even attached…and weren't they those…??

—∿—

'Mum… Dad…Toby… Mr. McZed' said Jules in a small voice.

'Yes dear?' said Liz absently. Like the rest, she was busy.

'There's a bloke looking in the front window and he's got a camera.'

The crew rushed forward to stare at the space-suited figure floating in front of Ladybird's nose. Highly agitated, he was waving, smiling, filming and shouting silently. The effect was comical; the crew laughed. A scowl passed briefly across the face in the helmet, but he got the point. He let the camera float on its cord, pointed and tapped the golden name tag on his chest and, amazingly, pulled an A5 pad and attached pencil from a leg pocket. Timothy's spacesuit was custom made to his own specs.

'His badge says Timothy Branston, CEO Galaxy News Corp, Paragon Air, Command Transport.... Something Something Something...there's lots,' said Julie, squinting.

'Of course!' said Liz, 'I read about him buying a trip into space from the Russians, cost millions. Boasting he would make it back from the stories. Says his personal carbon footprint is bigger than King Kong's. Dreadful man.'

'A top capitalist carnivore,' mused Toby, 'but he may be useful. What's he written?' he asked Jules, who had unearthed Liz's opera glasses.

'I know who u r Can do yr media Give me interviews On yr side'

'On our side? Branston? Bollocks! The stories I've heard about Branston! That gutter-press baron is only ever there for himself.' snorted Ned.

'Maybe so,' agreed Toby, 'but if we could tie him to straight reporting, the coverage he can organise is huge. He's got papers and TV in every country.'

'Tell him we'll do a series of interviews, but the first sign of editing or spin and we stop. Get an email address,' snapped Liz. Solly floated back with his sketchpad and a big texta.

Branston nodded enthusiastically and gave the demands a big thumbs up. They weren't even asking for Money! He scribbled clumsy messages (damn gloves), asking for posed photos, names, messages to loved ones, dangers faced... the torn off sheets drifted away in their own orbits. The little kid even bought a wide-eyed cat to the window, how perfect was that! Along with the family group, the two intrepid pilots, the woman's note to her Mum. Tim the Newspaperman was in his element. When the buzzer told him his space walk was up, Branston scrawled his last page

- T1@branston.net- back in 30. our secret !!!-

then hauled his way off around the radiator, desperate for transmission time while a lackey topped up the air in his tanks.

—∿∿—

The crew got back to their tasks. Just another day in space. Sean struggled and yowled piteously in Solly's arms and was assisted back into his cat box refuge. He backed into the corner, hissing. Liz and Toby set to work on a brief compiled release to email to Branston and fired it off unencoded on the Dekko. Liz bought up 'All the News from Ladybird' and added a copy of Branston's release, along with a cover note to Shirley and Maria, instructing them to monitor the Branston rags. Jules swung over from her pilot seat to download her camera's contents; the whole package was then set to auto transmit.

Solly explored the food situation. Loved how you could eat a muesli bar without holding it.

Meanwhile, the mutterings and shufflings behind the engineer's station grew in volume, culminating in an explosive set of oaths. Steve's head appeared above panel.

'The bastard! It just isn't going to work! Sorry folks, we've got big problems. We're losing air pressure and I don't know where from, maybe the seal on the new aerial or the generator exhaust. I've pumped silicon around all the sleeves but it's still leaking like buggery. I can keep us going for maybe ten, fifteen minutes with the oxy cylinder but after that… we don't get to breathe. We must go down, now! Sorry.'

Without a word the crew scrambled to their seats and strapped in. A curt 'ready?' from Ned and they lifted, rotated and peeled away from the ISS. Timothy Branston, just re-merging from the airlock, had only enough time to film Ladybird accelerating up and away, disappearing into the stars. Nice shot, but no fucking second interview! He looked at the built in Jaeger-LeCoultre chronograph, set to London time. Back inside, and they better have a channel open for him…

—∿∿—

Things got very hectic and not a tad frantic on Ladybird.

'We've cut about 8000 kph off our ground speed but the batteries have dropped right down, we'll need the generator as well, Steve' called Ned.

'That's all very well if there was some air out there that I could suck in, but there aint. If the pressure gets too far down, we start blacking out. You might notice y'r ears popping?'

Steve was desperate; all his calculations pointed at disaster. Solly spoke softly to Jules, she unbuckled and arrowed over to the large fire extinguishers.

'You're right Sol, propellant's nitrogen.'

'Gawdallmighty, don't let those off, we'll choke to death on the powder in them, it'll go everywhere!' bleated Toby, with visions of a thick, floating toxic chemical fog.

'Don't stress, Princess. We're on top of it' retorted Jules. 'Our beefed up bubbler will get the powder out.' She thrust the hose into the intake, pulled the pin and started spraying.

'Could be an interesting reaction' said Solly cheerfully, 'considering the ingredients, but not to worry, nothing too explosive. I think.' He started talking with Liz to get some flight data. Toby rolled eyes to Steve.

'Always told you they were bright little buggers, Tobes. Keep it feeding in, Jules. I'll add a bit of oxygen... Hey presto, an atmosphere!'

The generator purred into life, Ned warned Jules to wedge herself in, dropped the nose and started to pull the power on. Ten minutes later and the altitude was down to 110 kilometres and ground speed was cut back to a more sedate 13,000 kph. The horizon was still running away from them, but not quite as fast. Jules was started on the second extinguisher; Steve reported the pressure was still dropping, but much slower.

'Any idea whereabouts we might come down?' asked Toby.

'Probably somewhere west of Tajikistan, up on the Tibet Plateau,' replied Liz. 'Lots of very cold, isolated spots to pick from, but the shopping's lousy if you want spare parts.'

'Or a decent latte,' murmured Toby.

'Should be down to zero groundspeed in around five minutes, then we can do a vertical drop... bit less chance of getting spotted. Provided all goes well.' said Ned

'Six minutes fourteen seconds' added Solly with exactitude.

'Sorry to say this, the leak's worse and the petrol in the generator is low.'

'That's the second extinguisher empty.'

'Batteries at about 15%.'

'Bugger all oxygen.'

Toby was not happy with the grey look from Ned.

'Three hundred thousand feet up and Mach 10. We might be in a bit of trouble Toby. Any bright ideas?' whispered Ned.

Toby wrinkled the brow, checked the options. Oh dear. Aerial emergency. Repairs. For some bizarre reason, the heroic Arthur Brown clambering out on the wings of the first trans-Atlantic Vickers Vimy bomber to chip ice off sprang to mind.

'I'll just duck out and get Captain Sven's big battery then,' said Toby absently.

Ned began a comment about stupidity but became thoughtful instead. The light bulb had come on.

'Liz, Jules, Solly, remember how we linked up to Ladybird 1's system through the mini Dekko so we could fire the pyrotechnic bolts and dump her if need be... could you patch through to the other LB1 controls from here? Hook it into our flight deck?'

Jules and Solly conferred, Liz powered up the Dekko. Jules ran a temporary lead across, added a switch. The minutes ticked by.

'210,000, Mach 8, 10%, won't talk about the air' called Steve.

'OK Ned, switch over, we'll operate LB1 from here.'

'Thanks. Make sure you're strapped in because this might get a bit uncomfortable, bit of upside down negative g I'm afraid. Cut the field on LB2 back to minimum…' He rattled off instructions, inverted and powered up Ladybird I to push on the roof. Toby's vision turned red and his problem with reflux came up. 'We have to try some old fashioned re-entry now we're in the stratosphere to save power… keep our field on low but I'll cut LB1's. I'll need to juggle a bit to stop tumbling.' They watched through the roof panel as the McZedmobile lost its blue tinge and the tips of its stubby wings turned a dull red. 'Toast the other side now…' A quick revolve and Ned reversed the thrust so that LB1 pulled, slamming the crew back down in their seats. He cut the field on LB2 to zero and the ever-thickening atmosphere started to tear on its underbelly. It began to become distinctly cosy. The smell of scorched lining started to fill the cabin.

'Ned, you're remembering us arriving at the Stubbs' farm, aren't you? Free form power dive and all that?' asked Toby.

'Don't fuss Biggles,' muttered Ned, 'everything is working fine. One more shot.' The third rotation was one too many, the tumble was quick and vicious. Earth, Sun and stars flicked past in a kaleidoscopic blur, Ned powered up and fought the controls, the rest held on against the buffeting. The spinning slowed, settled. 'Think we might give that a miss,' said Ned with regret. 'How're we doing Steve?' Steve looked up from the paper bag and swore. Luckily, the slight gravity was keeping its contents in place.

'You owe me a lunch, you bastard.' He looked around and checked. 'Amazingly, the generator kept running through all of that madness, though it's packed it in now. Batteries are back up to 15% and I can suck some air in, so pressure'll come up a bit, soon.'

'80,000. Mach 3.2,' called Toby from the instruments, surprised his voice didn't wobble.

They soon slowed to a hover, and then dropped vertically. Liz checked their position and confirmed they were a long way from any known big military bases, radar stations, towns, villages, or anything at all, really. Somewhere above Ngari prefecture in Northern Tibet, which Solly informed them was generally very cold because of an average altitude 4500 metres and population about a quarter of a person each square kilometre. Toby looked down and shuddered. Far below he could make out a jumble of massive mountain ranges clad in white, with vast brown tundra between them. Desolation.

—᠁—

Transmissions had been intercepted but the squirming technicians were still unable to translate them, apart from the ones to search engines. The Principal Arranger had, of course, recognized 28,000 kph, southeast, northern arctic in the as the speed and orbit path of the International Space Station. Capable of space flight! The vast potential, if only the Alliance had control of such technology... but Ms. Montague did not countenance 'if only.' She had implemented an immediate launch sequence, only to cancel it when the second data showed the machines to be rapidly slowing over central Asia. Far better if they landed there for a clean removal as the nuclear destruction of the Space Station would have created... what was the term? A hue and cry. Ms. Montague had been exploring the nuances of language.

As soon as this annoying, pestiferous blowfly landed for long enough she would crush it.

—᠁—

Chapter Fourteen

Homer Spiggottt looked at the map of The Democratic Republic of The Congo, scanned the record of active units and added some final scribbles to his Spigott big picture mind map. As his boss said, Goddamn! Africa was always difficult. Operations were easy to bury afterwards, but took forever to implement. Kelvin's last communication had been quite specific: ASAFP. The Ugandan unit? Homer shuddered at the prospect. Expensive, inefficient, too much collateral damage. An older file emerged; Colonel Francis Pewter in Angola? Hmmm. The colonel was retired, had built a vast cattle ranch and settled his small mercenary fighting unit there. He would only be two hundred odd miles away, owned a large ex-military helicopter and had recently filed a standing request:

'Although we are getting on, the chaps and I keep in training and are as keen as mustard.'

He was also quite certifiably mad. Perfect.

—⁓—

Ladybird settled gently in the centre of a rolling, empty landscape. Dry, flattened tussocks of grass glumly endured the biting wind and occasional flurry of snow.

'Could we not go somewhere tropical for a change?' complained Toby. Steve quickly switched off the field and checked his instruments.

'We've got about 2% or less in our batteries and Captain Sven's is dead flat. We might be good for a hundred kilometres or so. After that we'll have to call the NRMA. No lights or heating,' he warned. Already the cold was creeping into the steel hull and past the insulation. Tracksuits, socks, jumpers and coats were pulled on.

'There's no towns but might be a road about 30 kilometres east… could be people if there's a road, maybe. Not much of a map though,' apologised Liz from the Dekko. They gently lifted and sauntered east, the crew scanning the plain for any sign of habitation. Ned and Toby nursed Ladybird along at two hundred feet, all too aware that the sustaining blue glow might falter at any moment. The low sun behind them cast lengthening shadows on the undulating ground. Soon it would be dark to add to their woes, observed Toby: only to be told to shut up and concentrate.

Fifty kilometres later and the supposed road had still not been found when Jules spotted a faint glimmer off to their right. Creeping forward just off the ground, they watched as a small, low hut and squat shed emerged from the gloaming, a soft yellow light coming from its one window. Nobody was to be seen as they touched down silently.

'Well it looks friendly enough' said Liz after a while. 'They wouldn't get a lot of visitors out here so I might knock on the door with only one of you men?' Steve was none too happy, but could see the sense of what Liz said. Ned, who of course claimed to speak a little Tibetan and some Chinese, nominated to go with her.

'We'll push a wall down if there's any trouble' said Jules, slipping into Ned's seat.

'Gently like,' agreed Toby.

While Ned optimistically cleaned one of the empty petrol cans, Liz gathered some possible gifts and trade items.

'Jeans, they're mad about jeans,' suggested Toby, offering his oldest Levis. Liz was sceptical but added them to the chocolate, tea, sugar, analgesics and baked beans. Jules and Solly added some comics and a Tin Tin book. Lots of pictures. While Solly restrained Sean, the others watched the emissaries set off into the night. They knocked, the door opened a little, some conversation and they disappeared inside. For a long half hour Jules and Solly became increasingly anxious and Steve rattled through his tools for the most lethal ones. Toby tried to remember what hostage negotiators did; that didn't help. At last, Liz returned, climbing the steps with a glass flagon and chuckling.

'Petrol, Steve! About three litres and dubious quality, but it was all they had. Oh my!'

Steve busied himself happily with the generator while Liz told her story. 'Well! It's a family with a mother, a father, three kids, and a grandmother. We were very polite at the door and were waved in. They all sat staring at us as if we had just arrived from outer space, quite understandable really, while Ned ran through all of his Tibetan phrases and was starting with Chinese when the father held up his hand and announced: "Perhaps, sir, it would be far easier if we conversed in English? Francais? Deutsch?" Liz laughed. 'He introduced himself as Rhabten and it turned out he had been a tour guide in Lhasa for many years before he was closed down and had moved back here with his family. They are so poor! Everything they had has been taken by the army, including the old taxi he used in Lhasa to run tourists around. This petrol he had hidden away. He said they had been planning to escape to the foot of one of the passes, then walk to India. How they would have survived, I don't know.' Liz looked sadly out across the dark plain at the looming wall of mountains to the east. Although the snow-covered peaks glowed warmly pink in the last of the sunset, she could imagine how jagged and bitterly cold any path up there would be.

'Did they like the comics?' asked Solly.

'Indeed. The oldest girl Pema took them and bowed, then all the kids scurried off to the corner. We could hear a lot of giggling.'

'The jeans?' queried Toby.

'Well… Rhabten said he preferred Fiorucci, but the grandmother Kurukulla was very happy with them. She was taking them up before I left. We are all welcome to come over for the evening meal and to stay the night, including Sean, provided he behaves himself.'

The packing and preparations accelerated when she added 'It's warm…'

Colonel Pewter's housekeeper looked disapprovingly at the crack platoon of troops assembling on the parade ground. Or rather, the ancient, mostly overweight, rag-tag gaggle of farm workers shuffling into the front yard. Across the way she could see the colonel's disreputable friend and pilot Pieter Cornelius supervising three men straining to pull the battered Russian helicopter out of its big shed. No good would come of this. She still remembered the state of himself when he returned from his last 'expedition' nine years ago, smoke pouring from the bullet riddled machine, two of the boys killed and him with his leg shattered. Mrs. Pepper shook her head and returned to the kitchen to shout at the girls.

She had food hampers to get ready.

Pieter walked beside his very old friend and grumbled as they supervised the troops helping themselves from the cases of guns and ammunition.

'You're a mad bugger Francis, agreeing to those American bastards to go on this trip. Look at this lot! What good are they now in a fight? Look at Bura, he's too drunk to stand up and can't even load the magazines for that Bren. And what about Gebhuza there; him a warrior? His wife beats him up every Saturday!'

'Have you seen his wife, Pieter?' countered the colonel. Pieter nodded grimly and conceded the point, then suggested they could leave him, take her. He stopped in front of a grey haired, well-rounded man solemnly polishing a Lee Enfield .303.

'Chimola! Francis, you're not taking your cook are you? Chimola… "breaker of things"… what a name for a cook! He'll break my helicopter!' Chimola looked impassively at Mr Cornelius, at his Colonel, then back down. He began to methodically load the box magazines for his gleaming, ancient rifle. A little further away, Gebhuza prodded the now snoring

Bura with his boot. The Colonel drew his pilot aside, decapitated a rose with his swagger cane to be sure he had the man's attention and spoke quietly to him.

'For starters, Pieter, it's our helicopter and not yours. Even though you stole it in India, I have long since paid out your share. Bura will be sober in an hour with Mrs. P's coffee, Gebhuza has killed more men than you've had hot breakfasts and Chimola is the best shot in my squad. He can head shoot an Impala at 500 yards with that gun of his. They come with us.' He bowed the cane for emphasis, turned and walked on.

'Hunting for impala then, are we?'

Together they walked over to the Mil Mi4 while Colonel Pewter outlined how the Americans wanted them to fly to a map reference in the DRC, a bit out of Matadi, locate what may be a rocket launching site and destroy it. Very straightforward, in, a few mortar rounds and out, ...

'The Congo, man! That's serious country for fighting. Every bugger there sleeps with a Kalashnikov. And us with eleven fat old soldiers who have been farmers for too long and a helicopter that mightn't get us out the front gate! Barmy, Francis. No way.'

'Two hundred thousand dollars, US,' murmured Colonel Pewter.

Pieter Cornelius walked on silently.

'Then it's a good thing I did an overhaul when we took that politician on tour last month,' he conceded after a while. 'Not that he's paid us yet.'

'Good chap. We'll land close by using that satellite navigation gadget, double march over and lob some grenades and a phosphorous bomb or two... home for breakfast. Damn sight easier than the old days, eh? And if I'm not mistaken, here's Mrs. Pepper with the hampers. We'll have dinner on the way...'

Pieter unscrewed the cap on his silver hip flask and they toasted the excursion.

The troops shambled over and formed ranks for inspection.

———∿∿∿———

Ms. Montague looked at the data sheet and almost smiled. Obviously in the same position for at least an hour, night set in, happy to be on solid ground no doubt.

'Signal Matadi for immediate launch.'

'Ummm, slight technical problem Ms., they signalled that being on standby for so long they had to recharge the fuel...' The technician blanched before the glacial look.

'How long?'

'Four, possibly five hours Ms. I'll signal immediately about the absolute urgency for speed of course Ms. I'm sure they will try their hardest. I'm sorry Ms.' He scuttled off.

Four hours. The missile's flight would add very little to that. The target would most likely be sleeping and dawn was a good ten hours away. It would still be a satisfactory outcome.

———∿∿∿———

Shirley bounced the borrowed Falcon up a fire trail off the Mount Hay road while Bobby and Brad busied themselves on the Dekko. She dictated her message for the Hendersons, outlining the 'possible' support of Kelvin and his agency and warning of the mysterious Alpha group; their power and apparent ability to locate Dekko transmissions. The Falcon pulled into a secluded clearing where they set up the aerial and went on air.

'There's a big transmission downloading,' said Bobby, 'and wow, even looks like there's some photos attached.' Shirley quickly scanned the decoded text and swore.

'It says they're all going to stay the night in a hut with a nice family, in the middle of Tibet. Omigod. They must have set their Dekko to transmit when we came on line. Send our signal and close down Bobby, and we just have to hope that no-one else is listening in.'

'And that they're too far away to get there quickly,' added Brad hopefully.

The image of the joined machines in a forest somewhere, with four adults, two children and a cat in front. This was followed by interior shots, views of the earth from a great height and the International Space Station being approached. The last image was of a small house sitting on a featureless plain. Tibet perhaps? Ms Montague took in all the useful data but missed the soul of the photos: the pride of Ned and Toby pointing up at Ladybird, the bright glow of enthusiasm in Solly and Jules, the love of Liz and Steve as they looked down on them. Liz and Steve at their stations, the rapt attention of the pilots as they approached the ISS. The lonely beauty of the little house against pink mountains.

'These last signals have a lot of uncoded text and a separate coded version with some of the same material' announced the technician excitedly.

'Why is that important?'

'Because we can identify the original base text and then have the key to decoding their messages. The section we've worked on appears to be a conversation between a small pig and another person about a birthday. Nobody in our section knows this text.'

Ms. Montague frowned. Something stirred uncomfortably, a long lost ghost from far away... Ludicrous. She felt anger stirring.

'The last transmission came from the same location in Tibet?'

'Yes, Ms. There is no movement.'

'Leave the code for now. Ensure the launch proceeds immediately re-fuelling is completed. There will be no delay.'

The single room was crowded with twelve inside, but all the warmer because of it. The bubbling pot on the dung fire had been augmented with Ladybird supplies and the unusual meal was consumed with hot sweet tea. Jules and Solly retreated to a corner with their new friends, big pad and textas. The grandmother, despite ominous protests from her daughter-in-law, bought out a dusty brown bottle and small cups. Steve declared after the second cup that he could probably run the generator with it. In the afterglow, Rhabten told them of the family's return from Lhasa to northeast Ngari where his brothers still lived. All had been peaceful until two years ago, when the army had set up a small garrison fifteen kilometres away on the main road, taken most of their yaks and horses and left worthless paper money in payment. Worse still, they had recently taken Rhabten's old taxi and when their oldest son Ketu had protested, he had been arrested.

'When he is not working for them they keep him locked in a small cell on the edge of their camp. It has no heating and I fear he will die when the cold comes. They are wicked and do not care.' Rhabten and his wife looked away to hide their tears from the guests. The crew studied their cups in silence. Eventually Liz made a decision and spoke firmly to Steve.

'We cannot sit by and do nothing to help these people. A rescue is called for.'

Rhabten looked horrified and waved his hands in negation.

'No, no, you must not go near near them! There are more than thirty soldiers and they have many guns. They have killed people before. You must not go there!'

'Do a bit of house renovation then, Liz?' said Steve. 'No worries!' Ned put his hand on Rhabten's shoulder and spoke reassuringly.

'Don't you worry there young feller-me-lad, we're used to getting people out of tight places. Besides, we are going to need more petrol and these scoundrels would have it. We would be paying them a visit anyway.'

'I fully agree we must help,' said Toby, 'but wouldn't the soldiers come straight here? The family would be in great danger.'

'Yes,' agreed Liz, 'and for that reason, they must come with us. Ladybird needs repairs before the next long leg of our flight and I think I know just where we will be able to take refuge and get help. I would say it is also where the family wishes to go.' She carefully explained her proposal to Rhabten, who conferred in great excitement with the family. The grandmother embraced each of the guests in turn then made a brief, animated speech to Liz. Rhabten and his wife Amrita laughed and agreed.

'My mother wishes to give you her name, Karukulla. It means "Dances the rhythms of Wisdom." She says it suits you far better than her.' Liz blushed and thanked her. Pema, the oldest daughter, whispered to her father, who nodded gravely.

'My daughter asks what will happen to our two horses and the yaks. She does not want them to be killed by the Chinese soldiers. We must kill them ourselves.'

'Could you not give them to one of your relatives?' asked Ned.

'They live two days walk away. It is too far.'

'Hmmm. Well I don't suppose they are very big animals, and they would be used to being inside at night... Are they quiet? Right then! We'll drop them off on the way. Should only take another half hour at the most. Toby, Steve and I will take Rhabten as soon as the moon comes up and you and the kids stay and help pack, Liz. It's the only way, and we should be back well before dawn.'

'Never was a quiet way to travel, Francis' yelled Pieter Cornelius to Colonel Pewter as they climbed out of the Mil. He patted the aluminium flank fondly; his Russian friend had been as reliable as ever.

'Active patrol rules from now Pieter' said the colonel, finger on lips. He quickly allocated jobs; two with bad arthritis to guard the helicopter, Gebhuza and Bura on point to scout forward, the rest in staggered double file. Off to the east, the full moon was just clearing the horizon as they set out, Pieter with the GPS, Francis with compass and map pad. Between them they decided thirty minutes to the target. Better make that forty-five said Francis ruefully as he accepted some beta-blockers from Pieter.

—–ᴧᴧ–

It was a very mixed bag of technicians who worked in a chaotic rush to get back up to operational status. The initial stage of the project some four years ago had been hectic, with the secret transporting, rebuilding and setting up of the liquid propellant missile in it's 'grain silo', but since then life had been very, very easy. Guarding in shifts, a bit of repair and maintenance, but mostly, the good life in various African cities. Not a finely honed instant response team, the Chief Executive regretfully realised. He knew the price of failure too; three of the original group had 'disappeared' over a minor security breach a year ago. Judging by the last message from his mysterious employer, he could be next. Quickly checking the target coordinates for the third time, he returned to the silo to scream at the Russian supervising the fuel re-loading.

—–ᴧᴧ–

Homer Spiggottt's anxiety was six crotchets past high doh. If his information was correct, a nuclear missile was about to be launched from Africa into Tibet and he doubted if his geriatric land based hit squad would get to the launch site... may not have even left the farm! The Senator would not like his next phone call.

'So where the hell are they! What do you mean they took the car for a drive! Get onto that goddamn Denzil woman now Horowitz, and if she can get onto her buddies in Tibet, tell them to get the hell out of there. They are about to get nuked!' bellowed Kelvin at Graeme.

Rhabten's brother was bewildered by the sudden doorknock in the middle of the night, the unloading of livestock, his brother's brief explanation and the tearful farewell. He was left holding the leads of the yaks and horses, surrounded by his round-eyed family as they watched the strange, glowing barrel lift silently into the air and disappear across the moonlit plain.

Shirley and the kids were playing tourist and a quick trip to the other side of the Great Western Highway had landed them at Sublime Point lookout. Fifty metres from the car park and Bobby's sharp ears heard a familiar ringtone.

'That's your mobile, Mum. Will I go and get it?'

'Forget the mobile luv, it'll just be Graeme getting his knickers in a twist. Time we had a break. Five minutes walk and I'll show you one of my favourite vast vistas. Better than the Three Sisters and no crowds!'

And so it was.

According to Francis' map and cross references, the big grain silo and squat concrete bunker four hundred metres down the slope were their target. Pieter's GPS had them floating in a sea of nothing. Only good for visiting N'delatando, Francis had said. They were conferring in whispers on a plan of attack when a muffled yell and a burst of automatic fire erupted forward right.

'Gebhuza! Damn! I'll warrant that he left his glasses off to go creeping forward and bumped into a sentry! That's the ball up on the slates then.' Colonel Pewter deployed his men left and right, and then signalled a cautious advance. An apologetic whistle indicated Gebhuza was alive and presumably, the sentry was not. Another hundred metres were gained before a machine gun opened up, joined by rifle fire from several directions and the Expeditionary Force dived for cover. Pieter swore; the rock he had chosen had prickles and the fire was uncomfortably accurate. Floodlights came on.

'What now, Great White Hunter? We're pinned down here and there are lots of those buggers down there. Not quite a stroll in and out, eh!'

'The men know what to do, Pieter,' said Francis calmly, 'take out the lights then pick off the guards. Might take a little while.' There was a single shot from a clump of boulders to the left and a light shattered.

'Well done, that man!' shouted the Colonel.

Ladybird skimmed silently across the moonlit plain with the two pilots guided by Rhabten. Toby was freezing: the back doors were open while Steve swept the last of the straw and dung out into the night. The purring generator spluttered and stopped.

'That's Rhabten's petrol done. Twenty percent charge, should see us through but we better make sure we score some more fuel mate' called Steve.

'What I have in mind, Rhabten, may involve your taxi being a little damaged, or a lot damaged actually,' said Ned. Rhabten smiled and shrugged. He no longer owned it.

'This riverbed will take us to the edge of their camp. My son is in a small hut near there. The guardhouse is over the other side and they do not come out at night. Too cold.'

Too easy, thought Toby. They crept along the depression then slowly rose to find a cluster of buildings before them. Ladybird slid forward to the hut, gracefully pirouetted and backed to the solid timber door. Rhabten knocked, whispered urgently then nodded to Ned; Ketu was out of the way. Steve passed a towrope around the steel bar securing the door, Ladybird edged forward with sharp little pops and cracks as the rope tightened. CRASH!!! The door resolutely remained closed but the entire wall pulled away. A young man in rags staggered out and fell into Rhabten's arms, just as the roof and remaining walls collapsed.

'Quickly!' called Ned, 'Cut the rope, get the boy aboard and get the doors shut. I think we may have woken a few folk!' Lights were coming on, figures were running and a bell was ringing as Ladybird drifted silently over the camp at fifty metres. No one seemed to be looking up.

'Can you see your taxi Rhabten? Over there? Good-oh. Lets collect.' Toby looked at Ned, very anxiously.

'Ned, there's a whole bunch of angry, armed soldiers down there. You're not planning on landing, sneaking over and milking the petrol tank… are you?'

'Watch and learn, my boy. Better still, keep a lookout and tell me immediately if any of these laddies start setting up anything like a rocket launcher. Rifles are OK.' Bullets started to spang off the hull; they had been noticed. Leaning forward to look down, Ned dropped Ladybird quickly to straddle the taxi, paused for a count of five then lifted up and away in a hail of rifle and small arms fire. Toby glanced down; the roof of the taxi glowed blue in the observation window.

'You bugger McZed! You let the field spread over and it lifted with us!'

'Oh yes. Thought it may work,' said Ned with a touch of smug.

'Home, James. Which way, Rhabten?'

The Chief Project Officer roared across the bunker at the technician.

'It's ready! Lose the roof! Get the bastard going. Go, go, go!' He shrieked as a rocket grenade slammed into the wall. Not that it did anything; the walls of the bunker and silo were nearly a metre of reinforced concrete…

Colonel Pewter frowned as the steel silo roof appeared to slide sideways and plummet to the ground. Damn! There was a deep rumble and smoke boiled out of the base of the silo. They were launching!

'Drop a mortar into there, rocket grenade, anything!' he bellowed. Pieter cursed him for a fool; if they succeeded in blowing up what he suspected was in the silo, he wanted to be a good fifty kilometres away! The rocket launcher team was under sustained machine gun fire thanks to their pot shot at the bunker but Bura was ready with the mortar and carefully lined up on the top of the silo. The shell dropped in then blasted up into its trajectory. Pieter heard it go and prayed feverishly.

Where the shell went, no one was sure, but it missed. The Expeditionary Force and Defending Militia were both cowering behind rocks as the rumble grew to a bellowing roar, flames jetted out from vents and the ground shook. Like a dreadful insect emerging from its cocoon, the missile tentatively poked its head out from the silo then slid its body up into the air. One soldier alone attempted to obey orders during the maelstrom; Chimola the cook valiantly loosed off two shots before being bowled over and scorched in the backwash.

An airgun to stop an elephant.

Colonel Pewter and Pieter Cornelius watched the fiery tail of the missile as it climbed far away into the night sky.

'Does this mean we don't get paid then, Francis?'

'Not even to cover expenses old chap. And we still may have a fight on our hands.'

'Not a problem. The mercenary contracts just ran out with the rocket, I'd say.' This proved to be the case. After some customary profanities and threats, the South African in charge of the opposition quickly agreed to a revenue neutral cease-fire, provided the intruders buried the initial casualty and returned his weapons.

Everybody began packing up to go home. In a well guarded manner.

Ned and Toby cautiously settled Ladybird down in front of the hut, Rhabten wincing as his taxi was partly compacted. Liz gave Steve a full compaction then hurried off to help Pema prepare the last supper. It would take around two hours for the army to re-group, work out what had happened and get a truckload of (very annoyed) troops out to the farm.

—⁓—

'Target relocated twice, within twenty kilometres, but returned to original site and is stationary. Message from Matadi, Ms. Montague. The site is under armed attack, but they have successfully launched the missile and estimated impact twenty-eight minutes'

'Good. Monitor the target area. Message Matadi to destroy the site, then terminate their contract.'

—⁓—

The well-singed Chimola, since hostilities had ceased, was able to salute his Colonel.

'Two bullets in that big bastard Sir. He's wounded but I can't track him to finish him off.'

'Well done Chimola. Good shooting. Get yourself patched up.'

'Head shot was it?' asked Pieter, sneering, 'I bet it's bleeding like…' He didn't get finished.

Four hundred kilometres away and near-orbital, a new star was born, flared and died. Lit the valley up quite well. Indeed, lit up most of the DR Congo, Cameroon and the Central African Republic. The first 174 grain metal jacket bullet had finished bouncing around inside the electronics casing and neatly shorted out the firing circuit… Colonel Pewter pulled himself up to attention and gravely saluted his cook.

'Very well done indeed. Excellent. Worth a bonus. Ten thousand, eh Pieter? Five percent. Very fair. Leaves one-ninety.'

Pieter knew he would get nowhere arguing. He smiled and offered his hand to Chimola.

'You can give us a slap up feed when you open your restaurant in N'delatando, man!'

―∿∿―

Mother, Grandmother, twins and sister finished cry-hugging Ketu and loaded their meagre belongings into Ladybird. Ned and Toby screwed down a bed frame and bolsters, along with very basic safety harnesses from horse girth straps, belts, ropes; anything that came to hand. Steve and Rhabten were able to siphon around thirty litres of petrol from the crushed taxi and two discovered army ration packs went into the pot; another McZeddish meal.

―∿∿―

Three a.m. Tibetan time and Ladybird lifted away from the empty hut, turned northeast and climbed to fifteen hundred feet. Kitsi and Pabu slept soundly, well rugged and strapped on the bed between their Mum and Gran. Ketu begged to sit next to Jules and watched the take off procedure, fascinated. Liz suspected hormones were also at play. Solly attempted to explain the motor monitoring panel to Pema while Ned and Toby discussed maps with Rhabten and the caged Sean growled over a lump of dried, unidentified meat. Thirteen on board. Fourteen including Sean, Toby quickly decided. Off in the distance the headlights of an approaching truck could be seen.

'Mr. McZed, Is it possible to crush them under, like our taxi?' asked Ketu politely.

His father scolded him for unworthy thoughts.

'Don't even go there, Ned!' muttered Toby.

―――

'No… but it reminds me we still have the taxi with us. Only fair we should return it.'

Ned made a wide, climbing turn, located the truck and flew a little ahead of it. 'It may be a little bumpy but just hang on and nothing to be worried about.' With that he cut the lower fields; the taxi roof lost its glow. Still wedged. A bit of a shuggle and the crunched Ambassador disappeared.

'Ned? You didn't?' asked the horrified Toby.

'Don't fuss, it'll miss by miles.' In the truck cabin, the Officer and two NCO's gasped as the blurred impression of a car impacted into the road fifty metres ahead and disintegrated. With all six wheels locked they pulled up at the edge of a sizeable crater. Ladybird banked back gently to the northeast. The twins slept on.

Liz switched on the Dekko to check the mail.

—⁓—

Homer spoke rapidly to the Senator and agent Horowitz, explaining the sequence of events of how the missile had launched, the panic it created because it couldn't be intercepted and then its mysterious destruction over central Africa. Either malfunction or possible damage inflicted at the launch site; he was waiting on more information. An intercepted report indicated the Alpha's DR Congo operation was closing down.

Kelvin grunted, snafu but sorted, and asked where the hell was his plane.

—⁓—

Shirley was ashen faced when she had finished listening to her mobile messages.

'Jesus wept! Bobby! Brad! Get the Dekko set up NOW!'

'But Mum,' said Brad, gesturing to a minibus of adventurous Japanese.

'Just do it,' said Shirley, 'there's a nuclear missile on its way to Tibet!'

While her sons worked feverishly to re-assemble the Dekko, Shirley keyed in Graeme's number and paced the car park. Where the hell was he? A tourist walked over to the car to watch the boys putting the curious device together. Very interesting.

'Science experiment' mumbled Brad. 'No photos please. World War Two radio. Lookout's down there. Closing soon. Go!'

'Graeme! What the Hell's happening?' Graeme quickly explained the crisis and its resolution. Had she spoken to Ladybird? Shirley said no, but would do so as soon as possible, then bring the car back. Sorry. She thought rapidly as she walked back to the car.

Time for a long Dekko phone call to her mates.

———

'Winnie the Pooh by A.A.Milne. Eeyore has a birthday. Page 76. Why didn't you use the Internet earlier!' snarled Ms. Montague at her attendants.

She was in a foul mood. Seventy-five million dollars and four years, and the missile had not even got half way.

———

Liz had started to read the decoded messages when Shirley's direct call came through.

'Read the messages and go to code 2 before you reply.' Liz called Jules and Solly over.

'So what's this code 2 then?'

'Yeah right,' said Jules, 'Code 2 type situation then. Solly wanted Winnie the Pooh, so fair enough, but Brad and I thought we might need a different base that wasn't as widely read or known. We scanned two issues of the Cambrawarra Pastoral Times. Heaps thick and it took ages. They use it on gardens for weeds.'

———

'Because nothing gets through the Cambra. Good thinking.' They read through Shirley's earlier signal, calling out salient points to Ned and Toby. On top of it, the prospect of an all powerful, secret enemy capable of tracking them did not appeal. At all.

'If they tracked us from the Dekko while we moved, they'd know our direction, like radar,' said Ned, 'so let's give them a bum steer.' They reversed direction, accelerated quickly to Mach 3 and flew back to well to the west of the family farm.

'Now set course for Moscow, comrade!' suggested Toby, as Jules re-set the Dekko and opened a trans-global Pastoral Times dialogue with the Sublime Point car park.

'How the hell could a private organisation get a nuclear missile?' demanded Steve later.

'Enough money and arms dealers will sell anything you want. We were all very lucky,' replied Toby. 'I think that now we're off air, we better turn around and get to Liz's proposed refuge. Very quickly. That lot, the Alphas or whatever, may have other tricks up their sleeves. If Rhabten knows of a wild, unguarded pass through the Himalayas, lets do it!'

'Yay!' agreed Solly, 'get down low and go, go, go!'

'Not too low. There's big rocks in these mountains…' said Ned.

—∿∿—

The American astronaut was suitably apologetic.

'I'm sorry but that's a definite no, Mr. Branston. Everything sent from the ISS has to be cleared through Mission Control. We can't send it to your Editor and no, your mobile phone won't be released. You have to wait forty-eight hours until the Soyuz arrives. Sorry.'

'Mr. Timmy, we can send you down without the shuttle,' suggested the Russian, 'you'd be back to earth in about half an hour.' His jokes were always a bit ponderous. Timothy struggled to contain his rage.

'All right then. I won't send my other stories but forward this to your control. The big explosion we saw over Africa, and the shots I took of it.' Branston's luck again, right place, right time.

'Umm… we heard there might be a security problem about that too. Sure, we'll send it, but it mightn't get very far. Just mentioning it,' he added. His paying guest's face deepened from red to purple. In space, however, no one seemed too fussed at all if you scream…

—⁓—

Shirley found the Senator and offsider drinking and casually dropped the keys on the bar. She ordered herself a beer, since no one offered.

'I managed to get in touch with Ladybird and passed your messages along. Used the Internet café. They were flying out and were OK. They'll contact back in a day or two.'

Kelvin glared at her suspiciously.

'Do a lot of Internet in the middle of Tibet, do they?'

'Satellite thingy. Quite secure, we use a code.' This was only going to get more difficult, thought Shirley.

'Next time, agent Horowitz stays with you. Nothing to say those bastards won't send another version of Capaldi along.' They drank in silence.

'Must be time for lunch,' said Graeme hopefully.

—⁓—

Chapter Fifteen

'Of course,' said Ned, raking through his iPod, 'has to be Pavarotti's Nesun Dorma!'

'Wonderful, but not quite accurate McZed' said Toby, pointing across to the compact pile of sleeping family. 'Best keep it soft.'

The flight out of Tibet was relatively uneventful. They were not attacked by the Air Force or surface to air missiles, the motors worked perfectly, the batteries slowly built to full charge and stayed there. They flew low, making for a slow trip, but all the more beautiful for it. No radar, no GPS, just compass and maps. By the light of the moon they carefully threaded their way across the northern Tibet plateau and joined the glittering expanse of the Banggong Co Lake. If there were troops guarding the frontier, they were doing it indoors, next to a warm fire. Solly joined the sleeping Tibetans, the others stared out the windows at the spectacular, icy mass of the Himalayas as Ladybird wove around valley after uninhabited valley through the Ladakh night.

'We live to fly another day' announced Ned, pointing forward to the pink tinge of dawn.

—⁓—

Lama Sri Rinpoche Laputa Taransai meditatively sucked on his teeth and reflected on his breakfast. From his raised dais he surveyed the bowed shaved heads of the young monks absorbed in the rolling harmonies of the morning chant. The sun had crept over the mountains to warm his back. He raised his eyes a little to contemplate a large bird, floating far away on the horizon, no doubt searching for his own breakfast... Life was indeed good.

A big bird. A Lammergeier perhaps? Even a Golden Eagle? No, it was not a bird. Nor was it a plane. Sri Rinpoche had travelled on many planes to all parts of the planet to meet his followers. Nor was it Superman he thought with a silent chuckle. He settled to observe its flight, rising higher in his vision until it was directly above, then slowly growing in size; it was descending. The possibility that this silent, glowing cylinder may hold visitors from another world came to mind. How interesting that they would choose to arrive here! A good choice however, as the Zanskar valley was the centre of the universe. The callers stopped to remain suspended a hundred feet above the crowded courtyard. Silently. Politely. Patiently.

Sri Rinpoche was pleased to see none of the shaved heads had lifted. He extracted his glasses from the folds of his robe. There appeared to be a downward facing window framing a smiling face and waving hand. Without big glassy eyes and tentacles. Not extra-terrestrial beings then, he thought with a little regret. He waved back to the human.

Rising to his feet, Sri Rinpoche clapped his hands loudly. The chanting faltered into a ragged silence as the bliss filled minds were recalled. He made sweeping motions with his hands to clear some space, then, as the confused monks were a little slow, smiled broadly and pointed upwards. That certainly worked! Numerous vows of silence were broken in the scramble to the sides. Nodding merrily, Sri Rinpoche bade them to form orderly rows, and then be seated. Looking up, he offered his courtyard to Ladybird.

Liz had explained her choice of destination en route. Her discovery of Buddhism had taken her to a retreat in Sydney run by the younger Lama Sri Rinpoche and a dalliance with nundom, before being hauled back to Jamanka by her mother. Liz had continued to follow his teachings, attending his visits to Australia and communicating on the net. At this time of the year he would be in residence in the secluded monastery he had built in Zanskar, and they had found the adjoining village on one of Ned's travel stained maps.

There is always a path in any wilderness.

'Left hand down a bit and don't squash any. They mightn't be allowed to move,' said Ned while Ladybird rotated and settled slowly onto the stone flagged terrace. Shut down proceeded as Steve swung open the rear doors. Sean sprang down, stalked forward, leapt up on the dais and sat, tail lashing and looking at the Chief Lama. After the steps were run out, the crew and Rhabten's family emerged and stood as a self-conscious group. Sri Rinpoche gathered his robes, cautiously walked around Sean and stepped down to greet his visitors. Liz came forward and the Lama smiled broadly in recognition.

'Oh-ho! Elizabeth; a long way from Australia. Welcome to our little monastery!'

Liz embraced her teacher and then formally introduced him to all in turn. The Tibetan family stood in awe; never before had they met such a high-ranking Lama.

'I can see you have been travelling. We shall have breakfast!' he announced, patting his stomach. 'Second breakfast for me, as the hobbits say' he added, with a wink to Solly.

The monks were set to finish morning meditation as Sri Rinpoche led his guests into the eating hall.

—◦◦◦—

Two hours, a wonderful meal, and all had been explained. The Lama was a good listener, asking few questions and allowing the story to unfold at its own pace. Early on he summoned attendants and gave rapid instructions; Ladybird was to be covered with tarpaulins, its shape changed, and outside communication was to be shut down. Four monks were to go to the village and discreetly find out if the arrival had been noticed and reassure any concerns. Quick off the mark, thought Toby.

When Sri Rinpoche heard of the plight of Rhabten and his family, he warmly told them that Zanskar was now their home for as long as they wished. Many Tibetans had sought shelter here; they were among friends. The family, struggling to comprehend events but overjoyed, were led off gently to meet other refugees and be settled in.

'Come then, to my quarters,' he said to the crew, 'for we have much to talk of. What you have told me is most amazing! So many perils, so many openings!' Sri Rinpoche rubbed his hands in delight. He loved the unusual, the complicated and the many-layered quandaries life sometimes presented. So far away from the quest for simplicity, but still needing simple resolution.

'Knotty!' he shouted aloud as he strode along.

'A bit random' commented Jules.

'He's all right. He's like a big Yoda' said Solly. 'Jedi Master Rinpoche.'

―⁓―

Miss Lorimer and students were busy working through the 1964 school songbook while Maria, Arabella and Jim had set themselves up in her storeroom. Shirley had emailed to Tilda Primary as they suspected anywhere in Barangan would probably be monitored. The ASIO agents had been easy to lose, after Jim did a bit of bush-bashing on the tracks around Barangan. Stick out like dog's balls and can't drive for nuts was his comment. Now they stared in wonder at the screen of the Principal's unused computer, stunned by a two minute video of Liz and Solly, the grinning pilots and the approaching International Space Station, framed in Ladybird's distinctive front windows. With planet Earth glorious as background.

'Nicely shot' said Jim, after a while.

'This has to be the world's biggest ever mega-nova story' whispered Arabella, throat dry and face pale.

'Omigod,' added Maria, 'they went into space? When was this? Bloody Shirley! All she sent me was "Go to TPS and download Florence's latest. Now back down safe. S."'

'Well,' said Arabella, 'We've looked at the nice pictures; perhaps we should look at the text? Always helpful, I've found.'

'I know dear,' retorted Maria mildly, 'I was one of the ones who taught you reading.'

Together they skimmed the fourteen pages; Liz's cover note, the Branston release, a re-run on goals, risks, economic impact and environmental potential. Neck Snapping Performance figures for the blokes. The full description of their flight from Australia, Ned's escape, The Snares, naval altercations, and the flight up to the ISS. Humorous anecdotes. Everybody's Love. Regards from Sean, the first cat in space. Well, the first free cat in space.

'What to do with this then?' asked Maria. 'You're right of course, Arabella. Absolute Blockbuster story. Problem is, there's a lot of people out there working very hard to keep it squashed. We have to hit everywhere, hard and at exactly the same time.'

'Well, after the Paris Match story,' said Jim, 'I've had lots of interest from Europe…'

Suave. Urbane, even. Arabella pursed her lips, thought again and agreed.

'Yeah, great Jim. Lets do a package release to them all. Every newspaper we can come up with as well, and I'll ring all the editors I know to get some help.'

'Lovely,' said Maria. 'I'll get onto Roger the Director, that mob from Channel 7 and see what I can do with my old address book for European television. Some of them are a bit resistant to being censored. Quite exciting really! Only problem is where we can send it from. Not much point going back home.' They thought again for while.

'Cambrawarra. Only place that passes for a biggish town aound here. There's even two Internet cafes!' declared Jim.

'All right then. Arabella, I'm sure your Cambra Times editor is eating out of your hand nowadays and will let you use his distribution network, providing he can publish as well. There's a motel in Cambra with Internet, we'll use it, and the two cafes as well. I'll sidle into the Department of Education's Regional office too, do a general mail-out on their system… should get it well started down the forwarded chain mail!'

Arabella held up her USB. 'This morning our thumb drives, this afternoon the world!'

'I reckon,' said Jim, 'that the clip of the Space Station will go berserk on You Tube. It's even got some great music going with it' said Jim.

'Ah yes… the Blue Danube Waltz. Bit before your time, Jim. Now off to Cambrawarra, Kiddies!' ordered Maria.

———

Shirley smiled at the discomforted Senator as she slid the thumb drive into his laptop.

'Don't worry Kelve; the kids reckon there's no viruses in it. I would have given it to you earlier but it took them a while to download it and I'm not much good with this technology stuff… Oops, did I just wipe the hard drive…? No, only joking… there you go, how about that then!'

Mr. Strauss's new dance tune laid 'em in the aisles.

———

For Toby, the four days in Zanskar were a delight of regular meals, comfortable beds and relative warmth. Space and Tibet had already helped him get used to the altitude, while the radiant monastic peace eased away the dramas of the past week. He dabbled between working in the vegie gardens with the monks, helping Steve and Ned repair and rebuild the Ladybirds in the monastery's large workshop, exploring the library, or just sitting still. Sri Rinpoche had spent time with him, listening, talking, laughing, and even showing him some basic meditations. Toby felt serene. Tranquillity was something he had never experienced, indeed, something he had belittled in the past. Nice stuff, he decided.

Sri Rinpoche drifted gently from one crewmember to the next. Ned was left shaking his head in awe after a long conversation ranging from New Guinea tribal customs to advanced alloy bond characteristics. He proudly showed Toby the Lama's gifts of a 12th Century central Asian trade map and several ancient handwritten recipes. Ingredients would be a problem. His Ladybird I had been separated to get through the workshop door, fitted with extra batteries, oxygen tanks, a new scrubber, and several components scavenged from the Lama's ageing Beechcraft. Ned announced proudly he could now reinstate his role as long-range fighter escort.

Steve and Sri Rinpoche solved the problem of air leaks in Ladybird 2, re-built the pressure regulator and carbon dioxide scrubber, installed a conventional CB radio to communicate with LB1, added a supplemental solar array and discussed zen and the art of Ladybird maintenance. A radical engineer and great bloke, commented Steve.

Liz appeared to walk on grass without bending the blades after sessions with the Lama.

On the third day, the Lama had invited Julie and Solly to an afternoon of kite flying. Ketu, now dressed in the robes of a novice, carried a large case out to the hillside.

'The Lama has told me that in three years I can go to Delhi and learn to fly aeroplanes!' he whispered to Jules proudly. 'Awesome!' He liked new words.

Sri Rinpoche lifted out four brightly coloured small kites.

'These are Indian fighting kites. The string near the kite has been coated in powdered glass so be careful, it is very sharp. It can cut the string of another kite if handled well. I will teach you to fly them, then we shall have conflict!'

'Isn't that a bit, well, not Buddhist?' asked Jules, dubiously.

'Yes! But it is great fun! In our hearts we shall only see it as a game of skill.' Sri Rinpoche was very pleased with his kite students and after a while the combat began. It was highly energetic, the kites weaved, there was much shouting and surprisingly, the Lama's orange kite was first to part company, cut loose by Ketu. He was appalled and tried to melt into the hillside, but Sri Rinpoche laughed uproariously and clapped him soundly on the back.

'Oh well done! Yes, you have great skill! You will be my good pilot in four years!'

Ketu's red kite was next to fly free, cut a little too easily, she thought, by Jules. Boys!

She saw the way of it, Sri Rinpoche allowing defeat by the young novice, Ketu sacrificing his kite to the girl guest and now herself to do the big sister bit? No way.

'Gunna chop you down, little brother' she muttered to Solly.

'Airight Duke,' he replied with Holloway gravity, 'Let battle commence!'

Jules ran some fancy loops, swoops and figure of eights, moving closer, crowding. Solly appeared not to notice, kite stationary. She swooped down, across and up to catch the string… but his kite had gone! Where? He was still holding the string, eyes almost closed, smiling. Jules tried to track where the string went, then swore as Solly's blue kite flashed down out of the sun, caught the line, a quick tug and her kite fluttered away in the breeze.

'I read about that in one of Mr. Buchanan's Biggles books,' he explained.

Sri Rinpoche and Ketu applauded while Jules ruefully shook the victor's hand. Ketu set off as kite runner while the Lama lifted several neatly tied parcels from the case.

'This is a kite I have just finished and it may or may not work. It needs two pilots and an anchor. I make a very good anchor! Help me to assemble this prototype.'

The kite slowly grew as they fitted box sections, snapped out wings and added struts. Two double side strings linked to flaps were attached while Sri Rinpoche hooked a strong line and reel to a padded belt around his hips. Ketu had returned and helped keep the kite grounded while the others walked down the hill into the breeze.

'If this flies too well, you may need to fetch me back from Kashmir!' joked the Lama as he wedged himself behind a rock.

At a signal, Ketu carefully lifted the nose. The wings shivered and the giant bird leapt into the air; Sri Rinpoche grunted and leant back to take the strain.

'Left hand down a little Julie, let out more line Solomonder... yes, now we will let out another fifty metres... slowly... ah, very good... nicely balanced...'

At four hundred metres the line ran out and the trio settled to talk and play. A Lammergeier drifted over and maintained station well above the kite, interested but wary of this new big rival for his airspace. Monks gathered on the walls of the monastery to watch. Sri Rinpoche invited Solly and Jules to outline for him the evolution of the Ladybirds, the field and their hopes for its future. Simply. They chatted; he nodded and listened intently, occasionally steering further down paths. The monk was lost in admiration for the beautiful simplicity of the concept, could see a vast and ever expanding field of possibilities. He gravely recognised the changes, the challenges, the resistance and the risks that the field would bring. Sri Rinpoche then offered himself to help them in their great task. Solly and Jules grinned widely and shook his hand.

They took breaks to discuss and try new aerobatic manoeuvres, which their big bird performed with ease, eliciting enthusiastic applause from the monastery walls.

'This field will eat away at the shell of this big crab you fly in. I understand that it also protects you from the wind and prying eyes, but later, when you can be more sedate and open to the world, could it become a strength contained within?' asked the monk.

Jules and Solly looked at each other. Of course!

'Yes, thank you,' said Solly, 'we could...' he began, but stopped as a strong gust of wind caught the kite, ripped the strings out of their hands and levitated the startled monk over the rock. He began to be dragged helplessly up the hill. Ketu raced ahead, grasped the line. A knife appeared in his hand, he looked to his master who nodded. The kite soared, steadied itself then drifted majestically over the monastery, off on its own voyage. Sri Rinpoche stood up, brushed his robe down and smiled at the disappointed children.

'Our toy flies better when it is not held down! Time for some lunch. You have given me much to think about.'

—◦◦◦—

'Well Mrs Denzil, it's crunch time' said Senator Dobrovich.

'The Cougar has landed?' she asked. 'You must be happy to have your toy back.'

'Yes. It's at your Bankstown Airport. Pack your bags because we're off to catch up with your pals and have some serious conversation. Assuming you know where they are going.'

'Got a rough idea, Kelve, we'll zip across the water. Paris would be lovely this season. Another thing, to keep up with you boys, I would feel happier if I had a gun as well. Graeme can take a run out Mount Hay road and show me how it works.' She smiled sweetly.

'Well' muttered Graeme, 'I don't know if having an extra pistol packing person is such a good idea... Senator?' Kelvin grunted. Anything to please. Graeme went off to rummage in the artillery bag.

'Cool,' said Bobby, 'Is your plane like a Lear jet, Mr Dobrovich?'

'Better. Faster. Learjets are a hairdresser's aircraft...' growled Kelvin.

'Can we have a go flying it?' asked Brad.

'No worries,' said the Senator.

—◦◦◦—

Timothy Branston paused briefly for the obligatory publicity photos with the Soyuz crew, pushed past the debriefing officers and found his way back out to the tarmac. Well aware of consequences, his Paragon Air staff and private, very large executive jet were waiting, motors ticking over and clearances sorted. An anxious aide tried to take his bag and was told to fuck off. Timmy ran up the steps, growled 'London' and slumped into his Diffrient Computer Suite. Cabin staff quietly arranged food and drink on the periphery... Mr B was on a roll: the first six directives were fired off before the plane left the ground.

—⁓—

The delivery pilot, introduced as Hank who's with us to Paris, nodded to the company then climbed back on board to set up. The Senator's Cougar F750 had been waiting on the tarmac at Bankstown Airport when they arrived, and it was less than impressive. Unpolished, no paintwork to speak of and with distinctly suss additional patches spoiling its otherwise graceful lines. Shirley boarded, then sniffed as she surveyed the interior. She turned to Brad.

'Reckon this would be on a par with our ute don'tcha think Brad?'

'The upholstery's about the same, but it's got a toilet and a bit of a galley, Mum.'

'Lifted out of a caravan probably. Emer-Ritz, it aint.'

'Mightn't look much, but this plane is totally rebuilt, is now 50% more powerful and would be the fastest private jet around, dammit!' Kelvin looked annoyed.

'Bit like the Millennium Falcon!' said Bobby encouragingly. Kelvin, still disgruntled but smiling, waved vaguely at the seats and moved up front.

'At least the seats go all the way back' shouted Shirl from horizontal. She made herself comfortable, unstrapping the shoulder holster and carefully tucking her new weapon into her leather bag. Brad looked on.

'Awesome, Mum. You don't suppose...'

'No way Bradley. Don't even go there. Bad enough that I'm carrying one.'

The Cougar howled down the runway and sprang into the air. First stop Dubai.

—⁓—

Homer Spiggott scanned the e-mail dotpoints from Colonel Pewter quickly.

* a) His gallant troops had overcome a superior force and had taken the DR Congo rocket site with a loss of several men.

* b) Realising the risks to American and World Security of leaving a nuclear device, they had attached a timed explosive device and forced the site technicians to launch the rocket, resulting in its safe destruction in space.

* c) In consideration of:

i) The significance of the actions undertaken

ii) Additional risk and expenses, including casualty compensation

iii) A termination agreement /payment after years of faithful service

iv) The foregoing of the publication of his most interesting memoirs

* Then: a final termination payment of $600,000 would be appropriate.

Homer shrugged. It worked… problem sorted. He organised a bank draft, then replied:

My Dear Francis,

Enclosed termination payment as specified, congratulations on a successful enterprise and my condolences to the families of the departed. I need not elaborate on the complete meaning of 'termination' should there be any breach of section c) part iv). Thank you for your faithful service. Adios amigo.

He deleted the last two words; too frivolous.

Homer then turned to face the Very Annoyed Executive person, impatiently waiting between two armed guards. Standard opening gambit.

'Mr. Charles Jackson? Before you begin demanding rights and lawyers, you cannot access either. You are the head of an organisation that is a direct threat to our national security and are in our custody for as long as we choose. If you ever want to see your comfortable lifestyle and family again, you have one option: cooperate.'

'Very spooky I'm sure, you asshole. By the time my people finish with you, you won't have a life, full stop. You know nothing, Sergeant Schultz!'

'On the contrary, your own life is probably more at risk from your associates. We know enough of their methods, along with the extortion, blackmail, arms shipments, as well as the latest little nuclear project in the Congo.' Homer smiled and leant back.

Nuclear? The Congo? What was Ms. Montague up to? New York swore silently. Deep shit.

The office door splinted inward as the hard faced killer with a blazing submachine gun sprang into the room. Plaster lumps spat from the roof, the guards returned fire as the gunman lined up on the paralysed Jackson. Blood sprayed as holes appeared in the assassin's overalls. He sprawled, gurgled horribly and died.

'Goddamn!' screamed Spiggott, 'Get this man down to a secure room!'

The white faced Charles Jackson was dragged quickly out the door.

'You can get up now Simpson. You've been practicing that gurgle, haven't you.'

Agent Simpson grinned sheepishly. Good enough for the movies, he figured.

Homer surveyed the wrecked ceiling and sighed. More expense again. This small charade was embarrassing but effective. Amazing how loud, intense and attitude altering real bullets were. The urbane Mr. Jackson should unravel quite quickly now.

—⁓—

Mrs. Alison Jordan looked at the First Class menu and settled for the fish. Ms. Montague preferred lighter food while flying. And fly she must, for all her deliberations told her that this ladybird machine and crew were headed to Western Europe, probably seeking scientific support. Which they must not obtain. The sole meuniere arrived for her to pick at.

—⁓—

In 'Dunwandrin', the cream and green weatherboard bungalow at twenty-five Wallaby Street, Barangan, it was noted that the Internet, newspapers, radio and TV all had exploded. Ballisticly. Gargantuanesquely.

'We've had over two million hits on the ISS video clip!' announced Jim with suitable awe. 'As soon as they block it, someone else loads it back on. Four rock bands, a car company, eight travel firms and a soap manufacturer have used it for their ads already, and that's just on the sites that I've found. Wow!'

'The Cambrawarra Pastoral Times has syndicated our articles worldwide and Frank says he hasn't been to bed and reckons he's going mad. He must be, says he's giving me a $500 bonus' announced Arabella gleefully. Only thing, this thing's so big its a bit scary…'

'Yes indeedy,' said Maria with wide eyes, 'haven't had this much fun in years. My Barangan Correspondent Reports have blitzed world TV as well. Quite a few folk still try hard to put the stoppers on, but its not working quite as well for them. Our mates Evangeline Parsons QC and Senator Kelly have challenged and removed all the suppression orders. Billy Styler has been squashing the other radio shock jocks. As for the real scary bits, Ken Baker and Ernie Harris are taking turns on guard. No Problems.'

Out on the front porch, Ken chewed a black cigar, watched the street with snake-slit eyes and cradled his automatic shotgun. Hoping someone would make his day.

—ᴧᴧ—

Senator Dan Kelly sat down and mopped his face, exhausted, oblivious to the hands clapping his back and the thunderous standing ovation. From both sides of the house. Best speech in living memory.

Dan had picked his slot well; there was an appropriations bill up that afternoon so the chamber was full and lunch was just past, so many of the senators were quite… mellow. He had started out softly, outlining the scaffold. He gently courted an inept heckler from the far right, then delivered an elegant riposte to disembowel the fool and wake those who were dozing. Dan warmed to the task. "Could be a potential problem" was stoked up to "Total Catastrophic Disaster". The best to be on the safe side aspects of Climate Change were bundled with our cringing dependency on imported oil. The exultant exuberance of our own clean power source, at little cost. Carefully managed of course. The murmurs of agreement grew to a rumble. Australia as a Nation of Innovators, with stirring examples. An enthusiastic description of the bush battler Tilda family workshop, with Henry Lawson overtones. The youth of Australia, excelling despite gloomy predictions, inventing a wondrous, new, Australian Technology! That young, virile drive which every member of the chamber possessed! The chorus of Hear Hear echoed around the panelled walls. The Kelly voice dropped to a dangerous growl and he slammed a bundle of papers down. The gallant Henderson Family with their friends, setting out to make a go of it but against such odds! Documented Evidence of Foreign Conspiracy! Our Armed Forces duped into pursuit and attempted destruction of the flying machines! The abduction and assault of a respectable woman schoolteacher! Attempts at discrediting the Australian invention! This was not to be tolerated; it was a strike at our freedoms! And despite all this, our Aussie adventurers, like Kingston Smith, have flown on. And up! Dan thumbed the chamber's audio-visuals and Ladybird's approach to the ISS sprang out on the screen as he thundered into his finale. The spirit of the Southern Cross, the impertinence of colonial confidence, the courage of Kakoda! The legends, icons and myths were laid on with a shovel as Dan worked the senators up to a froth.

'Blind Freddy could see that this Senate MUST unanimously vote its full support behind these heroic Australian battlers. Not to do so would brand every bastard here forever as timid, lily-livered, indeed, as PUSILANIMOUS!'

Dan had liked the Barangan briefing paper.

He put the motion, they voted, it passed.

Historically unanimous.

―⁓ⱽⱽ―

Ms. Juliette Overmyer, aka Jordan, aka Montague had taken a very fast train from Paris to Munich, to be met at the station by the German Head Factor and his Head Arranger. Soberly dressed and visibly anxious, they fussed over her single suitcase then schwooshed her away in an obligatory black Mercedes. On arrival, Ms. Montague took control without a whimper of protest. Munich, now the nominal Principal Factor, respectfully briefed her regarding the arrest of New York, arrangements for his removal and the security upgrade.

The Principal Arranger had been very busy on the flight and train ride, researching.

'There is no recorded information of how these machines were built. If we can destroy them and their crews in the air, there is a high probability the technology will be removed permanently. From reports they appear to be un-trackable by the usual heat signature weapon or by radar, however, there is

271

an Israeli missile that uses electro-optical imaging. We need a high-speed jet armed with these missiles ready in Northern Europe, for I believe they are headed for Britain, Germany or Scandinavia to have the technology validated and checked for safety. We need immediate access to any reported sightings, and a back up armed team. Review all the information and if there are any other options, I am to be informed immediately.'

Ms. Montague turned on her heel and stalked off to her allocated office, followed closely by her personal and technical liaison aides.

—⁓—

'Your friends in Australia have been very successful,' said Sri Rinpoche, laying newspaper transcripts on the table while he selected television and Internet segments to run up on the smart board. He translated the French, German and Japanese items for the Ladybird crew as his fingers flickered on the laptop. Adept. Liz, Jules and Solly were pleased to see their own fed in material added to the Barangan releases.

'This is most amusing too!' chuckled Sri. 'There was a very determined effort to prove that your approach to the Space Station was a hoax! Reports from the crew that no-one had visited, experts saying the video clip was a fraud... then this came out!'

The front page of Branston's flagship Galaxy News sprang up on the smart board.

Headline 'I WAS THERE!' Timothy holding space helmet. Ladybirds nestling next to the radiators. Crew smiling out of the front windows. More inside!

'He made me seven years younger! Thank you Mr Branston' exclaimed Liz.

'Didn't tell me you were thirteen when I met you,' complained Steve.

'Nice one of Sean,' said Jules, 'though he looks totally freaked.'

'Aussie Space Corps pilots McZud and Buckenen. Looking cool' added Solly.

'Oh,' said Toby, 'that's all very well, great publicity and all that, but this meeting's about where to go next? We're a bit vague on that if I remember. Like, we can't just wander around the planet getting shot at.' Despite the tranquillity, his level of disgruntle was rising a little with the lack of direction. Lama Sri Rinpoche Laputa Taransai spoke.

'I have thought on this. You wanted to find and appeal to a reputable research facility in Europe to test your device for its safety. This would be appropriate. I have a friend from my student days in Stockholm who may be able to help. My tutor. It was from a lifetime ago, but we have always been in touch. A physicist. It is Dorte Andersen.'

'Swedish is he? Big white beard and a red suit?' asked Toby.

Solly was shaking his head in wonder. 'Doctor Dorte Andersen from the Leksveriksnia Institute? Wow. I have read heaps of her articles. She should have won the Nobel Prize for her work on The Harksvent Reactor Project. Potential isometric transition factors relating to the Helium-4 nucleus stuff. She's amazing!'

'Dorte is Danish for Dorothy, Toby' said Sri. 'She does not like Wizard of Oz jokes but does laugh at many things. She calls herself Doktor Dot. She retired and lives out of Narvik in Norway, but still consults and attends on many committees.'

'The Norwegian Nuclear Physics Committee, the Science Research Council, Oslo Physics Olympiad Committee and the Nobel Committee and heaps more,' said Solly.

'If it is agreeable, I can e-mail her suggesting a visit, without mentioning anything which may raise alarums. Yes?' Sri looked to the Hendersons.

'Bewdy. Any mate of yours is all right by us,' said Steve. 'The 'birds are ready to go anywhere, anytime. New filters and remote links, even more batteries, stacks of oxygen and fuel and both as watertight as duck's bums.'

'Thanks Steve,' sighed Liz, 'to be sure. So how do we get from A to B?'

'Well, there's a thing!' announced Ned, unrolling a large world map onto the table…

—∿∿—

The two lines of monks chanted as they pulled on silken ropes attached to Ladybird 2's landing skids. They didn't have to pull very hard; Jules hovered the blue glowing craft a fraction above the stone flagging. Toby was impressed however; in the sunset afterglow it could have been Vikings hauling a Knarr down to the sea for a North Atlantic voyage. He shivered. Not the best image. At least all the prayer flags were nice.

Sri Rinpoche spoke briefly to the monks, who were not overly happy but accepting in silence. He turned, and with Ketu following, ascended into Ladybird 2. Toby smiled, remembering the arguments Ketu had put up to accompany them, as the chief monk's aide and Personal Assistant, trainee pilot, cook, clothes cleaner, dish wallah, porter… the LB2 crew had become seven. And a cat. Eight was a good number for small group work, thinking back to counselling, a hundred years ago it seemed. Ah well, the last leg! Giving a small wave to the impassive saffron ranks, he trudged up the steps carrying Sean.

Four puncture wounds treated with the handy pocket disinfectant spray; Toby joined Jules and Ketu in the pre-flight check. Sri Rinpoche looked on and chuckled as Liz fussed around with his seatbelt. 'Do you have an in flight menu and movies?' he asked genially.

'Perhaps some biscuits soon, and the view may make up for the movie,' replied Liz.

'All clear on runway four' announced Toby.

'Passengers are not permitted to smoke on the aircraft, the emergency exit is the back door,' called out Solly, standing and gesturing, 'but we don't have any life jackets to demonstrate.'

'Siddown and put your seatbelt on Sol' growled Steve.

The CB radio lifted from Sri's plane crackled with Ned's impatient voice from Ladybird 1.

'Do you think we might leave today then?'

The monks watched and prayed as both Ladybirds rose gently into the good night.

—⁓—

Heinreich Gunter dabbled in many things during his twenty year backpacking travels. Becoming a Buddhist monk ticked one of his boxes and he had allocated three months towards that in the tranquil, not overly arduous setting of the revered Sri Rinpoche monastery. Scored an extra twelve months on his visa as well. Kool. With the departure of the Venerable Sri, the blanket communications ban had been lifted and Heinreich hurriedly reclaimed his satellite phone from storage. Sick mother. Although not really the one bad apple, Heinreich had put his finger in many freelance pies to fund his voyage. Now in his room, his SMS finger prodded away rapidly on a lengthy description of the 'spaceship' arrival, its crew, their doings at the monastery and their departure with his leader. He had not been able to glean their destination, but the story as it stood should earn something. Completed, he fired it off to the news bureau and assorted government agencies in his string, then just on spec, to the new lot in Munich. He had heard from a fellow entrepreneur in Bangkok that they were interested in anything political, industrial or economic…

—⁓—

'Most interesting!' observed Sri Rinpoche Laputa Taransai. 'It is very like the gentle ascension to heaven which one reads of. We have a splendid view of our mountains and all of Ladakh since you set the machine in a slow spiral. Rather like a revolving restaurant,' he added hopefully. Dinner had been missed. As all was well and the slow climb allowed it, the crew was able to open one of the large hampers from the monastery kitchen and stroll around with their evening meals. Sri declared it quite the most comfortable and civilised way to travel. In an orbit twenty metres away, Ned cheerily waved parts of a roast chicken from the village. To the annoyance of Toby and Steve, who were feeling somewhat carnivorous by now. Back to the felafels.

The ascent over the next two hours into space, and then, as Jules and Solly announced gleefully, into Deep Space, was uneventful. Not that you could call the slow panoply of a planet shrinking beneath you a non-event. Sri Rinpoche and Ketu were mesmerised as continents emerged, lit by the strings of pearls of humans at night. Gazing, praying, pointing, chatting, sighing happily. Contented passengers.

'Having a good time then?' asked Steve. 'The seals we worked on and the changes with the scrubber are working a treat and Ned says that LB1 is tip-top too. Thanks!'

Sri nodded absently, then pointed to the moon creeping out from behind the dark earth. He smiled enquiringly. Solly grinned and nodded.

'Not this trip though...' added Jules.

At 6,000 kilometres up, the Ladybirds were far above the low earth orbit spy satellites, albeit not the rest such as geosynchronous ones in high orbit. Solly stated 45,000 kilometres up was a bit too far to go. Their monastery table conference had decided that although still observable by telescopes, this would be the most secure route. Did security agencies use telescopes? A wham-blam super-fast trip was also discarded in favour of 'leisurely'... Bugger it; they were sort of on holidays, as Steve put it.

The Ladybirds set course for the Arctic.

———∿∿∿———

Ms. Montague scanned the Gunter SMS and demanded an immediate probe on history, contacts, influence and finances of the Zanskar monastery along with a full brief on the leader who had flown off with the enemy. She was pleased when this, as well as transcripts of all phone and email traffic over the past week was provided in less than twenty minutes. The Munich office loved technology, speed and efficiency as much as it did hierarchy, orders and control. Ms. Montague liked Munich. The email from Sri Rinpoche to Dr. Dorte Andersen and notes regarding her background in physics leapt out of the page at her; she knew immediately this had to be the destination of the machines. She referenced the address then quickly summoned her underlings.

'The target will arrive near Narvik in Norway at this map reference very soon. The aircraft I commissioned should check if they are already there, and if not, maintain surveillance nearby. Is it armed appropriately?'

'Zey are permitted to fly anyvere in Scandanavia, to be photographink zer liddle migratory birts,' stated the Munich Arranger smugly. 'Ve ver able oso to obtain only two of zer special missiles and equipment but zer correct installink vas difficult. Zis vas difficult because zer civilian jets before do not haf zer missiles. It vill vork howeffer, ve know.'

Ms. Montague sighed.

'Get the back up team to Narvik' she growled.

———∽∿∿∼———

Twenty-five Wallaby Street, Barangan, was causing problems with the neighbours. Five television vans, a dozen foreign cars and numerous plastic gazebos housed reps of most of the nation's media. Nature strips were suffering. Potential conflicts were being averted by negotiation: little spots of interview celebrity being were traded for kerb space, access to power points / taps and occasional toilet use.

'Jeeze,' said Jim. 'When do we do the next conference? There's more journos out there than flies around the footie club's dunny.'

'Two hours. We've got a few unreleased shots from the Snares, along with the piece that Toby wrote from Zanskar. Senator Kelly is about to send me a report on the Senate Special Committee. Lengthy deliberations, I suspect' said

Maria. 'It would be nice if Shirl or Liz could send some new stuff to feed the chooks,' she added wistfully. All those hungry outlets waiting.

Just inside the front gate, the two ASIO agents sat in their negotiated space under Maria's beach umbrella. On the porch, Sergeant Ken Baker raised his clinking glass to them and grinned. Ernie sat on the back verandah and watched the fence.

———

Charles Jackson, ex New York, smiled at Homer, apparently back to unruffled.

'Nice presentation Homer but probably wouldn't work in a boardroom. I guess it shows you're keen to do a deal however...' He paused and looked confidently across the table. 'Interested in a little insurance package I've put together over the past few years?'

Despite his avowed commitment to The Alliance, Charles was a modern businessman. Company loyalties changed. How did it go? Circumstances change your chances? Different faces for altered cases? Charles settled for both. Midstream, he would jump for the biggest horse. Twelve years as Principal Factor made him well acquainted with Alliance policy on executive failure and he knew he would be in great need of both protection and money.

Homer smiled back. He could do pragmatism.

'I thought you may come around, somehow. What have you got and what do you want?'

'Everything, and lots.'

Four hours saw Charles walking out with a smile, his lawyer, a stuffed briefcase and a temporary bodyguard. Homer was still shaking his head in wonder at the retrieved, very secure website. Enough tied in with their own discoveries to establish bona fides and the rest... the size and multinational complexity of this 'Alliance' was boggling! Running, according to Jackson, since the 1600s. Charles' insurance package was very attractive, with over 50 web pages of history, structure, finances, staffing, current projects and codes. Homer recognised an uncomfortable number of highly important faces in the recorded meetings, people who were beyond prosecution but would become useful assets to the Department. Charles had also given Homer a full briefing on the current program to obliterate the Tilda Project. Homer looked at the steely-faced cell phone snap of the 'Principal Arranger'. The first task would be to track this Montague / Jordan person and set up full surveillance on the Alliance Munich section. Send the info to the Senator, who should be in Paris by now then on to pruning the other branches of this rotten tree.

Homer Spiggott rubbed his hands, called in his very closest staff and set to work.

—✺—

'I think,' said Liz, 'that it might be time to send some more pikkies and chat to our mates Shirley Liz. And the rest of the world. Hmmm?'

'Yair,' added Steve, 'the reverend here can earn his keep, set up his office studio and give the planet a bit of a sermon. Be a first, from deep space!'

Sri Rinpoche happily unpacked the video camera and equipment and instructed Liz on its operation. Settling himself in Sukhasana pose, he began with a short prayer. As he chanted, Sri gently floated up off the carpet... and realising what was happening, burst into laughter.

'My friends!' he announced, wiping away the tears, 'I am the Lama Sri Rinpoche Laputa Taransai, and I am not demonstrating the power of levitation through perfect meditation! I am speaking to you from space. Allow me to introduce the people who have bought me to this weightless place in their wonderful craft...' Sri went on to present the crew; give a succinct account of their objectives and to state his complete support. Ketu kept him from floating off.

Liz then took a tour around Ladybird, feet schtikking with each step. Jules had visited the monastery's tailor and had traded the last of their lollies for his supply of Velcro: with practice, the crew could now move about the cabin. Additional carpet, glued to the walls and roof, added to the floor space and made for some interesting camera angles. First stop saw Steve extolling the virtues of the carbon dioxide scrubber and generator exhaust system, then Jules and Ketu floated the audience through kitchen and food arrangements. Toby, Captain's cap firmly pulled down, ran through the flight deck controls and instruments, adding that the passengers were now flying at eighteen million feet and enjoying calm weather. Liz commended the grand view of an Earth that filled the front windows then called Ned and LB1 in close to wave and say hello. A pirouette to show his pride and joy. And just to show off.

Solly and Sean then stole the show. Carefully supported by Solly, (no-one else would attempt such a thing), Sean had been talked out of his cage a half hour earlier to creep tentatively forward, clinging to the carpet. Sean was never one to be intimidated by a new environment for long and had since made great progress.

'Sean,' called Solly, 'Time for a drink?' He held up Sean's own squeezy pushbike bottle and gently eased a large globule of 'Pusso-Milk' out to wobble mid air. Sean uncurled, completed an elegant Adho Mukha Savasana while calculating trajectories and gently launched himself. Slow motion mid-air Tiger pose, a wide smile and jaws closed silently around the creamy gobbet. A leisurely aerial cat full twist with somersault and Sean was clamped onto the further wall, licking a paw.

'No need for Velcro with him,' muttered Toby. Sean had found that his superb agility, array of cat moves and natural attachments made him well suited to space travel. Spotting the remains of his final stuffed mouse floating in the kitchen area, he went into full charge Attenborough mode...

'I would say,' said Liz after the three dimensional soccer, 'that that's a wrap. We'll fire off the lot to the Denzils. Lunch anyone?'

The Ladybirds motored on to their Arctic drop zone

—⁓—

'Graeme, and Kelvin, maybe you're interested in this?' Shirley led the pair to the adjoining Denzil suite of their Champs Elysees hotel. Brad and Bobby stood back from the Louis XIV walnut sideboard.

'This is our third generation Mini Dekko Omnitron, made by Solly and Jules' announced Bobby proudly. The Americans looked nonplussed into the battered plywood case at the keyboard, jumble of dials, switches, slots, plugs and winking l.e.d.'s. The lid contained a glowing flat screen.

'Your portable TV?' hazarded Kelvin.

'Does that too. We've just picked up a message from Mrs. Henderson, who's about 6000 K that way,' said Brad, pointing up, 'and we've downloaded a video file. Should be cool.'

'But... it's too little. Where's the power plant? Your transmitter? You would need a massive satellite dish as well, like a small radio telescope!'

'Yeah,' agreed Bobby, 'I always said we needed the bigger vegie steamer.' Shirley could trace with her finger the doubt written on the Senator's brow.

'Are they still on line Brad? Open up the link. With the camera on.'

Switches were flipped, the screen popped into life and Liz looked up. Behind her a Buddhist monk appeared to be in conversation with a floating boy and cat. Beyond them, stars glittered around a quarter-framed view of planet earth.

'Aahh... is that the Senator and agent Horowitz with you then, Shirl. I was wondering when you would introduce them.

Welcome aboard!' Graeme smiled broadly and waved. Kelvin swore loudly, apologised and did likewise.

'Not the best thing for security, but we don't have much choice,' said Shirl to Liz. 'These good old boys are hard at work protecting us all, so we figured it's time to bring them into the loop! Bye.' She cut the link and looked levelly at the two men. 'Now before you start carrying on Senator, Yes, we have been able to chat with them on occasions and we didn't tell you about the Dekko, but tough. Didn't quite trust you. And you're still a bit dodgy…'

'About goddamn time you let us know, Ma'am. I could have done my negotiations face to face, for a start.'

'And bought them into the fold like a good shepherd. Sure, Kelve. I hate to say it, but we have another problem as well. The opposition seems to be able to locate the Dekkos when we transmit, although we believe the buggers can't open the coded text we use.'

'Specially after we went to Code 2' added Bobby, with a conspiratorial wink.

'Yes. The visuals aren't coded yet, so they've probably seen all the j-pegs and our last little chat…' She let them mull that over. Graeme mulled quicker.

'Need to be out of here then. Probably within fifteen minutes, Sir.'

Senator Dobrovich chewed his cigar, hawked and spat absently across the room and into the waste paper basket.

'Two points…' whispered Brad to Bobby. Shirl glared. Don't take it up.

'Well Mrs. Denzil, maybe we should now go where your friends are going.'

'The north of Norway is very nice this time of the year, Kelve. Narvik is pretty.'

—∿∿—

'Whacko the chook! We're on again!' announced Jim Dobson, looking over Maria's shoulder into the Dekko. The beaming face of a Buddhist monk, sitting in the middle of Ladybird 2 came up. He began chanting and rising.

'OMG! It's just great, Miss. Wicked! The world will love it!'

———

Reports of arrests and surveillance meant that New York had traded his knowledge, confirming the information from her Overseas Security sleeper.

The Principal Arranger was in full control. The incredibly complex task of moving The Alliance into defensive security mode would have overwhelmed another, but Ms. Montague did not do daunt; her directives flowed rapidly and seamlessly through the covert Arranger network for emergency shutdown. Principal factors would be warned to close surface operations and make their own security arrangements.

Her technician passed her the iPad and she watched the short clip. The Denzil family, Senator Dobrovich and an agent in Paris. So. She fired off an order for an immediate attack to an aide who almost clicked his heels before hurrying off. Back to the larger task. The office entrance was sealed; anonymous white vans were gathering outside. Munich had it's own underground exit four blocks away and they would soon evacuate to their secondary site. Secondary sites were Arranger-only knowledge, not compromised.

She would then move north, to ensure that the Australian threat was dealt with. Permanently.

———

Far below, the dark mass of the Arctic was lit by the flickering green swirl of the Aurora Borealis.

'Well, aren't we lucky then!' said Ned, calling from LB1, 'The Dance of the Spirits to light our way. Sailing down on a solar wind. The light might even mask our own little blue glow from anyone looking.' They gazed down on the shining wisps. Toby looked to Solly.

'Umm, Sol, the Aurora is an electricky thing isn't it? Ionic? Not likely to affect the field is it? Like suck it up or something?'

'Probably not.' said Solly, busy taking pictures. 'If it did, we might lose all our power.'

How reassuring, thought Toby, as he maneuvered to follow Ned through the ionosphere.

Ned, of course, chose to drop down the middle of one of the emerald green curtain folds, surfing a vertical, phosphorescent pipeline. The Atlantics came crackling through his CB radio link with 'Bombora'… there was nothing that man wouldn't do for emphasis! The kids squealed happily while Liz filmed. At least there appeared to be no problems with the field. Different colour maybe. The Ladybirds dropped to the Barents Sea, cold, dark and dotted with ice.

'We're a bit south of Bjørnøya, Bear Island' said Liz, bringing up an interactive map. 'We've got about 400 kilometres to get to the Norwegian mainland. We could go up this fjord at Sommaroy to the end 'cause it looks a bit less populated, then loop around southeast through this mountain area down to where Dr. Andersen lives beside Trollvatnet. If we see activity we can cross the lake underwater, like Ned did, and pop out at her house.' Toby shivered. The prospect of an underwater trip in an icy Norwegian lake called Trollvatnet in the early morning did not appeal.

'This is a good plan' said Sri Rinpoche. 'If I can send an email, Doktor Dot will have a big breakfast ready for us!'

The debate was brief. Possible security difficulty versus a hot breakfast. Tough call.

'Excellent.' said MS. Montague. 'Have your aircraft take off at dawn and patrol, tell the team to start moving up towards

this Lake Trollvatnet. An isolated house you say? Good. You have your instructions for further operations. Arrange my transport to Narvik.'

'Immediately, Principal Arranger!' Definite heel click.

Homer Spiggott looked at the securely shackled, nondescript woman who sat glaring at him. Agent Simpson, machine pistol at the ready, stood behind her.

'Shouldn't have used the office email, Mrs. Baker. Put you right in the frame, along with the laptop in your car. Guess you felt it was a bit urgent? We broke that particular Alliance code two days back. Anything to say?'

Homer managed to dodge most of the spit. The mole was removed, and to be interrogated. Homer had more pressing matters; it appeared that two Israeli Python air-to-air missiles had been tracked to an airfield in Tromsø and that the Alliance had an aircraft nearby. The Senator and his party were on their way north as well.

Everything was happening in Norway mused Homer, as he fired off a message to his boss.

The Ladybirds crept past the lights of Sommaroy, Sandvik and then on to the end of the fjord as dawn broke. No traffic on the E6 as they slid across and on past the little village of Skjold. Ned drew back and higher in order to direct the larger LB2 around any habitation, but there was not much; this was a rugged, isolated area. Very quiet. Anyone with sense was still in bed asleep. Ned was about to comment on this as they cruised through the Hogskardet pass when a flicker to the right caught his attention. Small plane maybe, banking, about 4 kilometres away.

Liz read the text message out to Toby. 'Urgent. Armed aircraft in Tromso area. Python missiles. Senator says dangerous.'

'Never heard of them, but Ned's up on all of that stuff. Shouldn't be a problem though, we're well away from Tromso. Let him know.' Ned was definitely up on Pythons.

'Buggeration! Absolutely deadly! If they're fives, those bastards are a whole new generation, work on an optical system. Not radar! If it locks on, we're stuffed. We've got a visitor too, off to the right and seems to have spotted me, at least. Might just be a curious pilot, I'll lead him off and lose him. Drop low Toby.' Toby did so, trying to catch a glimpse of the intruder. Must be behind that peak. He edged in toward the slope.

Ned banked right, keeping the aircraft in sight and increasing speed. It was definitely steering towards him, a small jet and closing fast. Some boxes under those wings? Damn. Ned left his hand on the throttle and watched keenly as the plane moved closer. Abruptly, the craft banked steeply left, diving directly toward LB2, creeping around the side of a mountain. Must have an observer.

'Toby! Up 45 and full power! Get the fuck out of there!'

As Ned watched in horror, concealing covers blew off from two very lethal looking AAM's mounted under the wings. One dropped, flames spurted and it arrowed toward its target. Going helluva fast. LB2 was powering up and away, but seemed like a snail. The smoke trail was curving toward the dot with a locked on, mathematical, intersectional certainty.

Ned watched, hooked in dismay. The other pilot was far more practical and had wheeled back on him. One to go. A puff with a speck in it appeared. Ned's pilot instinct took over as he banked away and dived. Bad, bad scene, the range and angles were wrong for him. Port rear, Mach 4 and gaining quickly. Ladybird not as fast yet and getting low…Ned slammed port, cutting across the face of a cliff, knowing the missile would react as swiftly. Narrow cleft ahead. Ned barrelled in, slowing rapidly as he prayed for a bend. There! Ned turned hard to starboard, entreating deities furiously as the g's piled on. It worked. The missile, deprived of its rapidly approaching target and faced with rock instead, angled up and out of the chasm.

Within milliseconds its advanced scanning spotted and rejected its own host aircraft, put the missile into a wide circle and searched anew.

Ned was very lucky. With eye bulging deceleration he managed to stop before the cliffs closed in, then sank to the bottom. Even so, he was very exposed and needed an overhang. Nothing. Sit it out. A thousand feet above, the Python flicked overhead and registered the finned cylinder. Stationary. Locked on for terminal chase it lined up... and at that moment ran out of fuel. Even so, its tiny wings tried valiantly to maintain target course but alas, Gravity called. Obedient to programming, the AAM blew itself to pieces.

—⌇⌇⌇—

Boiling mad, Ned rocketed up out of the cleft, looking for his enemy. Plate steel would make short shrift of aircraft aluminium. Having seen their remaining missile self-destruct however, the jet had disappeared. As one would, thought Ned.

Bitterly, he began the search for LB2, or what remained of it.

—⌇⌇⌇—

Chapter Sixteen

Ned's words of 'absolutely deadly,' 'locked on' and 'stuffed' were still ringing in Toby's ears when the shout to 'get the fuck out of there!' reached him. He probably shouldn't have, but yelling to hang on, he hauled the throttle back hard, snapping the plastic safety gate. The window in front went to an intense blue and Toby was slammed back into his seat...

Had the missile been even smarter, it would have plotted Ladybird's trajectory ahead, changed course and easily intersected. It was however, obsessive. Lock on; stay on target, go where it goes. Consequently it found itself behind the designated but shrinking cylinder and lost the race. Three hopeful circles, pffffit went the solid fuel and with an expensive bang, termination.

Toby and the crew were oblivious to this as the seven g acceleration bought rapid blackout. Faces contorted, their sightless eyes missed seeing the sky darkening from blue to black, the stars appearing and brightening as Ladybird's tremendous power hurled them once more into space. Faster and faster. One pair of eyes, though seeing all through a dark brown haze, came back to functioning after a while. Generations of very high altitude living had left Ketu with a bloodstream jam packed with red corpuscles, enough of which were making it to his brain. He croaked to Julie and Toby to slow down, but no response. Even moving his eyeballs was hard, but a very slow sideways glance showed him his Lama's blank face in a hideous rictus grin. Were they all dead? Straining, he moved one hand to his seat belt buckle and unsnapped it. The belt whipped back of its own accord to hang mid-air, rigid.

It took five minutes of superhuman effort for Ketu to claw his way forward between the pilot's seats and inch his arm forward to grasp the throttle. It was like swimming through his Grandmother's sweet-rice-with-extra-condensed-milk. Pushing with his legs, hauling back on a chair frame that was buckling under his fingers, he slowly forced the throttle forward. The force pulling him back, stopped. He fainted.

Jules came around slowly to the largest view of the moon she had ever seen. She could see the craters quite clearly. She puzzled painfully as to why they were getting bigger.

'Omigod Toby, we're going to crash!' But Toby was still emerging. Quickly she rotated Ladybird sideways and reached for the throttle, fingers closing around Ketu's clenched fist.

'Let go you dork' she yelled, pulling. The hand came free and she could ease the throttle on again. Ketu slid back to wrap around his seat.

Was it enough? The moon, now framed in the side windows, was starting to creep back, even as it grew larger. She pulled on more power, fighting the brown edge in her vision. Hyperventilating seemed to help. A bit more throttle. Bloody hell, power was down to 5%! Jules could only sit and wait, sometimes yelling at Toby or anyone to wake up, at other times swearing while she watched the moon. A race between the looming surface and its outside rim. All she could think of was the advice of Barangan's only surfer: never swim against a rip, swim across it. The rip that could turn them into moon powder at the bottom of a new crater.

Good advice as it turned out. For a few heart stopping moments Ladybirds swooped at incredible speed across the surface until the moon's horizon quickly slid past. Jules eased the throttle back to zero, set the field at minimum and cried. There was a general moaning and stirring as the rest of the crew swam up out of the dark. Jules gently rotated until the dwindling moon was in full view. Beyond it, Earth also shrank. She explained the situation to Toby.

'Oh God, sorry everyone, used a bit too much throttle I daresay.' He noticed the power readout. 'Bloody Hell! Is that 1%! Steve!' The lighting was down to dull glow, the field on the window grids was the faintest of blues and it was getting distinctly colder. Steve worked on the generator, priming, checking, and pulling the start cord but to no avail. Bloody lawn mowers, thought Toby, never start. Steve was more patient, checked and cleaned the plug, two more pulls and the motor purred into life. There was some feeble cheering as the lights brightened. Solly asked some questions, made some calculations and estimated they would be moving away from earth at around point triple-oh four.

'Point point triple-oh four what?' asked his Mum.

'Light speed.' Toby was about to about to say that it didn't sound tooo fast, when Solly added 'About four hundred and thirty thousand kilometres per hour.'

Nearly three hours at 1.5g bought them to stationary, a long way from home.

'Just keep pointing at that little blue marble, if you please Miss Julie,' said Toby.

'Maybe we should try messages to Ned and Shirl now we're heading back,' suggested Liz.

'Could we perhaps go past the moon on the way back?' asked Sri Rinpoche politely.

'Provided the generator holds out...' muttered Steve, patting the motor.

—⁓—

Ned had estimated the direction of LB2 when last seen and flew on for ten minutes, searching for wreckage. A thin column of smoke ahead proved to be a small cabin, much to his relief. Nor could he see any sign of smoke in the sky above. From memory, the Python was a relatively short-range missile; if his friends had kept ahead of it for 20 kilometres or so, they may well have survived. Perhaps... He switched on his Dekko and sent out a call, but there was no response. Heading back to the start point, Ned set his craft at a guesstimated angle and opened up the power. Chances were, they had gotten away but ended up in a low orbit, hopefully in one piece. Where the hell were they?

An hour later and still no sign. Had they gone further into space? Had LB2 gotten away on them? Still no Dekko replies. He would wait in a high, Arctic orbit and hope. Ned settled in with a squeeze pack of whisky and his first cigar in space.

'We got through to Ned! He's asking where the hell are we.'

'Tell him about half a million kilometres out, but on our way back home. An excursion out back of the moon,' said Toby in his resigned voice.

'We've missed breakfast.' said Sri, equally resigned.

'We should be in about tea time though' said Solly, mouth full of bread.

Liz relayed the messages. Ned's coded message came back.

'Well my dears, have a nice time and take lots of pictures. I'll need to go and meet Dr. Dorothy as I'm running low on things. Give me a call and I'll tell you how to come in. Don't just come straight down. See you for tea.'

The crew settled back while Steve (successfully) topped up the generator's fuel bladder with a squeeze bottle of petrol. Bit like a reverse urostomy quipped Toby.

They all agreed to try 2 gs for a while. It would be a long trip.

A relieved Shirley relayed the LB2 Dekko message to Kelvin as he came in on final approach to Narvik airport. Both Ladybirds had escaped after missile attacks, would call before landing at their destination.

'Which this Alliance crowd must be aware of, if they were waiting for them. Homer tells me there was an email from that Buddhist guy to a certain Dr. Dorte who lives next to a lake out of Narvik. Like, security? We gotta get there pronto.'

Shirley could but agree.

'If there are still messages coming from two separate sources, obviously your aircraft has failed! Fools. They will still go to Lake Trollvatnet. Make sure our team is there. How long before we land?'

'Twenty minutes, Principal Arranger.'

Ned carefully pushed the nose of LB1 out of the water and surveyed the rambling timber house. The small blue rowboat was tied to a pier as Sri described, so this must be the right place. Smoke from the chimney. He scanned the shore and as much of the backdrop forest as he could see, but there was no activity. Ladybird slid dripping out of the water, over the tussocky foreshore and sidled in under a massive pine tree. Ned opened the rear door and peered cautiously around.

'You would be Mr. Ned McZed then! Welcome to Trollvatnet! You are a little late, and there is only the one of your curious machines. I trust that the other is all right?'

The voice came from a small, stocky woman in a bright floral dress, lounging over the verandah railing.

'Doctor Andersen I presume. The others will be along in a few hours. I must apologise for the delay, we were... held up a little and became separated.'

Ned was given a large mug of coffee and a light lunch, a self constructed grand pile of smoked salmon, cheeses, pickled vegetables, meats and oddments on dark rye.

'You build an interesting Smørrebrød, Ned McZed,' said Dorte admiringly. Ned nodded, mouth too full to reply. Space had made him hungry. Over the meal he gave Dorte a full account of their trip from Sri's monastery in Zanskar, the wonders of the Aurora, the clash with the missile armed jet, their lucky escapes and the joy of hearing from LB2 far out in space. Ned stopped eating and talking as his host became distracted. She spoke rapidly into a small, unnoticed microphone on her lapel. An earphone too? What was this?

'I am sorry Ned. I have some friends outside in the woods who suggest we continue our lunch under the table. If you please, now.' Ned complied, taking his sandwich. 'I have been following the stories of your group and its machines with much interest,' continued Dorte, 'and can see how they would cause considerable conflict with the established order. You appear to have been attacked in the media, chased and shot at all around the world! After my good friend Sri Rinpoche sent an e-mail, I realised you were all on your way to me here to gain support. Most flattering!'

'Young Solomonder and Sri agreed you were the best person. World Leading Physicist and all that. Sol is very keen to meet you.'

'And I him, indeed! We have much to discuss,' she said thoughtfully. 'But we digress. In case there may be some trouble, I requested a little help from our citizens' militia in Nordtin. They are very serious army type people and were quite enthusiastic when I suggested I might be in danger. They came out at 4.00 a.m. and now say we have some visitors.'

Ned and Dorte continued to eat and chat quietly. After a while she stopped to listen to her earphone. Motioning Ned to stay put, Dorte collected a large iron skillet and moved to crouch beside the back door. Luckily she was low: several bullets smashed through the wall, a loud explosion rocked the house and there was much yelling. The door crashed open, a black clad figure staggered inside with a machine pistol at the ready. Ned winced at the dull spang of cast iron on bone then looked out at the gleeful Dr. Andersen.

'Well skilleted Madam!' Dorte was listening again.

'That's the last one then. Too easy. Come and meet the neighbours, Mr. McZed.'

The unwelcome visitors were in various states of disrepair with two on hands and knees from the stun grenade, one near the car having leg wounds bound up and the fourth still unconscious on the kitchen floor. An elderly captain hurried up to Dorte and apologized for the intrusion. She patted his arm consolingly, thanked him and introduced Ned. Prisoners secured and transport called for, Dorte bought out a bottle of akevitt and tray of glasses. Health was politely toasted and then the ten man squad departed, Captain Fossen telling Dr. Andersen that the police would perhaps be out tomorrow, or the following day. Or they would phone.

'Very sensible and low key, most remarkable!' said Ned in a follow up, follow up toast. He was expecting helicopters, sirens, cameras, forensic squads.

'Yes, well, that's everything settled before the others arrive then' said Dorte, dismissing the morning's excitement. 'Come back inside Mr McZed, you can tell me everything about this enterprise you are on, then show me around your Ladybird machine. Much more interesting.'

———

The group at 25 Wallaby Street settled back with a collective, contented and weary sigh. The Buddhist monk rising, tour around Ladybird, space views and Sean's aerial gymnastics had been massive hits. The most recent shots and dialogue were quieter, with the crew obviously very tired and stressed. Their story of another attack, the pell-mell flight and slow voyage back from what could have been an icy grave in oblivion was counterpointed by some beautiful shots of the far side of the moon and some uplifting philosophy from Sri Rinpoche. It was wound up with a cryptic comment from Liz that they should reach their destination within a few hours and would get back soon. Good stuff; it was keeping the kettle boiling nicely. The support website had an enormous, planet wide following and thanks to Evangeline Parsons, Billy Styler, Senator Dan Kelly and Co., no one was blocking access…yet.

———

The Cougar taxied beside the Narvik runway with Bobby having his turn as 'co-pilot'. The Senator was obviously a family man, somewhere, reflected Shirley. Brad was packing up the Dekko and Shirl didn't have a job, so she cracked open a beer and relaxed. Not bad, for American beer. At least the fridge worked.

'The Alliance Munich office was empty when they finally broke in, Sir. Underground exit. A janitor thinks he recognised the Montague woman arriving,' called Graeme.

'Right. Tell Homer to track where they went if possible, though I suspect she would be traveling private now she's in Europe. Work through all their transport files. I would not be surprised if she comes up here, since they set up an air ambush and blew it. Find out what Norwegian Security we can link up with. Bit twitchy about outsiders as I remember.'

Maybe we could be a bit twitchier at home as well, thought Shirley, thinking about Maria's abduction and themselves being chased through the back streets of Leichhardt…

———

After a few more akevitts, to become accustomed, they had adjourned to Ladybird I for an inspection. Doktor Dot the Physicist was taken aback when she was shown one of the engines and had naturally expressed disbelief. Ned, naturally, shut the door, fired up and edged over the shoreline.

'Oh no! We're sinking!' announced Ned gravely. Dorte looked away fearfully from the rising water on the windscreen, then swore and clipped the grinning idiot over the head. Obviously part of the show. A large fish swam past and Ned gave chase, deeper into the lake. The CO_2 scrubber was switched on to bubble away. At fifty metres they parked on the bottom while Ned explained the controls in lengthy detail. Ghostly shadows flickered past the windows.

'Would you like some afternoon tea? Back on shore?' asked Dorte eventually, hopefully.

———

LB2 finally dropped down through the fading dusk to the isolated shores of Trollvatnet. If this 'Alliance' already knew where they were heading, no point in sneaking up to the place. Toby and Jules peered through the mist forming on the lake surface and made out faint lights, roughly where Ned had said they would be. Skimming the water, they drove directly towards them, not really caring if they had the right place, lake or even country. As Steve had put it, they were spaced out to the point of knackered.

Two figures waved from the shoreline and steered LB2 with torches into a berth next to its sister. Doors swung open, Sean leapt gracefully down and looked around, followed by the heavier landing of the saffron robed monk. Dorte ran to help Sri Rinpoche up.

'Hello my good friend! Thank you, I am not quite used to our Earth's gravity as yet. I have been floating. Very strange,' said Sri, leaning on her arm. The steps came down and after joyful hugs and not a few tears, Ned helped the remaining crew stagger into the house.

Doctor Andersen could see that the pilots and Steve were flagging during the evening meal. Although Solly, Liz, Ketu and Sri had caught some sleep between the moon and Earth, the others had not. Sean did not have a sleep cycle to disturb and was roaming; new place, therefore explore. Spare beds and bunks were soon loaded with bodies and Liz, Sri and Dorte settled in for a talk while Solly taught Ketu the joys of the Internet.

'I take it that McZed explained the purpose of our visit? That we need some solid scientific testing and assurance of safety behind us to present the field to the world? There will be a lot of attempts to discredit this invention of Sol's,' said Liz quietly.

'Yes, I agree. When I first heard of your Ladybirds, I could see the challenge they would bring to conventional power. And power is … power. Radical innovation will always face conservative opposition, but for the good of the world, this must win through. Norway's scientific community, though better than most, is not without its vested interests. However, they also have a quite insatiable curiosity. I will do all that I can.' There were some excited stirrings in the computer corner.

'Mum, we're on the Internet big time! I googled Ladybird and there's heaps. Miss Scott must have been really busy!' Liz, Dorte and Sri lifted their cups and came across and watched various of the postings: photos and clips from the Barangan Wool 'n Hops Festival, The Snares, Tibet, their three broadcasts from space and a plethora of commentaries, discussions and Ladybird spin-offs. The Parramatta Road car yard advert was particularly bad; Maria and Shirley's news bulletins and Senator Dan Kelly's speech were particularly good.

'That reminds me, I better check in with Shirley and let her know we're safe. Our last call was as we sailed past the moon.' Liz giggled as she said it. It sounded ridiculous. Rugged up against the night chill, they all went out to LB2. Sri set to work making cups of tea while Solly warmed up the Dekko

'So, with this you were able to broadcast back to earth, from nearly a million kilometres?' asked Dorte, amazed.

'More like 800,000,' said Solomonder, shyly proud. While Liz fired off her message, he happily explained the Dekko functions, its construction and theoretical base. Doctor Andersen tried valiantly to keep up; not her field, but in the end she got the drift.

'Remarkable! Even this would be a lifetime's work, Solomonder, let alone your motor. Perhaps it might be time…' Dr. Andersen paused, looking to Liz Henderson. 'If your mother agrees, perhaps you may explain a little to me about the field generator. If I can, I will need to understand what you have here.' She tapped on the plain timber box covering the central floor motor. Solly looked at his Mum, who nodded. He began to talk, trying to find terms for the incredibly complex field concept. It was like trying to unravel Christmas decorations.

'So it's a little like an ion propulsion motor but utilising the waterfall effect? I heard that was being developed in Australia but I thought it only worked in space.' Solly looked blank; Dorte explained.

'Oh I see how that works…a bit, but no not really. You know the basic Lorentz force thing; well it's not like that either. Its like it's two layers down from that. The whole skin of the metal becomes the propulsion surface… it's a bit difficult to explain.'

'Please try. I will keep my mouth shut…' An hour later Dr. Andersen was shaking her head in wonder.

'It shouldn't work like that. It's impossible. But I think I can see… just the start of how… but if it does that then…' Sri Rinpoche put his arm around his friend's shoulders and hugged. 'This will come to you in time Dorte. You will understand. Now we must return to the house before everyone freezes.' He gestured to the others, huddled around the pathetically small fan heater.

'Oh goodness, I am sorry. Of course. Tomorrow! Thank you Solly. Tomorrow.'

—*∿*—

Shirley walked into the American's room and interrupted their gun assembling.

'You're a bit late to play Rambo, Senator. Apparently the Alliance sent their boys in this morning, but got cleaned up by some local part time Norwegian soldiers recruited by Dr. Andersen. No deaths, although one was a bit battered by the good doctor with a cast iron frypan.' She looked disdainfully at Kelvin's rocket launcher. 'Anyway, both Ladybirds are safely down and everyone is going to bed. We can visit in the morning for a chat. If we arrive before then, the Norwegian army might have something to say. Sleep tight, dears!' She smiled mischievously and blew a kiss.

—*∿*—

In separate, discreet accommodation in Narvik, the Principal Arranger listened in silence as the aide attempted to explain away the failure of their German elimination team in Trollvatnet. The site was obviously guarded by a top echelon commando unit and difficult to approach unobserved, the team was outnumbered, out gunned, out...

'Halt die fresse, dorftrottel! Thanks to your dumme arsch agents, I will have to personally attend to this matter.' Ms. Montague had many languages when needed. 'Find me a hairdresser, a clothes shop and shoe shop within two blocks of this hotel. Out! Geschwind! Schnell!' she snarled.

———

Two soldiers with submachine guns waved them to a stop. Graeme's practised eye could see at least two more in the shrubs, another in the mirror, all with weapons at the ready.

'Step out with your passports please. With care.' The visitors complied, Brad and Bobby with the appropriate movie posture. The captain, a little embarrassed, moved them from spreadeagle-on-the-bonnet to stand with their mother. Kelvin and Graeme's heavily embossed diplomatic passports and Shirley's New South Wales driving licence were glanced at. The boy's Barangan North and Tilda Addison Bus Pass raised some interest, but the unpacking of the Senator's alloy suitcase had the greatest appeal; soldiers clustered around to debate the merits of the Anschluss 25AZ rocket launcher and quiz Kelvin over the assorted guns. Devoid of all weapons, the group continued up the track in the back of the Civil Defence truck.

———

Shirley, Liz and the four kids were tied up in a melee of greetings while Ned and Toby warily introduced each other to Kelvin and Graeme. Sri and the chattering adolescents disappeared early from the crowded lounge room to set up food, with Ned being dragooned into providing soft drinks, coffee or akevitt for those who wished for Refreshment after their travels. Dorte answered a call; Graeme noted her pressing a discreet button before she moved outside with the phone. Shielded? Kelvin launched into damage control.

'Mr. McZed, Mr. and Mrs. Henderson and Mr. Buchanan, I would like to sincerely apologise for the… um… over-reaction shown by my country earlier. This was before we understood the true nature of your mission. I trust there are no hard feelings. We only want to help you achieve your goals with this wonderful new technology.' This was reinforced with warm, open, friendly handshakes and Sincere smiles.

'Jeez Kelve, cut the bullshit!' called Shirl, 'We've all got a good idea what your country would 'only want', and a corporate backed, good old unilateral tied up monopoly is not where this particular wonderful technology is going!' There was a chorus of agreement around the room. 'Ned might take you up for a burl in LB1 a bit later on however, If you play your cards right and don't get too pushy.' Kelvin brightened visibly.

'I would much appreciate that, Mr. McZed. I understand that your flying, like mine, goes back some…' The senator moved to the safety of side room hangar talk.

—◦◦◦—

A very wide and tall (for short order) breakfast assembled itself out on the back verandah and over this adventures were exchanged. The pine forest soughed, the lake sparkled, Vivaldi floated outside and Sean dozed on the railing in the sun.

'Thanks for your warning about the Python missiles,' said Ned, 'otherwise we may have tried sidestepping them. Wouldn't have worked. Tricky little buggers.'

'Well, since I'm going for brownie points, let me tell you a bit more about the Congo rocket which nearly dropped on you in Tibet. Bit bigger than a Python.' Kelvin related Homer's version of the Colonel Pewter expedition and the 'mysterious' nuclear blast high over the Zambian Border. That caused a lull for digestion.

'A nuclear missile exploding on sovereign Chinese territory. My god, Senator!' said Toby in awe, 'those silly bastards could have started World War Three!'

'Yes' said Kelvin, satisfied. 'Very dangerous and unpredictable. We are up against people who don't have boundaries, or apparent limits to their resources.' He was pleased to have slid the 'we' in.

'The Opposition,' said Liz eventually, 'including this Alliance bunch, have not stopped us yet. We seem to be protected at the moment, Senator. Almost as peaceful as Zanskar' she added, smiling at Sri. He nodded and beamed.

'But can you get the support you need here?' said Senator Dobrovich, still trying.

'Kelvin my dear,' said Dorte, giving him a benevolent Doctor/Grandmother look over her half frames, 'It may appear that not a lot has happened, however, I have not been idle since the arrival of Mr. McZed. I have a very secure phone line, and thanks to working within the nuclear research area for a long time and Mr. Nobel's little award, I am well acquainted with most of this country's scientists, administrators and politicians. All appear aware of our world famous visitors.'

'Not that it isn't bleeding obvious from the net,' said Steve.

'Indeed. Also that you are here at Trollvatnet. Several government departments in fact are tied up in knots. Air Defence is aware of the air battle to the north; the two pilots were arrested and questioned. Your two boilers out under the tree were observed landing, the Minister for Defence is politely asking about future movements and which scientific institution I was planning to use. He seemed to have worked out most things.'

Kelvin gave a palms-up-sigh. Oy vey, almost.

'Let us know if we can help, anytime,' Graeme put in, covering the retreat.

—◦◦◦—

'The Minister is Gregers Balstad, and I believe he is ready to help you. He has organised the Luftforsvaret to patrol this region and requested that you limit future flying to within a 20 kilometre radius of here, however you can go up and down as you like.'

'Oh good,' said Ned, 'Not much of a run, but we can do a few circuits and bumps if you want, Senator.'

'Swell. Call me Kelvin. Lead on Sir.'   Ned and Kelvin departed, chatting.

'This … um….Greggers…?' asked Steve.

'Gregers. It is Norwegian for Gregory,' said Dorte helpfully.

'Same in Australian. D'ya reckon he might be in a good spot to get us a few spare parts? Two of the batteries are stuffed, oxy tanks need filling, I need some relays and the kids want a few bits too.'

'He can probably track something down for you, Steve…'

———

Ms. Montague was taken aback, indeed, challenged by the reflection in the full-length mirror. Logic had dictated a full swing from her normal conservative attire, but this was... dissonant. What jarred most was that the blonde, cleavaged diva in the crimson dress appeared to be smiling. Ms. Montague caught the eye of the stunned mullet aide, staring inappropriately.

'Pay them, fool' she snapped, 'We have more shopping to do.'

She had an idea.

———

Kelvin strapped in the doubled lap sash car seat belts and looked dubiously at the instruments, controls and fittings of LB1. His Cougar was rough and ready, but at least everything was new and in the right place. The control stick (if that was what it was) looked to be from a kid's computer game, and that strange cylinder off to the side resembled a plumber's nightmare.

'Carbon dioxide scrubber' said Ned, while working through the pre-flight check. He switched on the radar and gave it its customary slap to start.

'That looks familiar,' said the Senator. 'Where from?'

'An early F-111A model, I've got a friend who rebuilt it. I didn't ask where he got it though. The dish is set up in a ceramic box outside the field. Lots of other bits from the wreckers...' said Ned, waving vaguely around. 'You ready?'

Kelvin was glad for the soft foam headrest on the car bucket seat as Ned, after a gentle lift off and angling up, cracked on the power and rocketed up to 50,000 feet. His contacts had wangled him several flights in front line fighter aircraft, but none were capable of the climb rate this tin can showed! Slowing a little, Ned performed a few of his favourites, then after a slow 360 rotate and dip, continued climbing with the earth receding in the front windows.

'You sure know how to give a man a good time, Mr. McZed,' grunted Kelvin, hanging from his harness and wondering about his breakfast.

'So did your navy...' muttered Ned, cutting the thrust and adjusting attitude. The scrubber started with its customary gurgle.

They cruised a little in the stratosphere, Ned giving his guest a bit of a shot at the controls. The Senator flew carefully at first, and when nothing went wrong, with more boister. The quiet was punctuated with many goddamns and holy sheets.

'Ned, something this fast and manoeuvrable shouldn't be so damn easy to fly! What speed have you been up to already?'

'Myself? Probably a bit over Mach 6 in LB2 when we were chased out of the Snares by your missiles.' He paused for the Senator to digest. 'Of course, Solomonder estimates they were going at around Mach 420 when they put the brakes on out the back of the moon... Not sure if they've got a top speed.'

'Shit,' said Kelvin. He slid his thumb down onto the top of his hand-tooled cowboy boot, ran the nail across the micro-sealed seam. Felt for the handle of the flat, razor sharp ceramic blade. Good. 'What sort of range? S'pose this machine would make it to the States?'

'Not too far for it, I suppose' agreed Ned.

'Would be a honey of a deal in it for you to just to zip across...' mused Kelvin, 'but I guess you've made yourself clear on that. What I can't quite figure why you took me up for a flight though. You know how much I would like to get a hold on one of these gadgets and take it home. Would be easy for me to do, too.' He looked closely at the pilot. McZed did not appear ruffled by the veiled threat. Ned dropped the nose of LB1 down a little.

'We're well north of Trollvatnet, no population to speak of,' said Ned conversationally. 'See that flat spot, left of the mountain? I estimate that would be our impact point, Senator. Even if I was already dead, not that I think you're a cold-blooded killer. Maybe you would pass me over whatever you're fiddling with in your boot and then I'll demonstrate my security device. Now.' Ned's voice had dropped to a low chill.

Kelvin considered his options, realised his bluff against this uncompromising lunatic was worth Jack Shit. He slid the translucent blade carefully out and handed it, apologetically, respectfully and slowly to McZed. Ned inspected it with interest, tossed it into the toolbox.

'See that little green light there?' he said, with a conjurors tap on the dash. It blinked twice and went out. As did everything else, instrument lights, scrubber, and as they watched, the blue, glowing field. Momentum slowed, they dropped and as the thin atmosphere gripped on the stubby wings, went vertical. Down. 'Both Ladybirds are fitted with one,' explained Ned, 'they cut in automatically after five minutes flying unless cancelled by a code. In case someone was thinking of nicking one.' He reached under the dash and appeared to press buttons, frowning thoughtfully. Speed was building up, it was getting warmer, and the rugged ground was closer.

'Now, how did it go? No, that's not right... Maybe... no, that's the laptop...'

Ned smiled at the familiar scorched smell, glanced at the American's strained face. He reached surreptitiously under the seat for the kill switch with his left hand.

'Ahh, that's it.' The green light flickered on, the comforting blue glow spread.

'My apologies, and remind me to never play poker with you, McZed' said Kelvin, as they settled back down next to Trollvatnet.

―~~―

Negotiations by Dr. Andersen hovered over Oslo, then Bergen and finally settled on the NTNU in Trondheim. With 20,000 students, it was the second largest university in Norway, had excellent resources, was central but set in a smaller town. Dorte said that she trusted them, they owed her some research time, and the accommodation was comfortable. It had lots of ticks.

'Norges Teknisk-Naturvitenskapelige Universitet. It's very good,' agreed Solly.

'Can we just call it Norway Tech?' asked Toby.

Defence Minister Gregers Balstad arrived personally in a helicopter with the batteries, two loaded oxygen tanks, the diverse materials requested by the crew and a few extras. Ned carefully packed his present of three bottles of vintage Bruichladdich in cotton wool under the pilot's seat of LB1. In LB2 Jules and Solly rebuilt the starboard lateral engine, Steve fitted the new batteries, oxy tanks and relays while Liz and Toby restocked the larder. Sean mostly slept, mostly in the way.

―~~―

Four days later, with a dozen Royal Norwegian F16 fighters as escort, both Ladybirds took off to fly south. The Luftforsvaret Wing Commander shepherded them down to the fjord and out to sea, 'for security reasons', and they enjoyed a leisurely flight down the spectacular Norwegian coast. Outside Trondheim, a group of army helicopters took over, politely guiding them to a NTNU sports field. Dorte, Sri Rinpoche, Solomonder, Jules and Ketu disembarked at this point, and with the Ladybirds gliding stately behind, took the procession down a wide boulevard leading to the Department of Physics. Police had erected barricades, and just as well, for from the moment the unmistakeable flying machines had entered Campus airspace, a tidal wave of texted students poured across to line the road, clapping and calling. The Physics Department, ever conscious of status ranking, had organised a large media contingent, a brass band and a podium with all staff suitably attired.

Staff, students, police and the media were a bit puzzled upon closer viewing. How could these rough welded recycled boilers being led down the path be the same ones on their TV and Internet? Ned, ever the showman, lifted to twenty feet and did a slow pirouette for those at the back. Roar, went the crowd. Definitely the ones! Camera phones sparkled. Oh to have chosen Physics and have a chance to work on this revolutionary new technology!

The Department of Physics staff seemed to think so, and after the effusive official welcome, all jostled and vied to offer their own particular branch of laboratory services. The Department Head ushered off Dorte, the Hendersons and Ned for a planning meeting, while Toby elected to stay with the Denzils, Sri and Ketu. The Ladybirds had been guided into a large workshop; the Tildans and Buddhists decided they would have an early lunch sent in while keeping an eye on the machines. Nobody was quite sure what this new situation would bring, despite Dorte's assurances and the cosy reception... Smiling and friendly, but heavily armed, soldiers patrolled outside the workshop doors. For security.

The Head of Physics, Professor Fredrikstad Lilleström, was flanked by The Minister for Defence, Gregers Balstad and an aide.

'Were the materials I delivered satisfactory?' asked Gregers politely. General agreement.

'If you would be liking some food or drink, please to help yourself,' said Fredrikstad, gesturing to a side table. Solly and Jules drifted over, Steve loaded up some plates and returned.

It fell naturally to Liz and Ned to lead the negotiations across the richly glowing rosewood.

'Dr Andersen has told us you would be in a good position to extensively test the field for us, to determine if there are any biological or environmental hazards,' began Liz. 'She sent you the limited testing data which Mr. McZed completed earlier. Was this useful?'

'It was very interesting of course, and I will need to ask more questions of Mr. McZed. As you stated, it is limited but it does indicate that your 'field' is benign. It does not explain how the field works to produce such energy from so little input however?' replied Prof. Lilleström, leaving a small question mark to swing.

'Yes, the theory and mechanism behind this remarkable invention, along with its future development would be very good to explore…' agreed Gregors Balstad, adding bold, italic and underline.

'That as it may be,' rumbled Ned, 'and it may be a path which we tread at a later date, Sir. Until then, would you be prepared to help us establish the safety aspect? We can link one of our motors to an iron sample in the workshop if you move your test equipment into there. Shouldn't be too difficult.'

'Well…' said Fredrikstad after a hurried consult with Gregers, 'it would be far better if you could dismount one of the motors so we can… inspect and test it in our main laboratory. We would need to dismantle it as well...' There was a muffled snort from the side table.

'Perhaps,' said the Professor sourly, 'Solomonder and Julia may be bored with this talking. We have an excellent Child Minding Centre within the Department. It has computers and other children to have games with.' There was a chilly silence. Steve winced as he saw the gathering storm in Liz's face.

'Mummy,' said Jules, 'Is the nice man saying we can go out and play?'

'Is it like Småland at Ikea, Daddy?' asked Solly with equal sincerity. Ned and Steve roared with laughter, and after a moment, Liz joined in.

'Not sure if the kids are keen on that idea, Fred!' said Steve. Gregers spoke quickly to the red faced Lilleström in Norwegian. He bit his lip and nodded curtly.

'I apologise for being stupid. Of course, you must be here.'

'Vi godkjenne din unnskyldning, herr' said Jules quietly. The Hendersons looked puzzled. Dorte nodded and smiled.

'I lent Julia a Norwegian phrase book and CD. That was very good; she just accepted the Professor's apology.' Gregers frowned slightly, recovered. English only, then.

'My friends, I am sure that the Physics Department would be very happy to test your field. Most of this can happen in the workshop, and if the test equipment cannot be moved, you can supervise bringing an engine to it. Then we will discuss sharing further information. Agreed? Then let us eat properly, rather than this party food!' The affable host, Gregers graciously shepherded the crew off to a private room.

'Oleaginous again...' muttered Solly to Jules on the way.

—⁓—

Senator Dobrovich and Agent Horowitz drove out of Oslo, bound for Trondheim. They had been 'not required on voyage' for the Ladybird flight, had taken Kelvin's Cougar to Oslo, paid a visit to the embassy and were now going to attempt to renew their tenuous relationship. Certainly tenuous between McZed, and myself reflected Kelvin with rue, should never have tried to push the issue. He was hoping that Graeme's credit with the Denzils would get them back in the game.

Sergeant Baker lifted the glass of champagne in a toast to the madness of the flying boilermakers. He had been invited in to 25 Wallaby Street to observe the Trondheim procession and celebrate the Ladybirds safe arrival.

'Those Hendersons are a long way from home,' he observed. Maria topped up the glasses.

'So what's our job now that they've got there? With all that media hanging around will they still be sending stuff to us?' asked Arabella Swift, with a touch of pre-emptive petulance.

'Reckon, we're the only ones they can trust,' said Jim Dobson. 'And how else would they get headlines in the Camby Pastoral Times?' he added with a smirk.

'Enough already!' growled Maria. 'Liz will be sending us an update on Trondheim soon enough, meanwhile, I want your story on the new legislation on my desk in an hour, Miss Swift, along with your historical photo compilation, Mr Dobson. And aren't you on duty, Sergeant?'

'This is a complete shambles! Four of our sub branches have been turned over by MI5, our investments are all going sour and it is costing a fortune just to stay ahead of the police! Why hasn't this mess been sorted out yet?' demanded the remaining London Head Factor.

Munich, the new Principal Factor, squirmed uncomfortably but rallied.

'We have also been under attack and had to move our operations. Unfortunately, we have been unable to capture or destroy this new technology, due to operations organised by the Principal Arranger having failed...' He left that one floating in the pan.

A new, sallow and thin face spoke. Pittsburgh.

'As you are aware, our main American office was completely lost, along with many of our agents. I am pleased to tell you however, our previous Principal Factor, New York, has been located and terminated.' Munich blanched a little, Pittsburgh continued.

'After great cost we have contained the damage caused by his information and are working to neutralise the source of the attack, the Overseas Security Agency. The rest of this failure will need to be dealt with in Europe.'

'As it shall be,' added Munich hastily.

'As it must be,' added the Shanghai chorus and Singapore.

'Meanwhile, we shall all be transferring as much of our oil holdings as possible into gold and defensive assets,' announced London. 'Without causing a major collapse in that area' he added, in deference to the ashen faced Dubai Head Factor.

It was like being a blind pensioner needing to cross a road at a Boy Scout Jamboree thought Toby as he fended off another coffee offering post-graduate student wishing to discuss something esoterically Fysikk. For three days they had been harried as various teams, desperate and full of energy, obtained their ration of access to the magic blue field. He had never seen so many white lab coats. With careful diplomacy, Doctor Andersen had negotiated limited access for the Department of Biology into the Physics buildings. It made sense, she explained to Professor Lilleström, to explore any aspect of physiological, neurophysiological, cellular and molecular toxicology blah blah blah, using a script prepared by Solly from the NTNU sitemap. Jules and Solly had second thoughts when the biologists turned up with cages of assorted cute small mammals...

Ned and Steve had temporarily unbolted two of the LB2 engines and carefully guarded them in the cyclotron equipped main laboratory, trying to keep track on the equipment and experiments performed over the ten allowed hours. They were then quickly returned to their rightful places and checked. No damage. All the adults slept shifts in the Ladybirds at night, with doors bolted. At their daily closed, screened meetings they decided that their security measures at least limited the amount of information on the engine workings. Despite feeling that to be too paranoid was unhealthy, some communication was kept to scribbled notes on folded scraps of paper. Burnt, not eaten. Sean guarded the doors.

—⁓—

'So far, this field effect has been tested as completely benign,' began Fredrikstad Lilleström to his audience of one. Gregers Balstad nodded. The Professor continued, putting up three-dimensional tomographic models on the screen. 'We were able to secretly scan both of the motors while in the main laboratory, but it is very difficult to identify the components used in construction. Some we recognise, others we have no idea. My friend Bernt in Materials Engineering thinks they may be a mixture of older electronic parts and can make no sense of the structure.'

'But you at least have the beginnings,' said Gregers, waving to the models.

'We would have if there was any logic in this craziness ' said Fredrikstad angrily. 'Both of these lunatic machines are completely different to each other! It was as if children at play built them! They were not built to any plan. All this is in the heads of those children. How can we work with this insanity!'

Gregers steepled his hands and reflected. All in the heads of these children...

—⁓—

'It would be really helpful if you could organize it, Shirl, and I'll call when we're on the outskirts. Best to Brad 'n Bobby.' Graeme switched off his mobile and explained to the annoyed Senator that Shirl said she would get to it. Eventually. That she had also been talking to Ned and was not happy. But he was confident. Kelvin continued driving though the Rondane mountains in silence.

Lunch time and after considerable negotiation through Dr. Andersen, the unarmed party of two with large plastic clip-on visitors passes sat in the University canteen with Liz, Shirley and the kids.

'I'll just pass on my usual hugely increased government guaranteed offer for the rights...' began Kelvin conversationally, 'One point two billion...ish and open to negotiation of course. We'll better any other offers etcetera. Meanwhile, how's the testing been going?'

'Pretty clear bill of health, Kelve,' said Shirl, 'according to Dorte. She's on top of it. Meanwhile, back at the ranch, what's happening with the Mad Alliance? Blown any more of them up?'

'Making progress, Ma'am, and much of the Alliance has been shut down. At the moment, our people are concentrating on Europe, and it appears there is a hidden cell in Norway.'

'Would have to be in Norway, wouldn't it,' said Bobby. 'Did you get some more guns and things when you went to Oslo?'

'The Norwegian Defence Department looks after security issues on the campus. Rest assured, we are without guns or other weapons,' said Kelvin, ignoring Shirley's pointed look. 'Not even a letter opener.'

'Armless' commented Jules.

'Apart from what's in the boot' added Bobby, 'of the car, that is.'

'And got lots of money for bribes' said Solly.

'And sort of not really on the dark side' concluded Brad.

Graeme later explained the great Australian pastime of shit stirring, and that they did actually have a foot back in the door.

⌇

Ms. Montague took in the cool appraising look from her visitor, crossed her long legs and languidly lifted her latte.

'The equipment and passes you required are here' he said. 'You are clear on what is to be done if they are not cooperative?'

'Disposal.'

'Good. Do not fail. There have been too many failures.'

Gregers Balstad stood, turned and left.

⌇

Pittsburgh drew the meeting of Head Factors to order. London, Shanghai, Dubai and Singapore dutifully looked to him from the split screen. Munich, the recently deposed ex-Principal Factor glared sulkily but also complied.

'We have come to a crossroad. The full Court of Proprietors and I have decided that a major re-structure of the Alliance is needed if we are to advance to our rightful place in the new millennium. We have the resources and organisation to become the world's dominant multinational corporation!' Pittsburgh paused, satisfied the Factors were hooked. 'We are in a position to now do this openly. No longer skulking behind the scenes, but with an unassailable power that is clearly visible to the so-called leaders of business and government. Commanding all! We will be in a position to set the world's agenda, set the world's rules.' There was an eruption of applause from the Head Factors.

'To do this, the Court of Directors and Court of Proprietors will merge to become the new Global Board of the Alliance, which will be publicly listed. The Global Board will hold all of the shares. The Council of Arrangers will be disbanded; its

---

313

members incorporated as salaried employees into the administrative structure of our company. They have been useful in the past, but in too powerful a position. Some of the Council may be opposed to this, so I have established a new Security Section from selected arrangers under my management, as Principal Director...' he looked coldly at each of the faces, daring dissent, *'...of the Global Board. The Security Section will deal with any problems. A particular problem I am aware of will be removed, as soon as it has served its purpose...'*

In several very quiet settings, some 'unselected' Arrangers were hooking into their own, private communication systems. After ensuring their own security.

'The Human Physiology Department wish to complete some blood tests and brief scans of your people who have flown and had the most exposure to the field,' announced Professor Lilleström. 'They are particularly interested in the younger people, as they would be more susceptible to any effects. They say the tests do not involve any radiography or anything harmful. It would take twenty minutes. This they have told me, I do not know, it is not my field.' He shrugged and gestured to the uniformed nurse and two lab-coated assistants. The nurse came forward, smiling.

'Yes, that is the case. My name is Ingrid and I am very pleased to be meeting you' she said in heavily accented English. 'If the children could come with us first to our room I can take some small blood samples for the laboratories. I am very experienced with this procedure.'

She looked expectantly toward Liz. 'These are your children? I think you would be very worried that they would be in the best health. I am knowing this as I am a mother too...' She looked at Jules and Solly and smiled again. 'It is like the injections at school yes? I am much better than the nurses at school because I have bought you some comics and some gingerbread...and these Bars from Mars?'

'Mars bars?' asked Jules and Solly. The nurse laughed.

'Yes, that is it. If you are afraid of course your mother could come with you.'

'That's OK' said Solly airily, 'You don't have to come, Mum.' Jules shrugged agreement.

Liz sighed. She was inundated with technicians, students, researchers and professors.

'All right then. There will be a full report for us, of course?'

'Of course, Mrs. Henderson,' said the nurse quietly, 'By this afternoon you will know.'

———

Chief of Overseas Security Spiggott was mortally offended at being four inches off mortally wounded. Homer had been crossing the park on his regular path to work yesterday morning. Pleasant, sunshine, slight chill in the breeze, joggers, mothers with baby buggies, a dark suited man reading a newspaper on the bench... then Shot in the Back! Like Wild Bill Hickok, except not in the head, and in a park, not in a saloon.

As luck would have it, Agent Simpson was researching surveillance dressed as a hippie, making him curiously invisible. He had witnessed the first shot and had quickly emptied the magazine of his P90 through the cloth rainforest-rainbow shoulder bag. Luckily too, there were no innocent park persons in line of fire. When the initial action and screams were over, calm returned; everyone had seen it all before on TV and knew exactly what to do. Several of the medically inclined mothers, with and without training, helpfully staunched Homer's bleeding and held him up until the ambulance arrived. Agent Simpson pressed the smoking shoulder bag over the worst of the assailant's two holes, answered mothers' questions politely and attempted to stop the phone cameras. Later, after removing the tightly taped nappy, the Doctor said Homer had done well, only a deep flesh wound to the shoulder, just some stitches and cleaning up. Agent Simpson said it was a very John Wayne

———

315

wound. Luckiest of all, the assailant also survived to help in inquiries.

Normally of a peaceful, if somewhat anxious disposition, Homer was now livid and working feverishly, albeit one handed, to rip the guts out of these Alliance bastards. Their operative was very cooperative after his near death experience and provided some good new avenues. Somehow, mused Homer, the Alliance security wasn't as good. Probably because the wicked witch Montague/Jordan Principal Arranger was away chasing his boss and the Tildans. In Norway, which was interesting, because a faint path also led to certain high placed officials there. Best get on the phone about that one…

'Shirl, have you seen my kids around?' asked the worried Liz. 'They went off to have some tests, but that was over an hour ago. Supposed to take twenty minutes.' Shirl hadn't, nor had anyone else. Spare Physics students were sent to search; they were not in the building. Steve bailed up the Norwegian security at the entrance doors; had they seen a nurse and two assistants leave? Yes, with two unconscious students from the biomedical laboratory to have x-rays after an accident. All had the correct passes. Liz stifled a scream when she recognized Solly's joggers on the cut.

Under Secretary Senator Kelvin Dobrovich called the meeting to order.

'Norwegian Security tracked Solly and Jules to a van which was found empty in Trondheim. They blocked the city exits, but maybe too late to stop them getting away. Does this look like the nurse?' He passed Liz a photo.

'Ingrid… she called herself ' whispered Liz. 'Will she hurt them?'

'Sorry Ma'am, don't know. We think she may be a head agent of the Alliance. They would want information about the field, of course, so they would keep them alive. We need the chance to negotiate their return and are trying to get messages through the links we have discovered. Unfortunately, until then, the children are untraceable.' The tight-lipped Norwegian head of security could add nothing.

'Well maybe not quite…' said Brad looking at Graeme. He nodded.

'Mr. Horowitz there gave all of us some little tracking gadget thingies, like some insurance in case we got lost.' He fished in his pocket and held up a small disc.

'Also because we hassled him for them. They were part of his spy kit' added Bobby.

'They're a bit like toys,' said Graeme lamely. Kelvin glared and looked at the disc.

'These are good for about 15 miles, if they get activated. It means that Horowitz and I need to get driving in a big circle, and you all stay here and talk to these people if Homer Spiggott does manage to get some contact. He'll phone on this.' finished the Senator, handing Liz a large cell phone.

'Perhaps I'll come along with you' said Ned McZed. Kelvin couldn't really argue.

—⁓—

Ms Montague stared at her laptop, re-reading the email. The source was the trusted Munich Arranger, sent through a secure coded link, and the content was devastating, unbelievable. The ultimate betrayal! That the Proprietors and Factors would combine to destroy her centuries old Alliance, purely for greed and convenience. That the Council of Arrangers would cease to exist, its more pliable members buried in clerical positions, the less pliable, buried.

For the second time in her life, Amelia Montague wept.

Uncontrolled, desolation driven sobs.

The grief slowly pooled into a glassy black obsidian shell, a crucible for growing molten rage. Ms. Montague deleted the email, carefully selected a list of recipients, and typed a statement, a proposal and instructions. She knew with certainty the replies; she knew the minds of every correspondent. Sent. She then worked for an hour on another document. Ms. Montague could type comfortably at 130 wpm: the flickering fingers were driving at closer to 175, without stop. She loaded the document to a USB drive.

Dressed in the red linen suit, Ms M loaded a full clip into her small automatic, directed the aides to complete packing and walked downstairs. Now to deal with these children.

—⁓—

Jules and Solly regained consciousness on a rug, handcuffed to a steel ring in the wall. A garage, empty and quiet apart from the whirring of a small electric heater. If Jules had been able to speak through her taped mouth, she would have told Solly they were in big trouble. He nodded that he already knew. The door opened, and the nurse, who had been so careful in taking 'blood samples' swept in. Looking incredibly fashionable, Jules thought.

'I trust you were warm enough?' asked Ms. M, unlocking the handcuffs and removing the gaffer tape. Quite gently.

'What are you going to do? Are you going to torture or kill us?' demanded Jules. She moved in front of Solly, looking around for weapons. A rug and a plastic heater.

'That is no longer relevant' said the ex-nurse, 'you will not be harmed. Sit down please,' Chairs, a table, two cups of hot chocolate and a black coffee appeared.

'I believe I'm expected to test this first' she said, smiling, sipping then grimacing. She did not like chocolate.

'Good. The poison is undetectable. A little joke,' she added.

The totally confused Jules and Solly accepted the drinks. Warm, rich, comforting. Sweet. They drank and watched warily. Jules checked the weight of the table.

'You and your friends have done very well to avoid being killed' began Ms Montague, attempting a polite compliment with limited success. 'There may be further threats, but they will not be as strong because the Alliance is losing its most effective people. You will survive, I believe. Good.' Jules and Solly nodded. Where was this going?

'I have a favour to ask. I was able to have some of your earlier messages decoded... the structure was simple but the base text used was unusual. It was a story of a donkey, a bear, a small pig and a birthday... Could you tell me some more of this story please.'

She waited. Solly and Jules conferred. Totally weird, but they could do weird.

'If it was our signal from Tibet, we took that from Chapter six, In which Eeyore has a birthday and gets two presents' said Solly.

'...Gets two presents' murmured Ms Montague.

'We know it very well' said Jules, fascinated. The woman in the red dress appeared to have gone into a trance. She nudged Solly. He usually did the first bit.

'Eeyore, the old grey donkey,' he began...

———

'Yes, I remember,' said Christopher Robin' chorused Jules, Solly and Amelia Montague.

In the silence that followed, Julie pondered the past twenty minutes. She and Solly were used to recitations, could run a good show with Winnie the Pee... but both had been blown away when the lady in red had stepped, word perfect, into the voice of Eeyore. Gloom, resignation, the gradual climb up through sadness into excitement... she was Eeyore!

Ms. Montague looked at them steadily.

'I don't suppose anyone ever forgot your birthday.'

Jules shivered. The woman's hand was hovering near the bulge that spoiled the superb line of the red jacket. She gripped the chair. 'Never mind that. I need to go now.' Ms. M reached into the jacket pocket and passed two flat metal buttons to Solly. 'These are your transmitters; they have been activated. Do not do anything silly like running off, this is not a very good area and your friends will be here soon. Give this to Senator Dobrovski with my compliments' she added, handing Jules the USB drive.

'I suppose' said Solly 'we can be polite and say goodbye. I didn't like the abduction and the being drugged bit, but you do a great Eeyore. Better than my Dad's. Were all of the attacks like the rocket plane and the missile because of the field to stop it because the business side of your gang didn't want it to stuff up their business things?'

Again, the steady look. Ms. M considered the question, Solomonder and Julia.

'Quite so. They wished to own it or destroy it. I am no longer part of that particular organisation. I have not yet decided how my colleagues and I will approach this interesting change yet. Goodbye.'

And she walked out, without doubt to a prepared car, a chosen path, a certain destiny.

—⁓—

'We have a signal! Head left at the next, about twelve miles. Two signals!' Graeme called excitedly. Ned heaved a sigh of relief, Kelvin hunched over the wheel and hauled left.

A very rapid roar through a quiet industrial section of Trondheim and they pulled up outside a garbage strewn laneway.

'Twenty yards down, off to the right, must be behind that green roller door.'

'If I get enough speed up and hit full lock I should be able punch it in' growled Chief Agent Dobrovich, putting the large Volvo SUV into gear.

'You'll be bloody lucky to get this thing into the laneway, let alone turn it. Will we have a look at that little door next to it instead?' suggested Ned.

Kelvin and Graeme kitted up with a variety of weapons and Ned suggested he would like a revolver or similar. Just to fit in. They walked cautiously down the lane, Graeme ready with the explosives, the senator studying the tracker. Ned quietly opened the small door, obligingly stepped out of the way and watched as Graeme and Kelvin went in high and low. No gunfire, so Ned walked in to find Jules and Solly grinning at them.

'I bet that you would use a robot camera. Nice moves though,' said Solly.

'We didn't think you would be too long' said Jules.

'We were tortured dreadfully, but they've gone now' added Solly to Graeme, who was grimly covering the internal door with his Uzi.

'We had to tell her everything... chapter and verse' said Jules.

'Chapter six and Cottleston Pie' added Solly gleefully.

'I can't keep up with you two' muttered the senator.

'Well you should try harder then,' said Jules primly, 'but never mind. We've got a present from the lady for you as well...'

———

Tearful greetings from mother, father and friends and it was back to work, completing the laboratory field testing. Liz grudgingly gave blood samples, along with the rest of the adults. The two Bio-Medical post grads, covered in identification badges and escorted by Norwegian Security, were pathetically grateful and apologetic. Unlike Professor

Lilleström and the urbane Gregers Balstad. Graeme and the Senator (unarmed) were allowed to remain as 'security consultants.' Kelvin had frostily introduced himself to the Norwegian Minister as Senator Dobrovich, Head of Overseas Security. Although Homer had put the finger on Balstad, he had little real evidence, and as well, Gregers had all the soldiers.

The Tildans and company had an evening meal and general meeting in the canteen courtyard, with Graeme lending them a localized cone of electronic silence. Nearby students were swearing at their mobiles, so it had to be working.

'The testing is finished, although Professor Lilleström will insist that there is more to be done. Thanks to my friends at NTNU, I have a full breakdown of the testing, staff involved, results, everything. It is all good. Congratulations!' said Dorte, raising her coffee in salute.

'So the field is safe then,' said Solly. 'Like we figured.'

'What happens now?' asked Toby.

'Maria tells me we have an enormous number of private and government offers to buy the technology,' said Liz, 'apart from what the Senator has offered. There have also been a variety of injunctions, counter patent claims, sponsored legislation, direct threats, the works. Mostly from the oil industry, power companies, defence, transport; all sorts.'

'All sorts who would screw it up' said Steve.

'Timothy Pickle' said Ned, 'says he will sell Paragon Air, Command Transport and a few other things, will give Solly and Jules a half billion over anyone else and make us all Senior Executives in 'Nova Levitron Inc'.

'Obviously wants to float a new company,' said Toby. 'He's a man with a plan. Maybe the CSIRO might be a goer, but there's not much left of it I suppose…'

'The path is not clear' pronounced Sri Rinpoche, 'But there definitely is a path.'

They contemplated on that until they saw the neutral faced Gregers Balstad and the unusually beaming Professor Lilleström making their way across the courtyard. Jules switched off the cone of silence.

'We have wonderful news!' announced the ebullient Prof. 'All of the experiments have been very positive, so far, and we are well on the way to completing the… program. Again, I apologise for the little incident with the children, but that will never happen again.' He waved expansively at the four visible guards. 'I would like to be the first to tell you that my Department has nominated your two children for…' he paused and looked benignly down his nose at Jules and Solly, 'for Honorary Doctorates!' Expecting delighted handclaps, he only got raised eyebrows. The Lilleström lips pouted a little. Ungrateful little elendig.

'Yes,' intervened Minister Balstad hurriedly, 'and that is good. I have also spoken to some of the members on the Nobel Prize Physics committee. You would be the youngest people to ever receive this. I cannot guarantee the award of course. Meanwhile we must consolidate the patents and protections on behalf of the University and yourselves. '

'On behalf of the University…' said Liz icily, 'what exactly do you mean, Mr. Balstad?'

'Well of course,' said Gregers smoothly, 'since the University has had a major part in the development of this technology they would be entitled to part ownership.' Behind him Professor Lilleström nodded enthusiastically. All politicians needed one. 'The Universitet has many connections to private industry who are all very happy to take over the application and marketing side. You would be major shareholders of course…'

'There was never any agreement made regarding this.'

'Nevertheless… You are here now, and this technology is more important than what you might believe are your rights. As aliens you have no rights. You did not enter this country legally so you can also be detained. These soldiers are not here for just your protection. I trust, however, that you will be very comfortable remaining within the boundaries of this Physics Department. To continue your invaluable research.' He smiled thinly. 'Besides, which country in the world would you trust more to release this knowledge in a responsible, environmentally sensitive and beneficial way? Is this not why you came to our wonderful Norway?' Balstad didn't wait for an answer but turned and left, Lilleström trotting behind.

'I am so very sorry' said Dorte, tears in her eyes, 'this is not what I expected or wanted. Den jævelen! He has no right to do this.'

'Not the right, just the power. As Minister of Defence' said Toby.

'I think,' said Ned McZed,' that we might need another meeting, perhaps in the workshop where The Denzils, our American friends and the Ladybirds are...'

———∿∿∿———

Everyone was gathered inside LB2, conferencing. Steve figured that the plate steel would be enough to block any prying electronic ears, but just to be on the safe side, set the field to a soft blue glow. When told of the Balstad ultimatum, Graeme was outraged, the Senator resisted saying I told you so and Shirley was all for doing a bunk immediately.

'That's an interesting point' said Toby, 'because it would be dead easy to push our way out. Why has Balstad allowed us to be all together in the one spot? With our own getaway vehicles that are unstoppable?'

'When we looked out the window, there were two big tanks outside the workshop doors. They might be there to stop us.' announced Jules.

'Yes...' agreed Sri Rinpoche. 'That is the case. However, their large guns are pointed away from us. Why would this be so? Very curious. Is this politeness?'

'Maybe Mr. Balstad hasn't told them that we're the bad guys yet?' put in Brad.

'Balstad is part of the Alliance and the Alliance wants these doohickies wiped off the planet. They have to have a back up plan...' said Senator Dobrovich reflectively.

Steve was muttering to himself and moved to the back of the craft. They could hear him moving equipment, unscrewing bolts. He swore loudly.

'It's the bloody oxygen tanks the bastard brought us! There's an aerial tucked away to the side of the valve. I bet he's stuffed a radio control or an altitude sensor thing and enough explosive in there to blow us to kingdom come. I won't open it up to have a look though.'

'Yes, please don't. Sure to be a nasty surprise if you do' warned Ned. 'We might just move all our presents from that gentleman out to the back of the workshop. There's a toilet there. Jules, can you knock up some large signs in Norwegian about bombs and the suchlike; we'll put them on all the doors a bit later.'

The next hours were a busy time. Appearing subdued and cooperative, the crew et al chatted with technicians and helped in experiments while quietly gathering equipment and supplies. Steve announced that the batteries and the original oxygen tanks were fully charged. He had earlier scrounged chemicals for the carbon dioxide scrubbers and petrol for the generators. Sean was located, pampered, fed and settled in his cage. Filled, he slept.

Dorte spoke quietly to Liz, Jules, Solly and Ned.

'This thumb drive has all of the experiments, the data and conclusions from the Physics department. I will also attempt to release this and make statements, but if Balstad and Defence block me, you will also be able to put it up. I will then be in a position to confirm it, along with my colleagues. Sri and Ketu will stay with me, and I am sure the venerable Lama will be happy to broadcast your good news as well. When and how will you leave?'

'Well now,' said Ned, 'I have been giving this some thought...' The Hendersons mock-groaned and eye-rolled.

'Yes, easy, fire alarm; roll up the door, fly out. First of all though, Doctor Andersen, are you aware of an organisation called the Guinness Book of Records...?'

—∿∿—

Senator Dobrovich looked incredulously at the LB1 key in his hand.

'You understand that this is only a loan, mind you, to get you home?' said Ned.

'But...'

Ned ticked off points on fingers.

'You were interested earlier in taking it for a run across the Atlantic and I know you can handle the machine. You may need to leave the country in a hurry, to stop any political difficulties. Besides, I need to be with everyone else in LB2. I'll be taking the Dekko out, but your super-spy radio phone things will work when we hook them up to the aerial. And don't you worry about the death-dive security device that cuts in after five minutes... It was just a bit of foolery with a cut out switch under the seat. I'll show you where it is.'

Kelvin held his hand up.

'Why? Why are you giving me a free run with this? You know I will have this drive pulled to pieces as soon as we get home.'

'Maybe so. I do want it back together afterwards though. The receipt you'll sign says as much. I'm attached to this machine. Perhaps I want someone who is on our side over in the States and prepared to say the field is safe to use... I was also pleased with you jumping in to rescue Solly and Jules and your protection from this Alliance bunch.' The Senator shook

Ned's hand warmly and thanked him. 'The other thing, I would quite like Ladybird I to hold the trans-Atlantic world speed record for a while. Dr. Andersen has made some calls and will time your start. I'm sure you can arrange someone to notice when you arrive home…' Kelvin's eyes widened and a huge smile cracked his face.

'Goddamn!!! Mr. McZed sir, it will be my pleasure!'

Gregers Balstad looked down with satisfaction. As he could have predicted, the Ladybird crew had triggered the fire alarms to clear the building, now the large metal door of the workshop was slowly cranking up and behind it he could make out the blue glowing leg of one of the machines. He turned and made his way downstairs, keying his phone. Lilleström followed.

'Balstad here. You have your instructions; make sure they are carried out in full.'

LB1 and 2 glided slowly out to the courtyard and hovered in the dawn's early light. The army lieutenant, unsure of what he was to do, approached the smaller craft and considered knocking on the door. The bright blue glow put him off. His only instructions were to prevent the visitors leaving on foot… too late he called on the tank crew to turn their gun around as both Ladybirds lifted majestically up and headed west. The few earlybird students present twittered and cheered. Off to the side, Dorte Andersen registered the time and sent her text to Guinness HQ.

The Wing Commander radioed instructions as his scout aircraft tracked the two craft, flying sedately at 15,000 feet. His fighter wing slid into place, above, below and beside. The box was closed firmly. He moved his F16 down to fly alongside the bigger one and opened communication.

'This is Luftforsvaret Wing Commander Halvorsen. You do not have permission to leave Norway and must return to

Trondheim immediately. Turn 180 degrees to port slowly, now.'

'We have no intention of returning anywhere. I suggest you go back home' came the measured tones of Ned.

'Negative. We have direct instruction that you will be stopped unless you comply immediately. You are surrounded by 30 aircraft, fully armed. Turn to port.'

'First sign of trouble we'll leave you behind. Your weapons won't touch us.'

'Negative. Armaments include cannon and visually guided missiles. Each of your aircraft is fully targeted. You must turn port, please.' The Wing Commander sounded a little anxious.

'This is Senator Dobrovich here' boomed out Kelvin's voice. 'If you shoot down a United States Senator, my country is going to consider this an act of war! Do you want that responsibility, flyboy?' There was a long silence. The countryside crept past below. The coast appeared ahead.

'You must turn or I have no choice!' pleaded the Wing Commander.

'Bugger off' said McZed.

'One and two squadron, arm missiles...'

'Excuse me if you please, Wing Commander Halvorsen' came the quiet, calm voice of Liz.

'Please allow me to explain a few things before you fire your missiles. Firstly, everything which has been said so far has been broadcast over a radius of 500 kilometres by us. My daughter is also translating this into Norwegian. We are unarmed, of no threat to Norway, moving slowly, away from any towns or flight paths. There are four children on board who are having a lot of fun filming and broadcasting everything. Including you. You look wonderful in your big fighter.' Brad and Bobby with the camera waved cheerfully at the Luftforsvaret F16. 'We also believe that the person giving you your instructions may not be doing so in the interests of your country.'

'But he's the Minister of…' The Wing Commander zipped the lip with a gulp.

'Defence' went on Liz, relentlessly, 'but as the Commander at the scene, you are fully responsible and can make your own decisions. Or perhaps consult again with your own boss? Norway has been very supportive and welcoming so far. It would be a shame to change the positive image the world has…' she concluded with not a little wist.

The Wing Commander appeared to be talking, with many gestures, on his radio. Nodding. Eventually he turned and slowly raised his thumb.

'Thank you' breathed Liz. She was crying.

The planes peeled off, the sky was empty.

———*w*———

Outside the empty workshop, Balstad swore loudly and profusely. A clump of students, filming the gaping door in hope of a YouTube Hit, recognized the Minister and re-directed their phone cameras but he didn't notice, was intent on pulling a bulky satellite radio out of his jacket and extending the aerial. 'No matter,' he muttered to himself and the hovering Lilleström, 'I have a little surprise for our friends.' Holding the radio up, (conveniently for the phone cameras) he keyed the signal…

———*w*———

Nobody was fatally injured. The students, further away, were blown off their feet but recovered themselves and some of their still functioning phones. Log on, load up, bingo! Fantastisk! Fredrikstad Lilleström copped a large chunk of lab bench, which broke an arm, leg and three ribs. Balstad ended up with a major head injury from a sizeable lump of concrete. Although it didn't improve his looks, it would later prove useful for his recall when he was called to answer questions regarding abuse of ministerial privileges, damaging national prestige and blowing up Universitat property.

Politically, socially, he was dead.

Chapter Seventeen

The two Ladybirds hovered at 60,000 feet and conversed.

'Remember to stay sub orbital or you won't qualify. You shouldn't run into anything else at this height. Have you radioed your pals in the States? Keep an eye on the battery levels and remember to use the scrubber. Stay under Mach 12 and watch the spark plug lead on the charger, it's quite loose…' fussed Ned.

'All right already. Horowitz has got that all under control. Where are you guys off to?'

'We are going home, Senator' said Liz. 'All of this danger, all these threats… are finished. Our children will be back at school or playing. Steve and I will be back at work and everything will be normal. Everything.'

'Yair, too right!' shouted Steve across. 'Youse better bugger off , Kelve. See ya Graeme!'

'Take it easy Graeme,' called Shirley and the kids.

'We'll Skype when I'm homeside. You can meet the wife and kids! Thanks for everything, great fun!' replied Graeme.

'So I just point this doohickie east and pull back the throttle, McZed?' said Kelvin.

'Pedal to the metal is the current terminology I believe, Dobrovich. Cheery-bye.'

Ladybird I peeled off to port and rapidly shrank to a dot.

'I suppose we best set course for Tilda then,' said Toby. Ned began to key in the Satnav co-ordinates and check off the instruments.

'Not quite' said Liz. 'When I said all this was finished, that is what I meant. Solomonder and Julie have some things to say. They have made several decisions. Steve and I agree.'

'Reckon,' agreed Steve. 'Every other bugger has been coming up with ideas about what and how to do things but its all about what Solly and Jules want to do with their invention. It belongs to them and they haven't said anything much yet.' The advocate sat down. There were murmurs of agreement and all heads turned to Solly and Jules. Ladybird cruised on with a quiet hum. After some squirming, Solly and Jules looked at each other and nodded.

'Well, we have actually been talking about it for a while' Jules began uncomfortably. 'Now we know for sure that the field doesn't actually hurt people, then they should be using it as soon as possible to try and cut down on pollution because of the greenhouse thing. People can make cars and planes and ships run with it and we think it would run power stations too. So we just want to give it to everyone. Free. Bit like a project for the world to do.'

She turned to Solly.

'Absolutely' said Solly, nodding vigorously. There was a moment's silence as everyone took this in. Toby began slowly clapping and nodding and one by one the assembly enthusiastically stood, cheering and agreeing. Solly and Jules blushed crimson.

'Well bugger me, how truly proper and simple and clever is that!' said Ned McZed, wiping his eyes. There was widespread concurrence.

'Thanks' said Solly shyly, 'we decided a fair while back, actually. We used Jules' school laptop. She reckoned that was OK 'cause they said it could be used at home for things. Don't know if you're allowed to take it into space though,' he added.

'It's not too big a download,' said Jules, 'and we put all the script on a few different formats and all the diagrams onto tifs and jpegs. Should be easy.'

'What should be easy? What did you download onto what?' asked Shirley eventually.

'Everything' said Solly, holding up a thumb drive. 'Onto this.'

'Circuit diagrams, bits and pieces you can use instead, some ideas for an electricity generator, how to assemble a field motor, hook it up… all that sort of stuff. Useful stuff ' said Jules.

'And What do you do with that then?' asked Shirley, pointing at the USB.

'Mum! Like, what would you reckon,' chorused Bobby and Brad in exasperation.

'I know. I just want to hear it from them,' said Shirl quietly.

'I would hazard a guess to say that you intend to distribute the field to the world then?' said Ned. 'Despite all the obvious problems?'

'We talked the whole lot over as a family, Ned ' said Steve levelly. 'Every bugger wants to get hold of the field and bury it or take over the planet. We've all been targets too often, and that won't stop until it's out there. Besides, if we can knock up the field generators at somewhere like the Top Ace, anyone can make one. Just need the electronics and a soldering iron. Too easy. If everyone owns it, no one can hog it.'

'The prospect,' said Toby after a while, 'of meeting a red P plater doing Mach 4 doesn't fill me with joy.'

'Agreed,' said Liz, 'but they'll work it out somehow. Limits and rules and things.'

'And what's to stop a big company scurrying off with the information and patenting it and then stopping everyone else using it?' asked Ned.

'We took some copyrights on line and Sri Rinpoche walked down to Trondheim a couple of days ago and put his whole legal team in New York to work as well' said Jules.

'He said they were very good' said Solly.

'They would be, as well as ethical, green and omniscient, knowing Sri' said Liz.

'We'll add a bit saying the field is public property, but if someone tries to pinch it, they've got a fight on their hands' pronounced Jules, with Solly nodding happily.

'But all that stuff we talked about, the huge economic crash when all the big companies fold and transport and power and…all that has to change, like overnight?' asked Toby.

'Well,' said Solomonder, 'It has to change anyway.'

'Or we end up wrecking the planet completely and not being able to patch it up again,' added Jules.

'You see Toby,' said Steve 'although some big businesses may be forced out, there will be so many little ones springing up to soak up the workers and with so much new stuff to make. The big industries will need to downsize and change, if they're smart enough.'

'But!' called out Ned and Shirley together. 'What if…

As Ladybird drifted high over the Atlantic, the arguments were fielded, fed, rebutted and put away in the shed. The questions ran out as well, apart from the one 'was the world ready?' It was left hanging in the wardrobe.   As Toby later observed,

> Logic, sense and heartfelt feeling
> Spread like Solly's field and conquered all.
> Conventions left could only stand alone, then fall.
> Nothing else was left to do.
> Ladybird turned west, to chase the sun.
> The download of the knowledge had begun…

—∿∿—

Graeme read the messaged email and chuckled. The Senator was up front, whistling, scanning the radar for obstructions and cracking on the pace. An hour out and they were halfway there. This should make him even happier.

'Sir, message from McZed. He says that there is a bottle of Bruichladdich sitting under your seat and that we're to go on the net and look at any of their websites or their broadcast channel. What do you think that's about?' Kelvin looked at the boxed bottle and two crystal glasses. Nice one, Ned. Cheers. He poured two hefty shots and passed one to Graeme. The Senator had been thinking.

'My guess is that they are about to unleash the biggest goddamn change this planet has ever seen. There won't be a thing anyone can do about it! And do you know what Agent Horowitz? Good luck to them!' The crystal clinked. 'Meanwhile, back at the ranch, get onto the New York Times, CNN, CBS, NBC and anyone else you can think of and tell them to get their butts down to Times Square. Clear a spot in front of One Times Square for the biggest Ball Drop they've ever seen. Damned if I feel like flying this baby quietly into some Air Force field when all hell is going to break loose anyway!'

'Yes Sir! I suppose I better let our wives know to watch the show too…'

—␣—

Chapter Eighteen

The clouds slid dancing under the wheels of his old station wagon as Tobias Stanley Buchanan banked and dropped down towards Tilda. Fred Astaire offered advice of picking up, dusting off and starting all over again from the six speakers of the newly installed mini Dekko Omnitron Entertainer. Sean purred contentedly on the back seat as the early morning sun warmed his fur. Maria smiled across at Toby and he felt like purring as well.

'Been a hell of a rushed month since you got back, Buchanan.'

Surely had been. Most of it had been spent at the Top Ace with the Hendersons, Denzils, Ned and Maria where they stood on the sidelines and watched the world go into a free fall of reorganization. Road access had been restricted by the police under the direction of Sergeant Ernie Harris, the Army patrolled the surrounds and the Air Force cruised the boundaries. Better late than never. Steve's Monaro was restored to its flying glory, along with Ned's Land Rover and Toby's Camry, so the roadblocks didn't matter. Along with the Dekko, the faithful Camry now had two of the new Sri Concept Internal Field SCIF-1.1 motors and a great paint job in Emerald Green.

Best of all, Maria had agreed to move into McZedcroft with him.

'Driving through the baseclouds
in the early morning light
My lover's by my side and ain't life grand
When all goes well...' he murmured.

'So far, so well' reminded Maria, 'but what will this Inaugural Grand Meeting of the Top Ace Solfield and Dekko Omnitron Company bring? Apart from your mates Graeme and Kelvin turning up with LB1, Shirley says that Senator Dan Kelly and Evangeline Parsons QC are sitting in, as well as the

---

High Lama Sri Rinpoche Laputa Taransai flying in! What a collection. Who knows what madness they will come up with.'

'Time will tell, light of my life, time will tell…'

Indeed, thought Toby as he found a clearing amongst the rusting junk to settle.

Yes, indeed.

###